The Crumb Snatcher

An Erotic Murder Mystery

By

Deana Walters

The Crumb Snatcher

ISBN: 978-0-9793171-2-5

Dedication

This book is dedicated to my James for giving me that gentle nudge of encouragement to revisit this story and share it with others.

Prologue

It was barely 5 a.m. when Matthew McNulty stumbled sleepily downstairs. The late night planning sessions were beginning to take a toll. Being careful not to awaken his wife Allison, he turned the television off and gently opened the door to his home office. As he fired up his computer he thought how his life had changed over the last few years.

He pulled up the country club floor plan and set about diagramming the seating for the annual fundraiser ball. Five hundred well-heeled guests would dine on a meal suitable for royalty. Three years ago if someone had told him he would be doing this he would have blown smoke from one of his favorite cigars and let out a hearty chuckle. Years of college and designing thermonuclear applications for a prestigious think tank had led to a challenging career, but had not prepared him for his current position as Executive-In-Charge of Corporate Fundraising. His division at the think tank had been unexpectedly and unceremoniously phased out, and he had joined the ranks of the well educated, senior experienced unemployed.

After several months of searching the Internet classifieds looking for something close to his field, and after too many fruitless interviews, and with time working against him, he accepted the offer with Pushman and Associates. As the low man on the totem pole he did not have the option of bowing out of his current assignment; coupled with the fact that Henry Pushman had personally requested his presence on the committee.

The cobwebs in his head were like a dense fog this morning. Massaging his temples, Matt alternately viewed the screen with first his left eye, then his right. A mild attack of iritis had necessitated wearing his glasses instead of his contacts. He sorely needed a caffeine jolt, and on his way to the kitchen he experienced a brief moment of anger as he once again passed the sofa.

He thought back to the time when he had a life, at least the life he thought he wanted. In retrospect it reminded him of eating the last spoonful of his favorite ice cream; it always left him wanting more. However, like the carton, his life seemed empty. Then he thought about the day he met HER.

How funny she was- polite, cool but not distant, and willing to accept a challenge.

Mentor to the romantically confused, Lydiel Sommers spent most of her life these days on her computer; so much so it had become the equivalent of a life-saving elixir being titrated slowly over an eighteen hour period of time on a daily basis. On more than a few occasions she had tempted fate in search of a partner, someone not so unlike the characters in her novels. A strong but gentle man- loving, compassionate, intelligent and hot! For the most part her search usually ended with less than satisfactory results. Her relationship talents were more effectively utilized helping others. She seemed to be a miserable failure in that area and destined to die alone in her widowhood, bent over her keyboard typing the next erotic mystery.

On one of her worst writing days an online instant message window opened and there he was - Mr. Wonderful. Weren't they all? Cute, humorous, married and apparently normal - most married men online did not equate with normalcy. Matthew McNulty blazed across her screen and into her life.

Having abandoned the "want to find a mate" mission, Lydiel was no longer in the market to meet anyone, yet she agreed to meet him.

Tall, warm, cuddly, and one hell of a good kisser, she let it begin and it was wonderful. He was also smart, sexy and reasonably honest, and their personalities complemented each other. They shared similar interests, and in time, deep feelings of mutual respect, appreciation and affection interspersed with generous helpings of good old-fashioned lust. She was his sounding board and accommodating distraction. She had a place on the periphery of his life, perhaps never to become a part of his inner circle.

For his part, Matthew McNulty knew that whether he liked it or not, this was a woman whose devotion and loyalty were without question as was her fidelity. He was her core and everything else in her life became a satellite. He knew her so well that at times it was as if he whispered to her heart, and there were times when she knew him better than he knew himself. When things seemed hopeful on the home front there was emotional distance between them; but when the sting of rejection was fresh and painful he sought solace from her. Without question they made each other happy.

Book One

It's All About Allison

Chapter One

> "Something as small as an unguarded and casually tossed remark can serve as an undoing when inadvertently intercepted."
> ~TLM

Doreen Bell was an early riser. Growing up, the house rule was when you woke up you got up. Every morning at exactly 7:13 a.m. Lydiel's Sommers' phone rang, and every morning she answered it to answer the same question.

"Hey Ma, just checking on you. Are you okay?"

This was Doreen's first contact of the day.

"I'm wonderful as always and I have been working for at least two hours. How are the girls and how is work?"

"Hold on Ma, I've got a call."

Lydiel was used to being put on hold by Doreen, her clients, her editor, her publisher and of course by him.

"Okay, I'm back. Now where were we?"

"I was telling you that I am wonderful as always and I should really get back to work. Don't worry about me so."

"Ma? Are you there Ma? Ma? Ma?

Damn phones always did this. Doreen's frustration with the telephone service was building daily. There were many times her mother could hear her clearly and other times not at all.

"I am here Doreen. Stop shouting, please. I may be old but I am not deaf."

For the life of her, Lydiel never understood why this happened. It was irritating as hell and she really wanted to get back to her story. She knew that he would be calling soon.

"Did you hear that Ma?"

"Hear what Doreen? You have been wearing those head things too long."

"No Ma. I hear another conversation mixed in with ours. It happens all the time. I hear other women talking."

"I tell you what kiddo, you listen to the ghosts. I need to get this story down before I lose my thoughts. Talk soon."

"Ma wait! Don't forget to take your medicine and eat something please."

Lydiel decided that the only way to get back to work was just to agree with her overly concerned offspring.

"Will do Doreen. I promise. Bye."

Doreen did not disconnect right away. The "ghost conversation was now louder and clearer.

"I'm telling you this Allison, we need to discuss things. Let's do lunch. I'll call the others. How about noon at Mirelli's?"

"What others? The time for discussion has long passed."

Allison McNulty's voice was trembling as the venom spewed forth.

"That bitch needs to disappear and I mean forever!"

There was a loud click and a pop that terminated the conversation. Doreen was shaken by the exchange but before she could give it more though her lines began ringing.

Lydiel's work was once again interrupted by the telephone. A quick check of the clock told her who was on the line.

"Good morning handsome?"

"Hi babe. How are ya?"

No matter how bad her day was, hearing that voice created instant sunshine and always brought a smile to her face.

"I'm wonderful now. How's your day going so far?"

"Same stuff, different day. I'm sleepy today. I was up late at a committee meeting and then up early to work on the seating arrangements for the ball. I need more caffeine I guess. I barely noticed that I slept alone again…Do you hear that?"

"Hear what?"

"When you talk it sounds garbled as if someone else is talking over you."

"How strange. Doreen said just said the same thing."

"How is she doing these days?"

Lydiel bit her lower lip before answering. "Struggling as usual sweetie, but working now."

Lydiel's heart felt a twinge of sadness, but she realized there was little she could do to impact the situation. Living alone, sleeping alone, eating alone was her version of same stuff, different day.

"I hate to see you working so hard, I'm working hard too, pounding out the new book. I miss you Matt."

Pangs of guilt tugged at Matt, but they both knew the score and they also knew things weren't likely to change anytime soon.

"I miss you too babe. I will see you soon, though. Good luck with the writing. I need to go here. Talk soon. Kisses lover."

"Bye sweetie and take care. Kisses back."

No matter how long they talked it never seemed long enough, and no matter how many times they were together they always needed and wanted more time. It was the little things he did that made the biggest differences in her life. Lydiel closed her eyes briefly and relived their last warm embrace and kiss. Oh well, back to the keyboard and the book.

Chapter Two

For her entire life Allison Woodall McNulty wanted to be in control, demanded to be in control, needed to be in control. If it were not relinquished voluntarily she would wrest it away and make sure that whoever refused her would be very sorry he or she had crossed her. There was nothing she wouldn't do to get things her way. The word "no" did not exist in her vocabulary. Disarmingly engaging, she wrote the book on manipulation. Every grade, every job, and every relationship was a direct result of her devious scheming.

As a child coercion and cajoling always resulted in her getting her way - from the expensive bicycle to her mansion-like dollhouse. Once she entered her teens Allison knew how to play people like finely tuned fiddles. She remembered old Mr. Slavinsky, her high school history teacher, and Rodney Christopher, her not ready for primetime boyfriend.

Rodney had previously been dating one of her friends. Between relationships herself, she decided he would fill the bill temporarily. What an easy target he had been to seduce! One day during lunch break she and Rodney had been going at it hot and heavy in the band instrument room. Pinned against a wall, his hands were up her skirt and hers were down his pants. Right in the middle of a seriously deep lip lock who should amble in but Slavinsky. Allison laughed out loud as she recalled the look on the old buzzard's face. Rodney took off like a bat out of hell and Slavinsky reported them both to the senior advisors. Threatened with being expelled, Allison did the only thing a girl in her situation could do - she turned the tables.

One week before the hearing she requested a "meeting" with Mr. Slavinsky. As she entered his small office, she noticed a group of her classmates milling about. Always the gentleman, Slavinsky rose from his desk and walked around to face her as they talked. Allison approached him so closely they were practically nose - to - nose. As she attempted to put her arms around him he grabbed her arms, pinning them to her sides. As luck would have it at that exact moment, Mr. Witcher, the gym teacher entered the room. Needless to say there was no further discussion of expelling her or Rodney, and poor Mr. Slavinsky took early retirement.

As she grew older Allison became a master of the game, developing agendas for life, tweaking them as needed. Her goal was to get married, do the wife and mommy thing, and enjoy all of the pleasant trappings that went with it - on her terms.

In her previous relationships she turned in performances Hollywood would admire; warm, sexy, whatever she needed to be, whatever she needed to do. When it seemed no longer worth her time and effort she opted out. Allison remembered the day she first met Matt. It didn't take her long to decide he was to be the one. He was smart, fun, lonely, and not too bad in the sack either. She definitely had a plan, an investment to protect and no one was going to interfere with that. She wasn't going anywhere and neither was he.

Allison felt renewed anger as she drove to Mirelli's. Just what she needed- another interloper! Allison Woodall McNulty knew the game. For years she had played the role of a wife - a warm, soft, loving creature who knew sex of any type was the best lure. The proof was her now nearly totally sexless marriage with Matt. Never one to completely enjoy the sexual side of a relationship, she gave just enough of herself to keep him around. There were times she was so turned off she needed a stiff drink before bedtime, but he never knew. That was before the kids. Afterwards it was definitely grin and bear it time until she finally decided why bother. Her agenda had been met and her goals all realized. Matt was a good provider, helped with the kids, and best of all he tolerated her devotion to the church. Who needed sex when there was…?

She knew there had been dalliances in the past, all short-lived with the exception of the last two. As long as it was hit and run sex with a virtual stranger there was no real threat posed to her marriage, and she thought she had done a relatively good job of controlling his free time. Between work and her outside commitments, the majority of his free time was spent at home enjoying the company of the kids, and nothing and no one was going to change that!

Damn him! Damn him! Damn him! And

damn the bitch he was screwing. In some ways this one was worse than the last one who nearly caused the end of their marriage. At least he still approached her for sex when he was seeing that one. Of course he knew it was usually not going to happen. He would get over it, poor thing and keep trying. Lately, however, he genuinely did not seem interested in bedding her anymore, and it was this slight that made Allison Woodall McNulty realize that perhaps for the first time in her life, someone was saying no to her.

Chapter Three

Henry Pushman looked out at the crowd of people and cleared his throat.

"Good afternoon associates. As you know our largest fundraiser is less than six weeks away and we here at Pushman and Associates expect to exceed all projections. I want to thank you for your tireless energy. I realize the hours have been long but the end is in sight. Today's meeting will focus on Matt McNulty's presentation"

Henry was a company man and this company represented his lifeblood. It was also his safe haven. Here there was no unpleasantness nor did he have to vie for control. Each associate was a shareholder so each had a vested interest in the success of the company. They were like one big family. Several of the men played golf together, and many of the wives knew each other and met regularly for their card parties; some it seemed to the exclusion of everything and everyone else.

Nattily dressed and well spoken, Henry epitomized the over fifty corporate executive. His home life was just the opposite. Trapped in a loveless marriage with twins off to college in the fall, he dreaded the end of each workday. Dinner was like eating in a vacuum. His wife Connie was so self-absorbed she was clueless as to what was going on in the world. Their conversation was confined to the upcoming ball, redecorating the cabana, and her calendar of events that would take her away from home. Although Connie was a fairly decent cook, the menu recently consisted of half-baked casseroles, microwave dishes, and lots and lots of flavored margaritas. He knew that mentally digressing served no useful purpose, and this fundraiser was important to both his company and the community. Once again he addressed the associates.

"So let's see what Mr. Matt has come up with shall we?"

Matt's attention had been on her. He missed her. He missed touching her, kissing her, holding her. He missed making love with her. He was tired, irritable and horny, and this presentation had turned into one big pain in the ass. His eyelids felt as if concrete weights had been taped to each one. With one final gulp of the now lukewarm coffee, he made his way to the podium. Lowering the lights, he clicked through the slideshow presentation and entertained questions, comments and criticisms. Much to his surprise the presentation was well received and he was asked to move forward to the next phase of the planning. The presentation ended right on time for the lunch break. He received kudos from his co-workers as they filed out of the conference room.

Henry gave himself a silent pat on the back as he listened to Matt. He was convinced he had done the right thing in taking a chance on him. Matt was the husband of one of Allison's old school chums and Henry had taken a giant leap of faith in hiring him. Excellent references aside, there was a huge difference between working in a think tank and dealing with boards and committees. His was a very demanding key position in the company.

"That was an outstanding presentation my boy!"

For Matt McNulty it felt strange to have a contemporary pat him on the back and refer to him as "my boy", but the accolade was much appreciated. Maybe this was a job he could get into after all.

"Matt, thanks to you our timeline is running faster than the country club can keep up with so take the rest of the afternoon and tomorrow off."

Thanks Henry, I appreciate it."

"Have a good evening Matt. Enjoy your day off. I think this just might be a good fit for both of us."

The morning had gone perfectly for Lydiel. The interruptions had been minimal and the book was coming along great. Writing was her passion, right behind the passion that overwhelmed her every time she was with Matt. As if on cue, the phone rang.

"Hi baby. Is everything okay? How did the presentation go?"

"Everything went great. They liked the presentation and it was approved unanimously."

"That is such wonderful news, Matt. I'm happy for you. Are you sure nothing's wrong?"

"No, no, maybe very right if you are going to be home this afternoon. I have some time and I miss you."

"I'm always here for you. You know that, and I miss you a lot."

"See ya soon babe."

"See you soon, sweetie."

Matt hung up the phone and thought about the softness of her skin as he left the building.

Lydiel always had to stop and breathe after talking to Matt. She was in the most awkward position a woman could find herself in. She was in love with another woman's husband. That was a choice she had made and suffered no remorse over it. She turned her thoughts to how good it was going to be to see him again, kiss him again, hold him again and better yet, lie naked in his arms again. He was always so warm and cuddly, and the best hugger in the world. When they kissed each other it was as if nothing else existed and they could love the world away.

She saved the file she was working in and moved away from the computer. She had just enough time to take a shower, do her hair and find something sexy to put on, for him to remove. It felt so good when he undressed her…

No sooner had his key turned in the lock than Lydiel greeted Matt wearing nothing more than a purple apron and chef hat. Her arms went around his neck as he slid the hat off. That first kiss between them was the way it had been since the day they met. Mistletoe from Christmas past still adorned the doorways in the apartment and they had warmly and deeply kissed each other under every piece. His hands rubbed her back and the curve of her hips as she stood on tiptoes. There was such hunger and such passion between them and it never cooled.

Taking her hand he led Lydiel to the bedroom. It was her house, but their room. She had declared it so months ago, and he knew no one ever shared it with her but him. As she leaned over to turn back the covers Matt entered her slowly and deeply. He immediately felt her response, grabbing him tightly and massaging him with each throbbing contraction. Putting his hands on her shoulders he thrust gently and then withdrew. There was much more love to be made this afternoon. Gently standing her up and untying the strings, he removed the apron and joined her on the bed.

Chapter Four

Connie Pushman arrived at Mirelli's a little ahead of schedule to secure a quiet rear table and order the wine. As she exited the new BMW, she carelessly tossed the keys to the valet. Two women standing just inside the outer doors joined her as she entered the restaurant. Since they were having a late lunch, it was relatively quiet inside. The Maitre 'D smiled as he walked towards her.

"Ciao, Mrs. Pushman. It's very good to see you again."

"Ciao, Giorgio. I need a very quiet table for four for lunch. I am expecting another guest to join us shortly."

Giorgio Pieri had been the Maître D at Mirelli's for over fifteen years and he had never seen the two women with Connie Pushman before. They seemed uncomfortable and out of place.

"Would you like a wine list Mrs. Pushman?"

"No Giorgio, why don't we stick with my usual and several refills?"

Allison was more than mildly irritated. On top

of everything else, that bastard husband of hers wasn't answering his phone. Repeated calls to his office resulted in repetitions of "Sorry, Mr. McNulty is not available at the present..." or "You have reached the office of Matthew McNulty. Currently I am unavailable..."

What the hell kind of place was Pushman running? Connie had better have a plan or else she was taking matters into her own hands. Little Ms. Interloper was on her way out, out of her life, out of bedding her husband and out of this world. No one, absolutely NO ONE was interfering with that agenda.

Allison knew she was in a state. How dumb was Matt? What part of this scenario didn't he get? Her mind went back to that day Connie's phone call came about Matt cheating. They had arranged for it to come in at just the right time. Her mother had arrived to babysit and took the call. She and Matt were out to dinner and when they arrived home her mother told them about the call and had a few choice words for Matt as she left. She had to laugh. She had been at her all time her tearfully dramatic best. Matt had seemed mildly irritated and a little confused, but the effect was long lasting. He never stayed away from home for long after that. He knew better, but lately things had changed between them, and she didn't like it. She would have never known what was going on were it not for her dear friend Connie Pushman.

After arriving at the restaurant, Allison took a deep breath as she strode quickly inside. Giorgio appeared instantly.

"Ciao Bella"

"Save it for someone who cares, prick. Where is Connie, or is it still Mrs. Pushman to you?"

"This way, madam."

Giorgio's voice was tinged with obvious disdain at Allison's treatment of him. After all who the hell did she think she was? If there was one thing Giorgio had learned it was that Allison McNulty was a selfish, obnoxious bitch of a woman and he always had to restrain himself when dealing with her.

As she walked towards the table Allison was surprised to see the two women sitting on either side of Connie. They were definitely not a part of their circle. Without waiting to be introduced, Allison began her pronouncement.

"This had better be good. I have no time for bullshit and you know it Connie"

Connie Pushman knew her work was cut out for her. Allison was out of control as usual. Gritting her teeth, she motioned to her to sit down.

"Allison, get a grip and shut up! We are in a public place!"

Unable to control her own irritation, Connie offered her a glass of wine and introduced the two women with her.

"This is Francesca Sommers and her sister Remey Anderson. They are Lydiel's daughters."

Allison was more than surprised for many reasons.

"Are you crazy? You bring her family here to discuss why I want to see her dead?"

As Allison stood to leave, Connie grabbed her wrist firmly.

"Sit that stupid behind of yours down, have some wine, shut up and listen."

It didn't take Francesca long to realize they had a loose cannon on their hands. Remey was beginning to have second thoughts also.

"Do you remember the phone call, Allison? You know the phone call to your dear mother-in-law about Matt's infidelity? Francesca made the call. Do you remember how the other situation rectified itself? Remey was responsible for that. It was by sheer friggin' coincidence that your Matt and their mom found each other, and believe me there is no love lost between them and Lydiel."

Allison looked at the two women and felt as if she missed a chapter somewhere. Ignoring them she chose to address Connie instead.

"I don't understand. How did you meet them and why the animosity between them and their mother? How do they know Matt and why are they helping me?"

"Ah, but that is the beauty of it all. Lydiel has no idea they feel this strongly. Miss Goody Goody still welcomes them into the fold. As to how we met, that's not a topic for discussion at this time. They are what we need to eliminate that thorn in your side. On a rare visit to Lydiel's they noticed a picture of a guy on the nightstand. They were teasing her, asking if that was her boyfriend. She didn't say anything and they never met him, but Francesca hacked her computer and they started e-mailing him. It seems they all had fun talking to each other. They made the connection when they saw Matt's picture in the newspaper when he joined Henry at the firm."

Although she personally hated Lydiel Sommers and the threat she presented to her marriage to Matt, Allison was trying to understand how these two women could conspire to kill their own mother. Her mother was less than fond of Matt and had suggested that she dump him, but never ever suggested having something permanent happen to him. As angry as she was about the "cheating" phone call, all she ever said was "learn to control your husband."

Francesca was the first of the odd twins to speak.

"The bitch should have been dead long ago. She adopted me when I was 8, and I came there with the idea of killing her. When I was 12, I tried to poison her but she wouldn't die. A few months ago she had a bleeding problem. I switched her pills and made her bleed more. After the operation I had someone make threatening calls to her house and switched her pain pills with the bleeding medication. She still didn't die. Matt was so upset when she was sick. He acted as if he was going to lose the love of his life."

Allison was unimpressed. Poor Matt - the love of his life, indeed! He hadn't begun to be upset, and there would never ever again be love in his miserable, pathetic life. The girls' ambivalence towards their mother had piqued her interest, and she was curious as to what was in this for them. What was the real motivation behind their assistance? As if reading her mind the other odd twin, Remey spoke up.

"My mother, Lydiel Sommers- she's a writer. People know her. She has money somewhere. We want it. Of course what we know can help you too but it isn't free. Now where's lunch?"

One look at Remey and Allison knew lunch was only an appetizer for her. What a lump of lard. Allison looked at Connie through new eyes. There was something strange about how she knew these two.

Chapter 5

Matt loved the way Lydiel felt in his arms. Wrapped up so tightly that they seemed as if they were melted together, and running his fingers lightly across her nipples, he felt the shivers run through her. She felt him harden in her hand as she gently stroked him. This is the way their afternoon had gone; her mouth on him, his mouth on her; teasing, tasting, licking and sucking. He took her over and over in every way imaginable. She was like a runaway train and he was the engineer steering it.

Lydiel lived for the times with Matt. For her making love with him was like having the Fourth of July each time. He was the consummate lover, but the best part of their trysts was how they always made time to talk to each other. She loved the sound of his voice and they discussed every subject imaginable. No one had ever made her laugh like he did. He was her world and he made her happy. Lying there quietly, listening to the sound of his heart beating, she knew that their time together was about to end. Lately, however, it seemed as if he hated leaving her as much as she hated him leaving.

Matt knew Lydiel well, and as if he were reading her mind, at that same time he turned to kiss her - the warm, soft, gentle kiss of leaving.

"I was thinking babe. Since you are working so hard trying to meet the deadline for your book, maybe you should consider hiring someone to come in and help around here at least one day a week."

"Oh? Now I seem so old that I can't care for myself? Seriously Matt..."

"No and you know that's not what I'm saying at all sweetheart. I care about you and I worry a little, more since the surgery."

"I'm fine, really, Matt, I am."

"Just think about it, okay? I need to get cleaned up. Family will be home soon and I need to be there."

"I know. I know."

Lydiel wondered if she would ever get used to him leaving her like this. Would they ever spend a night together, eat dinner together, or spend an evening cuddling together? Grabbing a robe, she talked to him as he dressed. She walked up behind him and rested her head on his back for a brief moment. Taking her hands he turned around to face her. He thought he saw the glint of a tear in her eye.

He kissed her. He wanted her again but duty called. He wanted to just hold her and tell her what was in his heart but… He held her hand as they walked to his car. What once was easy now was difficult. Opening the car door, he kissed her deeply once more, sat down and started the engine.

"Take care sweetie. Talk tomorrow."

"You too baby. I miss you already."

"I miss you too."

As Matt drove off, Lydiel experienced a myriad of emotions. Still feeling his wetness inside her, she turned to walk back inside. It seemed as if when he left, life inside the house left with him. Walking towards the bathroom she realized once again how much she loved him.

The wine had served to calm Allison quite a bit as did the lobster ravioli. She had willingly donated her salad to Remey who apparently had no difficulty devouring it. Things remained amicable until Francesca spoke.

"Why is your hubby wubby screwing my mother, Allison? Doesn't he get any at home? He seems awfully cute judging from that picture. I'd do him in a minute."

Allison felt the anger rise once again. She did not want to "do" Matt, but she knew that sooner or later she would have to. Yet, she did not like the idea of anyone else "doing" him or him "doing" them. He didn't need or deserve anymore than she was willing to give him. She didn't want to sleep with him, bathe with him or touch him unless she had no choice. Every day she gave him his generous doses of "I love you", or "I love you lots and lots", because she knew that was what he wanted to hear, and needed to hear. When she thought about it, she doubted if she ever loved him. She used him. When they got married she was almost thirty. She needed to get married, establish roots, have kids, and Matt was her social prop. Everyone else was with someone and she could not be the odd girl out, so she got Matt to marry her; her first major fait accompli.

Allison did not like Miss Francesca Smart Mouth at all, and responded to her inappropriate question in a very clipped tone of voice, choosing her words carefully.

"He and I no longer share a bed regularly, not that it is any of your business. He screws your mother because she is a cheap whore who wants what belongs to me and she can't have it. As for you 'doing him', I don't think so."

Connie knew it was time to head trouble off at the pass.

"The guys will be getting home soon Allison, and I need to defrost something. Are we still on for the card game later or are you babysitting tonight?"

"If Matt has plans I will spoil them and be there for the card game, if not I'll stay home and watch movies."

"I wish you would come. You're the best whist partner."

For the first time since mentioning lunch, Remey spoke up.

"Francesca is a great whist player."

Remey had spoken out of turn, and Francesca knew how patronizing the two other women could be, and socializing with Connie tonight might be a good thing.

"I would love to play cards with you Connie."

One look at Allison's face and Connie knew she had to act quickly to diffuse the time bomb without alienating Francesca. She was going to be the linchpin in pulling their plan off.

"Perhaps another time dear. Allison and I have a few things to discuss before our next meeting and the card game would give us that opportunity. Let's talk more in the morning, Allison. I need to go."

After taking care of the check, Connie was gone.

Allison waited until Connie left the restaurant before attacking Lydiel's two daughters.

"Let's get something straight. With or without the two of you, the bitch will go away, by whatever means necessary."

With a wry smile and an icy stare, Francesca was beginning to see a very dangerous side to Allison McNulty, but she was a pro at playing the game and remained calm in her response.

"Don't get your panties in a bunch. Allison."

Connie Pushman loved her husband in a very

special way but she hated being married. She hated being married to Henry. He deserved better. She hated having sex with Henry or any man for that matter. She was beginning to wonder if it had been wise to introduce the girls to Allison. The three of them had enjoyed a comfortable relationship for over a year, and there were also her mixed feelings about Matt. There was a small part of her that empathized with him. He walked blindly into a relationship with Allison and never knew the kind of woman he was married to. Many times in the past she herself had been on the receiving end of Allison's need to control. Before she could continue her train of thought, Connie realized Henry was home already.

"Good evening dear. Sorry I'm late. I'll find something for dinner."

Henry had grown used to the hours Connie kept, especially the ones that did not include him or any explanation of where she had been or what she had been doing.

"Don't worry about it love. I ordered take-out and I have eaten already. I washed it down with a fine Chianti and I am set for the evening."

Henry's mind was someplace other than his living room. He barely heard Connie's mundane chatter. He wanted to run fast and far. He wanted to meet a really hot horny woman who would screw his brains out and revive his dormant cock. He wanted to hug, kiss, cuddle and more than anything he wanted to feel wanted. It had been so many months since he and Connie "got naked" as she called it, that he was beginning to lose it. He truly wanted to get laid. He thought he heard his wife's voice coming from the kitchen.

"How is Matt working out, Henry?"

Connie always felt that small talk with Henry was a weak attempt at filling the empty space between them. Every question was rhetorical.

"Matt is working out quite well. I was very impressed with the outstanding presentation he turned in today. He has been working so hard that I decided to give him the afternoon and tomorrow off."

The cogs and wheels in Connie's brain were suddenly set into motion. Sooo, Mr. Matt had the afternoon off to play with his little writing whore; no wonder Allison couldn't reach him.

"That was very generous of you dear. Since you had dinner already and the twins are with friends tonight, would you mind if I played cards with the girls? It seems as if it has been ages since we were all together."

"I see no problem at all. Enjoy yourself dear."

Henry often wondered exactly how stupid Connie thought he was. 'Girl time' was her excuse for everything, and he suspected the leading cause Allison McNulty was away from home so much lately. Excusing himself he headed for the quiet of his bedroom and a very gentle up close and personal relationship with himself. Before he could make it to top of the stairs, Connie was gone. It was at that moment that Henry made the decision to change his life and the lives of the McNultys as well.

Chapter Six

Matt leaned against the garage and toyed with his cigar. He never felt more closed-in in his life. He needed to get away to think. Before he could decide anything he saw Allison coming towards him. He was not in the mood for her.

"The ball committee is meeting tonight and I was wondering if you would..."

Matt cut her short. He knew what was coming next.

"Actually I do mind. I have something I want to do."

"And pray tell exactly what is more important than spending time with YOUR kids?"

Connie Pushman checked her watch one final time and realized something must have happened with Allison. As much as she dreaded confirmation, she placed the call. After one ring she heard the voice that roared.

"Allison? I thought you were coming to play cards."

"The bastard wouldn't watch the kids and just

drove off."

"Oh dear, I'm sorry. I wonder where he went. Henry gave him the afternoon off and the day off tomorrow."

The loud click of the phone was almost deafening as Allison slammed the receiver down repeatedly. Perhaps it was time for Matt to disappear as well as his slut. Once again she dialed Connie's number.

"Connie, where can I find the girls?"

"What girls?

"The two from today, at lunch."

"Remey has a family, so she is home. Francesca hangs out at Charley's. Why the sudden interest, dear?"

"Just curious. Talk tomorrow. Bye"

"Allison?"

Even from a distance, Allison had managed to spoil Connie's evening.

As soon as she hung up, Allison scrambled to find a sitter for the kids. Ten and thirteen year olds were not to be trusted home alone, and even if she considered it, if Matt returned home to find them home alone there would be a "discussion" as he called it. He couldn't even argue with her. She finally had no choice but to call their grandmother.

"Hello Mother? I hate to bother you but I need someone to be here when the kids come home. I have a very, very important committee meeting tonight."

Hannah Woodall knew her daughter well enough to know that she would use anyone to get her way, to do what she wanted to do when she wanted to do it. It made her heart sad to see how selfish her daughter had turned out to be.

"Well, where is that husband of yours, Allison?"

Allison could feel a small trickle of blood as she bit her lip. Hannah was rapidly approaching her limit, and she spoke very slowly and in measured tones.

"He had something he needed to do, Mother. Not that it is of any concern to you."

"Getting laid comes to mind. Really Allison, how long is this going to continue? Men need sex. You know this. You also know that he is whoring around and has been for years. Why won't you just let him go and get on with your life? Give him the kids too. You never spend any time with them lately anyway."

"I really don't need a lecture, mother. No one ever leaves Allison Woodall McNulty. Daddy was the one and only person who ever did or ever will. I know the game and I never lose, not ever."

There were times like this that made Hannah wonder about her daughter's sanity.

"Is winning worth it Allison and what exactly are you winning? There was a time when Matt truly cared for you but your isolation and selfishness forced him elsewhere."

Her mother was beginning to grate on her one remaining nerve.

"Now what time shall I expect you mother?"

Sighing heavily, Hannah Woodall realized a horrible truth. No one ever said no to her daughter.

"I am on my way."

What the hell was wrong? Had the world gone mad? People dared to say no to her - Allison Woodall McNulty? This was unacceptable on any level. She was distracted from her thoughts by the arrival of her children.

"Hi mom!"

Spoken in unison as always, Liam and Sean hugged her like two little bear cubs.

"Grams is on her way to sit with you. I have a meeting to attend."

"Where's dad?"

That unison thing drove her crazy. How was it possible for kids born almost two years apart to share the same thoughts and speak at the same time?

"Your father is out for the evening."

"You are never here anymore, mom."

Sean was such a whiner. Allison hated the tinny sound of his voice and the tears. Boys shouldn't cry and at 13 he was too old to act like such a baby.

The doorbell was the saving grace. Allison opened the door for her mother.

Hannah Woodall always had a smile for her two favorite little men.

"Hi boys. How are my loves?"

As much as they loved Grams, she was the last person the boys wanted to see tonight. They missed their mother.

"Hi Grams."

"I'll be back later, mother. Matt will probably get home first."

"Don't be so sure Allison. Don't be so sure."

Damned old crone. What the hell does she know? Matt had better get home before her. The biggest question was where the hell was he this afternoon? Was he "doing" HER?

Matthew McNulty lit a cigar, leaned back on the huge rock and watched the sunset at the lake. It was blissfully serene here. He looked on as a couple of die-hard fishermen pulled in a few resistant bass. The fish reminded him of himself; Allison baited the hook and he continued to swallow it all, hook, line and sinker. It was getting old and he was getting tired. Lydiel had offered him a no strings opportunity to travel, have fun and feel good about himself. He hated the fact that she got the crumbs-the leftover energy, the leftover time; but if that were a true analogy of his relationship with her, then indeed Allison was the crumb snatcher. Tomorrow he would surprise Lydiel and she and he would partake of some mighty fine crumbs.

Chapter Seven

Henry Pushman decided he needed to be around people. Shedding his corporate blues, he donned his favorite pair of Dockers, the first oxford shirt he put his hands on, and decided to spend the evening at Charley's.

When he arrived the place was jumping as usual and as usual Henry felt like a fish out of water. No matter how hard he tried to shed his business persona it followed him like a second skin.

As he approached the bar, he noticed a young woman sitting alone. Taking the stool next to her, he ordered a double tequila. It had been at least five years since he had been here alone, and he was out of practice with the ladies, but decided to give it his best shot.

He wanted to say something to her without sounding like an old fogey or worse yet a letch. His twins would laugh hysterically if they could read his thoughts now. With trepidation and no swagger Henry Pushman decided to give it the old college try

"Excuse me, may I buy you a drink, Miss?"

The young woman didn't seem frightened or intimidated in the least. In fact she seemed eager for company without fishing for compliments, which to Henry's way of thinking was a very good thing.

"Sure, why not? An apple martini would be fine."

"Put it on my tab, Charley."

Charley Williams blindly acknowledged Henry's request without passing judgment.

"Sure thing, Mr. P."

"I'm Henry and I am certain that your name is every bit as lovely as you are."

Francesca could tell right away how old the guy was with that old school pickup line.

"I am Francesca Sommers and thanks for the drink."

"You are quite welcome Francesca Sommers. Do you come here often?"

Francesca knew enough about men to know this one wanted to get laid. The clothes and the watch meant money, and that little band of gold meant there was a Mrs. P somewhere who was obviously not on top of her game.

"I am usually here every Thursday and occasionally on a Saturday. I don't remember seeing you here before, Mr. P."

"I'm usually with my friends when I come here, Francesca, which I must admit isn't very often."

"Flying solo tonight are you? That's good sometimes. I do it quite a bit myself, Mr. P."

Henry was out of his element and felt lost trying to make conversation with a woman young enough to be his daughter, but he was doing his awkward best.

"Come now. A sexy young girl like you, flying solo? I find it difficult to believe that you would ever be alone. Something seems amiss, my dear."

"No more so than a handsome married guy like you, here alone, talking to me."

"Ahh, I see you are observant and beautiful; a great combination."

"Tell you what Mr. P, how would you like to put the moves on me on the dance floor. I think this is your kind of music."

"I'm not much of a dancer."

"I think this is one of those you lean into me and I lean into you numbers. C'mon, let's give it a try."

Leaving the barstool and following Miss Francesca Sommers onto the dance floor, Henry's eyes sized her up quickly and he liked what he saw, maybe a little too much. Holding each other close, Henry was beginning to come to life in more ways than one.

"How old are you Miss Francesca Sommers?"

"A whopping 24 years old, Mr. P."

Turning her back to him, Henry put his arms across Francesca's small breasts and felt himself harden as she did a little bump and grind.

She knew he wanted it so bad he could taste it and if he was a good boy she might let him have it.

Henry wanted her. Stranger or not, at this point nothing could be stranger than his wife, whom he had not felt in so long he had lost track. He leaned in closer and felt the heat of her through his Dockers.

Francesca knew this could be an opportunity of a lifetime. Whoever Mr. P was, he was horny and he could afford her. As the song ended she led Henry to the darkest corner in Charley's, kissed him and unzipped his pants. On any other occasion Henry would have recoiled at the thought of being publicly fondled but tonight he found it seductively exhilarating. This was proving to be a night to remember in more ways than one.

Allison never liked these places. They seemed to always be dark, smelling of beer, unacceptable music playing and unacceptable men. Making her way to the bar she asked the bartender if he knew a Francesca Sommers. Pointing across the room, Allison's gaze landed on two figures in a corner. She could make out the form of a woman who appeared to be hugging a man. Not wanting to disturb her here, she sat on a barstool hoping to get her attention before she left the place.

Henry removed Francesca's hand from the now noticeable bulge in his trousers. The erection was becoming too painful and he was close to a release.

"Where do you live, Francesca?"

"Two blocks east. I don't have a car."

"No problem. Here, you pay the tab and I am in the gray BMW outside."

While Francesca took care of the check, Allison got a good look at the man. He closely resembled Henry Pushman. It couldn't be. Henry wouldn't be caught dead in a place like this. When she looked up again the man was gone

"I need to talk to you Francesca and. it won't wait."

"Sorry Allison, not now. I have a hot date with a very hot guy. Talk tomorrow?"

Not tomor…"

Francesca was walking towards the door. Watching from just inside the entranceway, Allison saw Henry Pushman open the car door for Francesca Sommers and drive away. Someone else had told her "no". Someone else would have to pay.

Chapter 8

This was turning into one hell of a morning! Lydiel was rapidly losing track of the interruptions today. First her attorney called regarding her will. Then her editor called with a "few" changes that she needed to make ASAP. The business calls were then followed by one from her mom that lasted all of two minutes, one from the doctor reminding her that with the oppressive heat she needed to pick up fresh refills for her inhalers, and finally one from a potential candidate for the position Matt mentioned to her yesterday. Why he thought she needed a domestic assistant for a five room apartment was beyond her. The interview was scheduled for 10:30 a.m. She would give anything to have Matt with her today. She needed to be inspired. There was the phone again!

"Good morning, this is Lydiel Sommers.

"Good morning Miss Lady. How are you?"

There was no mistaking the syrupy sweetness of that voice.

"Hi Francesca. To what do I owe this uhm…?"

"I'm just checking up on ya. How's Mr. Gorgeous?"

What was she up to now? Francesca gave less than a damn about anything going on in Lydiel's life unless it was of some benefit to her. As she recalled during her last phone call and e-mail she'd wished her mother dead.

"My life is just wonderful thank you. Francesca, exactly why are you calling me? You and I don't have the type of relationship where we call each other and I really am quite busy today."

Francesca needed information but her mother was not buying into her Miss Nice persona.

"It's a nice day and I thought maybe you and Matt had plans."

"That would be something that would never concern you. I need to go. Try to have a good day."

Damn that bitch! Francesca wished she had been successful all those years ago when she tried to kill Lydiel. She needed to know when her mother last saw Matt. Miss Hot to Kill the Whore was on her case early this morning, threatening to tell her sister in crime about her and Mr. P.

That poor guy. It didn't take much for him to blow; a few deep sucks, massaging his balls, and as soon as he was inside her, that was it. It must have taken all of ten minutes. Talk about a guy who needed a piece of ass...

Lydiel was puzzled and upset. Why the sudden interest in Matt? Francesca was up to something and it definitely did not bode well for her. As the phone rang once again Lydiel realized that writing was not on the agenda for today.

"Good morning. This is Lydiel Sommers."

"Hi mommy. How are you?"

"Hi Remey. This seems to be my day to hear from my errant daughters. What can I do for you?"

"Are you having a bad day or something? I just called to see how you were. I saw Francesca yesterday."

The plot thickens. First a call from her would be murderess and now a "hi, how are you" from Remey, who never calls.

"That explains it. Your sister just called. Now you. Hatching new schemes are you?"

"Ha ha ha ha. You are too funny. Matt and I were online earlier this morning. He is so fine. We had a nice chat."

"I am very happy that you and Matt have become chat friends Remey. As for your assessment of him, he is quite wonderful; a very nice person."

Like her sister, Remey was fishing and for what Lydiel had no idea.

"That must be old people talk for hot. Matt is a hot guy. I think married guys are so cool. You can have fun and then just walk away. No harm. No foul."

Lydiel felt suddenly ill. Remey's words were like collective bee stings, each one more painful than the last. Once again she was made to feel like an accommodating distraction in someone's life.

"I never think of relationships as child's play Remey. They include real people with real feelings and hardly a game. Causing someone pain or anguish is never "no harm" or "no foul", quite the contrary. Speaking of married guys, how is your husband?"

"Doug is Doug as always. It feels strange to live together."

Lydiel was growing weary of Remey's inane chatter and it was almost 8 a.m.

"Was there anything else Remey? I need to get back to my writing"

"No mother. Perhaps you need to see Matt soon. You seem cranky. Talk soon."

As soon as Remey hung up Lydiel began to dissect the last two conversations. Both girls seemed so interested in Matt this morning. As she prepared to shower and get dressed for the day, the damn phone rang again.

"Hello?"

"Sorry ma. Are you okay?"

"I'm fine Doreen, just agitated. I heard from Francesca and Remey within a few minutes of each other."

"What do they want now, to try another new poison? "

"They seemed interested in Matt"

"Are you still there ma?"

"Of course I am, Doreen."

"Ma? Did you hear that?"

Lydiel just wanted to scream, to stand naked in the middle of the floor and scream. She had no idea what her daughter was talking about hearing voices.

"Hear what Doreen?"

Doreen had no idea what was going on and when she told people about the ghost conversations no one believed her. She only heard them when she talked to her mother. She needed proof that she was not crazy so she purchased a device to record her conversations with her mother.

"Hear the two women talking, ma?"

"I don't hear anything but you talking. I hate to cut this short but I have a few things to do and I am running behind this morning. Can we talk later?"

"Sure, uhm, okay. Have you spoken with Matt this morning?"

"No, but it's still early." Talk soon. Bye."

Like before, Doreen could hear another conversation going on over hers. Clicking on the tape recorder she continued to listen in:

"Hello? Connie?"

"Allison. I thought you were coming to play

cards last night. We really could have used you."

Doreen recognized the voices as the same two women she heard talking before. Clicking off the recorder to answer her other line she knew one thing - whoever they were, they sounded miserable and some poor guy was in big trouble.

Lydiel checked her watch and noticed it was 8:30 a.m. and no word from Matt - no e-mail, no instant message and no phone call. Henry Pushman must be quite the taskmaster. There was a little part of her that always feared the worst. That tiny little area of insecurity that was always so disconcerting. Oh well, maybe now she could get that shower in. After talking to Francesca and Remey she felt she needed one more than ever

Chapter Nine

Lydiel stepped into the shower, closed her eyes and imagined him there with her, soaping and massaging her shoulders, washing her back, teasing that button.... The warm water felt wonderful as it gently cascaded over her. Unconsciously she started to sing one of her old favorites by The Captain and Tennille, Do That To Me One More Time.

Matthew McNulty had left strict instructions with his secretary yesterday that were anyone to call for him she was to play the recording or simply say he was unavailable and to take a message. He had big plans for today and nothing and no one was going to spoil them, not even Allison, and when the phone rang he knew it would be her.

"Hi, it's me. I'll be home late so you'll have to fix dinner for the boys. My mother will stay with them after school until you get home."

"Sorry Allison, no can do. We'll be going to the party center after work for dinner and then afterwards we are going to discuss the seating arrangements for the ball. Either you or Hannah will have to take care of the boys."

It's too late for me to change my plans. People are counting on me."

"And this is my job. I won't be there for dinner. Goodbye Allison."

Matt McAllister was on a mission.

Allison gritted her teeth so hard her head ached. What a liar! LIAR! LIAR! LIAR! She knew where he was going and why. Allison had no choice but to call her mother.

Hannah Woodall was having a grand day! Her arthritis let her know she was still among the living. She heard the phone and for the briefest of moments she considered not answering. Who else could be calling her at this time of day but her daughter.

"Hello?"

"Good morning wonderful person. How is the best mother in the world feeling today?"

"Whatever it is Allison, the answer is no!"

Bristling and trying desperately to control her voice, Allison responded in measured tones.

"Excuse me. I don't recall asking you for anything. All I said was good morning."

"Allison, I, better than anyone, know when you want something."

"You agreed to meet the boys after school, mother, and I was wondering if they could come over for dinner. I need to do something important after work."

"Allison. You are my child and I love you. But over the past few years it seems that everything you want to do is important. It's always about you. No one matters but you; not your husband, not your children, and certainly not me. You use us all. Liam cried so much last night it broke my heart. Sean did a wonderful oil painting that you never saw, and of course I'm absolutely certain you didn't kiss Matt goodnight, and probably didn't sleep with him. Tonight is my poker night and my friends and I will try to break each other's banks. I cannot fix dinner. And Allison? Don't even think of not being home by 7 p.m. Goodbye."

With a barely audible click, Hannah Woodall had regained control of her life and it felt good. She had stood her ground against Allison. Were it not for the arthritis she would have done an Irish jig at that very moment.

With her breathing reduced to short gasps, Allison Woodall McNulty put her hands on the kitchen counter, bowed her head and pondered what had to be a conspiracy. For forty-six years she had maintained absolute control over her life; forty-six friggin' years! Forty-six years! If there was a God in heaven, this madness would end, as would Matt, his whore, and anyone else she deemed unworthy. She was so engrossed in her anger she never heard the boys come into the kitchen.

"Hi mom. We're hungry."

In unison again, Sean and Liam rushed towards Allison like two 2 year olds.

"DON'T YOU TWO EVER HAVE AN INDEPENDENT THOUGHT? DON'T YOUR LITTLE MOUTHS EVER WORK SEPARATELY? DON'T YOU KNOW WHERE THE CEREAL IS? DON'T YOU KNOW ANY FRIGGIN' THING AT ALL OTHER THAN MOM, MOM, MOM?"

She regretted the words as soon as they left her mouth. She was just not in the mood to deal with the boys this morning. Normally she would be at work by now.

Liam cowered in the corner as tears silently rolled down his face. Sean opened the cabinet door and removed two cereal bowls. He then took the cereal off the counter and filled the bowls. As soon as he opened the door to the refrigerator the carton of orange juice fell out spilling onto the kitchen floor. As his mother reached out, the horn on the school bus sounded. Before she could apologize Sean reached for Liam's hand and the two boys left the house and boarded the bus.

"Dear God in heaven, this too shall pass."

Allison Woodall McNulty began the arduous task of cleaning the spilled juice.

Chapter Ten

It was a great morning for a drive and an even greater one for Matthew McNulty. The knowledge that he would be holding her soon brightened it even more. Matt parked the car on the parking pad behind Lydiel's house and let himself in. Closing the heavy door as quietly as he could, he stood in the kitchen and listened to her off key singing. It was nice to hear her happy.

Lydiel stepped out of the shower and turned to reach for her towel. In an instant a warm towel and two strong arms enveloped her. Matt dried her off and then held her close. He held her hand as they walked through the house.

"Where did you come from? I thought you were at work. Nothing happened did it?"

Matt silenced her with a deep, warm, extended kiss. Letting the towel fall to the floor, he turned her back to him, wrapped his arms around her breasts and kissed her neck and her ear lobes. He gently rolled her nipples between his fingertips as she melted into him. Their interlude was rudely interrupted by sharp rapping on the front door.

"Are you expecting anyone babe?"

"Oh no. I totally forgot. I took your advice and placed an ad for a domestic assistant. Can you help with this please?

Matt reluctantly opened the door and came face to face with Lydiel's applicant.

"And who might you be?"

"I could ask you the same thing. She said nothing about a husband."

"I'm not.. er, her husband. Please come in."

"Matt? Who is it sweetie?"

Lydiel had a bad habit of leaving clothes in one place and robes in the other. Her clothes were in the bathroom so she was forced to put her black satin robe on. It was the embroidered one with the kimono sleeves and a favorite of Matt's.

"It's your 10 o'clock babe."

Turning back to the woman, Matt decided to play host while Lydiel made herself presentable.

"Would you care for coffee or tea, Ms…? I'm sorry I didn't get your name."

"No, you didn't and I didn't give it."

Matt was irritated by the woman's surly behavior. Any other time he would have excused himself but this he had to see.

As she emerged from the bedroom, Lydiel was somewhat taken aback at what she saw.

"Good morning Sarah? I am Lydiel Sommers and I am pleased to meet you.

Turning to Matt, Lydiel informed him that Sarah was interested in the domestic assistant position.

Lydiel and Matt had agreed long ago that were they to encounter anyone she knew or didn't know well, he would introduce himself. In what capacity was never made clear. That would have been considered TMI as Matt called it or too much information.

Sarah was unimpressed by a woman wearing a bathrobe at this time of day. The apartment didn't seem large enough for help but it was a job, and one for which she would be double dipping. He was obviously HIM.

Sarah Turner's presence was putting a crimp in

Matt's plans. The job was not that detailed so he decided to cut to the chase and get the interview over with.

"It is nice to meet you Sarah. I'm Matt. Have you done this sort of work before and could you provide references if need be?"

Lydiel was surprised at Matt's take-charge attitude but she liked it and decided to sit back and watch him at work.

"What days are you available and what rate of pay are you expecting?"

"Right now I have open availability and Ms. Sommers stated $9.00 per hour."

Matt decided he was on a roll and pushed the woman for more details.

"Do you have adequate transportation and do you have any children?"

Sarah was becoming increasingly more uncomfortable. No one told her that he would be interviewing her and his rapid fire questioning was beginning to rattle her a little.

"I have a car and my children are grown."

"You hardly seem old enough to have grown

children, Sarah. If Ms Sommers decides to hire you when could you start?"

"I have a question, Matt, is it? Whom would I be working for?"

"Ms. Sommers of course, but as her friend I certainly have concerns about her safety and well being, which brings me to my next question. Can you provide a copy of a nationwide background check along with verifiable references?"

"I'm sure I can… Matt. I would need a day or so to get everything together."

"Fine, why don't you set up another appointment with Ms. Sommers and if you ladies would excuse me…"

Lydiel didn't want Matt to leave. She wanted to spend time with him and she wanted to get rid of Sarah.

"I'll just be outside, Lydiel. Not to worry."

"Sarah, why don't we agree to meet again with the necessary paperwork on Thursday at this same time?"

"Sounds good to me, Ms Sommers. See you then."

Lydiel extended her hand but Sarah was dismissive. A few blocks away Sarah Turner tried to control her trembling. No one told her…She steadied her hands as she made the call.

"I need paperwork and the job is mine."

This was the best news Allison had had all day. A slow, wicked smile crossed her face as she headed off for her meeting.

Lydiel closed the door and looked around for Matt.

"Matt? Matt? Where did you go?"

Lydiel heard his voice just outside the back door.

"I'm here, lonely and horny, Can you help me?"

"Only if you come closer."

Back inside the apartment, Matt held Lydiel as if he had been away for a very long time. He looked into her eyes and kissed her deeply as his hands snaked up the kimono sleeves. Holding him felt so good and so right and she needed him. Matt undid the belt of the robe and eased it off her shoulders. She unbuttoned his trousers and reached inside. He missed her all right.

Lying naked together and talking about everything and nothing, Lydiel had to bite her lip to stop herself from saying the words. Rolling her onto her back and starting at her eyelids, Matt kissed every inch of her. She was hot and she wanted to feel him inside her but not yet. She reciprocated in kind. He liked to watch her as she teased and tasted him. He also liked how she responded to his response to her. Matt had a way of pushing Lydiel to the edge, but he never let her fall and he never left her hanging. Today was no exception.

As she tried to slow her breathing, Lydiel continued to experience the mini tremor-like orgasms as her head rested in the crook of Matt's arm. Kissing him lightly, she needed answers to her earlier questions.

"What is it babe?"

"I didn't say anything."

Snuggling closer with her arm across him, Lydiel waited for him to tell her.

"Well, I'm here because I miss you and I wanted to surprise you. My presentation went so well that Henry gave me yesterday afternoon and today off."

"Oh wow! I get to be with you two days in a row. Be still my heart."

Matt took a long look at Lydiel before speaking. "I want your heart to keep beating and for a very long time."

Lydiel felt the sting of tears welling in her eyes. She knew that love hunger was in control of her life. She always tried to hide it from Matt but there were those times, moments like this that got the better of her. She fought with her better judgment and softly asked the question she always asked.

"How long do I get to keep you today, lover?"

"Until I decide to go home Lydiel, and right now I am in no particular hurry to get there."

Lydiel could not believe what she was hearing. This was not like Matt at all.

"Matt, is everything okay, at home I mean?"

"Things haven't been right there for a very long time. Hey, I've got an idea. What say we get cleaned up and go for a ride someplace?

Put on some comfortable clothes, your tennies and grab your camera."

Whatever was going on they would talk about it later. For the first time Matthew McNulty and Lydiel Rosemary Sommers showered together and left her house together.

Chapter 11

Connie Pushman rubbed her temples as she poured over the new figures for the upcoming ball fundraiser. She was already beginning to regret drinking the bottle of Pinot Grigio last night as she waited up for Henry. It was after 1 am when she heard his key in the lock, and wherever he spent the evening it appeared to have agreed with him. She had no questions and felt it best to let sleeping dogs lie. Allison had spoiled her evening of card playing with her paranoid ideas about Matt. Wherever Matt was, he was lucky to be away from her. As long as they had been friends she never understood why Allison was so bitter. For the time being, however, this ball had to be her priority for many reasons. Deep in thought the sound of the intercom buzzer startled her.

"Yes Louise, what is it?"

"Mrs. McNulty is on line one, Mrs. Pushman."

Oh joy! Just what she needed this morning. More angry diatribes.

"Thank you, Louise. Put her through."

"Hi Allison. How's your day?"

"Same stuff, different day. Matt looked me in the eye and lied to me. Apparently screwing that bitch is more important than his kids. I can't make the meeting this evening. I have no sitter for the boys."

"You HAVE to be there. Our guys are meeting us. This is their only available date. We can't do this without them. Remey and Francesca will also be there. This was your idea and we are all risking a lot for you. Personally I don't know why things have to be so drastic. So he is getting some on the side. Why can't you just let it be? You don't want to sleep with him anyway."

"I am not rehashing this with you Connie. I want her dead! I want him gone, and you are going to help me as agreed. Sarah had her interview and it looks like she's in, so get your paper guy to have background checks and verifiable references done by this evening. I want to move forward as quickly as possible."

"Allison, why can't your mother watch the boys?"

"Don't mention that crone to me. She and her old fogey friends are having poker night and she doesn't want the kids there."

"I don't get it. She wanted grandchildren, you wanted kids, but neither of you wants to be bothered. I am holding up my end of the bargain and you had better be there or else I am OUT, and I am taking everyone and the money with me. Your choice, Allison. I need to get back to crunching numbers. See you this evening at Mirelli's and don't be late."

Connie was beginning to disappoint Allison. They had been friends for over 40 years and yet it was becoming more and more apparent how little Connie really knew her. Her relationship with Matt had been in a steady decline for several years. It was funny how at one time in her life she really thought she could pull it off and have it all, but over the years she had come to realize that the responsibilities and expectations that went along with marriage and motherhood made her feel as if she were in a trap with no escape.

For the first few years she did a good job of playing wife. Of course she had to. Everyone was pressuring her to have kids, and her mother had assured her that this was the best way to secure her future with Matt. Actually it had destroyed the relationship between her and Matt. She didn't like sex on a regular basis. Even occasional lovemaking almost turned her stomach; so much so, for the most part she no longer slept with him. She didn't like him touching her in any way. Keeping busy with outside activities was her plan of avoidance and it seemed to be working. He was a good person, too good in some ways, just not for her, forever. She loved the kids but at times they were like two little millstones around her neck. The older they got the more demanding her role as a mother became.

Matt was a very sensual and sexual person full of warmth and charm who craved intimacy. Allison found that type of closeness unnecessary, and she had realized a certain sort of satisfaction in the status quo. She had church and he had his hobbies, but at the same time she had become increasingly disturbed with his dalliances. The latest one was totally unacceptable and for the first time she truly felt threatened.

Chapter 12

Henry Pushman was having the best day he had had in a very long time. Life could be so good sometimes; so warm and so damn hot - like Miss Francesca Sommers. He could still feel how wet she was and how good it felt to let go inside a warm, willing body. It had been far too long. He wanted to see her again, and again and again. He was surprised to see that Connie had waited up for him as it was well after 1 a.m. when he arrived home. He noticed an empty wine bottle as he walked past her to the kitchen. No words were exchanged as he went up to bed.

Now where did he put her number? He had called his office late last night and left it in a voicemail, and as soon as he arrived at work he had retrieved the number, written it down and now he couldn't remember where he put it. The whirring ring of his private line distracted him briefly.

"This is Henry."

"I hope so. I would be very disappointed if it was anyone else."

Connie's attempt at facetious humor always amused him. She was so transparent.

"Oh, hello dear. How's your day going so far?"

"Busy as always. I am still crunching numbers so I won't be home until very late. Perhaps you might want to grab a bite to eat on your way home."

"I see. I'm sure your hard work and dedication will be rewarded handsomely dear."

"Being married to the boss certainly helps. Take care, Henry."

Ordinarily he would have been slightly irritated but today was different- very different. Henry found the number and immediately called Francesca.

"Hellooooo"

"Good morning Miss Francesca Sommers"

"Hi Mr. P! Nice surprise."

"You, my dear were the nicest surprise I have had in a very long time."

Francesca thought she had heard every pickup line in existence but there was something so sincere about Mr. P's flattery. For an old guy, he was very hot and very nice.

"I was wondering if you were busy this evening?

"I have plans."

"I see. I wonder if you would you change them for a nice dinner and a night of wild sex with a guy old enough to be your father, and horny enough to seriously screw you silly?"

"Hmm, let me think for a moment. Wifey is unavailable. Daddy is hungry and wants to be fed. Is that about right?"

Henry's shirt collar suddenly felt tight and the bulge in his trousers was hard to ignore.

"Uhm…, Yes, in a manner of speaking. Wear something nice and meet me at 8 p.m. at the Renaissance Square. I am looking forward to seeing you again, Miss Francesca Sommers."

"I'll be there. See you soon, Mr. P."

Francesca needed to get a move on. She was meeting the girls at Mirelli's at 7 p.m. and would have to leave no later than 7:45 pm to walk the two blocks to the Renaissance. Better yet, save the wear and tear on her feet from the stiletto heels and take a cab.

Henry placed a call to Executive Services at The Renaissance. Pushman and Associates held a long-term lease on two executive penthouse suites at the hotel, and he left instructions to have the elite suite prepared for two guests for the evening. For the first time in years he was excited. Everything had to be perfect for his evening with Miss Francesca Sommers!

Chapter 13

Lydiel never expected this day to come. The weather was perfect as was her companion, and she was happy. Matt had never seen Lydiel so quiet and he wondered what was going on in that writer's mind of hers.

"Are you okay babe? You are so quiet."

"I'm wonderful sweetie. I was just thinking."

"Dangerous thing - a thinking woman…"

"I am just very, very, very happy Matt.

"I'm glad sweetie. This was long overdue."

"Matt, what's going on? You and I talked about a day like this but you always said it was not doable. Now all of a sudden I see you two days in a row and we're finally having our day together. You are taking a big chance and I don't want to make things more difficult between you and Allison."

"Not to worry babe. There is no danger of that happening. I have come to realize that nothing could make things worse between Allison and me. I also realized there is nothing that can make things better."

Lydiel heard the disappointment and

resignation in Matt's voice and it further burdened her heart. There were times when she felt like Matt's transition woman. The bitterness and unhappiness were beginning to take their toll and she wondered if they were together today because he wanted to be with her or as an overt act of rebellion. For whatever reason, it felt wonderful to be with him.

Matt turned off the main road onto a short dirt road. He switched the engine off and got out of the car. He retrieved an oversized backpack from the trunk and walked around to open the door for Lydiel.

"We're here babe. Come with me."

As Matt took her hand he turned and kissed her. Was there ever a time since he entered her life that Lydiel had not wanted him? She craved intimacy with Matt the way some people craved sweets. Taking a quick look around she noticed what looked like an entrance to the woods with lots of tall trees and a well-worn path that seemed to go on forever.

"Where are we Matt? What is this place?"

"This is Whistler's Woods and the realization of one of your fantasies."

Lydiel was excited and confused at the same

time. She was afraid that if she blinked it would all be a dream. Holding his hand tighter, she walked down the path with him, every now and then glimpsing a clearing. The ground was a soft carpet of pine needles and fallen leaves. The sun peeked out between the branches creating unique shadows, and her heart was racing.

"Where are we going Matt?"

"We're there."

'There' was a small secluded clearing between two stands of trees. Matt removed a blanket from the backpack and spread it on the soft ground.

"Care to join me, lover?"

"When did you have time to plan all this?"

Matt was full of surprises today.

"When I realized I had the day off. You told me once that you had never made love outside. Today that all changes; that is if you want it to."

"I more than want it to."

"Then lie here with me babe and hold me, kiss me, and be with me."

For the rest of the afternoon Matthew McNulty indulged Lydiel Sommers in a warm, intimate realization of one her fantasies, and in so doing made her a very happy woman. The ride home gave her ample opportunity to take wonderful pictures of the countryside, but the best pictures of the day were the ones that would remain as warm memories in her mind and her heart.

As he kissed Lydiel goodbye, Matt could only imagine what would be waiting for him at home. Unfortunately he didn't have to wait long.

Chapter 14

When he pulled into the garage Matt noticed Allison's car. Bracing himself he opened the pass through door and was greeted by the cacophony of little boy voices-his little boys.

"Dad's home! Dad's home!"

Matt had to laugh. The way the boys spoke in unison was so irritating sometimes but also very funny.

"Hi you two. How are ya?"

Allison was unimpressed with the father and sons reunion, and the urge to rip into Matt was getting the best of her.

"Boys, I need to speak to your dad. I think the movie you wanted to see is in the DVD player."

"I don't really feel like this now, Allison."

Matt hadn't been in the house five minutes and it was starting already. Allison was wound up tighter than a drum and raring to unleash on Matt. He didn't want to spoil the good feelings of the day by entering into a "discussion" with Allison.

"You knew how important this evening was to me, yet you chose to spend it with the slut of the month. The boys are your responsibility as well as mine. Now I'm late. I fed them already and the homework is done. I should be home by 10 or so. By the way, I know you didn't have to work today."

"Allison, wait… The boys need their mom too. All of these meetings are taking a toll on them. Can't you skip this one?"

"I have nothing more to say to you, Matt McAllister! If you want someone to talk to, talk to your whore."

With that Allison turned on her heel, slammed out the door and drove off. Before Matt could adjust to Allison's verbal barrage the boys were nagging him.

"Come watch the movie with us dad, please?"

Matt sighed deeply, took a seat between his sons and for the next two hours revisited the exploits of Godzilla.

Lydiel decided a warm, luxuriously fragrant bubble bath was in order. Popping in her favorite classical CD, she stepped into the lavender scented bubble bath, closed her eyes and relived the day. She would never forget how thoughtful Matt was. She was concerned, however, about what was going on between him and Allison. Just as she was enjoying the relaxing properties of the lavender, the phone rang.

"Good evening, this is Lydiel."

"And just where the hell have you been Missy? I have been trying to reach you for hours."

Who could mistake the whiney nasal tones of her flamboyantly gay agent, Jack Bass. Lydiel always had fun with Jack and could give back as good as he gave.

"Keep your pants on sugar and tell that tall drink of Latin water to give your dick a break so you can talk to me. I was out this afternoon. Now tell me what is so important?"

"The publisher wants your book, and they are offering a more than acceptable advance. There may be a few minor revisions and the deal is done. I will be in touch, and tell whoever was in those panties of yours to keep it up-no pun intended. Ciao Bella."

Lydiel Sommers was indeed a happy woman tonight.

Connie Pushman was mentally taking Allison to task. For a woman who was trying to arrange a murder or two, Allison certainly was playing fast and loose with keeping dates. It was 7:20 and no sign of her. Everyone at the table was getting a little antsy, especially Francesca.

"Connie, I need to leave soon. I have another engagement."

Francesca was not about to miss out on what she felt certain was to be an evening of hot steamy sex with her new horny hottie of a guy in a very posh hotel. She had come far recently and she was not going to blow it waiting for Miss I Want To Kill My Husband's Mistress to show up for a meeting.

As wicked and as cruel as she was, Francesca never realized how a person could devote so much time to planning to murder someone. That is what poisons were created for. Of course they didn't seem to work well on a certain person. A few weeks ago it could have been her Allison wanted dead. Matt would have done her if she had played her cards right, but like always she blew it. Now they rarely e-mailed each other. At any rate that was all water under the bridge. Allison was right about one thing, Miss Goody Two Shoes Lydiel had to go. Connie's questions interrupted her dreams of Lydiel's demise.

"You have a date Francesca? With whom?"

The two men seated with them at the table with them seemed unduly nervous. Neither man made eye contact with the women nor did they speak to each other. All Francesca knew about the men was second hand information gleaned from her sister. According to Remey the taller of the two men introduced only as the pharmaceutical guy, was a strange man who was always quoting scripture while dealing industrial strength toxins, and who definitely did not come cheap. He had a mortgage, three kids in college, a high maintenance ex, and a little unaccounted for cash on the side. Francesca assumed the other man was the paper man.

Connie found it hard to concentrate on the business at hand. For some reason she was irritated by the change in Henry. She hoped that whomever the little tart was that was spicing up his life would keep him so busy that he wouldn't look too closely at the budget for the ball.

Remey could never understand why people met at a restaurant and then waited forever to order food.

"Are we going to eat soon? I fed Doug and the kids but I didn't eat dinner myself."

Poor Remey. Were it not for her special talents, she would not be a part of this at all. Her overwhelming obsession with food obscured any other thought processes until she was fed. Sensing her restlessness Connie decided dinner shouldn't wait.

"Why don't we all order now? I'm sure Allison will be along shortly"

Connie was not good at stalling and right now she was very angry with Allison. It was obvious that the paper guy had places to go and things to do, and joining in girl talk among the co-conspirators was not among them. Connie read his face and knew that the time was up.

"I'm afraid I can't stay for dinner Mrs. Pushman. I'm meeting a very important client for dinner. I wanted to make the acquaintance of Mrs. McNulty, however, her presence here isn't necessary. I believe you'll find these in order."

As he slid the box towards Connie, Francesca was busy clock watching. Opening the envelope, Connie was satisfied that the papers were in order and pushed a thick envelope towards the paper guy.

"I believe our business here is concluded ladies. Have a good evening."

"I need to leave as well, Connie. I don't want to be late for my date."

"Must you leave us too, dear? You never answered my question about your date."

This was the first time in over a year that Connie had heard anything about Francesca dating anyone. Francesca slid her chair back, stood and smoothed her dress.

"We'll talk tomorrow, Connie. I think I see Allison coming in. Enjoy dinner and see to it that my sister is well taken care of. Good evening, everyone.

Hailing a taxi, Francesca was off to meet her hot, hot Mr. P.

As she feigned any true sincerity, Allison

approached the group offering her usual apology.

"I am so very sorry to be so late. Was that Francesca I saw leaving?"

"Well if it isn't Princess Allison."

Connie's cryptic greeting told Allison that she was just slightly pissed off at her late arrival. As luck would have it Giorgio was working and hovering as usual.

"Can I get anyone anything?"

Speaking for the group, Connie ordered their usual libation and found it difficult to hide her anger with Allison. The success of the plan hinged on a full commitment from each of them. Lately Allison had become lax in that area. The pharmaceutical guy adjusted his horn-rimmed glasses, checked his watch and addressed the group.

"Ladies, I really must leave. Remey knows how to utilize the product. She's quite proficient, really. I believe there is just one piece of business to take care of..."

Allison reached into her purse and pulled out a small zippered bag that she passed to the pharmaceutical guy. Matt would never notice the money missing and it was just as much hers as it was his. He had been so preoccupied lately he hadn't had time to check the emergency account. If she made the deal she was working on she could replace the money very soon. After Lydiel and Matt were taken care of, she would control the finances and be able to repay Connie.

The man made brief eye contact with Allison as he pushed back his chair.

"It was a pleasure doing business with you. Remey, ladies, have a good evening."

Making sure he was gone, Connie started in on Allison.

"You almost blew it! We are so close and you almost blew it! What the hell were you thinking?"

"I was thinking I had to wait for my husband to get home to watch the kids. I was thinking about him screwing his whore. I was thinking that more than ever I want her dead! I was thinking that I don't want to see any physical harm come to Matt but I want him to pay for what he has done to me."

Remey viewed Allison with total revulsion, a hypocrite of the worst kind. Here she was plotting the murder of her mother while at the same time whining about what the man who never gets sex at home is doing to her. Remey wondered why Matt was even still living at home. Allison was a cold bitch with a cold heart who thought everyone had to jump to for her.

"Why do you care what he does and exactly what is it he has done to you Allison? He comes home every night and you don't want to screw him anyway. Matt needs someplace warm and wet and that definitely is not your slit."

That was the first non-food related remark Remey had uttered.

"It's the principle of the thing, nothing the likes of you would know anything about. You people lay down with anyone and anything. A one night stand is one thing but when the one night stand goes on continuously, that constitutes a relationship, and that's threatening and unacceptable."

At that moment Connie Pushman hated Allison McNulty. Her lack of sensitivity was appalling as was her entire demeanor. Allison always thought her father's Nordic background somehow made her better than other people, but her lack of social graces made her quite the contrary.

Remey bristled at Allison's remark, but kept the conversation as civil as possible.

"But why do you want to kill the woman instead of your husband Allison? It takes two remember?"

"We are no longer having this conversation, Remey. Now when will the things be ready?"

In her heart Remey was more than ready to abandon the project, but she also had an axe to grind with Lydiel that went way to back to her childhood. She also did not want to disappoint Francesca.

"Give me a few weeks Allison and it'll be a done deal."

"Why do you want to kill your mom Remey?"

"We are not having this conversation, Allison"

Connie apparently had misread Remey. She was far more capable of handling Allison than she realized and the more Allison talked the more she jeopardized the project.

Chapter 15

Henry was nursing a rum and coke as he waited for Francesca. Just the thought of her smooth warm skin and the heat she generated made him hard. He felt flush and this was a momentary source of embarrassment for him.

Francesca watched Mr. P from a distance for a few seconds before approaching him.

"Looking for me were you?"

"Not anymore darlin'. How is Miss Francesca Sommers this evening?

"She is very well thank you and happy to be in the company of a very sexy and very hot guy."

"I have a surprise for you, my dear."

"What girl doesn't love a surprise Mr. P?"

Henry stood up, took Francesca's arm and led her to the elevator. She had never been inside the hotel and was somewhat apprehensive. Mr. P was major league, and definitely out of her league. The elevator stopped at P1 and the doors opened into the most elegant penthouse Francesca had ever seen. Of course it was the only one she had ever seen.

"Oh my! This is all for me?"

Henry loved the look on Francesca's face. It was like the joy of watching a child at Christmas, only she was no child.

"It's for us, at least for tonight, I hope. I have another surprise for you. Come in my dear."

As Francesca entered the bedroom area she noticed a little pink shopping bag on the bed. When she opened it she found a black lace crotchless thong and peek-a-boo bra.

"I hope I didn't offend you but I learned that you were a dancer once and I thought perhaps you would do me the honor of dancing for me"

So, he had been checking up on her, had he? It was probably standard operating procedure for a guy like him. After all one could never be too careful.

"I would be happy to. Where can I change?"

"Right through there."

As soon as Francesca left the room, Henry installed the titanium pole, got undressed and seated himself in his favorite chair. When she re-entered the room she noticed the pole.

" Ooooo what a kinky boy you are, Mr. ***P.***"

Turning the music on, Henry urged her on. Grabbing it with both hands she swung her body onto the pole, arching first one leg and then the other in an air walk. Pulling herself further up the pole she swung her hips from side to side and then effortlessly changed positions, all the while to the tune of the music. Dismounting and walking over to him, Francesca stooped down and teased him with her tongue. His response was immediate. Turning her around and bending her over slightly, Henry ran his finger along the cleavage between her butt cheeks and just inside the crotchless thong touching her gently. Francesca slowly moved away from him and mounted the pole again. She began a series of gyrations that Henry only imagined to be humanly possible. As he gently stroked himself, beads of perspiration formed on his upper lip and forehead.

"Francesca, come sit on my lap please."

Slithering over to Henry, she eased herself onto his hardness, rocking gently.

"Was this what you had in mind sweet P?"

Henry was now totally oblivious to his

surroundings and fighting with everything in him not to explode inside her at that very moment.

"It is more than what I had in mind, Miss Francesca Sommers."

Lifting her up, he turned her to face him as he buried his tongue halfway down her throat. He felt her hard nipples pressing against his chest and he knew he needed to lay her down. Throwing back the covers with one hand, he eased her onto the bed and rolled her onto her back. With her legs parted he kissed her hard as his fingers squeezed her nipples. His tongue teased her belly as he made his way to his favorite places. Parting her fleshy lips his tongue toyed with her button until it was hard and throbbing, as he tasted the juices of her hot pink wetness. He was so hard he could stand it no longer. He draped her legs over his shoulders and took her deeply, over and over, each time a little harder as he felt her muscles grab and hold him. With her arms around his neck Francesca pushed upwards as Henry continued to ravage her. He felt as if his release was coming from a place deep within him as he let go. Francesca was still as she felt the orgasms, hers as well as his. Pulling away from her, he kissed her once more as he rolled onto his back. He held her close as if she would disappear if he didn't.

"That was so very good. Thank you Miss Francesca Sommers."

Francesca had been with many men in her young life, but this was the first time she had made love with anyone. She closed her eyes and snuggled close to her Mr. P, and for the first time she felt safe

Henry sat in the easy chair and watched Francesca sleep. He wondered how such young a woman could be such a sexual tigress. He saw her reach for him and awaken when she noticed he was no longer there."How long was I asleep, Mr. P?"

"Not long dear. I thought you might want to freshen up before dinner."

Francesca was thirsty and famished and no matter what time it was, dinner sounded like a very good idea, so did a warm bath to relax her overused muscles.

The bathroom was awash in scented candlelight and the tub was filled with a softly fragrant bubble bath. A black lace negligee and matching robe were hanging on the door; yet another display of caring from Henry. She wondered how any woman could reject a man so kind and loving.

Taking into account the lateness of the hour, Henry ordered a bottle of 1996 Salon Blanc de Blanc, Truffle Bresaola Salad and petite Chocolate Crème Brule. He decided to teach Miss Francesca Sommers more of what the good life could offer.

Just as Francesca joined Henry in the living room, the elevator buzzed and Henry keyed the doors to allow the Room Service attendant to enter the penthouse.

For the first time in her life, Francesca had an idea of what it was like to be rich. She would never have been able to afford the things Henry had purchased for her.

"You look amazing Miss Francesca Sommers. Care to join me for a late supper? And you can tell me a little about yourself Miss Francesca Sommers."

"There isn't much to tell Mr. P. My brother and I were adopted when he was 11 and I was 8. I have many sisters and brothers. As to employment, I am currently employed as a personal administrative assistant. (This is how Francesca rationalized her involvement in the plot to kill her mother)".

"Are your parents still alive?"

"My father is deceased. My mother is Lydiel Sommers, the writer. You have probably never heard of her."

"Quite the contrary, my dear. I have read some of her early work. We have never met but it is my understanding that she is rather reclusive."

She was reclusive all right. Lydiel put a twist on being reclusive by screwing the brains out of Matthew McNulty every chance she got. Francesca wondered how people would feel about her mother if they knew she was a mistress.

"She and I don't have a close relationship and rarely see each other. Okay, now it's your turn, Mr. P and by the way, since we have made love more than once, maybe you can tell me your name."

"Well, Miss Francesca Sommers, as you know I am encumbered, so to speak. I have two children, a set of twins who will be entering college in the fall. I am the president and CEO of a large firm here in town. I have been married to my wife Constance for

22 years and we no longer share a bed. I am 56 years old and enjoying the company of the hottest woman I have ever known. Oh, my name is Henry Pushman."

Francesca choked on her salad. Her head was swimming and she suddenly felt almost ill.

"Oh my, my, my. Are you okay, my dear? Drink some wine and take a deep breath."

All the wine in the world wasn't going to change the fact that she, Francesca Sommers had just seriously fucked Connie Pushman's husband! Not to mention that Henry had no idea that she, Francesca Sommers had been screwing his wife for over a year. She was in way over her head and up to her sweet ass in Pushmans.

"I hope everything was to your liking, dear."

"Everything was wonderful, Henry, and please just call me Francesca."

"Francesca it is."

As they returned to the bed, she found a perverse pleasure in sucking the cock of Henry Pushman. He was by far the better lover of the two. How ironic.

Chapter 16

Allison turned off the engine, locked the car and closed the garage door. She was exhausted. Opening the front door she could tell by the darkness and quiet that everyone was asleep, including Matt, which was a very good thing. Feeling her way, she found the sofa. It was definitely going to happen! Everything was in place- almost.

Connie and Remey were the only ones remaining from the meeting. There was something unsettling about the "pharmacist" as Remey referred to him. He didn't seem to be as much of a stranger as Allison let on. He left Connie with a bad taste in her mouth. As she waited for Remey to finally finish her dessert, Connie decided to check her messages. The first one was from Henry.

"Hello dear. I'm sorry to disturb you at this hour but I fear that I have overindulged tonight and will be staying over at the club. I will meet you in the conference room for the 9 a.m. meeting."

In 22 years of marriage Henry Pushman had only spent the night away from home when traveling on business. Perhaps he had found a playmate at last. No matter. Connie had plans of her own.

"Remey, would you like to stay over at my house tonight? It seems Henry drank a little too much and is spending the night at the club. The twins are at a sleepover and I really hate to be alone tonight."

"I guess that might work. Doug is traveling on business and the kids are with his ex. Sure, why not."

At least a part of the evening could be salvaged. She missed Francesca, though. It had been weeks since they were all together. After paying the tab and leaving the restaurant, Connie and Remey discussed the plan as they headed towards the house.

"Where did you meet the pharmacist, Remey?"

"He used to be but isn't a pharmacist anymore. Francesca and I were at a convention and he was there. He's a very interesting, smart geek. I expressed an interest in unique applications for some of the chemicals and he took me under his wing. This is how I supplement my income."

Connie realized how little she really knew about Remey, other than the obvious. Turning into the drive, she noticed that once again she forgot to set the timer. Retrieving the flashlight from the trunk, she and Remey entered the empty house. As soon as she switched on a lamp, she saw the message light blinking on the phone. She decided to let the messages go until tomorrow.

"Would you care for something to drink, Remey?

"Maybe just a glass of wine, Pinot if you have it"

"Make yourself at home. I'll be right back."

As long as they had known each other, neither Remey nor Francesca had ever been invited to Connie's home. After removing and folding her jacket and skirt, Remey relaxed on the massive sofa. It must be nice to have so much money.

Connie poured the wine, and took the bottle back to the living room. Handing Remey a glass, she placed the tray on the table. Remey stood up, placed her glass and Connie's glass on the table, put her arms around Connie and kissed her lips softly. How long had it been, Connie wondered, as Remey removed first her jacket, then her shirt and finally her bra. Pulling Connie down onto her lap Remey slowly squeezed first one breast and then the other. Her fingers trailed lightly across her nipples feeling them harden under her touch.

Connie's pulse quickened as Remey laid her down on the sofa and removed her nylons, kissing her thighs as she did so. She knew Connie was wet and she inserted one finger beneath the lace panty and lightly caressed her between her lips. Connie moaned softly as Remey removed the skirt, and then the panty, teasing her with her tongue. Connie unhooked Remey's bra and felt the warm weight of her ample breasts as they touched her thighs.

Connie decided that before the foreplay continued, it would be better to move to the playroom which served as the guestroom. Once inside, Connie buried her face in Remey's cleavage as she let her hands roam over her equally ample behind. Lying on the bed, Remey once again tongue teased and fingered Connie until she felt the contractions signaling Connie's orgasmic release.

Never one to leave her lovers hanging, Connie found the double strap on, stepped into the harness and inserted one end into Remey's pink wetness. Turning both ends on, Connie rode Remey until they both came several times. As the two women lay spent in each other's arms, Connie realized how much she missed the girls, especially Francesca.

Chapter 17

Matt had no idea how long he had been awake when he found himself staring at the ceiling once again. The clock read 4:15 am, and he decided he may as well get up and review the figures for the meeting later. Walking softly to the bathroom, his thoughts turned to the day before. Stepping into the shower and soaping up he thought about Lydiel and how warm and wet she was, and how good it felt to finally shower with her. As he dried himself off, his mind continued to wander. After finishing his morning routine, he took a long hard look at himself in the mirror and he knew...

The meeting of the executive committee necessitated a suit and tie, which he hated. Tiptoeing quietly down the stairs, Matt made his way to his office. He knew the house well enough in the dark to avoid any dangerous obstacles. As a diabetic he knew the dangers of a cut or severe bruise. A fleeting moment of anger rushed through him as he watched Allison asleep on the sofa and fully clothed. Was he really so terrible that she couldn't bring herself to at least sleep in the same bed with him? Why did he subject himself to this? It was time to accept it, grieve the loss and get on with his life. He needed caffeine.

After turning on the under cabinet light in the kitchen, he made coffee and tried to focus on the events of the day ahead. Allison stirred gently in her sleep as her arm hit the floor. Thankfully this action was not enough to awaken her. Matt filled his favorite mug with the steaming lifeline and quietly entered his office. Slowly easing the door shut he switched on the lamp, turned on the computer and waited, and waited, and waited for the Pushman site to come up. An alert message was flashing on the site but as Matt attempted to access it he couldn't. He decided to read his e-mail instead.

Lydiel turned and hugged Matt's pillows tightly. They smelled of him and even as she slept, thoughts of him ran through her dreams. The alarm went off and she felt for the off switch. It was 4:45 a.m. Slowly climbing out of bed, with half closed eyes she made her way to her office, found her office chair and plopped down. Matt was always admonishing her about turning on lights and dispensing with the insane tangle of phone cords, cable cords and extension cords in her work area. He referred to her office as an OSHA nightmare. She ran her hands across the desk feeling for her glasses, found them and turned on her computer. As the screen came to life there was the familiar splash informing her she had mail. Squinting through her glasses she saw one from Matt. He was thanking her for yesterday. She sent a reply. An instant message window opened. Matt started the conversation.

MatMc: "Why are you up so early?"

Ly_Som: "I wanted to get an early start with the writing."

MatMc: "Go back to bed, babe, it's too early. You need to rest."

Ly_Som: "Thanks for yesterday. You are wonderful."

MatMc: "My pleasure sweetie and so are you."

Ly_Som: "What time is your meeting?"

MatMc: "9 a.m. I thought I would do a quick review but I can't sign onto the site.

Ly_Som: "Sorry"

MatMc: "Can you do me a favor? Can you try logging in for me?"

Ly_Som: "I can try. Give me the details."

MatMc: "The username is pushcoas. Password is wd40"

Ly_Som: "Okay, I am there. What do you need?"

MatMc: "Do you see an alert there?"

Ly_Som: "No"

MatMc: "Can you pull up the budget for the ball?"

Ly_Som: "I am there now, there seems to be something wrong but I am not a spreadsheet expert."

MatMc: "Babe can you do me a really huge favor?"

Ly_Som: "Anything for you."

MatMc: "Can you copy and paste that page and send it to me in an e-mail"

Ly_Som: "I can try,"

MatMc: "Thanks, I appreciate it."

Ly_Som: "No problem. It is on the way.

MatMc: "It's here. Thanks. Now please go back to bed. I will call you before the meeting. Kisses.

Ly_Som: "Kisses and more. Later sweetie.

MatMc: "Later lover."

Admittedly Lydiel knew practically nothing about spreadsheets but her assessment that something seemed out of place was correct. As he waited for the attachment to print, Matt was curious about the alert and why it happened when he tried to bring the site up, and not when Lydiel tried to access it. Matt turned off the computer, grabbed his jacket and woke Allison on his way out. His day was off to an interesting start.

Lydiel closed the instant message window and returned to her bed. Something was troubling Matt and she was sure he would discuss it with her later if he could. She was thinking about Jack Bass' comments last night. Could this be her big break finally? Matt would be so surprised and so proud of her but mum was the word until the check was in her hand.

Henry leaned up on his elbow and watched the

sleeping woman lying beside him. She seemed so innocent and child-like but he knew she had been around a little. None of that mattered. What mattered now was that she made him happy. It was nice to finally be able to do something for someone who genuinely appreciated it.

Silently extricating himself, he checked the clock. It read 5:15 a.m., and time to get his day started. He reached out from underneath the covers and grabbed his cell phone and saw the message light flashing. At this time of morning he felt certain the messages could wait. He walked softly to the shower. He had the 9 a.m. meeting on his mind. He was trying desperately to bring the ball in just slightly under budget. Matt's ideas and his presentation had already saved the company several thousand dollars and Henry liked his fresh ideas. What he did not like was the way Connie spent so much time with Allison.

The warm water felt good as he thought about his romp with Francesca. The more he was with her the more he wanted to be. Was this his mid-life crisis? After getting dressed he wrote a quick note to her, grabbed his cell and quietly left the penthouse.

Remey's snoring awakened Connie. She rolled her over onto her side and knew immediately she had slept through the alarm. She absolutely could not be late today of all days. As she looked at the peacefulness in Remey's face, Connie realized how much she hated sleeping alone. Now she need to take a quick shower, get dressed even quicker and get to the office.

"Remey! Remey!"

Connie had a difficult time waking the sleeping woman. She hated to disturb her but they needed to leave within the next 30 minutes.

"What's wrong, Connie?"

"Nothing dear but you need to get showered and dressed. We have to leave soon"

"Okay. What time is it?

"It is 5:30 a.m.

Dressed and ready for the day, Connie made coffee while waiting for Remey. She decided to listen to her messages and leave one for the twins as well. Just as the first message was queued, Connie heard the dog bark. Going out to the garage, she saw a squirrel tormenting Fluffer. Once back inside, Connie poured the coffee and within fifteen minutes she and Remey were on their way.

Yawning and stretching her way into the new day, Francesca Sommers was enjoying her last few moments of living large. As she reached to grab Henry's pillow, she found a note.

"Dear Miss Francesca Sommers,

Thank you for fulfilling an old man's fantasies. You are wonderful. I'm sorry I had to leave you this morning but I have a very important meeting. If you open the closet I believe you will find everything you need to start your day. I have also left instructions for a car to be brought around to take you to work. I miss your touch already. Have a wonderful day and until were are in each other's arms once more,

Soft kisses for you my dear,

Henry."

Francesca jumped out of bed and opened the closet door. Inside were a designer dress, shoes and bag to match as well as coordinated undies. Henry Pushman was a very nice man but very lonely. He was also quite the stud muffin. He was also very generous. She knew she would have to reconcile her relationships with both Pushmans and soon. But for now what a way to start her day!

Chapter 18

Matt and Henry arrived at the front desk simultaneously, laughing as they greeted each other.

"I didn't know you were such an early riser, Henry."

"I try to rise every chance I get, my boy."

Matt was always uncertain as to what his response should be to Henry's brand of humor.

"Sounds good to me, Henry. I'm on my way to check a few last minute details before the 9 o'clock."

"I shall let you get on with it, then. See you at the meeting."

Henry was impressed with Matt's dedication and due diligence, however, he suspected there was another reason his new executive arrived at work two hours early.

Matt turned on his computer and once again tried to access the Pushman site to no avail. He decided to check his e-mail and fiddle until time for the meeting. He also needed to call home and make sure Allison was up and getting the boys ready for their day.

"Hello? Allison, are you up?"

"Of course I am. I answered the phone didn't I? I am getting the boys ready for school. I have already broken up several arguments between them this morning. You really need to speak with them, that is of course when you can find the time."

Why did he even call? Was it just to irritate her? No matter. After last night Allison knew that in a short matter of time her two main sources of irritation would be eliminated forever.

Matt returned to his e-mails. Midway through reading them the chimes sounded indicating an instant message. Since he was not officially on the clock, he opened the window.

Dor_N: "Hey Matt. How are you?"

MatMc: "Waiting for my hug as always."

Dor_N: "LOL. I miss your hugs too. Have you seen my mom lately?"

MatMc: "LOL I saw her yesterday. We spent the day together."

Dor_N: "Wow! I bet she was happy. A whole day with you!"

MatMc: "We enjoyed each other's company."

Dor_N: "I'm glad. I have a question for you."

MatMc: "Sure, what's up?"

Dor_N: "Have you talked to mommy on the phone and heard another conversation or garbled speech?"

MatMc: "Yep. She and I talked about it. She said she was going to write a story about the munchkins in the phone."

Dor_N: "Lately when I talk to her I hear a conversation between two women and it sounds as if they are planning to hurt someone. I started taping what I hear. I know it's probably not a good idea but no one seems to believe me when I tell them what is going on."

MatMc: "Sorry Doreen. It's getting a little busy here. Maybe when I visit Lydiel again you can let me hear the tapes.

Dor_N: "I know how that works. LOL, but okay. Talk later.

MatMc: "Soon, I promise. Bye."

Matt knew exactly what Doreen was talking about. Just yesterday he experienced the same thing when speaking with Lydiel on the phone. Double chimes sounded indicating two instant messages. Well, if it wasn't little Miss Meanie-none other than Francesca.

Msquad: "Hiiiiiii Matt. Kisses hot stuff."

MatMc: "Hi Francesca. I need a minute, okay?"

MSquad: "Sure hot stuff."

Matt knew she was up to no good but he would give her a minute or two. The only time Francesca summoned Matt was to gloat over something. Out of fairness to Doreen, he would end his conversation with her and get rid of Francesca as soon as possible. He was not in the mood for her today.

MatMc: "So what's up Francesca?"

MSquad: "Since I'm not there, obviously not you. Have you seen mommy lately?"

MatMc: "No, why?"

MSquad: "Just thought you may have shown the old girl some mercy, a little looooovvveee."

MatMc: “What do you want, Francesca?”

MSquad: “I met someone. Horny old guy with lots of money and slams between the sheets.”

MatMc: “LOL I’m happy for you. How old is this guy?”

MSquad: “56 or so.”

MatMc: “LOL Go for it and try not to hurt him.”

MSquad: “So when are you doing the sympathy sex thing with you know who? You seem to be her only contact to the outside world.”

Matt detested this woman. Her hatred for her mother seemed to consume her. She never missed an opportunity to be negative. Whoever this new guy in her life was, he felt very sorry for him.

MatMc: “I need to go Francesca. Take care. Bye.

MSquad: “Whatever, hot stuff. Bye.”

Matt still had an hour or so before the meeting and he was bored. Maybe Lydiel was awake again.

As he punched in her number, he thought

about Allison.

"Hi handsome. How are you?"

"Hi babe. Did you go back to bed?"

"I did and slept for a couple of hours. Now I am at the old computer cranking out the lines. Did you find what caused the glitch?"

"Good girl. You needed the extra zzzz's. I have no idea what caused the glitch so I guess all that work I had you do earlier was all for nothing."

"Matt, I think you should hang onto the e-mail so you can compare it to the screen that comes up when you access the site again. Is everything else okay sweetie?"

No, everything else was not okay. Allison was acting stranger than normal and that damn Francesca worried him.

"Sure. I just miss you. When is the last time you heard from Francesca?

"I miss you too, baby. She called yesterday remember? Is everything okay, really?"

"Everything is fine babe. I will check in later. Get that book done and make us rich. Kisses.

"I will do my best. I love you Matt. Bye"

He knew she did. That was the problem. Damn her. He knew she did.

Connie Pushman pulled into her designated parking space, slid her access card and headed for her office. She had forgotten to leave the message for the twins. Once seated behind her desk, she fished for her cell phone to make the call. She had messages. Dialing in she heard the first message.

"To all executives of Pushman and Associates: During the routine account maintenance for your company, an unexplained discrepancy has been found in one of the operating budgets. Consequently the financial area of your website has been sealed and no access will be granted until the matter is resolved. We apologize for any inconvenience this may cause. An e-mail will be forwarded to all parties when the system is available again."

Connie shut her cell phone off and immediately went into panic mode. She was sure she had timed the withdrawal after the maintenance. Had Henry changed the dates without informing her?

She needed to calm down and think fast. It was only 7 a.m. and chances are no one had had time to check messages. Now where was his number? Where? Think. Think. The blotter! The number was under the blotter! With trembling fingers she keyed in the number.

"Please enter your access code followed by the pound sign."

This was easy; it was the twins' date of birth.

"Please enter the first three letters of the party you are trying to reach followed by the pound sign."

Connie hastily punched in the letters.

"I'm sorry. One of the letters you entered was incorrect. Please try again."

This time slowly and deliberately she punched in the corresponding numbers and hit the pound sign.

"You have reached the office of Walter Schmidt. Currently I am on assignment in Vienna. If this is an emergency please page me."

"Vienna? What the hell was she supposed to do with him in Vienna?

Frantic and frustrated Connie paged Walter. She had no idea what time it was there nor did she care. Just as she was about to hang up she heard a grizzled voice on the other end.

"I have no idea who the hell this is, but it had better be a matter of life and death."

"Oh Walter, thank God I found you."

"Connie? Her royal highness? What's up babe?"

"My ass…"

"It seems to me the last time I tried to get a piece of your ass, you told me that you were into the ladies."

"Please, I need your help!"

"Okay, okay. What can daddy do for his girl?"

"I need you to disable the entire Pushman website immediately including corporate e-mail and voicemail."

"You're asking me to disable several systems. This will take time."

"I don't HAVE time!"

"Hold on."

Connie must have checked her watch at least ten times before Walter came back on the line.

"Here's what I did. The website mainframe will be down for at least seventy-two hours or longer. There will be rolling outages on the e-mail and voicemail servers. You owe me, big time and I want my pound of flesh."

"I love you. You have it."

"Promises, promises. Now stop robbing your husband blind. I am back to bed. Ciao babe."

Connie was drenched with perspiration. She just bought herself time, but three days was not that long. How did Walter know what she had done? Lucky guess she supposed. As she hung up the phone she heard the morning message to the associates. With a deep sigh, she washed her face, reapplied her makeup and prepared herself for whatever the day held.

Matt tried one more to access the financial area of the Pushman site, only to realize the entire site was now inaccessible. He grabbed his jacket and legal pad and walked the short distance to the conference room.

Henry had wasted so much time daydreaming about Miss Francesca Sommers that he didn't realize it was 9 a.m. already. Armed with that Pushman smile he prepared to greet his associates and finalize the plans for the ball. He made a mental note to retrieve his voicemail messages before lunch.

Matt had sparked Lydiel's interest in the Pushman website. Drinking her morning tea she pulled up the site again. She had no idea why she was able to access it but she decided it might be helpful to Matt to have the information. As she was printing the last few pages the system suddenly shut down. Repeated attempts to access it proved futile. Closing the screen, it was time to pull up her book file and get busy.

Chapter 19

Allison let out a huge sigh as the school bus pulled up to pick up the boys. They saw it before she did. Normally they bolted for the door but today was different. They stood there for a moment and looked at each other and then at her, before speaking.

"Bye mom. See you later."

Allison's unison sons were at it again.

"No hugs guys?"

"Sure mom."

Liam and Sean hugged their mom tightly as if they didn't want to ever let go.

"Okay you two. The bus is waiting."

She had the day off and it was going to be a busy one. Since she and Matt never had their talk he had no idea she didn't have to work. Grabbing her purse, she was off in search of a whore. Remey had been more than happy to provide Allison with her mother's address and phone number the night before, along with a print out of a map with directions to Lydiel's house.

What sort of name was Lydiel Sommers anyway? Southern? Allison could just imagine Miss Southern Belle Lydiel dripping all over Matt, sounding like an overage Scarlet O'Hara, batting her lashes and in a voice like a human mint julep, whispering sweet nothings in his ear. "Oh Mr. Matt, I do declare. You say the nicest things..." It was enough to make her want to puke. She knew everything about Lydiel including what she looked like thanks to an old vacation picture Francesca had given her when this plan was first hatched. Allison felt ill at the thought of Lydiel and Matt together. In a few days it would no longer matter. Their days of screwing each other were coming to an unholy end.

Aisling Lavery was busy preparing her acceptance speech for tomorrow when Lydiel Sommers offered her the job. This was the first time she had never met her true employers in person before taking the job. Apparently Remey and Francesca had seen her in a play, and were impressed enough to contact her agent. For her, a gig was a gig was a gig. She didn't quite understand the cloak and dagger of it all. Lydiel seemed nice enough and Mr. Dreamboat Matt was nothing to sneeze at. She had the distinct feeling that she had interrupted something between the two of them yesterday.

The paperwork had been placed in her mailbox sometime last night and she was familiarizing herself with her new persona. She hated that homespun name they had given her. She had played many roles on stage including Ophelia and Juliet but never a domestic assistant named Sarah Turner; but the fact that they paid in advance was worth getting into character for.

Finding Lydiel's house proved to be a piece of cake. As Allison turned onto Spearhead Drive, she was somewhat surprised. It was hardly the sort of neighborhood she expected a successful writer to reside in. Parking was almost non-existent. She was hoping to get at least a glimpse of Matt's reclusive lover. She squeezed into a tight space close to a fire hydrant a few houses down and got out of the car. There was a huge gated parking lot across the street from the love nest which made the perfect secreted observation post. Standing behind a huge Rose of

Sharon bush, Allison had a direct view of the house. Unfortunately she did not have a view of the ticket being placed on the windshield of her car.

"Excuse me Miss, is there something I can help you with?"

Allison turned to stare into the face of the largest man she had ever encountered.

"No. Iiiiimmmm ffffine."

"What are you doing here? This is private property and one of the residents reported a strange woman apparently hiding in the parking lot."

Allison had to think on her feet.

"I'm sorry. I'm a reporter and I was trying to scoop a story on Lydiel Sommers. I understand she lives just over there."

Pointing to the house, Allison hoped the security guard was buying her story,

"Yes ma'am she does. She is also entitled to her privacy. I'm going to have to ask you to leave."

"Please, I just need a few more minutes."

"I'm sorry Ma'am, I have to ask you to leave now."

Allison couldn't risk an incident. What were

her chances of glimpsing a recluse anyway? She should have known better.

"I'm sorry officer. Let's consider the matter closed, shall we?"

"Yes ma'am. I'll be more than happy to escort you to your vehicle."

Lydiel raised the blinds in her bedroom just in time to see one of the hospital security guards escorting a woman down the street. There was so much going on lately, she hoped nothing was wrong.

Chapter 20

Henry took his place at the head of the conference table and opened his laptop.

"Good morning, everyone. Are we ready to begin? Let's all log on and see where we stand financially shall we?"

Connie bit her lower lip as she watched the others attempt to access the site.

"Henry?"

"Yes Matt?"

"I have been trying for hours to access the financial pages on the website and each time I received an alert message. Now I can't access the site at all."

"Let me try, Matt. Darn it, I am locked out also."

"Is anyone able to sign on to the Pushman site?"

Collective no's were heard throughout the room. Henry tried his executive password once more, to no avail. His first thought was perhaps a worm had infiltrated the system somehow, but that was virtually impossible with the firewall and anti-virus programs Pushman had paid a small fortune for to protect their assets.

"I don't know what the problem is but I will get our IT people on it. In the meantime it is such a nice day, why don't we table this, enjoy the weather and meet back here tomorrow for another go at it, shall we? Hopefully it is just something minor. Oh, I forgot to mention, you will be compensated for a full day's work. Enjoy all. Connie, may I see you in my office?"

Matt was beginning to like this job more and more. He needed to make two phone calls before he left. First he dialed Allison's number at work.

"You have reached the office of Allison Woodall McNulty. Currently I am away from my desk. Please leave a message and I will return your call as soon as possible. If this is an emergency, please dial 0 for further assistance."

For some reason Matt pressed 0.

"This is the operator. How may I direct your call?"

"I am trying to contact Allison McNulty."

"I'm sorry sir, Mrs. McNulty is not in the office today. May I connect you to someone else?"

"No, no thank you. Goodbye."

Matt now needed to add a third number to his list of calls.

Allison peeled the ticket off the windshield and stuck it in the glove box as she drove off. This day was not going as planned. Adjusting the volume on the radio she heard the bells on her cell phone. She was wearing her bluetooth and was unable to view the caller ID.

"Hello"

"It's me, Allison. Where are you?"

"Driving, where are you?"

"Must you always be so cryptic? Why didn't you tell me you took a day off?

"Maybe for the same reason you didn't tell me you had the afternoon off Monday and the day off Tuesday?"

Matthew McNulty felt the first indication of a headache. Now he was engaged in a tit-for-tat discussion with his wife or to be more precise an irritating circular argument.

"We should talk Allison."

"Perhaps you should make an appointment like you do with the slut you are sleeping with. I'll see you at dinner Matt."

With that Allison ended the phone call. Now it was time for the third phone call, this one to Lydiel.

For some reason Lydiel was not feeling the words this morning and she wasn't sure why. Maybe it was all the distractions, or maybe it was her writer's curiosity about the Pushman website. The ringing phone was just another interruption, albeit a pleasant one in an already non-productive day. She was puzzled to see it was Matt calling again.

"Hi baby. How was the meeting?"

"Darndest thing happened. The whole site went down so the meeting was cancelled. Are you free for lunch?"

"Matt, you and I never go anywhere. What's going on?"

"What a short memory you have. It seems to me we went out together yesterday,"

"We did and it was wonderful. What's wrong Matt?"

"I was thinking we could eat in?"

Now Lydiel was certain something was just not right. Matt knew her well enough to know that the only time she cooked was when he was expected for dinner.

"You know I rarely cook sweetie, but I could order some take-out I guess."

"I need to see you Lydiel. I can't stay past lunch but I really need to see you."

"Okay, I will order Chinese. When should I expect you?"

"Give me fifteen to twenty minutes. See ya soon babe."

"Okay baby, see you soon."

Lydiel took a deep breath and then dialed the Chinese restaurant at the plaza. After completing her order, she sat down and thought about recent events. Matt had not been himself ever since that day...

Chapter 21

Connie knocked softly on Henry's door before going in.

"You wanted to see me, Henry?"

"Yes, come in dear. I wanted to get your opinion on how you thought the budgeting was going for the project. As you know we have to stay on top of this. My IT people say it will be at least four to five days before the system is back up."

Connie felt her heart skip a beat and her palms were sweaty.

"I believe that we will come in under budget, Henry. Matt's presentation was excellent and revealed a way for us to cut at least six thousand dollars off the seating and catering."

"Really? I must have read my report wrong. For some reason I thought he could bring us in just slightly over fifteen thousand dollars under budget. Oh well, not to worry. We will check the figures when the system is available. Now, tell me how you are. It seems as if we have not spoken to each other in quite a while. How is Allison these days?"

Connie knew her discomfort was showing. Why did Henry pick today of all days to do this?

"Everything is fine. Allison and I have been working together on our little project and things seem to be falling into place nicely. We won't let you down. If there is nothing else..."

"Actually Connie, there is one more thing. You and I have been keeping up pretenses for quite a few years now. I never complained or tried to interfere with you and your little friends. However, recently I have met someone, and I have decided that I very much enjoy her company. Of course discretion is number one. There will just be times, evenings really that I will not be home. If you provide me with your calendar I will always be available when need be and help out with the twins until they leave for college."

Connie wanted to cry. Henry made her heart weep with his straightforwardness and honesty.

"Thank you for your consideration, Henry. Will you be home for dinner tonight?"

"Yes, dear, let's have a family meal, shall we?"

Whoever the woman was, Henry was a

changed man. Connie heard him whistling when she arrived for work. He seemed happy and for that she was grateful.

Lydiel heard the door open and without saying a word she threw her arms around his neck and standing on her tiptoes she kissed him. She buried her head in his chest as he held her close. For Matt, holding Lydiel like this for a moment made everything seem as if it would be okay.

"I was just about to put lunch together; beef lo mein and diet soda. No too romantic but filling."

"The fact that we are here together is romantic enough."

Lydiel was absolutely certain something was wrong. Matt rarely admitted when things were wrong. He was always stoic and just sucked it up, but this time was different.

"To what do I owe the divine pleasure of your company three days in a row? What happened at work?"

"I have the afternoon off, with pay of course. For some reason the mainframe is down and no one can access the site. I am getting a funny feeling about all of this."

"Matt, this morning after we talked, I pulled up the site and for a few minutes I had full access. I printed off what I could before it crashed. I don't know what it means or if it will help but here is the file."

The first word that came to mind was amazing. She always followed up on a hunch. It must have something to do with being a writer.

"I don't know what it means either babe, but thanks so much for the help."

"Now tell me Matt , what is REALLY wrong?"

"I need to talk to Allison tonight."

"Okay. You guys are married so I assumed you talked on a regular basis. Have things gotten worse or is that an inappropriate question for your mistress to ask?"

"She is playing games and I'm tired of it. It's become apparent that she is no longer interested in ever being intimate with me again, not in the true sense of the word. She took a day off and never said a word. Every time I'm away from home I get accused of sleeping with someone."

"I see. You and I have discussed this before. She knows that you are seeing someone and she is baiting you for confirmation."

"She is also spending a lot of time with Constance Pushman, Henry's wife. She claims it has to do with the ball project but I don't believe her. She is spending less time at home and with the kids. The only reason she was there the other night was because Hannah refused to babysit."

Holding Matt's hand, Lydiel looked into his eyes and did her best to hide her feelings.

"What can I do to help?"

"Just what you are doing now sweetie, listening."

"I am always here for you. I wish I could do more. Do you realize this is the first time we have been together and didn't make love? It feels strange."

"I know babe and I will make it up to you I promise. Lunch was great. I need to run a few errands before the kids get home. Thanks for printing that stuff off for me. "

"Take care of yourself, handsome. I need you

in my life."

"I need you too."

Lydiel walked Matt to his car, kissed him, hugged him, and walked away as he drove off. She wasn't sure if he was more troubled about work or home. The situation was ongoing and not likely to change anytime soon. Matt always gave a thousand percent and the fact that he suspected something was not right at Pushman would nag at him until he solved the mystery. Whatever was going on, she was enjoying the extra time they were spending together.

Allison's mood had changed substantially since she left home that morning. First the fiasco with the security guard, then the ticket and now Matt's phone call. The more she thought about it the more she knew she was doing the right thing. Turning into the mall parking lot, she headed for the electronics store. Armed with a printout she browsed the racks of software, searching for the one matching the picture. Her search was interrupted by one of the store employees who looked all of sixteen years old.

"How may I help you?"

Just what she needed, Mr. Super Friendly.

"I am looking for a certain kind of software. I need to monitor my kids' Internet activities."

"I quite understand. We have several types. Are you interested in remote access? Social networking, chats, e-mail and instant messenger transcripts?"

"All of the above."

"This is our top of the line. Guaranteed results or you will receive a total refund."

"Fine, fine, whatever. How much is it?"

"$149.99 plus tax, ma'am."

Ma'am? Seriously? Allison gritted her teeth and handed the clerk her credit card. She was rapidly approaching her limit.

"Thank you, ma'am, and if you have any questions, please don't hesitate to call."

Her mind was racing as she drove back to her office to drop off the software, but she felt better and she was smiling. Soon, Ms. Lydiel Sommers, very very soon.

Matt decided that perhaps now was a good time to investigate the possibility of moving some funds from the emergency house fund to a different type of emergency account. Explaining his plan, the bank manager pulled up all of the McNulty accounts.

"I don't think what you envision is possible Mr. McNulty. There was a significant withdrawal made just two days go."

"For how much exactly?"

"Forty-seven thousand dollars in cash by the other signer on the account, your wife, Allison Woodall McNulty."

"Thank you. You have been most helpful. I wish to close out the account and open a new one if that is possible."

As the bank manger handed Matt forms to fill out and sign, the pain of Allison's actions was slowly sinking in. Although it was his account he had added Allison in case of an emergency and he couldn't get to the bank himself. Now she had withdrawn forty-seven thousand dollars and for what purpose? Why would anyone need that much cash?

"All set Mr. McNulty and as per your instructions, no further information will be available regarding the previous account.

"Thank you."

Matt was almost overwhelmed with sadness as he drove back to Pushman and Associates. He felt it best if the banking information were kept in a safe place.

Chapter 22

Remey Anderson struggled to get the heavy apron on as she began the task of filling the small canisters. Wearing a full facemask equipped with a special rebreather device, she painstakingly placed several measured doses of commercial strength capsaicin into each of the small containers. Francesca led Remey to believe that Lydiel used an "extender" which was created for people unable to coordinate the squeeze and suck action using the inhaler alone.

After tapping the containers gently on the counter, she weighed each one to insure the correct dosages had been added, and in this case they had to be tripled. Next, came the labeling. The "paper guy" had provided pirated labels from a variety of pharmaceutical houses. The purpose was to delay tracking the source of the toxin. The final stage was inserting the canister into the inhaler.

Satisfied with her work, she placed the containers into the final packaging, which was also pirated, sealed them and placed them into a brown paper bag. Removing the apron and facemask, she grabbed the bag and left the room. As she returned to her office, she took several deep breaths and called Connie.

"Hello, this is Connie Pushman."

"Hi Connie. The packages are ready."

"Thanks, Remey. We will talk later."

Remey opened the bottom desk drawer, removed a flask and poured herself a double shot of tequila. As she downed the liquor she thought how she had sunk to an all time low in just a matter of months. Her recent marriage to Douglas Anderson brought with it additional responsibilities in the form of two little girls. Added to the one they shared, she was now raising three kids six and younger. To help Doug with his divorce she had nearly bankrupted her business. Several attempts to secure a business loan had failed and she was forced to ask Lydiel for help. It appeared that her "mother" was no longer in the business of financing the business ventures of her adult children. As a result Remey threw herself on the mercy of others and Connie Pushman was the one who picked her up.

Connie had given Remey the money she

needed to finance her consulting business from her personal account, and in return she and Connie became occasional lovers. One day as she and Connie were leaving The Renaissance, Francesca saw them together and set about insinuating herself in the relationship by threatening to tell Doug everything. Francesca's constant threats had ensnared Remey into the murder scheme.

It was Francesca who disclosed Matt's relationship with Lydiel. At first Francesca seemed genuinely sincere about seeing their mother happy. Then for some unknown reason everything changed. When Connie told her about a friend who had a little problem with their mother, Remey had no idea that it was Matt's wife, Allison, and that she wanted Lydiel dead. As always Francesca blackmailed her into participating. Now, here she sat, a key player in a murder plot against the woman who took her in when no one else would. If only Lydiel would have given her the money… Remey poured another double shot and pondered many things.

Chapter 23

Matt's emotions were all over the map. Sure things were bad. Sure he and Allison had grown apart, so much so he was driven to find intimacy elsewhere, but why did she take forty-seven thousand dollars out of the emergency account without so much as a "do you mind?" What sort of demon was chasing her to make her do such a thing? Was she planning to leave him? Gaslight him? Take the boys? What was going on? His mind was like a spinning top as he fought to maintain his concentration on the drive home.

For weeks Allison's frustrations had been getting the best of her. She took chances today that she never would have before and it was all Matt's fault. Why couldn't he have just let it go? Why was sex so important? Why couldn't he just be happy with what she had to offer and just be comfortable friends, an occasional hug and raise the kids together? She needed a drink.

Slipping on her favorite apron Connie Pushman started dinner-the family dinner that Henry had requested. As she sipped her third glass of Pinot Noir, she wondered how much time she had before the jig was up; before Henry discovered the missing sixty thousand dollars; before she was outed as a co-conspirator in the murder plot of a woman to whom she had no connection, before she lost her husband to a woman who would give him what he needed to be happy.

For the first time in her life Francesca Sommers was riding high and enjoying being in the driver's seat; bedding two of the wealthiest and most influential people in the city and a key player in ridding herself of Lydiel once and for all thanks to Matt's philandering. Life with Henry was good and she was also close to shedding that human fat farm sister of hers. What a loser!

Henry Pushman packed up his briefcase and laptop as he prepared for the drive home. As much as he enjoyed the company of Miss Francesca Sommers, tonight he needed to be there for the twins as they would be leaving for college in a few days. He needed to leave his new playmate a voicemail.

Lydiel was experiencing second thoughts at

having a stranger in her home even for a few hours a week. Her attorney suggested that the new hire be bonded as an added ounce of safety and she was hoping to reach Sarah before their appointment.

Aisling Lavery busied herself putting the final touches on her newest character - Sarah Turner. She felt confident that she would not let the girls down. She had her instructions and just as she was leaving the phone rang.

"Hello?"

"Good evening Sarah. This is Lydiel Sommers. I'm going to need one more thing from you, and that is a bond. I'm told they are quite inexpensive so if you would bring a copy with you to our meeting tomorrow we should be able to move forward."

Aisling was caught totally off guard. She chose her words carefully.

"I will take care of it and be there on time Ms. Sommers and thank you."

"Good bye Sarah."

As soon as Lydiel hung up Aisling phoned Allison McNulty.

"McNulty residence."

"It's me, Sarah, Allison."

Great. Just what she needed, a call from a wannabe actress. What the hell was wrong now?

"Lydiel wants me to be bonded before I can start to work and I need it ASAP."

"I will take care of it. I need thirty minutes or so and a courier will deliver the papers to you. Don't ever call me here again, is that clear?"

"Message received!"

As Aisling hung up she realized that Allison McNulty was one nasty bitch of a woman.

Allison had had enough for one day. She just wanted to relax before the kids came home. Maybe she could convince Matt to fix dinner. She poured herself another margarita and dialed Connie's number.

"Connie?"

"What is it Allison?"

Connie knew her irritation was showing and she made no apology for it. She was tired, especially tired of Allison.

"You need to arrange for a bond for Sarah

Turner and have it delivered by courier to her at her apartment ASAP. Miss Lydiel is now asking for a bond. Are you there?"

Connie Pushman drank the last of the wine, took a deep breath and wondered aloud when it would all end.

"It will be taken care of… and Allison? Don't call me anymore this evening. We are having a family dinner with the twins. Good bye."

Well la de da. We're having a family dinner with the twins. If things went as planned Allison would be able to divorce herself from Connie, Matt and the whole miserable lot of them.

Connie placed a quick phone call and then turned the phone off for the evening.

Allison heard the screech of the school bus and knew that the true madness was about to begin- the return of the unison twins.

"Mom, we're home! Mom?"

"I'm here boys and please don't yell."

"Are you sick mom?"

Allison was sick all right; sick of two little birds that always spoke as if they had one brain.

"No guys. I'm not sick, just resting. How was school and don't you dare both speak at once."

Sean spoke first.

"I need help with math and science."

"I need cupcakes for the party tomorrow. Are you coming mom? Please?"

"I will see what I can do Liam, no promises though. I have to work tomorrow."

Matt McNulty's head felt as if a tiny hammer were playing a symphony inside it, like the old Anacin commercial. He grabbed his jacket, and the file Lydiel prepared for him. He took two deep breaths and went inside.

The boys were watching a DVD, relatively oblivious to his arrival, and Allison appeared to watching the insides of her eyelids. Matt picked up the Margarita glass on his way to the kitchen. Bracing himself on the kitchen sink he felt anger surge to the surface.

"Hi guys. Why aren't you doing homework?"

"DAD!"

At least part of the McNulty family was happy

to see him.

"Keep it down to a dull roar. Your mother is sleeping. Tell you what. Let me change and the McNulty men will prepare dinner. What do you say?"

"Yeah, can we wear our aprons?"

"Sure thing."

Matt walked into the bedroom and felt overwhelmed by anger. Why? That was the question of the day. So many whys? No answers. After quickly donning a pair of shorts and one of his favorite t-shirts he changed his mind about dinner.

"Hey you two. I have a better idea. Let's have a guys' night out."

"Cool, Dad. Where are we going?"

"How about Mickey D's and then the library? Bring your homework with you.

Allison McNulty never knew when her husband came home or when her children left.

Chapter 24

Lydiel awakened with a start! Damn! She rarely overslept. She spent most of the night making the revisions requested by her editor and the book was finally finished. It was too late to e-mail Matt, and now she would have just enough time to take a shower and get dressed before her meeting with Sarah. Actually Matt's suggestion couldn't have come at a better time. It was just that one thing about Sarah that troubled her....

Matt woke the boys early, helped them get ready for school and took them to work with him. He explained to Henry that Allison was under the weather and he would need to get the boys to school. Henry arranged for a company car to take the boys, and Matt had to laugh at their excitement of being chauffeured to school, but there was nothing at all remotely funny about his situation. He knew the blowup was eminent. He needed to phone Lydiel. He had promised he would see her last night but things were far too crazy at home to chance it. This was just one more reason why he rarely promised anyone anything.

Lydiel was just stepping into the shower when the phone rang.

"Hi baby. How are you?"

"Oh I don't know, the usual I guess. Horny, disgusted and I miss you. I'm sorry about last night but things were sort of strange at home. I took the boys out for dinner, then to the library, helped with homework and stopped off for cupcakes for a school thing today. I also got them up early, brought them to work with me and sent them off to school in a company car thanks to Henry."

Lydiel and Matt had been together long enough for her to know that now was not the time to ask any questions. He needed a shoulder to lean on and to vent

"Hmm, busy boy. Guess what I am doing?"

"I'm not too good at guessing today, babe."

"I am standing stark naked in the shower all soaped up."

Matt felt a faint twitch. He could envision that scenario.

"Sarah Turner will begin work today. I asked her to secure a bond, just in case. You can never be too safe."

"That's my babe. I need to go here now, but I will see you soon. Bye sweetie."

"Bye lover."

Aisling Lavery had been up for hours fine-tuning her performance as Sarah Turner. She had no idea why this particular role meant so much to her. Perhaps it was because this was the first time she was being paid double for one role, and she didn't want to blow it. The radio said this would be an ozone action day, which was very bad news for a person like her.

Henry felt refreshed and content. Last night had reminded him of the old days when he and Connie slept together. He wondered when it was she stopped loving him as a wife loves a husband. The twins were so lively and enthusiastic about entering college, and gave him a list of everything they would need for their dorm rooms and all. Where had the time gone?

Connie decided to call the girls before she left for work to avoid any interruptions during her workday. Hmm, this was odd. Allison was not answering her home phone or her cell. Francesca answered her phone on the first ring.

"Hi Connie. Yes I think so too. The packages are ready, Sarah starts work today, and in a few days' time all of this will be behind us."

"Good morning dear. Everything is on schedule I believe."

It continually surprised her how cool and cavalier Francesca was in this whole scheme. If she didn't know better Connie would believe that Francesca had been the victim of horrible abuse but she knew that was not the case. She was consumed with hatred for her mother for some unknown reason. Remey was on vacation with Doug and the kids for two weeks; smart girl. She would learn of her mother's death while away from home.

Connie tried Allison once more. This time she got a response.

"Hhhheeellooo?"

"Allison?" Surely you can't be sleeping at this

hour."

"What time is it"

Connie could sense something was terribly wrong.

"It is a little after 8:30 a.m. Where are the boys? Don't they have school today?"

Allison was still wearing the clothes she had on yesterday and her mouth felt like she had been eating cotton. Speaking of eating, she didn't remember dinner, and where were the boys?

"Allison? Remember you are to make the exchange today with Sarah. Allison!

"Please don't yell Connie. I have a terrible headache. I am up now and after a shower and all I will be ready to meet Sarah if all goes as planned."

"It is too late for ifs Allison. I am up to my saltwater pearls in this and I don't plan to lose them. We'll meet at Mirelli's as planned. By the way, no matter what the situation, under no circumstances are you to call me at work. Goodbye."

Allison sat on the sofa and tried to clear her head. The last thing she remembered was drinking a margarita, three actually, and talking to the boys.

Where were the boys? Oh no… Damn! She forgot the cupcakes. Maybe she had time to stop at the bakery.

Chapter 25

Matt McNulty desperately wanted to get his day underway but first he needed to call home. He needed to get a few things said to Allison and to make sure she understood how he felt. He dialed her office number and reached the recording. He glanced at his watch and decided to try her cell phone. Again he heard a voicemail message. It was 9 a.m., surely... He dialed their home phone.

"McNulty residence."

"Good morning."

"Matt, you forgot to wake me up. Where are the boys?"

As always, Allison blamed Matt for any oversight on her part.

"I don't believe it is my responsibility to awaken an adult woman, especially one with children to take care of."

"You didn't answer me. Where are my boys?"

"OUR boys enjoyed dinner out with their dad, homework at the library and off to school this morning with cupcakes."

"Matt, I'm sorry. I must have fallen asleep on the sofa. I had a busy day yesterday and thought I would just rest for a few minutes."

Allison was sorry all right but not nearly as sorry as she was going to be. Matt noticed that she forgot to mention the margaritas and the recent forty-seven thousand dollar withdrawal.

"We will talk when I get home. Bye."

A resounding loud click terminated the conversation, but for Allison Woodall McNulty it would terminate much more.

Damn him and his smugness! Just who the hell did he think he was? He delighted in rubbing her nose in the fact that he remembered the cupcakes.

For Matt it was back to the business of the ball. The system was back up but the site was still down. He retrieved the single financial page Lydiel was able e-mail to him. As he perused the spreadsheet he heard his name called over the intercom. Duty called and he was off and running

Henry needed to review Matt's proposal and stopped by his office on the way to the conference room. He knocked and then entered the empty office.

As he turned to go he noticed a sheet of paper lying on the floor. Picking it up, he was surprised to see one of the financial pages from the site. Making a quick copy on Matt's printer, Henry replaced the page on Matt's desk and continued on to the conference room.

Lydiel Sommers was reading her e-mail and eating a light breakfast when the doorbell rang.

"Coming. One moment please."

Aisling Lavery took a deep breath. For the next few weeks she would live and work as Sarah Turner, a domestic assistant. As Lydiel opened the front door and stared at the woman standing there, a light shiver ran through her body. She knew it would take some time to adjust to having Sarah around.

"Sarah, come in please. I was eating breakfast. May I get you something?

"No thank you Ms. Sommers. I have the paperwork you requested including the bond."

"Thank you dear. Could you give me a minute or so to read over everything? Please feel free to familiarize yourself with the apartment, not that it is that big. For the most part I am relatively neat so it shouldn't be difficult to tidy up one day a week, wash no more than two loads of clothes and start dinner. There is a washer and dryer downstairs, and you may park your car on the gravel pad in the rear. Later I will need you to pick up my medication from the pharmacy."

Sarah had memorized the list the girls had given her and she immediately began mentally checking off the items. The bedroom was small - an easy chair, a couple of tables and lamps. There was a framed picture of Allison's husband, Matt on the bedside table along with an inhaler, an extender and two bottles of prescription medication. The office was just off the dining room, complete with organized clutter. The kitchen was at the rear of the apartment: clean and organized. Sarah noticed another inhaler. The bathroom was small but neat.

"Did you enjoy the tour. dear? Quick trip wasn't it?"

Lydiel startled Sarah. She was a woman who walked very softly.

"This room is my office and really my own

personal domain. As such there will never be a need for you to go inside. Your references check out, as does the bond. So, Miss Sarah Turner, if you are still interested, welcome aboard."

"It is my pleasure and thank you so much Ms. Sommers. I'm sure you won't be disappointed. "

"I'm certain things will work out Sarah. I had a key made for you and you officially start work tomorrow. Have a good afternoon."

"You too, Ms. Sommers."

"Please call me Lydiel, and until tomorrow…"

Matt would be happy. There was that one thing that Lydiel just couldn't get past, but oh well she would deal with it.

Breathing a sigh of relief, Sarah Turner walked the short distance to her car and called Allison. Now she knew why she had been selected for this job.

Chapter 26

Connie toyed with a paper clip as she waited for Henry in the conference room. Matt was quietly preoccupied and she found the silence deafening.

"Are you settling in and finding your way around okay, Matt?"

"So far, okay. Don't worry Connie, you won't be sorry. I appreciate the break but I'm very much my own person."

Connie sensed that she had touched a nerve and thought it best to change the subject. Dealing with Matt was much different than dealing with Allison.

"Did Allison remind you that she and I have a date this evening?"

"On occasion I am privy to my wife's plans for the evening, other times not until the last minute. Thank you for informing me of her plans for this evening."

Henry's timing couldn't have been better. Matt had grown weary of Connie and girls' night out. He had grown weary of lies and deception. He had grown weary of being married, feeling trapped and being unhappy.

"Sorry to interrupt your day. Since the site is still down, I thought perhaps we could update each other on our individual progress on the ball event. Why don't you start Matt?"

Always prepared, Matt had a slideshow presentation that was date stamped to document his progress from the time he received the project to the present with projected expenditures penciled in. He could tell Henry was impressed.

"Excellent, my boy, just excellent! I noticed that if we stay on course as you propose we would definitely come in under budget."

"Absolutely! There is a wedding reception the night before. What I suggested was that Pushman pick up the tab for an extra day of rental on the fountains, chafers, lighting and umbrellas rather than beginning a new rental of the same items. This will shave over three thousand dollars off the budget. I have also received concessions on the cost of food and beverages by entering into a retainer agreement with the caterers for any and all Pushman social events regardless of the location."

As Connie listened to Matt speak she was in awe. She had known Matt for almost twenty years through Allison's eyes. This did not sound like the insensitive, uncaring and inconsiderate husband Allison complained about. The man in the conference room was handsome, intelligent, articulate, persuasive and caring enough to see to it that his two boys arrived at school on time when their mother couldn't get up to do her job this morning.

Turning his attention to his wife, Henry asked for an update on the overall financial situation surrounding the event.

"Now my dear, can you bring us up to speed on how deep we are into this financially?

Connie's discomfort was obvious to both Henry and Matt.

"With the site still down it is impossible to get the figures from the spreadsheet. I need more time."

Matt knew Connie was hiding something and trying to buy time but he didn't know why. He knew a little about computers and earlier he had been toying with an idea to possibly retrieve some information.

"I have an idea Connie. Since the system is up but the site is down, maybe we can go back into your history and retrieve something that would help you, even if it was just one page. I'm not sure how much information was lost, if any."

"That sounds like a great idea, Matt. How about trying that after lunch Connie?"

"Whatever you think is best, dear. Now if you will excuse me, I have several calls to return."

Matt and Henry both stood as Connie left the room. As Matt prepared to leave, Henry stopped him.

"Care to have lunch with me, Matt? I need to talk and I don't want to do it here. By the way I have made arrangements for your boys to be brought here after school. I know Allison won't be home."

Matt had the strange feeling that Henry wanted to confide something in him. As long as they had known each other they had never socialized together so this would be breaking new ground, and he was not one to warm up to men easily. Lydiel was his confidante and he knew he could trust her.

"Sure Henry. Just let me tidy up a few things and I will meet you in the lobby. Thanks for looking out for my boys. That was very thoughtful of you."

"Glad to help, my boy."

That was something he would never get used *to.*

Allison McNulty chain-smoked as she waited for Sarah's call. Who did Henry Pushman think he was, having her boys dropped off and picked up from school? He could barely manage his own life, let alone meddle in hers and Matt's. She would definitely have to speak with Connie about Henry. The chiming bells of the cell phone alerted Allison to Sarah's call.

"It's about time. What took you so long?"

"Allison, stop with the sarcasm. You need something from me, remember?"

Not one to be talked down to, Allison bit her lower lip in an effort to hold her tongue.

Not one to be talked down to, Allison bit her lower lip in an effort to hold her tongue. The exchange was the important issue at hand.

"Very true Sarah Turner or whoever you are, and you were paid in advance to deliver."

Sarah realized that if she didn't take a stand with Allison she would continue to be steamrolled. She had no idea what was going on but whatever it was it was a burr in Allison's behind.

"For your information I was given the grand tour, a detailed overview of my duties and responsibilities and before you ask, yes I was given a key. Now where should we meet for the pickup?"

Through all of Sarah's inane chatter, the key was what Allison was waiting to hear about.

"Copy the key and meet me at the IGA on 12th and Western in twenty minutes. I'll be at the far end of row seven. Don't keep me waiting."

"Keep your shirt on Allison, I'm on my way."

Chapter 27

Henry and Matt arrived at Mirelli's shortly before the lunch rush. The seemingly always on duty Giorgio escorted them to a rear booth.

"Grazie, Giorgio. I would like to introduce you to the newest star at Pushman and Associates, Matthew McNulty. Giorgio and I go back a ways, Matt."

Matt surveyed the place that took Allison away from home on a regular basis now. Mirelli's had become the second home for Allison and Connie these days. It seemed strange how after all the years of their friendship they found the need to "reconnect" so frequently lately. Matt knew that Connie had put in a good word for him with Henry, but there was something else going on that he couldn't put his finger on. Matt extended his hand to the Maître.

"Nice to meet you, Giorgio"

"Should I bring you the wine list Mr. Pushman?

"Diet soda for me, please, Giorgio. What are you having, Matt?"

"Diet soda sounds good to me also."

This was the first time Giorgio Pieri had seen Allison's better half, and at first blush he definitely seemed to be the better half. God, what an unpleasant woman she was.

Matt wished Henry would get to the reason for having lunch together. He was uncomfortable with the situation and trying desperately not to let it show.

Henry was debating how to broach the subject with Matt. One of his weaknesses was his desire to see good in everyone, even when he knew it was not warranted. For some time now he suspected his wife of manipulating some of Pushman's financial accounts. What he found baffling was why? He was a successful businessman whose family wanted for nothing. Connie was paid handsomely for her work at Pushman, and occupied a seat on the executive committee. So why would she steal from him? He pulled the page from his jacket and placed it on the table.

"I stopped by your office earlier and there was a sheet of paper on the floor. It appeared to be one of the financial pages from the site before it went down.

I was hoping you could explain how you were able to retrieve it when the site was down?"

Matt knew that if Henry had the e-mail from Lydiel, he knew that someone outside the company had access to the financial pages. Clearly he was not in a good place now.

"I was up very early the day the system went down. I attempted to access the site. As you know all of the Pushman computers including our PCs at home and our laptops are tied into the mainframe. I used a friend's computer to access our site and there was no problem. However, I was only able to pull up one page. I e-mailed it to myself from my friend's computer. I tried several times to access the page from our offices at Pushman to no avail until the system went down completely."

While not being entirely truthful, Matt's explanation was plausible and he did try to access the site. He had never witnessed a system go down the way the Pushman system did. It crashed almost like a rolling blackout; first the site, then the voicemail system, and finally the entire system. He never had a chance to fully review the page in question or the file

Lydiel printed for him. Clearly whatever the issue was it was upsetting Henry considerably.

"Please don't take offense or misunderstand me, Matt. I am not questioning your integrity on any level. I examined the page in detail and even without the corresponding pages from the site I can ascertain a sizeable discrepancy in the figures presented at the meeting two days ago and the ones on the page. I have my suspicions but I need further corroboration."

If Matt was reading Henry correctly, Henry suspected someone was stealing from the company and the only person capable of manipulating the figures was…

Matt held that thought as Giorgio appeared with their lunch.

"Cobb salad for Mr. McNulty, and one for you, Mr. Pushman. Can I get you refills on the diet sodas?"

"Yes please, and thank you."

Matt had to laugh. He and Henry had responded in unison and it reminded him of his boys. It also seemed to lighten Henry's mood.

Chuckling, Henry did not let the simultaneous remark go unnoticed.

"Matt my boy, it seems that we are on the same page, even when it comes to Giorgio. I do need your help, however. Please come to see me after you take a look at Connie's computer. I will be most anxious to see if you can retrieve the records and what you find."

Matt had the sinking feeling that he was now in the middle of something very unpleasant between Henry and Connie.

Chapter 28

Traffic was moving at a snail's pace as Sarah inched her way to the rendezvous point. Had it not been for the fact that she had paid her rent two months in advance and purchased her ticket to New York, she would have walked away from this gig. She found Allison McNulty to be an obnoxiously arrogant control freak and she felt very sorry for her husband.

Allison turned the radio up as she drummed her fingers on the steering wheel. Impatient and anxious, she checked her watch for what must have been the umpteenth time. Where was that girl? She decided to touch base with Connie while she waited. She keyed in the number and waited through three rings before Connie came on the line.

"Hello, this is…"

"Skip it Connie."

"Allison? Why are you calling me here? I thought we agreed that we would talk about it later at Mirelli's"

Connie was uncharacteristically short with

Allison and that was something she was unaccustomed to.

"What's going on Connie?"

"I think Henry knows..."

"Knows what?"

Allison hated it when people left sentences hanging as if they were in the middle of some murder mystery or something. She had no idea what Connie was talking about?

"I think Henry knows about the money. The money I skimmed from the ball budget to help you with your little scheme for Lydiel. As a matter of fact your husband will be going through the memory on my computer in an attempt to retrieve the financial pages posted before the system crashed."

"What does Matt have to do with this?"

The more Connie talked, the more Allison felt her nerves fray. Matt was hardly a computer whiz and why would he be poking around files on Connie's computer?

"Matt made a suggestion at the morning meeting that it may be possible to reset my computer prior to the crash and retrieve the information on the site at that time which would of course reveal the discrepancy. Henry asked Matt to follow up on it after lunch so I have spent the last hour or so trying to see what I can find there."

"Where is Matt now?"

"I think he and Henry are having lunch together at Mirelli's."

"Perhaps I can enlist Georgio's help in a little eavesdropping?"

There were times like this when Connie shook her head in disbelief, and found Allison was both dense and tiring, and this was one of them. She could never leave well enough alone and her interference could throw a wrench in their plans.

"Leave it alone Allison! Just leave it alone."

Allison Woodall McNulty never ever left anything alone, except her husband whenever she could. If she weren't waiting on Sarah she would make a surprise visit to Mirelli's. She opted instead to call Matt.

"Hello, this is Matthew McNulty."

"Hi there. How are things going?"

Allison knew she was taking a risk. Matt had

not been very communicative as of late.

"Allison? Is there something wrong? Are the kids okay?"

"Nothing's wrong. I just thought we could talk for a few minutes."

"I'm sorry. Now is not a good time and as I told you earlier, we will talk later. Good bye."

Dismissed! Just like that, as if she were a child being sent to a timeout. Oh Matt, Matt, MATT! Didn't he know her at all anymore?

Sarah Turner deftly moved in and out of traffic for her meeting in the supermarket parking lot. This day was turning into a nightmare.

Allison was standing outside her car when Sarah arrived- a bad sign for sure.

"Well, Miss Sarah, you are only 10 minutes late but I'm sure you have a valid excuse."

"Well, Miss Allison, traffic on the interstate comes to mind."

Sarah Turner and Matthew McNulty had managed to give Allison a headache with their casually flippant attitudes.

"Let's skip the girl talk shall we and get on

with it. Do you have the key and the layout for me?"

Sarah handed the key and the roughly drawn diagram over to Allison.

"Remember, you are to call me immediately if she leaves the house or sends you on an errand"

Of all the roles Sarah played, she never envisioned herself playing I Spy.

Chapter 29

Henry knew Matt was upset and chose his words with due caution.

"Is everything all right Matt?" I couldn't help but overhear."

Matt was embarrassed. What in the world had possessed her to call him and why wasn't she at work?

"Everything is as fine as it can be, Henry. No need to worry."

Henry knew trouble when he saw it and he also knew his wife. If there was trouble between Matt and Allison, Connie knew about it. He began to wonder just how close those two were and he momentarily entertained the thought that perhaps…

"Glad to hear it my boy. In that case perhaps we should get back to Pushman so you can begin to unravel the mystery of the disappearing financial pages."

Henry motioned for Giorgio, whom he tipped generously, paid the bill, and he and Matt returned to the Pushman headquarters. He had no idea what action he would take if his suspicions were true. There was nothing he could do about any of it at this point. He decided that since Connie would be out for the evening perhaps when he returned to the privacy of his office he would give Francesca a call.

Connie was looking out onto the street below when she saw Henry and Matt returning from lunch. In just a few minutes her world may begin to spin out of control and she had no one but herself to blame. Since the day she met Allison, over forty years ago, she had never been able to say no and it was that weakness that would be the end of her.

Matt needed to make a call to Lydiel before dealing with Connie and her computer.

"Hi babe. How goes it?"

Lydiel was still dealing with Chapter 29. Writing was becoming a challenge lately. She seemed overcome by writer's block, probably caused by all of the interruptions. Right now she welcomed the intrusion.

"What's wrong Matt?"

"Nothing, lover. I just wanted to hear your voice, see how you are and if you miss me a little."

"I'm fine, sweetie. Sarah was here earlier and we got everything squared away. I miss you more than ever. I gave her a key, went over the routine and my expectations, and sent her on her way. She seems nice, there is that one thing that is so disconcerting. How is your day going?"

Matt needed to be with Lydiel, to take his time and sort things out. Too many puzzles in play at once and there were pieces missing from them all.

"Yeah, I know what you mean about that. It bothers me too. Are you sure the key was a good idea, though?"

"She needs to be able to get in if I am not here when she arrives or when she leaves."

"Lydiel, where else would you be? I can count the times you leave that house on one hand."

"Oh you never know; Prince Charming may come for a visit."

Lydiel knew this would drive him nuts but she was in a playful mood.

"For your information, I hear he comes quite often, due in large part to his Princess, and as a matter of fact I have it on good authority that he will be visiting the castle today."

Lydiel knew Matt well enough to know that something was seriously wrong and that he needed to talk. Now she was really getting worried. They had never spent this much time together.

"Matt? Is there anything I can do to help, now?"

Actually there was something she could do. He needed to go over the file she gave him but he did not want to go home to retrieve it. For some reason lately as soon as he walked in the door, Allison seemed to be walking out leaving him with the kids.

"Babe, remember the file you made for me from the Pushman site? Would you by chance still have the file on your computer somewhere?"

"No, something better. You were always getting on me about backing up the books and important things, so now I back up everything I print off but making two copies. There is another hard copy of the file here."

Matt wanted to hug his little, well not so little, idiosyncratic lover. Just when he least expected it, she always came through for him.

"I need to do some research on Connie Pushman's computer. I can't talk now. See ya soon. Kisses babe."

"Kisses back sweetie. Bye."

Lydiel retrieved the backup copy and started dinner for her Prince Charming. Matt needed to make another call and he dreaded it. With any luck Allison would be at work and he could just leave a message. Unfortunately luck was not with him as he heard Allison's voice come on the line.

"McNulty residence."

"Hi, it's me. I see you blew off work again. Keep that up and they will fire you. Anyway, it looks like our little talk will have to wait. Something came up with the budget for the ball, and Henry has asked me to review my presentation once more before the meeting of the full board. I won't be home for dinner this evening."

Allison's temples throbbed as she listened to the lies. She knew full well that the budget was Connie's area of responsibility and any questions about it would not have involved her husband.

"You know that I had plans. There is no one to

watch the boys."

Matt knew that his wife was more than just perturbed. He really needed to review the file and he needed to be able to concentrate. There was just no way he could do that home and truth be told he didn't want to go home.

"Why don't you cook a nice dinner for you and Connie, make a few margaritas and have your meeting at the house? Feed the boys early, help with the homework and let them watch a DVD."

"I use the girls' night out for a break, you know that."

"Anymore breaks and you would be coming home to get a break from Mirelli's. I have to go. Enjoy your evening with Connie."

And with that Matt was gone. Lighting a cigarette, Allison reached for the tequila and tried to think of what she could serve with the margaritas for dinner. As she emptied the glass, she reminded herself that in a very short time, her problems would soon be over. First things first; call Connie

Chapter 30

Matt knocked softly on Connie's door. He had mixed feelings about the task at hand. Henry was his boss and had given him a chance when no one else would, but it was Connie's relationship with Allison that started the ball rolling. Connie Pushman remained seated as Matt approached her desk. For the past two hours she had tried to access different files on her computer and she had also tried to find her favorite IT guy. Fear was gnawing at her like a rat with a big piece of cheese, and like it or not, she was the cheese now.

"You need to sign on for me Connie and then we can see how much information if any we can retrieve pre-system failure."

"I will try but I really don't think there is anything there. Usually when the system goes down all of the work and data is lost."

Matt noticed Connie's hands tremble as she typed in her password. He knew she was hiding something, but what? Surely she couldn't and wouldn't be stealing from the company. Suddenly his thoughts turned to Allison and the forty-seven thousand dollars and he sadly realized anything was possible.

"Let's see what we have here. If the crash occurred on the 12th, I will try to go back to the 10th which would allow for information to travel over various time zones."

Connie suddenly felt lightheaded. She could hear her heartbeat in her ears and her throat felt tight. As she relaxed back in her chair the phone rang.

"Good afternoon, this is Connie."

"Good afternoon yourself chickie. How are things?"

Just what she needed. Allison!

"I am in the middle of something. Can we schedule an appointment for tomorrow at say, 10 a.m.?"

"You sound funny. Have you forgotten about this evening? I have the key now. Things are going as planned."

Allison noticed how strained Connie's voice sounded strained as if someone were there with her. Then it dawned on her. It was Matt!

"Connie, is Matt there with you now?"

"Sure, I thought of that approach myself. It has merit and we can discuss it in detail if you like. Thank you so much. Goodbye."

Matt was pleasantly surprised to see the financial pages for the 10th appear on Connie's monitor, however, just as quickly as they appeared, they disappeared. The red alert arrow was once again on the screen. Matt was totally baffled. Just a few seconds ago things were fine and now it appeared the site was down again.

"Connie, can you try rebooting again, please. I was able to retrieve the information but suddenly the system went down again. There might be a worm in the system somewhere."

"Why don't we table it for today Matt. It's getting late."

"I would really like to try it once more Connie. It should only take a couple of minutes to reboot."

Before Connie could take any action, the phone rang again.

"Excuse me Matt. Hello, this is Connie Pushman."

Connie's voice was cracking under the stress of Matt's persistence to retrieve the financial files. She knew she had no choice but to comply for not to dowould certainly fuel any suspicions he and Henry might have.

"You owe me doll face. I just got your message a few minutes ago. This is a very temporary fix- 8 hours at the most this time. Whatever demon is chasing you, either kill it or find a better way to handle it. There is nothing more I can do. Ciao Bella."

Thank God for Walter! Every minute was crucial now. She rebooted the computer and signed on. Bolstered by newfound courage Connie suggested that Matt try to access the site again. Thoroughly frustrated by his inability to bring the file up once more, Matt sighed in resignation.

"I have no idea what is going on. I guess we will have to wait for the IT guys to take a thorough look at the system. Sorry, Connie."

"Don't feel bad Matt. These things happen."

After Matt closed the door Connie allowed a smirk to cross her face. That was a call too close for anyone's comfort. She knew she couldn't hold on much longer. It was time to call Miss Allison and get this show underway.

The cell phone rang once as Allison grabbed it from the passenger seat.

"Hellloooo."

"My aren't we in a good mood. Your husband nearly cooked my goose. God, is he tenacious!"

"So what happened? Did Matt find the file?"

"Thank goodness an old IT contact of mine came to the rescue with not a second to spare. He bought me a little time but you know how your husband is. He will not let this rest. He has an opportunity to score points with Henry. How much longer before we deal effectively with Lydiel? I am going to have to put the money back soon."

"Stop worrying. There is more than enough left in the emergency housing fund, and if things go right, Lydiel Sommers will cease to exist, and Mr. Matt will be cooling his heels in jail for quite a while. I will have control of things and you will be able to replace the funds."

Allison was amazing; so cavalier about the

whole thing as if it were a walk in the park.

"Let's talk about it this evening at Mirelli's."

"Connie wait! I forgot to tell you. I can't meet you at Mirelli's. Matt won't be home this evening and I have no sitter. I was wondering if we could have dinner at my house. The boys were just invited to a cookout in the neighborhood and we can talk."

Connie didn't like the sound of this but she agreed. She always felt uneasy discussing this particular subject at either house. She felt as if the walls had ears. At this point, however, she had no choice. Allison was amazing; so blasé about the whole thing as if it were a walk in the park,

"Okay, shall I bring the wine?"

"Don't bother. I am making margaritas."

"Sounds good, Allison. I will see you about seven or so."

The sooner this whole matter was resolved, the better Connie would feel about it. She was having misgivings about what was in store for Matt.

Chapter 31

Henry continued to surprise Francesca. A wonderful package had just been delivered to her from Chantrelle's, the most exclusive store in town, and as always, Henry's timing was impeccable.

"Good afternoon Miss Francesca Sommers, and how is the girl with the hottest puss this side of the Mississippi?"

"She is happy, surprised and missing the most amazing dicksmith her puss has ever entertained. Thank you so very much. It is beautiful."

Henry felt himself blush and aroused listening to Francesca's words. An old fart like himself rarely had his sexual prowess applauded. He loved pleasing her. She was so flexible, and the way she rode him was unbelievable. It had been years since he had come so hard, and so often; twice in a year maybe, but twice in one night? Not since his college days, more years ago than he cared to remember.

"I'm glad you like it dear. I was hoping you would wear it for me tonight at dinner or am I being too presumptuous?"

"I will wear it, and you are definitely not being presumptuous. I very much enjoy your company. Where is the most dynamic duo in town dining this evening?"

"I thought we could take a carriage ride down to the river's edge. It is going to be beautiful out tonight, and we could have dinner at the seafood place there with champagne of course. Then afterwards we could hold hands and take a short walk on the pier and gaze at the stars. Of course the brightest star will be with me."

At twenty four years old Francesca had no idea what it felt like to be romanced but she was learning fast. Guys her age considered a "date" going to the movies and maybe an all you can eat place afterwards. She knew the seafood place Henry was speaking of; crisp white linens on the table, Waterford crystal- the works. Never in her wildest dreams did she imagine a date like this.

"You are so good to me Henry. What time shall I be ready?"

"I am sending a car to take you to the Renaissance at 5 p.m. Accessories for the dress and anything else you need will be in the suite. I shall arrive by carriage at 7 p.m. so if you are in the lobby at that time it would facilitate matters greatly."

"I will be there will bells on Mr. P. Kisses until then."

"I am thoroughly looking forward to seeing you again my dear. Kisses back. Good bye."

At precisely the second Henry ended his call with Francesca, there was a soft tap on his door.

"Come in please. Oh! Matt, my boy. Sit down. Good news I hope."

One of the drawbacks of genius is the frustration experienced when there is neither a logical explanation of, nor solution to a problem. The fact that both of these eluded Matthew McNulty was unacceptable. He was so close to unraveling the mystery when the system had suddenly gone down again. He had the file at home but how could he explain the possession to Henry?

"Were you able to retrieve anything?"

"The strangest thing happened, Henry. I had the file on screen and then suddenly Connie's computer crashed. When she rebooted, the alert was back on the website. I think there may be a worm there. I think I can help in another way, however."

Henry glanced at this watch and noticed it was nearly 5 p.m. He needed to have the car sent to pick Francesca up for their date later.

"Matt, I have a dinner engagement later so perhaps we can table this for now and pick it up first thing in the morning. How does that sound to you?"

It sounded perfect, an unanticipated reprieve. That would give him a chance to review the file with Lydiel and gain her insight. Solving mysteries seemed to be her area of expertise.

"It sounds like a great plan, Henry. Have a good evening."

"Yes, you too, my boy. You too."

On his way to his office, Matt realized he left the single page in Henry's office. As he approached Henry's door he overheard Henry on the phone.

"Yes, this is Mr. Pushman. Please send the car to 852 Tower St. Have the driver pick up Miss Francesca Sommers and take her to the Renaissance please. Discretion as always, Joseph."

Francesca? As in Lydiel's daughter, Francesca?

Henry's dinner appointment was with Francesca Sommers? Matt hoped what he thought was happening wasn't. What kind of game was she playing now? Matt felt as if the world had gone mad in a day. Returning to his office he quickly dialed Lydiel's number.

"Hi handsome. How goes it? I miss you."

He was beginning to believe that stuff. Come to think of it, she was right. He was handsome and he missed her too.

"It isn't going well at all. I'll be leaving here shortly and I thought I might pay my favorite writer a visit if she isn't otherwise engaged this evening."

"Is that what I am now, your favorite writer? I'm sorry but Prince Charming called a little earlier and said he would be visiting the castle to see his Princess."

Matt had to laugh. There were times when she used so many words his brain could no longer absorb them all.

"I take it I know this man?"

"Matt are you okay? I'm cooking dinner now. You called me earlier remember?"

Matt was losing it. There was just too much stuff going on and trying to sort it out was becoming a bit overwhelming.

"Okay babe. I'm on my way. Do you need me to do anything on the way?"

Now it was Lydiel's turn to laugh.

"No sweetie. I'm fine. Just get your handsome self here ASAP."

"I'm out of here now. Lydiel? Did you get your inhaler refills?"

"Thanks for reminding me. I'll take care of it now. See ya soon."

"See ya soon, babe."

As soon as she hung up the phone, Lydiel realized the scripts had been called in to the pharmacy. Oh well, no problem. That would be Sarah's first task of the day tomorrow. Right now she needed to shower, tame her chestnut tresses, and get dinner started.

Chapter 32

Matt was experiencing brain gridlock as he maneuvered his way through the evening rush hour. The computer situation, the missing file, Henry and Francesca, and the nagging matter of the $47,000 were all competing for issue of the day. The more he tried to free his mind, the more cluttered it seemed to get. Turning onto the gravel pad behind Lydiel's house, he decided that for now the issue of the day was to do something for himself, and something to make his lady happy. As he opened the door, he loosened his tie and unbuttoned the top button of his shirt. The kitchen smelled wonderful.

"I'm here darling."

Lydiel had gone the extra mile to please Matt and she had an interesting surprise for him.

"Have a seat sweetie. I'll be there in a minute. I put a tape in for you. Why don't you turn it on?"

What was this all about? If he wanted to watch movies he could do it at home. What a day he was having, and now what was she doing? Settling himself in the overstuffed double chair, he grabbed the remote. What followed was something there were no words to describe. First there was music, old theatrical music. Music from Gypsy - Let Me Entertain You. Then suddenly there appeared a woman who had her back to the camera. She was wearing a red formal dress, long red gloves and her hair was in an upsweep. She began gyrating to the music as she slowly peeled one glove off and tossed it over her shoulder. Just what Matt needed, some old broad doing a strip tease. What the hell was Lydiel doing?

"What am I watching here, babe?"

"Just a tape I thought you might enjoy."

Matt turned his attention back to the tape. The second glove was peeled off and also tossed over her shoulder. The woman turned around and began to unzip the dress. Matt was almost dumbfounded. The dress fell away revealing a red lace corset straining to control a pair of beautiful soft round orbs of flesh, matching thong and thigh high nylons. Seating herself in a large rocker she swung a leg over each arm fully exposing herself. Matt felt himself harden as the woman licked her fingers and began masturbating. She reached around and undid the corset leaving a pair of red pasties covering her nipples. She sucked first one nipple and then the other. Standing up she did a little pirouette, bowed and crooked a finger inviting the viewer to "come hither". Just as the music and the show ended, she was totally nude. Matt felt two warm hands and lips on his neck.

"Did you like it baby?"

"You are something else Ms. Lydiel Sommers. When did you make this? I thought you said you would never do a video. Come over here and let me see you."

"Close your eyes first. I have another surprise for you."

Matt was unsure as to whether he could handle another surprise this day, but he felt it was best to play along.

"This is your game, Missy but I can't wait much longer to touch you."

Wearing a red silken gown with a plunging neckline and deep v- back with a matching robe,

Lydiel stood in front of Matt. She leaned over and kissed him softly at first and then deeper. He opened his eyes as he kissed her back. There were times when this woman literally took his breath away, and this was one of them. Red suited her coloring and her personality. He stood, took her in his arms and held her very close.

"You are very very beautiful. Hold me close darling and let me feel you."

Matt removed the robe and kissed each tender shoulder as he did so. Taking advantage of the plunging neckline he reached inside and gently rolled a nipple between his fingers as his other hand cupped her very supple ass. She felt so good, so very good and she was his. This was his woman and he was her man, and he was going to make outrageous love to her. Breaking the embrace he led her to their bed. He watched her slip out of the gown and all he could think of was being deep inside her, feeling her tighten around him.

"Come lie naked in my arms, lover and let me love you."

As Lydiel slid in beside Matt, it was as if they

had become one body. Deep kissing Matt as he gently stroked her always started the train of o's that took her from 0-10 in short order, while Lydiel moaned and writhed under his touch. His tongue teased her and made her clit hard while his fingers were inside her creating one orgasmic wave after another. Matt draped her legs over his shoulders and entered her gently at first and then harder. He felt her arch her back to meet his thrusts.

She needed to feel him and taste him. She sucked his nipples until they were erect and then slowly licked a path downward. She kissed the tender flesh of his inner thigh; the soft sensitive area beneath his balls, running her tongue as far back as it could go as she stroked his cock. She mounted him and rocked slowly back and forth. He pulled her close as her breasts hung in his face. Grabbing them he filled his mouth with her nipples and sucked deeply. His day was improving significantly. He didn't want it to end this way. He needed to be inside her. Coaxing her to her knees, he took her from behind, ravaging her as she backed into his every thrust. He felt her contract and release as he brought her to the edge over and over until with a few final thrusts he felt her come with him, throb after delicious throb.

Happily exhausted, they lay in each other's arms and for several minutes there was silence between them. Lydiel knew that Matt was troubled but she was not going to broach the subject with him. Instead she closed her eyes and thought how lucky she was to have him in her life.

Matt gently stroked her arm as it lay across his chest and he looked at the woman lying beside him and asked himself why? Why couldn't he? Why didn't he? Would there ever come a time when he did? She loved him and in many ways that was problematic for him. He couldn't give her the time and attention she deserved. Instead he lived with a woman who refused to share his bed, and on the rare occasions that she did, there was almost never any physical interaction. She was also a thief. Allison stole the essence of the marriage - the fire, and the passion, and the trust. But then there were the boys…

"Babe, are you awake?"

"I am, and very comfortable here but I know. You need to eat, and although I hate to move, I will put dinner on the table."

As Lydiel moved to get up, Matt held her close, closer than usual. He looked into her face and made a decision. She was one of the hottest women he had known. She loved him and she made him feel good about himself.

"I have an idea, let's both hit the shower and I will help you finish dinner."

Something was definitely wrong! Matt usually handed her a towel and a glass of wine. She decided to follow his lead tonight.

"What time do you have to be home, sweetie?"

"Lydiel, remember that day many months ago when I told you that one day I would stay until you wanted me to leave? Today is that day.

Chapter 33

Henry was relieved to see that no one was home when he arrived. Although Connie had full knowledge of his dalliance, it would be awkward to have her there watching him prepare for a date.

He tossed his briefcase on the bed and began to disrobe, neatly hanging up his suit and putting his shirt and underwear into the hamper. For tonight he would wear his new blue suit, striped shirt with the white collar and French cuffs, and his most comfortable leather oxfords.

Just as he was about to walk into the shower, the phone rang. He decided to let the machine pick it up. This was one date he did not wish to be late for.

No answer. Francesca had tried for days to reach Connie for a status update but seemed to miss her each time. Lying across the feather bed, she held the mirror up close as she eyed the sapphire and diamond necklace and earrings that Henry considered 'accessories', and a perfect match for the strapless beaded gown with the deep thigh split.

Leaving nothing to chance, there was a pair of matching stiletto strap sandals, bag and underwear. A bottle of her favorite cologne was left on the vanity.

Whatever guilt Francesca felt about her role in the upcoming demise of her mother seemed assuaged by the attention she was receiving from the husband of her co-conspirator. Henry Pushman liked her as she was. Admittedly the fact that he knew very little about her worked in her favor, but no matter how she felt, it was too late to turn back now. Lydiel deserved what she was getting and so did Matt. She and Matt could have been so good together.

The fact that Lydiel shared a husband did not mean that Francesca wanted a three way split. She had been that route before, and it was painful taking the crumbs that were tossed. Henry was married and never squeezed her in between other activities. When they were together he never looked at his watch or the clock. She was the most important thing in his life at that time. Hell, even when she was with Connie she had her undivided attention as well.

Then there was the matter of Lydiel's age. Matt cared for a woman more than twice her age and that was an insult to her ego. She was young, flexible and available, and no matter how youthful Lydiel appeared, she was old, and Francesca suspected, not very good in bed. Matt had no idea what it was like to make love to a real woman instead of some old has been writer. It was nearly six-thirty p.m. and time to get dressed and make herself beautiful for Mr. P.

Today was Henry Pushman's day to go blue, and that included the little blue pill –Viagra. He was not experiencing any real problems, but Francesca was a high energy young woman who put him through his paces. She managed to send his ego soaring and he did not want to ever let her down. They had known each other only a short time but she made him feel as if he had been recalled to life. She was just what he needed at this stage of his life. He tied his tie, looked into the mirror one final time and left for the carriage company.

"Matt, can you set the table for me? As soon as I put the salad together we can eat."

"Sure babe. No problem. Do you want some help with the salad?"

Matt set the table, lit the candles and realized

that this was only the third time they had shared a meal. He found the music and popped in the CD. From the way the kitchen smelled she had prepared his favorite beef and rice. Any other time he would have felt that twinge of guilt knowing that soon after they made love he would have to go back to his other life, but not tonight. Tonight belonged to them.

"No sweetie, I'm fine. You can put the salad and rolls on the table for me and I will bring the main course."

She looked rather comical with a purple apron over the red silk gown. He walked over to pick up the salad bowl but nuzzled her neck instead before spinning her around and hugging her.

"Have I told you lately how much I care for you?"

Matt was scaring Lydiel. She welcomed the attention but there was obviously something nagging at him.

"Hmm, now let me think for a minute. It seems to me…"

"Shhh."

Matt put his finger on her lips and kissed her

again. She turned and hugged him warmly.

"We need to eat baby. Then we can continue this. Here's the salad and the rolls."

"Thank you sweetie."

"For what Matt?"

"For everything. For this, for being you, just for everything."

"You never ever have to thank me for anything sweetie. You know how I feel."

"Yes, I do and I am slowly beginning to believe that you are sincere. It took me a while but I am beginning to get it. Dinner is very good, by the way."

"What is it Matt? What's bothering you? You and I talk about everything."

"Everything seems wrong. The forty-seven thousand dollar withdrawal is nagging at me. There is something very suspicious going on with the Pushman website, and I overheard Henry order a company car to pick Francesca up for a date."

"Francesca? For a date? Are you sure and why is she dating your boss? How does she know him?"

"I have no idea but I will find out. This is not

good for either of us. You are the relationship guru. Just off the top of your head why do you think Allison took the money? Things have not been good between us, even more so lately but we still talk about things or at least I thought we did. Do you think she is going to take my boys?"

"I know you want to see good in Allison and you find it difficult to believe that she could be deceitful or manipulative, but she is proving otherwise. I don't know why she took the money. It isn't enough to live on for very long. As for the boys, you and Hannah spend more time with them than she does and she seems to relish her freedom suddenly. Are you certain that these girls' nights out aren't gambling junkets or an affair?"

Matt knew that an affair was a possibility although highly unlikely given her devoutly religious beliefs. She seemed too selfish to give anything away including herself. She had been spending more and more time with Connie and less time with him and the boys. She had also been spending more time at church. Connie had never shown an interest in gambling other than lottery tickets and never to excess.

"I'm fairly sure babe. It is just so much money, you know."

Lydiel knew one thing for certain, whatever Allison was doing was hurting Matt and that was unacceptable. She felt that the alliance between Allison and Connie was unhealthy, but as a person with no standing she had to tread carefully when it came to discussing Mrs. McNulty with her husband.

"I don't think she is planning on taking the boys anywhere. They love you Matt and you are a great dad. All will be revealed in time my love. Trust me. My grandmother used to say it all comes out in the wash, and time may not be on her side."

Lydiel began to clear the table so she and Matt would have a place to work later.

"Come talk to me while I clean up the kitchen. I do some of my best thinking there."

Matt laughed. For most people moments of inspiration came while on the can. Only Lydiel could find inspiration in soapsuds. She was a funny one and a sexy one.

"Now lover, tell me about the thing with

Connie's computer and her ghost in the machine."

"As I told you earlier I suggested that if I could reset Connie's computer to a time just prior to the original problem I might be able to retrieve any stored financial pages, like the one you copied for me. For one brief moment today I had the site up and then all of a sudden the alert was back. I had Connie reboot her computer but it was no use. The odd thing is that the system was fine until I tried to access those pages. I thought if you didn't mind, you could go over the file with me so it would make sense when I talk with Henry in the morning."

"Sure sweetie, no problem, although you know I have a rather unorthodox thought process at times. I have a question and if it is none of my beeswax you can tell me. Does Henry suspect Connie of something illegal?"

One of Lydiel's more endearing qualities was her inability to think logically sometimes. She had excellent insight and logic had nothing to do with it. In her own inimitable way she understood people very well. Matt was counting on that now. He always referred to her talent as mystical mutterings.

"Henry suspects Connie of skimming from the ball budget."

"How interesting. The file is on top of my computer. Bring it into the dining room and we'll get started."

Over the next two hours Lydiel and Matt poured over figures and dates from the financial pages of the ball budget, projections and other activities of Pushman and Associates. What they discovered confirmed Henry's suspicions and raised new questions about Allison's recent activities. Matt felt overwhelmed emotionally and physically, and there was so much that he did not understand.

"Do you think any of this is related?"

Lydiel knew the answer but she wasn't sure Matt would believe her. She fielded his question as diplomatically as possible.

"Connie and Allison are friends. Perhaps one has encountered a financial problem and the other is helping out."

"Thanks babe. I know what you are trying to do and you don't believe that BS anymore than I do. Here are two women, neither of whom wants for anything, suddenly stealing large sums of money from their husbands. I could use a few of those mystical mutterings right about now."

"I think you might appreciate them more lying down. Care to join me in the 'muttering chamber' once more before you leave?"

Matt didn't need a second invitation. Holding Lydiel in his arms he tried not to think about going home or pilfered funds or any of the other why's in his life. Now was the time to immerse himself in the warmth of the woman who cared for him and wanted to be with him. They made wonderful love to each other and Matt lost all track of time. Lydiel was curled up tightly next to him with her back to him. He wondered what went through her mind as she slept. He gently removed his arm from underneath her and sat on the side of the bed. There was no use in prolonging the inevitable.

Chapter 34

Everything was ready. Allison poured herself another margarita and lit a cigarette as she waited on the deck for Connie to arrive. Things were moving along smoothly and with any luck Matt's little sexmate would be history soon. The only problem now was Connie, who seemed to be running scared. Speaking of the devil...

"Hello, hello, hello, anyone home?"

Never one to miss an opportunity to needle Connie, Allison saw her opportunity and couldn't resist.

"Just us axe murderers."

Allison's sense of humor was bizarre at times, and tonight of all nights Connie was less than receptive to it. She was jeopardizing all she had worked for to help Allison kill her husband's mistress.

"Very funny, Allison. Now tell me again why we aren't at Mirelli's with Giorgio hovering and spoiling us?"

"Your mind must really be going. Your husband has my husband working on that stupid ball thing."

"That 'stupid ball thing' as you call it is the largest fundraiser in this state, not to mention one of the reasons your husband has a job."

"My, aren't we touchy and in a bad mood tonight. I have some good news."

"Allison. Did it ever occur to you that there are other things going on besides your infernal obsession to kill Lydiel Sommers? My twins are off to college soon and they were the glue holding Henry and I together. He has found a woman who makes him happy and I am in jeopardy of losing everything and everyone to help a selfish, arrogant, cold fish of a woman. You and I are friends and I have gone the distance for you, but since I've known you, you have been a manipulator with an agenda. You never loved Matt and you never really wanted the boys. They were nothing more than a means to hang onto a man so you could save face in front of your family and the few friends you have."

Allison avoided Connie's gaze and bit her

lower lip. In many ways Connie was right. Being a mother seemed to validate her existence. Everyone else in her family and Matt's family had kids. Appearance meant everything to her and that is the main reason she never considered a divorce.

"You obviously are in desperate need of a few margaritas. How do you know Henry is having an affair?"

It never ceased to amaze Connie how Allison just blew off the truth. It was as if she was in some ethereal place where her feelings and opinions were all that mattered.

"Henry told me and I am happy for him."

"You're crazy. If Matt ever told me he was having an affair he would be out on his ass."

"So instead you know he is having an affair and since he won't admit it you make his life miserable, and you are going to kill his mistress. Makes a lot of sense to me, Allison. Did you ever stop to think what happens if and when he finds out? What happens if he discovers the missing money? In that case you would be cooling those well pedicured heels of yours in some hoosegow somewhere, a societal pariah who would never see her children again. Matt would then be free to be with whomever he chooses. The difference between you and me is that I love Henry in my own way.

When I was growing up and even into my college years all I wanted was to be a wife so I wouldn't have to do things alone or sleep alone. I would have someone to sit across the dinner table from me. Everyone around me was married or engaged, and I was tired of being the odd one out, always fixed up with the loser of the month. Then I met Henry- sweet, innocent, smart and rich. He liked me right away and I was always comfortable with him. Sex was a chore but I bore it as I did the twins. I have kept a secret for years while Henry and I moved further and further away from each other physically and emotionally, and as long as you keep your mouth shut he will never know. He has never hurt me, and I curse myself everyday now for taking that money because it will hurt him when his suspicions are confirmed."

Connie was becoming a spoiler. She always was the loyal one; the one who wanted and needed a friend so badly she put up with Allison for all these years. Here she was happy to have a key to the love lair and her best friend was raining on her parade.

"I got the key to Lydiel's house today. Sarah brought it to me this morning. I also have the canisters from Remey. Phase two will get underway tomorrow. It won't be long now."

Connie realized that this plot had reached the point of no return and she was in far too deep now. If she went against Allison it would not bode well for her, and the fallout would hurt a lot of people, most of all Henry and the twins. She was tired of the plotting, planning and scheming and decided to change the subject.

"Mmmmm, Allison, what smells so good? I am famished."

"Beef burgundy. I thought French as a change from Italian."

"Wonderful. Let's eat and discuss the plans shall we?"

Connie didn't fool Allison at all. She was worried that Matt would discover the missing money and report it to Henry. Perhaps Allison could do something to temper his enthusiasm.

Chapter 35

The carriage slowed and came to a halt as it pulled up in front of the Renaissance. The driver opened the door and placed the footstool on the carpet as he assisted Francesca inside. Henry could not recall seeing a lovelier sight in many years. She was stunning in the blue gown and the jewelry was perfect for her.

"Good evening Miss Francesca Sommers. May I say how incredible you look?"

The way Henry looked at her told Francesca many things. It told her that Henry truly enjoyed the pleasure of her company, and that perhaps it had been a very long time since he had indulged a woman.

"You cut quite the handsome figure yourself, Mr. P. Blue is my favorite color."

"Why thank you, my dear. Now tell me how does one so young know that line?"

Francesca decided to answer that question by planting a kiss on Henry's lips. He pulled her close and let his hand slide under the deep slit in the gown, massaging her thigh and the roundness of her hip as he returned the kiss. Francesca's free hand caressed Henry's crotch. Undoing his zipper, she reached inside and gently but firmly stroked his hardness. Henry closed his eyes and let her work her magic as the carriage lumbered along. He wanted to take her then and there but knew he couldn't. Instead he guided her head to his now throbbing cock and moaned softly as she engulfed him. Although he tried to hold back, this was new to him and he felt her swallow hard twice as he let go. Each time with her was an adventure.

The night was young and he was looking forward to reciprocating by sucking that little button of hers until it was rock hard, and tasting her wetness as he felt release after release. He wanted to hit the spot deep inside her that lifted more than her spirits; but most of all he simply wanted to make love to her. All in due time Miss Francesca Sommers, all in due time.

Connie was still uncertain as to why Allison wanted or needed a key to Lydiel's house. According to the plan that was why Sarah Turner was working for Lydiel.

"Why do you have a key to her house, Allison? Surely you aren't..."

"No silly. I am not going to do her in. That would ruin everything, although I would like to see the look on her face as she draws her last breath; to let her see me and to know that there will be no more trysts, no more sweet nothings whispered in her slutty ears, as a matter of fact no more anything. No, I have a key so that I can install the stealth software on her computer. The less Sarah knows the better. At the same time I will switch the inhaler canisters.

As Connie listened, she came to realize how much in control Allison always had to be. This all came to a head because Matt stopped beating a dead horse, and got a life. After all the years of patiently waiting for her to rejoin him in the marriage, Connie was surprised he hadn't found a lover like Lydiel before now. She knew there had been other relationships but none serious enough for Allison to want to eliminate the women permanently.

Before Connie had a chance to respond, the door opened and Matt and the boys were home.

Watching Allison's face, it was if a storm was approaching. She was underwhelmed to see her men.

"Hi mom! Hi Mrs. Pushman!"

It had been a while since Connie had seen the boys and they were growing like weeds. Matt looked exhausted and Connie thought it best if she left. Laughing, she acknowledged the way they still spoke in unison.

"Hello, you two or should I say you one. You guys are still speaking in unison I see, and getting so tall. My goodness, the last time I saw you were little grasshoppers."

The boys looked at Connie quizzically and searched her face for further explanation. Liam looked at Sean and then to Matt.

Matt knew they were being facetious and at their ages it was humorous. Before he could say anything Allison spoke.

"Boys, why don't you get ready for bed and I will be up later. Matt?"

"The cookout was winding down and the boys hailed me, so I decided to save you a trip and bring them home. It is a little late for them to be up, and I was surprised to see them out without one of us. Nice to see you Connie. If you two will excuse me tomorrow comes early. I will see to the boys Allison. Ladies…"

If she had any doubts before, Connie knew that was her cue to leave. Matt was visibly pissed off. Lately it seemed Allison was palming them off way too much.

"We will touch base tomorrow. Take care, Allison. Goodnight."

Whatever game Matt was playing, Allison had no intention of letting it go. She would check on the boys and then check Matt. After she put the last of the dishes away and turned off the lights, she poured the last of the margaritas and turned on the television. She brushed her teeth, and looked in on the boys who were both asleep. The light was off in the bedroom she and Matt shared, or used to share. He appeared to be sleeping but she wanted to know what he was up to. Slipping into bed she placed her arm across him. It was late and Matt was in no mood for Allison's feigned generosity.

"If you don't mind…"

"What if I said I do mind, and I want to be with you, and that I miss you?"

Matt knew this game all too well. She would wait until he was tired or asleep, come onto him, get rejected and then complain about how he was always too tired for her. Then she would go downstairs and fall asleep on the couch.

"I would say, get a grip, leave me alone, and learn to take care of yourself. Goodnight, Allison."

Storming down the stairs, Allison frowned and thought aloud

"When will they learn? NO one ever says NO to Allison Woodall McNulty. NO one!"

Allison downed a margarita in two gulps and took out paper and pen to make her selections from the offerings on QVC. They would learn. She would teach them all a lesson they would never forget!

After dinner Henry and Francesca took a leisurely stroll down the pier. The stars were out and the moon was full. It was a perfect night for making love to the perfect woman. Henry put his arm around Francesca and she put her hand on his butt, gently squeezing it as they walked. What a hot woman she was! He loved it. Connie was always opposed to public displays of affection, but Henry always thought that if they were discreet and in good taste, they sent a clear message to your partner.

As beautiful as the sandals looked, he had a feeling Francesca's feet could use a break. He decided perhaps a tour around downtown in the carriage was in order. Francesca rested her head on Henry's shoulder as the carriage wound its way around town. She was well fed and content and judging from the way his hands were wandering, it would not be too long before she was well loved. It had been more than three hours since they had eaten dinner and Henry felt that now was a good time to take his dose of blue. He slid the tablet into his mouth, and took a quick sip of the bottled water. He sat back and enjoyed the night air and his companion.

For the first time in over a year Connie Pushman was lonely. Henry was away for the evening, the twins were on a tour of the college campus, Remey was on vacation with her family, and

Francesca seemed to have dropped off the face of the earth. Connie tried her cell phone and reached her voicemail. Francesca's phone was on vibrate. She checked the caller's number and turned it off. She would deal with Connie tomorrow, but tonight belonged to the other Pushman.

The carriage stopped and Henry assisted Francesca out. The driver had promised to have someone deliver Henry's car and arrange for valet parking. Once inside the penthouse elevator, Henry's hands took license with Francesca's body. When the elevator doors opened into the penthouse, she was as naked as the day she was born. Tossing neatness aside, Henry soon joined her in the same state. Her nipples were hard, she was wet and they were ready for each other.

The bed had been turned down, the lights dimmed and soft music was playing. Locked in an embrace, Henry led Francesca to the bed. The passion and lust of the evening had created an urgency they both were ready to give into. Henry's hands and mouth found new ways to tease and please her. Having shown great restraint for most of the evening,

Henry had to have her soon. Kneeling behind her he very slowly entered her. His fingers teased and tweaked her button and before long he felt her tighten around him as he let go deep inside her. He had never been with a woman so perpetually turned on and one who always genuinely enjoyed being with him and pleasing him.

Book Two

The Murder of Lydiel Sommers

Chapter 1

Once again Matthew McNulty had no idea how long he had been awake and staring at the ceiling. These days he seemed to always wake up before the alarm clock sounded. He needed to get up but couldn't move. Yesterday had been unbelievable. First, there was the fiasco with Connie, then the video, dinner and outrageously warm and wonderful lovemaking with Lydiel. The way they read each other so well it was as if they were kindred spirits. They needed that time together and more of it. He had plans to do just that but with things the way they were at home, Matt never wanted to make promises or plans he may not be able to keep, especially with her. Sitting up, he collected himself and as he walked towards the bathroom, he covered the boys up and softly closed their door. He reminded himself of the biggest why in his life.

Fresh out of the shower, shaven and dressed, Matt was ready for his morning dose of caffeine. He walked past the sofa as if it and its occupant weren't there. He did, however, pick up Allison's keys from the floor. There seemed to be one more key than usual, probably to some door to the office she rarely visited. Lately it seemed as if she never went to work anymore.

While the coffee was brewing he decided to put the files in his briefcase, and quickly check his e-mail. Turning on the computer he tried to access the Pushman site but got the now familiar alert screen instead. As he started to read his mail, he noticed Lydiel was online. Didn't she ever sleep in? He needed that coffee before he could talk to anyone. Some auction show was blaring on the television. Normally he would shut it off but today he let it be. Returning to his office, he saw a new instant message box.

Ly_Som: "Good morning handsome."

MatMc: "Hi babe. Why are you always up so early?"

Ly_Som: "If you were here I wouldn't be. You know how I hate the bed."

MatMc: "One day we will have to do something about that."

Ly_Som: "I wish.......... Matt, be careful

today. I have a really funny feeling."

MatMc: "I am always careful but what's wrong?"

Ly_Som: "I can't put my finger on it but I feel as if something terrible is going to happen, so just be careful. Good luck with Henry."

MatMc: "More mystical mutterings, babe?"

Ly_Som: "I'm serious Matt."

MatMc: "Okay. I will. Talk later. I need to go. Kisses. Bye babe.

Ly_Som: "Kisses. Matt?"

MatMc: "I know sweetie and thanks."

Lydiel was rarely wrong and although he would never admit it Matt took her mystical mutterings to heart. He didn't say anything but he felt it also. Oh well, off to another day at the office.

Allison held her breath as Matt examined her key ring. He didn't seem to pay any attention to the keys as he placed them on the table. She waited for him to leave before getting an early start to her day. She had blown off too many days at work and Matt seemed to be checking up on her lately. That was not like him at all. She needed to get to the office early.

She woke the boys, checked to make sure they had everything and put them on the school bus.

On this day Allison McNulty chose her wardrobe very carefully; summer silk, flat shoes, no perfume and hair pinned up. Into her bag went the stealth software, one of Matt's favorite cigar lighters and a pair of cotton gloves. She checked the trunk to make sure the 'medication' was there and drove off.

Connie Pushman had been up since 5 am pacing the living room floor. In her heart she knew time was not on her side but she had to play things out until the last hand was dealt. She felt certain that the discovery would not come today and yet there was a sense of foreboding. It was one of those hard to explain uneasy feelings that hit the pit of your stomach like ice water on a hot summer day. Matt was not going to give up his search for the "lost" files, and his wife was not going to back out of eliminating his mistress.

There had been many times in the last few days when she just wanted to end it all. She wanted to tell Matt about Allison's plan and the money and all. She was tired, tired of living lies. This whole situation was out of control. Looking in the mirror she hardly recognized the woman staring back. She checked her purse, fingered the contents and left her home for another day at Pushman and Associates.

Literally up at the crack of dawn, Henry Pushman greeted the day refreshed and fulfilled. For the first time in his life he knew what it was like to experience lovemaking with a totally uninhibited woman who was as good at giving as she was receiving. As he dressed for work, he looked in the mirror and was pleased with the face staring back. There was life in his eyes and a sincere and genuine smile on his lips. He whistled softly while waiting for the elevator. Thanks to Miss Francesca Sommers he was ready to face whatever the day was to bring.

Chapter 2

Feeling the warmth of the early morning sun, Francesca's eyes reluctantly fluttered open. She reached out and realized Henry was gone. She hated to move but it was time to prepare for the day and it was going to be a long one. She pulled on her robe and walked into the living room to take in the view of the city at rush hour. Much to her surprise there was hot coffee, juice and rolls waiting for her. Staring out the window she asked herself why. Why couldn't she have met Henry years ago, even a few weeks ago before this whole THING with Allison started? Being with him made her realize how much she had settled for in her young life. It also made her realize that she much preferred his company and his touch to that of his wife. It definitely was time to have a serious talk with Connie.

The best part of Lydiel's day so far was remembering yesterday with Matt. He loved her little video, but she had a feeling that the reason was because he knew she did it for him. In the beginning of their relationship she always used her weight as an excuse but no more. The way they made love yesterday transcended every other meeting between them. Yesterday had been one of those body and soul experiences; the kind of pairing Danielle Steele wrote about. Today she was busy making up a little to do list for Sarah when the phone rang.

"Hey Ma, were you busy?"

Doreen was up and at it early also. She seemed to really like the phone job and that was a very good thing. No one knew better than Lydiel how difficult it was to juggle the responsibilities of motherhood and gainful employment.

"No more so than usual. I was just sitting here making out a little to do list for Sarah. What's going on?

"Ma? Ma? Damn I hate this. You are breaking up."

"I can hear you fine Doreen. Calm down. How is the new job working out?"

"It is working out fine. I can still hear another conversation while we are talking here. How is the book coming along and have you seen or heard from

Matt lately?"

Lydiel couldn't remember the last time she talked to her daughter that she didn't ask about Matt. He was that kind of man.

"The book is coming along well, actually better than I expected. Matt and I spent lots of time together yesterday. We had an opportunity to eat dinner together and work on a little project. I started missing him as soon as he was out the door."

"I know Ma, and I hate that you are alone so much. I wish the two of you could go out together and do things but I understand. Maybe I will get to meet Sarah one day."

After Lydiel hung up Doreen listened in to the "ghost" conversation. It was also a little garbled.

"Hi Conniem it's Francesca. I am just checking in and wondering how things are going with the plans."

"Things appear to be on schedule. What have you been up to? I miss you terribly."

Francesca knew she owed Connie an explanation and she didn't want to hurt her. They had been very good together but she needed to find a way to end it with her. She didn't want to lose Henry for any reason. This was her big chance to be happy.

"Is it possible to have lunch together today? I have a few loose ends to tie up here but I could meet you somewhere, say 2 o'clock or so?"

"That sounds like a plan. How about Charley's for a change? I hear they have excellent sandwiches."

Charley's was the last place Francesca wanted to be seen with Connie.

"I have a better idea. What about dim sum at that place in the IGA Mall?"

"That sounds great Francesca. I will see you there at 2. Bye."

That was just the phone call Connie needed. Her mood lifted and she was looking forward to lunch.

Doreen was more than surprised to hear her sister Francesca's voice. She wondered what scheme or scam she was involved in now. Whoever this Connie was, Doreen felt very sorry for her. She clicked off the tape recorder and went back to work.

Lydiel was enjoying the extra attention from Matt, but she knew that the missing money and the situation at work were taking their toll. How could a woman steal from her own husband, especially one that gave her everything she could ever want. Before she gave that and other things more thought, the phone rang and it was Matt.

"Here I am sweetie. How are things so far?"

Every time Matt heard her voice, a sense of relief washed over him. For some reason lately he felt that she was in some sort of danger. He couldn't put his finger on it, but that was one reason he was so insistent that she not be out at night alone, that she use a pen name and that no identifying information be listed anywhere. His new concern was also the reason he tried to spend more time with her. As independent as she was, she was far too trusting of people.

"Okay so far, babe. Thanks for last night. I wish I could have stayed longer. Has Sarah arrived yet?"

"Not yet. I was just making a to do list for her."

"Take care of yourself today babe. I need to get to a meeting. I will try to call you later. Kisses lover."

"Kisses back and thanks for thinking of me."

Hanging up from him was as bad as closing the door after he left and she hated doing them both. Sometimes she thought she loved him too much, and she always had to remember that she was sharing a husband - someone else's. She desperately wanted more of a life with Matt but she knew it had to be on his terms. For too long he felt trapped in relationships and she wanted to change that for him, but she knew in her heart she would never have the chance. Allison and the boys had at least a ten-year hold on him.

It had never been her intent to disrupt the marriage. She wanted more of a balance between time spent with his family, time to himself and time spent with her. This was the first time that they had spent quality time together and it felt good. Lydiel was not stupid. She realized that as soon as the crisis at Pushman ended and things settled down, Matt would move away from her a little and things would go back to the way they were before. Sharp rapping on the front door jarred her from her thoughts.

Sarah. Matt had locked all three locks on the front door so it took her a minute or so to get it open.

"Good morning Sarah, come in."

Sarah Turner was surprised to see Lydiel barricaded inside her own home in such a safe neighborhood. Maybe it was just a writer's idiosyncrasy.

"I tried to use my key but the locks…"

"I know and I apologize. I made a little to do list for you and I want to go over it with you. I would like for you to pick up my prescriptions from the pharmacy, and drop two reference books off at the library. They are both located in the IGA Plaza. Are you familiar with the location?"

If Lydiel only knew how familiar Sarah was with the location. Her meeting in the parking lot there had been the first of what she feared were several unpleasant meetings with Allison.

"I know it well. It shouldn't take longer than 45 minutes or so"

"Take your time. Here are the books. Why don't you get started and I will try to get a few chapters in before lunch."

On the surface, this job was going to be a piece of cake. Playing Sarah Turner was going to be a profitable little exercise. As soon as she pulled away from the house Sarah placed the call to Allison.

"Good morning, this is Allison McNulty. How may I help you?"

Sarah felt the sudden urge to vomit. Little Miss Control Freak sounded like Rebecca of Sunnybrook Farm on the **phone.**

"Ask not how you may help me, but rather how I may help you, Allison."

"Sarah? Please tell me you are NOT calling from the house. Where are you?"

"No Allison. Presently I am en route to the IGA Plaza to pick up prescriptions from the pharmacy and return reference books to the library. You asked me to call you when I left the house, so I am doing just that."

Allison's day just improved by a quantum leap. She could kill two birds with one stone or rather one writer with two inhalers.

"What time do you get off today?"

"Two-thirty, Allison. Why?"

This would fit into Allison's plans perfectly, if…

"Sarah, I need you to do something. When you get back to the house, try to encourage Lydiel to go out and enjoy the weather. Suggest a late lunch in the park or something. When you leave at two-thirty give me a call."

"That should be easy enough. We'll talk later then."

The wheels in Allison's mind were turning rapidly. She had managed to clear her desk of three days work and had put a substantial dent in today's jobs. A late lunch would allow her to totally clear her desk. That way she wouldn't need to return to the office. She needed to call Matt.

Matt added the final notes for his meeting with Henry. He knew it would be useless to try further attempts to access the file but the one Lydiel downloaded was more than enough to give Henry a clear picture of what was going on with the budget. The problem with Lydiel's theory was that if either Connie or Allison were in financial trouble why would they both need to steal? He was running two days ahead of schedule on his part of the ball project and with any luck he could wrap up his meeting with Henry, have a late lunch and get home in time to cut the grass before his big smoke event. Just as he was leaving his office the phone rang. He thought about not answering it, but it could be something about the boys, or Lydiel. He just couldn't shake that feeling and the last thing he wanted was to hear from Allison. He grabbed the phone on the first ring.

"Matthew McNulty"

"Hi there. How is your day going?"

Allison had wonderful timing. A few minutes more and they would have missed each other.

"My day is going just fine. I am on my way to a meeting. How are you?"

"Okay. I have an outside appointment. My mother is picking the boys up from home and taking them to dinner and a movie. I know you have the cigar thing tonight. I still have work to catch up on so I won't be home until nine-thirty or so. I just wanted you to know no would be home for dinner. I have to run. I love you. Bye."

Matt would decipher the exchange between

him and Allison later. Right now he had a very important meeting to attend.

Chapter 3

Henry's door was open and he was on the phone when Matt arrived for their meeting. Waving him in, Henry finished the call and appeared to be in a very good mood. Looking back, Henry had been in a good mood for the last week, and with all that was going on Matt wondered if Francesca had anything to do with it.

"Let's get started shall we, Matt? I have a late luncheon date. You said yesterday that you would have something for me today."

Matt took a deep breath and began to explain to Henry how he came into possession of the "missing" financial file. He recounted his activities on the day the system crashed and how he used Lydiel's computer to access the information due to the glitch.

Opening the folder, Matt took Henry step by step through the ball budget and the apparent sixty-thousand dollar discrepancy. It appeared that the same vendor had been paid three times for marketing publications related to the ball. When Matt finished

Henry leaned back in his chair and stared at him as if he were looking right through him.

"Matt, you are proving yourself to be a dedicated employee who has gone far beyond the scope of the job description. Your professionalism and honesty are above reproach. Now tell me what you aren't telling me and be straight with me. Did my wife take sixty thousand dollars from the company?"

Matt now found himself in a most unenviable position. Connie had been indirectly responsible for his being hired at Pushman. However, there was an unhealthy alliance between her and Allison, and he had firsthand knowledge that Allison's withdrawal of the forty-seven thousand dollars occurred the same day as the sixty thousand dollar payment authorized by Connie. He needed more answers to the myriad of questions surrounding the missing monies.

"I can't say for certain at this time. I need to check with accounting and do more research into who this vendor is. Also, I don't want to fall behind in my own area of responsibility. The ball is only eight weeks away and there is still quite a lot remaining to be done."

Matt's points were all well taken but Henry knew that he was buying time for someone. Sixty thousand dollars would not make or break Pushman but it could very well make or break the continuation of the Pushman marriage, and having Francesca in his life presented opportunities for him to be happy and to feel whole again. Connie was a very important part of his life and the mother of his children; however, he could not find it within himself to tolerate a thief and a liar. He had always been there for her and they had always worked things through together. Whatever issues she had now were putting them at odds with each other. The reality of the situation was that sixty thousand dollars of company funds could not be accounted for and Connie was the prime suspect.

"I have an idea Matt. You are running slightly ahead of schedule with the planning. Today is Wednesday. I want you to spend the rest of the week working away from the office starting now. Follow through with accounting and try to get a lead on the vendor. I don't want to see you anywhere near

Pushman. Check in with me as often as need be. I will inform Connie that you will be out of the office until further notice. I think you understand what I am saying here and I have no doubt that you and I are on the same page."

Henry was setting a trap for Connie and in a strange convoluted way Matt was the bait. The time away would hopefully help him solve two mysteries at once. Unlike Henry's situation the missing forty-seven thousand dollars was hurting him in more ways than one. This unexpected turn of events would give him an opportunity to brainstorm and have lunch with his favorite girl if she wasn't busy. Never one to make assumptions, he decided to give her a quick call.

"Good afternoon."

Matt always laughed when he caught Lydiel off guard like this. Her 'good afternoon' was so vintage, so classic.

"Well, good afternoon to you too. How are things?" I need to talk and I thought if you didn't have lunch plans we could drive out a ways and have lunch, say about 2 or so?"

Matt was taking chances lately and that was another big "why". They never went anywhere. It was a painful trade-off to be with him, but one she accepted and she was aware of his fear of being seen with her. After all, who knew where Allison's "eyes" were?

"Sure, just tell me where. I will have to stop for gas first and leave a note for Sarah if she hasn't returned from the errands I sent her on."

"No problem, Lydiel. You don't need to drive anywhere. I will pick you up in the back and we can ride together. Where did you send Sarah?"

"To pick up my inhaler refills and return a couple of overdue books to the library." She should be back before I leave. See you at 2. Bye sweetie."

Something was wrong. Since he had known her Lydiel she was never preoccupied when they talked. Getting away from the computer would be good for her, and it would give her a chance to enjoy the weather. He needed to pick her brain a little among other things.

He was preoccupied himself these days with the forty-seven thousand dollars, especially since he discovered that Allison and Connie both made the money transfers on the same day. What could they possibly need over one hundred thousand dollars for?

Lydiel had not planned on going out. That was her sole purpose for sending Sarah. She decided to bake a batch of cookies for Matt while she waited to hear from Jack Bass regarding the revisions to her manuscript. If this book deal went through it would mean worldwide recognition and solidly establish her as a writer. She needed that at this point in her life. These days with Matt were the best days of her life so far, but she knew where she stood with him. She wiped the tears away and set about making herself glamorous for the love of her life. She wondered if the day would ever come when...

Chapter 4

Sarah turned off the ignition and decided to return the books first. Since they were overdue she went inside to pay the fine. As she approached the desk, she noticed the employees smiling.

"I'm sorry these are late. Whatever the fine is, I will pay it now."

The woman behind the desk was a disgustingly pleasant librarian type: stodgy, bifocaled, bot smile in place.

"No problem. How are things coming along?"

Without thinking, Sarah replied that things were fine, paid the fine and left. Next stop was the pharmacy. As she approached the window, a rather exuberant technician greeted her.

"One moment and I will get your scripts for you. Here we are. There have been some changes and the new dosage is listed on the label. Do you have any questions?"

Growing up in a family of asthmatics, Sarah knew more about inhalers than she ever wanted to.

"No, but thank you. Good bye."

Sarah Turner wasn't exactly sure if there was something in the water or these people were scary bots from some horror film. The plastered smiles and overly generous assistance was nauseating. She grabbed the bag from the counter and practically ran for the safety of her car. Of all the roles she had played, this was shaping up to be the strangest one by far.

Lydiel paced restlessly waiting for the phone to ring. Her nerves were frayed and her heart was racing, pushing her towards a full-blown anxiety and asthma attack. The wheezing was getting worse and her inhalers were all empty. She needed to calm down. If Matt were here he would tell her to "slow down and breathe, babe." Just as she picked up the phone to call Sarah she heard her key in the lock.

"I hope I didn't take too long. The pharmacist said there were some changes and to read the labels. Are you okay?" You don't look well."

The contents of Lydiel's purse were spilled onto the table and she was holding an inhaler in her hand. Sarah brought her a glass of water and a washcloth. Within minutes her heart rate was back to normal and she felt almost like herself. The phone was ringing. Sarah picked up the receiver.

"Good afternoon."

"I have great news Lydiel. It is just what we have been waiting for!"

It was obvious the caller thought Sarah was Lydiel, as he continued to ramble on.

"One moment please. I will get Ms. Sommers for you."

Sarah handed the receiver to Lydiel and excused herself. Checking the refrigerator for something to fix for lunch, she tried to eavesdrop on Lydiel's conversation.

"Hello? Oh Jack. Yes. Yes, I know. Uncanny isn't it? I have been on pins and needles. Please tell me the news.

Whatever "Jack" was saying seemed to be a source of increased anxiety and agitation for Lydiel.

"I understand Jack but surely you must see my position. I do not see how what you are asking is possible. Yes but… Let me think about it and get back to you later today. Thanks, Jack. Good bye."

Sarah emerged from the kitchen carrying a tall

glass of iced tea while trying to think of a tactful way of engaging Lydiel in conversation.

"It's such a beautiful day out. I thought you might enjoy a glass of iced tea. You really should go out for at least a little while. Lydiel? Are you okay? You seem upset again."

Lydiel was thinking over the things she and Jack had discussed. What he was asking of her was totally out of the question.

"I'm sorry. Did you say something Sarah?"

"Nothing important but it is a wonderful day out and you should go out and enjoy it. Maybe you could take a break from the writing?"

"As a matter of fact, I have an appointment soon. Thank you for running the errands. You can leave early today. There really isn't much to do."

Lydiel didn't have to ask Sarah twice. Gathering her purse and keys she closed the door softly behind her. As soon as she was in her car she phoned Allison.

"Hello?"

"It's Sarah, Allison. Lydiel has an outside appointment this afternoon. She will be leaving soon and I am off for home.

"Sarah, wait! I need you to stay there until you see her leave. I need to be sure that she is gone."

How much did this woman want? Sarah surmised that Allison wanted to steal something from the house, but from what she could see there was very little of value there. She had hoped to enjoy the rest of the afternoon with a little mall shopping.

"I suppose I can hang around for a few minutes more. I did have plans."

Allison was beginning to tire of Sarah. She had been hired to do a job, paid up front and yet every task seemed like a chore. Sarah was just another expendable cog in the wheel of events. Allison needed her nicotine fix, but she knew that was a definite no-no today. Nothing could go wrong today. What was taking so long?

Lydiel decided to free her mind for a few hours. Just as she closed the windows she heard the back door open. Matt was the quietest person she had ever known.

"Hi baby. I'll be ready in a second. I am just making sure everything is closed and locked."

"You are always ready, lover. Come here."

Pulling her close he brushed her hair aside and kissed her neck and her ear. Lydiel held him close and once again the whys crept into her conscious mind. Looking deeply into the most beautiful pair of brown eyes she had ever seen, she felt it beginning and she knew that if they didn't leave at that moment, they would become lunch for each other. Matt looked around the kitchen and locked the door.

Sarah was parked a few houses down the street and had a direct view of Lydiel's parking pad. She was surprised to see Matt with Lydiel. As soon as they drove off she called Allison.

The sun was directly above and Allison was beginning to feel the heat. What was taking Sarah so long to call? Just at that moment the bells jingled on the cell phone and it was Sarah.

"What's going on? Did she leave yet?"

"She is leaving now and so am I"

Sarah deliberately withheld the fact that Lydiel did not leave alone.

Chapter 5

As she drove to the restaurant Francesca thought about how she was going to break things off with Connie. They had been very good together but it was never meant to be a long term or permanent relationship. The fact that she and Henry had become lovers was an uncomfortable complication, and one that compromised continuing on with Connie. Being with Henry was an unbelievable experience. The age difference didn't seem to matter. He was a better lover than the young guys she had been with.

Connie knew she was losing Francesca and perhaps Remey as well. She was beginning to regret her decision to introduce them to Allison. The three of them had become so enmeshed in her scheme that they didn't have time for each other, and now Francesca seemed to have simply lost interest in her. Allison was a spoiler in so many ways. This whole thing could not end soon enough for her. Tears welled in her eyes. In just a very short time, there would be no one there for her- no one at all.

Francesca arrived first and waited in the bar.

Sipping a glass of wine, there was a tiny place inside her that wept. Had she not met Allison she would not have become involved in the plot to kill Lydiel, she would never had met Henry, and in all likelihood she would not be breaking up with Connie.

Lydiel loved summer. It also seemed filled with so much promise and the sun and warm temperatures seemed to make everything seem better, whether it actually was or not.

"What's the matter babe, you are so quiet today?"

Matt had known Lydiel long enough and well enough to know that when that 40 mile an hour mouth wasn't moving something was wrong. The only times she was quiet were when she was sick, thinking, kissing him or making love with him. He could safely eliminate sick, kissing or hot sex.

"Nothing really, sweetie. I was just thinking."

Lydiel's statement was the equivalent of 'oh I'm just loading a gun'. She was dangerous when she was thinking, and it seemed that she had been doing too much of that lately. Something was wrong, he was certain of it

Matt parked the car in the parking lot of the park and walked around to open her door. Her hand was clammy.

"What is it babe? You can tell me."

"Nothing really. I was just so anxious to hear about the publisher's decision regarding the book that I had a slight attack. All of my inhalers were empty. I couldn't remember where the full one was."

"Lydiel, how many times... I offered to get the refills yesterday. Sometimes if I didn't know better I would think that..."

"You would think what, that I was trying to kill myself? Trust me I am not leaving your sweet cheeks here for a bunch of horny wenches to take advantage of. I have just been preoccupied. I want to make you proud of me. I want to be a successful writer whose works are well read and appreciated."

Matt sensed there was more but decided to let it drop for the time being. He knew the best way to ease and clear her mind was just to kiss her. Standing and walking to a very old maple tree, he beckoned to her.

"Come over here for a minute, babe."

As she walked towards him, Lydiel looked at him standing there and was almost overwhelmed by her feelings for him. This was one of those times she wanted to hold him close to her forever. What a complete and utter fool Allison was. Matt reached out to her and pulled her close. Wrapped up in his arms this way she felt as if everything would turn out well. As he leaned to kiss her, once again the question was raised within her - why?

Connie Pushman stepped inside the Loo-Long and waited for her eyes to adjust to the dim lights. A quick glance around and she saw Francesca sitting at the bar. She looked stunning, and so young. Just then the hostess approached.

"You want a table, maybe?"

"Oh, yes, please for two. My friend is sitting at the bar."

Francesca waved to Connie as she joined her at the table. She noticed right away how tired and weary Connie appeared. Before she attached herself to Allison at the hip, Connie had been lively and so much fun. Francesca recalled how she, Remey and

Connie sat around a bonfire on Halloween and told spooky stories, ate smores and made love. Life was wonderful then; adventures, stories, girl talk. There was always something to look forward to.

Life with Lydiel had been just the opposite. Francesca despised Lydiel and had since the day she was adopted. When she was 8 or 9 she had tried poisoning her but of course it didn't work. Her mother, (what a joke) recovered nicely and never said a word about it to anyone. Lydiel was not her mother. She was a woman who loved and cared for children, some hers and many from others. She was giving and kind, and the exact opposite of her biological mother who had abandoned her outside a crack house along with her brother, and never looked back. Francesca knew where her birth sister was and ran away numerous times to be with her, only to be returned back to Lydiel.

It wasn't that Lydiel treated her badly; it was just that she took away any possible chance of her ever reconnecting with her real family, and answering her question of "why". She always felt powerless because other people were always making decisions for her including Lydiel making her leave home before she was ready to do so. Lydiel believed that adult children should make their own way. During all those years she never felt like one of the "real kids". She just wanted her "mother" out of her life, for good and Allison was her ticket.

Chapter 6

Allison McNulty was on a mission. She decided to park in the visitor lot at the hospital and walk to Lydiel's house. She knew there was an alley and a walkway behind the house and decided there was less risk of being seen that way. Fortunately at this hour of the day no one was around to notice her.

The outside door was ajar making access to the rear door of the apartment easier than anticipated. Entering the hallway, Allison called out several times. There was no response. She pulled on the gloves, and using the key she let herself in.

As she stood in Lydiel's kitchen, the smell of freshly baked cookies filled the room. Assorted appointment messages dotted the sidewall of the refrigerator, and the top hosted the usual array of hard to place items found in every kitchen. Luck was with her. There was a brown paper bag on the counter that contained three small boxes, one of which had been ripped open and was empty. She removed the two boxes and replaced them with two from her brown bag. For some reason Remey had made four. After checking the bathroom to make certain there was no inhaler there, Allison walked to the bedroom. The air conditioner was running in an empty house-what a waste.

The bedroom surprised her. Everything was purple, even the damn silk roses. On the bedside table right beside a picture of Matt, (why did this not surprise her?) were two bottles of pills that were not familiar to her, and an inhaler. There was also an extender. Knowing Matt it was difficult to imagine him with a woman who had problems sucking anything. Allison placed the inhaler in her bag and replaced it with one of the remaining inhalers Remey had filled. That took care of three, but she still had one left.

So this was the scene of the crime was it? Taking a seat in the easy chair, Allison tried to imagine Matt making love to the faceless writer. Did she kiss him? Of course she did. Matt would never be with a woman who didn't like to kiss. He was passionate about kissing, almost to the point of obsession. He was also passionate about sex. He needed sex like other people needed food. Did she feed him well? Did he do things with her that they once did together? Did they cuddle afterwards and whisper sweet nothings to each other? Was she a knees girl or a flat backer? What she was, was an interloper; sharing a husband that wasn't hers. Being old and lonely called for desperate measures she supposed.

Allison tried to remember the last time she and Matt had sex on a regular basis. He was always more into it than she was. She couldn't count how many times had she given award-winning performances. In those days she needed to do it to get pregnant. Then he spoiled it all by taking matters out of her hands. Later she did it to keep him around, or as Hannah would say, 'keep him reined in'. For the most part she wanted to avoid sex with him at all costs now.

Contrary to what anyone thought she was not the embittered cheated-on wife. She had always known of his little "time outs" as she called them. Most of them were nothing more than eye blinking attempts to "get off". She recalled another one but whatever happened, happened and it ended, and Allison had been overjoyed. Her happiness had been short-lived, however. Once again that insatiable hunger needed feeding and he found the perfect nourishment in Lydiel Sommers. For the better part of a year he had been making love to, according to Francesca, a woman, ten years or so Allison's senior. What was it about a woman that age that made Matt keep returning to her bed? Whatever it was it wouldn't be for much longer. It was time to get a move on.

There was a cut crystal candy dish beside the television along with mail, books and other things lying about. Allison removed the lighter from her bag and placed it under a letter covering the dish. What she noticed most was the lack of personal touches in the house. It was as if Lydiel was a person who was just starting over, including where she worked.

Allison stood in the doorway of Lydiel's office and wondered how anyone could write in that mess. She seated herself in the big office chair and turned on the computer, inserted the software and waited for it to load.

Matt and Lydiel discussed various theories

regarding the missing money but one thing was certain, there were now two thieves instead of one, and they both felt whatever it was, Allison and Connie were in it up to their eyeballs. Was Connie helping Allison leave Matt? Were there gambling debts to cover? Matt was beginning to get a headache from the endless questions. He parked the car on the gravel pad just as he had done a hundred times before, and although everything seemed normal as usual, the feeling that something terrible was about to happen continue to nag at him. He pulled Lydiel close and looked into her eyes, as he mentally traced the outline of her mouth.

"You would tell me if something was wrong wouldn't you, Lydiel?"

"Of course I would, handsome. Can you come inside with me for a minute or two, please?"

Matt checked his watch. Allison and the boys were not going to be home and it would take no longer than an hour to cut the grass. He had a few minutes to spare.

"Sure sweetie. But you have to let me go when I need to leave, okay?"

Lydiel smiled. She thought of all the times she and Doreen had threatened to kidnap him.

It was obvious to Allison that Lydiel was a trusting person. Her computer was left on and this was a definite bonus. Allison inserted the disk and snooped through Lydiel's files while it downloaded onto the computer. She read boring e-mail after boring e-mail searching for one from Matt. Finally the disk was done. She slipped it back into her bag and just as she clicked restart she heard a key in the door. Damn! Her heart was skipping beats. No one could find her here. Clutching her bag Allison looked around the small room for a hiding place. Her only option was the closet.

Lydiel opened the door and Matt followed her inside and closed the door. Pinning her against the refrigerator he kissed her again. He was such a good kisser.

"I need to go babe."

"I know. I am just prolonging the inevitable."

Allison silently fought through hangers and clothes, looking and searching for any way out of the small dark space. Her hand touched what felt like a latch of some sort. The latch opened a small door, and she crawled through to another closet, falling as she did. Matt broke the embrace and eased away from Lydiel. He knew he heard something. Motioning to Lydiel to be quiet, he walked through the house with her in tow. Everything seemed to be all right.

Allison crawled over boxes and bins, snagging her skirt on something and spilling some of the contents from her bag. Scrambling to collect herself and her belongings, she wondered silently why in the hell people collected so much junk. The confines of the closet were becoming unbearable. She had to get out of there.

The phone in the office was ringing and Lydiel went to answer it while Matt checked the front door and the windows in the bedroom. Allison held her breath as she eased the closet door open. Escape was less than six feet away. As Matt sat on the bed and massaged his aching temples, Allison eased the kitchen door open and silently pulled it shut. Just as she began to relax and enjoy what she thought was the safety of the hallway she heard a voice behind her.

"Excuse me, who are you?

Startled and shaken, Allison did not lose her cool nor did she turn around.

"I am one of Ms. Sommers' clients and I seemed to have gotten the time wrong. Who are you?"

"I'm Kat, her upstairs neighbor. If you give me your name I will tell her you were here.

Allison desperately wanted to get away from this woman and this house. Thinking on her feet was one of Allison's strong points, and she pretended to search her bag for something to write as she mumbled inaudibly.

"I didn't catch that. Do you need something to write with?"

"Yes, that would be helpful."

"Just give me a minute; I'll get a pen and some paper."

As soon as the little snoop sister was out of sight Allison disappeared into the yard. She saw Matt's car in the lot and quickly made her way to the parking lot. That was a call far too close for comfort.

If he had any idea she was in that house … She tried not to think about the consequences. She was now one step closer to ending the madness between him and Lydiel.

Kat ran down the stairs with pen in hand and madly waving a sheet of paper in the air.

"Here ya go Lydiel's client lady. I have the pen and…"

Kat checked the hallway and the basement but the woman was gone. She would close her eyes and focus on what Lydiel's client lady looked like. She would give Lydiel the information. Perhaps it would be worth a few cookies and use of the telephone.

Allison sat in her car resting her head on the steering wheel and took several deep breaths in an attempt to slow her heartbeat. She had a bone to pick with Sarah Turner who neglected to mention that Lydiel did not leave home alone. Searching her bag she realized the cotton gloves were missing! Her hands trembled as she lit a cigarette and put the car in gear. It was time to leave this place.

Chapter 7

After placing their order Connie toyed with the skewered cherry in her drink as she waited for Francesca to speak. The ringing of her cell phone interrupted the deafening silence between them. She wanted to say something but didn't know what. Just when she thought the day couldn't get any worse… it was Allison.

"I'm sorry Francesca. Can you excuse me for a minute or so? I really need to take this call."

The call couldn't have come at a more opportune time. Literally saved by the bell, Francesca was having second and third thoughts about breaking up with Connie. The timing was all wrong. Connie had been very good to her and Remey, and the three of them were in this up their collectively beautiful necks.

"No problem. I need to use the ladies' room anyway."

Connie braced herself for the latest update from Allison. Lately everything was a "this won't wait emergency" with her. Things were beginning to take on a circus type atmosphere.

"Yes Allison, what is it now?"

"My, aren't we in a good mood this afternoon. Mission accomplished. I replaced the inhalers, installed the software and wouldn't you know it, just was I was rebooting her computer they walked into the house."

"Who is 'they' Allison? Are you telling me you were caught? Did you see them or worse yet did they see you?"

Connie's full attention was now focused on the repercussions that would ensue if indeed Allison had been caught inside Lydiel's house, especially with Matt there.

Allison knew this was typical Connie behavior - the ultimate alarmist, always thinking the worse. With her everything in life was anticlimactic.

"Of course not. It was a close call though. I escaped through a closet. It was hard to tell if I was behind door number one or door number two. It's a strange apartment with two doors leading to the same closet that is filled with junk. But I survived it all and now it's just a matter of time. We sit back and we wait. The funny thing is there were no pictures of her or anyone else except Matt in her house.

"Allison, I thought you said they were there. How could you not at least get a glimpse of her?"

"Do you seriously think that under the circumstances I was going to hang around and get a 'glimpse' of her?"

"Allison I am in the middle of lunch with Francesca so maybe we can talk more about it later."

"Fine. I need to do a few things anyway and Matt won't be home this evening. Bye."

"Good bye Allison."

Allison thought it best to keep a few things secret from Connie like the part about the neighbor seeing her. It was such an inconsequential thing and she had never really faced the woman. There was no way she would be able to identify her. For now it was time to make her other call. After what seemed like an eternity of aggravating ringing the phone was finally answered.

"Hi, it's me. Yes, I know I promised I wouldn't call you here but…"

"Alli, this is not a secure line. Give me a

number and I will call you back."

"989-7898."

"Got it. Stay put and give me about five minutes or so."

"Okay…"

Right now the thing that was bothering Allison the most was the fourth inhaler. According to Sarah, there were four but she could only find three, and she needed a little help with something no one else could help her with. The chimes were sounding on her cell phone and the number was unfamiliar to her so this must be him.

"Hello…?"

"Alli, you have to be careful. Don't evercall me at the other number. Now tell mewhat's going on."

Allison chose her words carefully and spoke slowly.

"I replaced the inhalers and installed the software. According to Sarah there were four but I could only find three. Matt and Lydiel came in while I was there."

"Is there any possibility that you were seen?"

He was deep breathing and rubbing his

temples as the migraine crept its way across his forehead. Nothing she was saying sounded good; he only hoped she was telling him the whole truth.

"No, I'm certain they didn't see me. I did rip my skirt in the closet but there was so much junk in there I'm sure the piece of fabric will never be found. It was such a small piece."

The fabric swatch was inconsequential compared to the remaining inhaler. He was almost afraid to ask her what she did with it.

"Alli, this is very important. Are you absolutely certain NO one saw you enter or leave her house and where is the remaining inhaler?"

She knew he was very aggravated and upset with her, and she bit her lower lip as she vacillated as to whether or not she should tell him about the neighbor. After all it wasn't as if the woman saw her face, and she seemed a little strange and confused, not representing any real threat to her. She did, however, still have the remaining inhaler in her bag,

"I didn't know what to do with the inhaler so I still have it, and I'm sure no one saw me."

"I need to go. My boss is calling a meeting. I

will be in touch."

"Okay, I understand. Goodbye."

"Alli…? Ditch the inhaler."

For the first time since the whole thing started Allison felt fear, nothing overwhelming but fear nonetheless. For now it was time to sit back and wait.

Chapter 8

From the small vestibule outside the restroom Francesca was watching Connie's face and posture changes, and knew right away that the caller was Allison, and Connie was visibly agitated by the phone call. As she watched Connie walk back to the table, Francesca was hoping to lighten the mood as well as change the subject.

"Are you alright, Connie? I hope the call wasn't bad news."

"I'm not sure Francesca. That was Allison. She exchanged the inhalers and while she was there Matt and your mother came in."

A variety of images, from the sublime to the ridiculous, ran through Francesca's mind -Allison startled and befuddled like a deer caught in the headlamps of an oncoming car; Matt –slow to anger and showing controlled ambivalence; Lydiel in full interrogator mode; or worse yet, Allison being discovered in the closet, unable to run, unable to speak. Oh, to be a fly on the wall in that house…

"What happened? Did they catch her? Did

she see them? Spill, Connie."

"Apparently just as Allison was rebooting your mother's computer, Lydiel and Matt came in. With nowhere to run so to speak, she hid in the closet in the office and ended up tumbling into another closet. The noise was just loud enough to arouse Matt's suspicions. At some point she sneaked out of the closet and out of the house without seeing them or being seen herself."

Francesca found this scenario even more hilarious and laughed out loud. She was picturing Allison tumbling head over heels in that junky closet and trying to be quiet at the same time. There was a part of her that wished they had confronted each other. Allison was like a runaway train with no engineer when it came to her obsession with eliminating her mother. Right now there were other things on her mind, however.

"Connie, I'm sorry I haven't been around much lately. Allison is a little overwhelming at times, and I seem to have been doing nothing but living and breathing the plan lately. I needed a break. I hope you understand, it had nothing to do with you or being with you."

Connie felt the beginnings of a big cry which she fought valiantly to control, but try as she might, a few errant tears rolled slowly down her cheeks. She missed Remey and Francesca. She regretted taking the money and truth be told she missed her husband's presence. She and Henry had had an understanding for several years and she never really thought the day would come when he would be spending his nights away from home. Life was no longer satisfying to her.

Appearances be damned, Francesca reached out and took Connie's hands in her own. The feelings were still there. It was obvious something was deeply troubling her. She signaled for the waitress and requested two glasses of water. She handed Connie a handful of tissues and watched as the tears flowed freely. Francesca had never seen Connie cry.

"I'm so sorry dear. I guess I'm not myself this afternoon. I was convinced that you wanted to meet today to break up and on top of everything else, I guess it put me on overload."

"What's going on Connie? There is more to

this and I want to know what it is."

"I have done terrible things lately because I'm weak. I have compromised the relationships that mean the most to me because I am afraid - afraid of Allison. I know how you feel about your mother but we are all now involved in a full-fledged murder plot and for what? People have affairs everyday and as well as I know Allison I am surprised she and Matt are still married. He stays for the sake of the kids, and like Henry, he wants love and passion and yes, sex.

From an early age they were both taught to see an obligation through to the end and that is what they are doing. In our case, the twins are grown and off to college soon and Henry and I are still young enough to enjoy life, but that is not the case with Matt and Allison. I have known her for over 20 years and she is showing her worst side these days."

"You still haven't told me what's wrong, Connie. Why did you sign on for all of this?"

"One day several months ago I apparently left a door unlocked and Allison walked in and saw you, Remey and I together. She didn't say anything for months. When she discovered Matt was seeing Lydiel it was if something snapped inside. She invited me to lunch at Mirelli's, and engaged in a long diatribe about your mother, how she hated her, what a slut she was and on and on. When I asked her what difference it made since she was no longer sleeping with Matt, she informed me that if she never slept with him again, he was not allowed to take another woman to bed."

"You mean she already knew us when we met at Mirelli's? She is a very selfish, devious person and I don't care for her at all. I'm sorry I interrupted you. Finish your thought."

"No, she didn't know it was you, just that there were two women in bed with me. One day she started talking crazy about doing whatever it took to break up Matt and Lydiel. Poor Matt, he clung to the hope that things would change and he could have his wife back. Instead his wife is plotting a murder and trying her best to frame him for it.

Allison needed money to pay the paper man, the pharmacist guy and Sarah Turner, which meant she needed a little over one hundred thousand dollars. She could only manage forty-seven thousand dollars and threatened to tell Henry everything if I didn't go along. I manipulated the budget for the fundraiser ball to the tune of sixty thousand dollars and I convinced Henry to hire Matt. I thought I had the dates correct but somehow misjudged the date the accountants would audit the ball budget account and did I ever underestimated Matt. Now it's only a matter of time before the missing money is found and then the end of life for me as I know it."

For Francesca this was new and troubling information. For the first time she got a glimpse of another side of Connie that made her heart sad. Connie was a good person but weak and desperate, and that made her putty in Allison's hands. As she continued to listen to the story, she began to hate the fact that Matt was being set-up as the fall guy for the murder, and Miss Bitch Witch planned on walking away scot-free. Francesca had no idea what she was going to do but that was just not going to happen. If anything happened to Matt, she would personally make Allison pay.

"This is the first time you ever talked about

your husband. I never saw any pictures of him or the two of you together, just pictures of the twins."

"Henry says pictures of oneself are a display of arrogance and they in no way portray the true person inside. Silly isn't it? He is a very good person Francesca and when the theft is revealed it will hurt him deeply."

No one who really knew Francesca Sommers would call her compassionate. Most people saw her as a mean spirited opportunist and to some degree that was true, especially when it came to Lydiel. In all honesty she never gave Lydiel a chance because she didn't want to. Unlike most of her previous friendships and relationships, her relationships with both Connie and Henry were warm and comfortable and there was loyalty to both.

"How much time do we have before the missing funds are discovered?"

"I'm not sure. Matt is a very thorough and detailed person and hell bent on solving the mystery of the crashing website. My guess would be a week at the most."

This afternoon had not gone as Francesca

planned at all. She needed time to think, formulate a plan.

"I see. The reason I wanted to have lunch with you was to tell you that I will be away for a few days. It's job related. I didn't want you to worry. Now let's enjoy our dim sum."

Chapter 9

As soon as she opened the front door, the first thing Allison noticed was the quiet. No kids. No husband. No demanding distractions. Her first stop was the kitchen for a sandwich and then to the computer. She had about two hours before her family would be home, just enough time to install the software on the home computer and begin to download the transcripts. This is what her life and her marriage had been reduced to -spying. Mentally flashing back to the day in the hospital parking lot where she had been hoping to catch a glimpse of Lydiel, Allison had squashed an overwhelming urge to just confront Lydiel and demand to know the nature of her relationship with Matt. She wanted to see the look on the mistress' face when confronted by the wife. As it turned out, her way was working out much better. Once she read the messages between Matt and Lydiel, all of her suspicions would be confirmed and she would have concrete proof of his infidelity.

Typing in the code she selected earlier, Allison decided to start with Lydiel's computer. She picked a date from the last 60 days at random and downloaded page after page after page of instant message transcripts and e-mails and printed them. While the printing was in progress, she decided to throw a load of clothes in the washer, vacuum and check her phone messages. She heard the printer stop. The no paper light was blinking. She reloaded the paper tray and finished checking the phone messages. The printer stopped again but before she could check the paper tray she heard Matt's key in the door. Scrambling to collect the pages, she quickly stuffed them into her bag and turned off the computer and the printer. She never noticed the blinking light indicating a paper jam.

"I wasn't expecting you home so early. How was the cigar outing?"

Matt noticed how flushed Allison's face was and that fine tremor in her hands, and he was absolutely certain that she wasn't expecting him home so soon, and he doubted if she cared about any cigar outing.

"Fine. I left before it ended. I've had a very long day. Are the boys back yet?"

"Not yet but they're on their way. My mother knows they have school tomorrow."

"I will leave you to whatever you were doing. I'm going to bed."

Watching Matt walk upstairs, Allison felt she should join him, at least for show, but the boys weren't home and they would probably be interrupted.

"Matt, wait. Maybe we can spend some time together tomorrow evening. It has been a while."

What in the world was she up to now? A while was months ago and he was in no mood for her antics. Promises made, never kept, and the little matter of forty-seven thousand dollars.

"I don't think so, Allison. I have a lot of work to catch up on. Good night."

"Does that work include that witch you are screwing?"

Without turning back, Matt walked upstairs, peeled off his clothes, turned off the lamp and went to bed. Sleep came quickly.

Ignore her would he? No one ignored Allison Woodall McNulty, NO ONE! He didn't have to answer her. She had seen his car at Lydiel's house. Reaching into her bag, she began to read the printouts. What a mush ball that woman was with her disgusting repetition of "I love you" and "I miss you". The man Lydiel described was the Matthew McNulty Allison knew and didn't love. Imagine that! Ms. Writer was not only having an affair with Matt but she was in love with him. How could an old woman be so silly and foolish? Didn't she realize that he would never be with her? He could never love her? For his part, Matt seemed to care deeply for his writer, but Allison had what Lydiel never would, her boys, and those were ties Matt would never sever, not for Lydiel, not for any woman. Putting the pages back into her bag, Allison turned on the television and waited for the boys to get home.

Connie Pushman fingered the pills in the palm of her hand and thought of her twins, so beautiful and handsome. She was very lucky, a boy and a girl the first time out. Her daughter was the spitting image of her father and her son, almost a mirror image of herself. She missed them since they left for school. She always knew the day would come when she would be an empty nester, but where did the time go? It seemed not so long ago they were just starting school; all the excitement of leaving home and making new friends, and now that scenario was repeating itself in a very grown up world. The house seemed almost tomblike. She missed the loud music, the teenage giggles and laughter, and the incessant ringing of the telephone. Three years ago Henry had insisted that a separate line be installed just for them.

The thought of how she and Henry once were was now a source of pain for her. In spite of everything, in the beginning they had been a formidable team. Henry's father was ready to retire and had groomed his son to take over. Connie was thrust into the role of corporate wife and she played it to perfection. A real people person, she immersed herself in the philanthropic area of Pushman and was a natural, and she enjoyed it. Lately everything was so different, she felt overwhelmed and in many ways she wished she were the target of Allison's wrath so it would be over with. The pain of loneliness had seemingly begun to consume her heart.

Francesca was concerned about Connie. She had never known her to be so dispirited. Connie was the good humor lady, always with a joke and a smile, until recently. She didn't like the way her friend looked as she left the restaurant. There was no answer on Connie's cell phone. She dialed the home phone; three rings, then on the fourth ring…

"Yes?"

"Connie? Are you all right?"

"Yes, Francesca, I'm fine, why?"

"You don't sound like yourself. What are you doing? Nothing stupid I hope. You upset me at lunch today and I was just checking to see if you were okay.

"I appreciate the concern. No need to worry. Good night, Francesca."

The line went dead and Connie returned the pills to the bottle. Perhaps another time but tonight she was simply too tired to die.

As much as Francesca enjoyed Henry's company, tonight was a night he needed to be at home, with his wife. The excuse came to her as she walked back to the table.

"Henry..."

"Francesca..."

They both laughed as they spoke at the same time. She deferred to Henry.

"You first, Henry."

"Oh I see, age before beauty is it? Well Miss Francesca Sommers, I was wondering if you would give an old man a rain check? For some reason I feel as if I need to go home tonight. It is no reflection on present company and I hope you don't take it as such."

Sometimes when you least expect it things have a way of working out. Francesca knew exactly what Henry was feeling.

"No offense taken. I understand perfectly. Let's talk tomorrow and firm up our dinner date, shall we?"

"Only if you kiss me right here and now."

"Gladly, Mr. P., gladly."

Henry quickly and quietly undressed and slid into bed beside his sleeping wife. He put his arm around her, kissed her shoulder gently and fell asleep. Connie touched the strong arm smiled and returned to her dreams.

Chapter 10

The alarm clock sounded loudly announcing that six a.m. had arrived. Reaching over to silence the buzzing,

Lydiel hugged the pillows once again. She thought about what it would be like to wake up and find him here with her; not every day but occasionally would be so nice. She glanced at his picture -that handsome face that did crazy things to her heart, but as she gently fingered the frame, she felt strangely unhappy. He was such a large part of her world.

The week had passed quickly because of him. Normally she had a love/hate relationship with the weekend. She and Matt would see each other for a couple of hours and then she would be alone again. No matter how she tried, the tears always came. It wasn't that she was afraid of losing him, but rather how to combat the ever-present loneliness. They wouldn't see each other this weekend because he would be away with the boys and Allison, and she had the book thing to deal with, revisions and all...

She wanted to tell him about her conversation

with Jack and at least a half dozen times she had thought about sending an e-mail but she felt it best to wait for confirmation. Before she could give it further thought the phone rang.

"Good morning…"

"Hey Ma. I know it's early but I was thinking about you. Are you okay? Are you going to see Matt today?"

"Good morning early bird daughter. How are you?"

"You didn't answer me."

"I'm fine and no I won't see Matt this weekend. He is doing the husband-daddy thing. I have a lot of research to do for the book and I will be in and out, so don't panic if you can't reach me by phone. My cell battery is dead."

"How many times have I asked you to get a second battery, Ma? With your asthma, you need to be able to call for help. Today is not a day for you to be out. It is going to be in the 90's and humid. Can't you have Sarah do that stuff for you?"

Lydiel knew that this was going to be a circular argument. Doreen had this way of mothering her mother. Perhaps she was right. Maybe she could ask Sarah to give her a few extra hours today.

"I could ask Sarah for a few hours today, I guess."

"Ma? You are fading out and garbled. I can barely hear you. You need to do something about that phone. Ma? Ma? Are you still there?"

"I'm still here Doreen. Maybe I will call Sarah and ask if she can give me a few hours today if she is available. It is the weekend after all."

"Well, try to reach her. I have to go. Be careful today okay?"

"Will do mother. Good bye Doreen."

Lydiel had to laugh. Everyone was too busy to come see her but always issuing admonitions about being careful. Oh well. First things first, check the e-mails. She put on the black satin robe and thought of him snaking his hands up the kimono sleeves and massaging her breasts as he held her close. She closed her eyes and savored a memory of standing in this same spot, holding each other, kissing each other and wanting each other. Enough already! She was acting like a smitten schoolgirl but he did that for her. He made her feel alive. He made her feel young and desirable.

The computer screen was filled with instant messages. Didn't people ever consider the fact that she slept? As she clicked them off one by one there was one from Matt.

"Hi babe. Sorry not much time here but I will miss you greatly this weekend. Be careful if you go out. Talk soon. Kisses…"

She would miss him too. There were no interesting e-mails so she signed out, turned the computer off, which was a very, very rare occurrence and phoned Sarah.

"Hello, Sarah? This is Lydiel. I'm sorry if I awakened you. I was wondering if you could come in for a few hours today. I could use the help."

Saturday was Sarah Turner's day to sleep in. She was less than thrilled to hear her employer's voice so early in the day.

"What time is it?"

"Just after seven a.m. I apologize for calling so early."

Trying desperately to awaken fully, Sarah sat

up, took a sip of water and cleared the fog.

"What time would I have to be there?"

"About nine a.m. would be fine. I have something I need to take care of so you will need to use your key. I will leave your pay on the dining room table, and thanks Sarah. Good bye."

So much for her weekend plans.

Lydiel stepped into the shower, sang her familiar off key version of Do That To Me One More Time, and mentally went over notes for the book. Just as she was stepping out the phone rang.

"Good morning."

"Hey chickie, its Jack. Are we still on for this afternoon?"

"We are. I am just getting things together here. I will meet you at eleven thirty as we agreed."

"Sounds good. You won't regret it I promise."

"I already regret not telling Matt. He and I don't keep secrets from each other ever."

"You make it sound as if we are eloping. We are just going to spend a few hours together and you will be a better person for it."

"I need to go, Jack."

Dressing quickly Lydiel packed her laptop, her tape recorder, and her notes on the book revisions and grabbed her bag making sure her inhaler was there. Feeling a little lightheaded she decided to make a quick sandwich and enjoy a little of the lemonade she had made for Matt. A creature of habit she checked and rechecked the windows and doors and left Sarah's pay on the dining room table. She still felt as if she was missing something. Everything in the bedroom seemed in order. She turned on the nightlight, blew a kiss to Matt's photograph, got into her car and left for her meeting with Jack. She was out of her comfort zone for the first time in a very long time.

Chapter 11

"Mom! Mom! What time are we leaving? Mom?"

Allison felt hands on her shoulders and voices in her head as she tried to escape the dream she was having. A few more minutes of sleep would have been a blessing. Opening one eye she saw Liam shaking her.

"Where's your dad?"

"He's loading the van. We are all ready, just waiting on you."

"What time is it?

"It's after nine a.m. Allison. Everything is loaded and the boys are ready and restless."

"I must have overslept. I'll be ready in a minute or so."

"Allison, I have asked you not to let the boys see you sleeping on the sofa. It confuses them."

"I will be ready shortly, Matt."

Matt knew this was going to be a very long and uncomfortable weekend for him. The misappropriation of the forty-seven thousand dollars was always in the forefront of his mind, and he knew that sooner or later there would be an ugly confrontation. He wanted to keep it from the boys.

Before all of this began he felt that Allison was not a bad person, just not the person he could live happily ever after with. Now that had all changed. She was being intentionally deceitful and hurtful. He no longer cared about her sharing the bed or her endless dates with Connie Pushman. What he did care about was money that he worked hard for and sacrificed to save, being taken without discussion or explanation. He had also grown weary of being questioned every time he left the house and having to account for every second of time spent away. He had grown weary of being married and not being able to be himself, except for stolen snippets of time spent with Lydiel or at work. Right now he wished he could take the boys and go on the camping outing alone.

Allison knew a big blow up was eminent. With any luck she could stave it off until after Lydiel was no longer in the picture. Then she would pull out all stops with the computer printouts, her firsthand account of seeing him at Lydiel's house, and make Matt feel so consumed with guilt that he was forced to openly confess his infidelity. If she played her hand right, suspicions would be pointed in his direction, and she would be able to kill two birds with two puffs of an inhaler. A smile crossed her face as she pictured a grieving Matt trying to stifle emotion at the news of his mistress' untimely demise.

"Mom, are you ready now?"

Sean was the impatient one, always ready to leave and the first one to ask if they were there yet.

"Another minute or so and I'll be there. Where's dad?"

"He's in his office checking his mail on the computer."

There was no doubt in Allison's mind that Matt was reading e-mail from Lydiel. Whatever it was, she would read it herself after they returned. It was going to be fun reading the "secret" mail between them. So far Matt always seemed non-committal in his responses, but it was blatantly obvious to Allison that Lydiel had made quite an emotional investment in the relationship. Too bad she wouldn't live long enough to enjoy it. She needed to talk to Connie but that would have to come later. Right now her family took precedence.

Matt briefly checked his mail, which was mostly junk. There was however, an invitation to a golf outing, which he attempted to print. For some reason the printer wasn't working. Small wonder, it was turned off. Hitting the switch he noticed the paper jam light was flashing. After clearing it, he once again attempted to print the invitation. Four sheets printed. There must have been a glitch somewhere. He collected the pages and was just about to discard the other three copies when he realized they were not the invitation but some sort of transcripts, probably from one of Allison's meetings. Maybe they would give him some insight as to the missing money.

"I'm ready guys. Let's hit the road."

Matt folded the pages and put them in his pocket. It was time to get this farce underway.

Chapter 12

The dream seemed to never end; caught in a vortex and sucked into a cold, dark abyss, Connie found herself face to face with a toothless old crone who continually beckoned to her. The woman looked strangely familiar -it was her eyes. In a very unsettling way it was like looking into a mirror. Connie reached out to touch that face…

Henry tried to move his arm and realized his sleeping wife was holding it in place. Awake or asleep, Connie was still a very striking woman. He remembered the day they got married. She seemed so happy, so full of life and promise. Then the twins came along and everything changed. He knew that the work and frustration of raising twins could be overwhelming and he had offered to hire someone to help, but she wouldn't hear of it. Instead the twins became her entire life and there seemed to be no place for him.

The rejections began to stack up like a deck of cards until the space between them overshadowed the love. He entertained the thought of divorce on many occasions but the idea of not being there for the twins was unacceptable. Of course looking back he realized that it was just a weak and pathetic excuse. Children deserve one good parent instead of two weak ones.

A second attempt to extricate his captive arm awakened his wife. It had been so long since they shared a bed that the night had been reminiscent of sleeping with a total stranger. Turning over, Connie stared into a face she had not awakened to in months. Why was he here with her now? Henry was the first to speak.

"Good morning dear."

"Good morning. I don't quite know what to say. This feels so awkward."

"Yes, I know, but for some reason I had a strange feeling last night that you needed comforting."

How did he know? He couldn't possibly know...and yet he was here, after months and months of sleeping alone, lying beside her, holding her.

"I have been very involved with the ball project lately and with the site down it has thrown me behind."

Removing his arm and sitting on the side of the bed, Henry knew there was more than she was telling him, much more, sixty thousand dollars worth of more.

"I'm sure we will get to the heart of the matter soon, dear. No need to let it spoil your weekend. I need to get my day started."

"Henry? Thanks."

"Not a problem my dear. I'm glad I could help."

After Henry left the room Connie began to experience guilt, remorse and fear. She had jeopardized so much and she knew that in less than a week she would be exposed as a thief. Matt would find the missing pages and the missing money as well.

Henry had Miss Francesca Sommers on his mind and the size of his cock and the familiar throbbing told him in no uncertain terms that he missed her. They had agreed to have dinner but Henry thought spending the entire day together starting with a long drive in the country would be just the ticket. He owed her for being so understanding last night. He also promised to help her with her sister's issues and for that he needed to talk to his banker. It was Saturday and Sam would be heading off to the golf course soon. Now was as good a time as any.

"Hello, Sam Sam here."

Henry always laughed at how his old friend answered the phone. Sam's mother had quite a sense of humor and thought it would be funny to name her firstborn and only son Samuel Samuels. All through school he had been known simply as Sam Sam.

"Good morning Sam, Henry here."

"Better to be here than there, if you know what I mean. What can I do for you Henry?"

"I have a friend who is experiencing some difficulty securing a loan so I need to establish a line of credit for her and Sam, I want this kept confidential."

"Anything for you old friend. Just tell me how much, whose name is on the account and when you want it established."

"Thanks Sam. I knew I could count on you. I

want a one hundred thousand dollar line of credit established in the name of Miss Francesca Sommers. There are to be no restrictions on the daily withdrawal amounts. When it is depleted you are to notify me immediately. Is that understood?"

"I got it! I got it! Thy will shall be done. I will need 24 hours and she will need to sign a signature card on Monday. Anything more I can do you for?"

"That'll do her. Have a good game and thanks, Sam."

"That is what bankers and friends are for Henry. Good-bye.

What was that damned incessant buzzing? Francesca realized it was the clock and once again she had slept through the alarm. Shutting it off, she rolled over and pulled the covers up. Sleep had not come easily and hours of tossing and turning had left her feeling tired and drained. She had a busy day ahead and languishing in bed wasn't going to help. Her concern for Connie was growing and her own ability to help her was questionable. She had to be very careful how she handled Henry. She would never hurt him or Connie. Yawning and stretching, she realized it was Saturday. She must have subconsciously set the alarm clock. Her preoccupation with Connie's situation was making it difficult to concentrate on anything else. Just as she dozed off the phone rang.

"Hello, this had better be good."

"Hello and it is always better than good.

"Hi Henry!. How are you and how are things this morning?"

"They are absolutely stellar, Francesca, my dear, and guaranteed to get better if you will agree to spend the day with me. I thought we could start with a ride in the country and brunch."

"Will I have to come home and get ready for dinner this evening?"

"Not to worry my love. Everything you need is at the Penthouse and I have a little surprise for you at dinner. Now please tell me that I have the pleasure of your beautiful and passionate company for the day."

"Where shall we meet?"

"I will send a car for you in thirty minutes or

so. Is that acceptable?"

"I will be ready. See you soon, Mr. P."

"See you soon Miss Francesca Sommers."

Chapter 13

Sarah Turner was really not looking forward to working today. She wanted to go to the mall and do some shopping and treat herself to lunch and a movie. That would all have to wait until after her visit to Lydiel's house. What could be so pressing there? Allison wanted to know whenever she was in Lydiel's house or when Lydiel was away. Dialing Allison's number, she braced herself for a new round of rudeness.

Although the trip had just gotten underway the boys were vocal and restless.

"Calm down you two."

"How much longer, Dad?"

The unison boys were at it again and Matt was not in the best of humor. Allison was strangely silent and that was unusual. Her jaw was set and she stared straight ahead. She was in punishment mode.

"We will be stopping soon for a bathroom break and a little leg stretching. How does that sound?"

"Must we stop so soon Matt? We have only been gone an hour or so."

"Yes, we need to stop and we will."

Before Allison could protest further her cell phone rang.

"Hello?"

"It's Sarah. Lydiel asked me to come over and clean a little. She is doing research or something."

"I see. Thanks for calling. Good bye."

Matt refused to buy into whatever was going on and resisted asking who was on the phone.

"That was Connie, letting me know about the weekly card game, Thursday. It was nothing really important."

There was no doubt in his mind that this was yet another one of Allison's lies.

"I don't recall asking Allison."

For the next thirty minutes there was absolute silence in the van.

Sarah threw a few things into her bag, checked her wallet for the right credit cards, grabbed her iPod and headed off to Lydiel's. She still didn't quite understand what exactly she was supposed to do but perhaps there would be a note or something. The sky was overcast and the air was thick and humid. She hoped Lydiel had remembered to turn on the air conditioner for her.

Matt eased into the sole remaining parking space at the rest stop and turned off the engine. He was desperately fighting a headache but knew the boys needed a break.

"Here we are boys. Come on and let's hit the john and then stretch our legs."

Sean and Liam were out of the seatbelts and the van in record time. As old as they were they wanted to hold Matt's hand and they marched off like the Three Musketeers, leaving Allison to her own devices. Exiting the van Allison took a seat at one of the concrete picnic tables and returned Sarah's call.

Traffic was light but as luck would have it there was no place to park either behind Lydiel's house or on the street. After three tries Sarah cut her losses and parked in the hospital parking lot. She secured her purse in the trunk and walked the short distance to Lydiel's house.

The street appeared deserted and she let herself in the front door. The house was shuttered tightly and it was muggy inside. She raised the windows in the living room, dining room and kitchen. There was no breeze at all but she didn't know how to operate the air conditioner. She decided to clean the bathroom first. While she was organizing the cleaning products there was a knock on the door and her cell phone was ringing simultaneously. She answered the phone first.

"Hello?"

"It's Allison and I don't have a lot of time. What's going on?"

"Hold on for a sec, someone is at the door. Who is it?"

"It's Kat, can I use the phone?"

"Sure, I'll wait out here."

"What is going on there Sarah?"

"Some woman wanting to use Lydiel's phone."

"Why are you there on a Saturday and where is SHE? Sarah? Sarah, answer me!"

"She's out doing research or something and she asked me to straighten up the place for her."

"Okay, while you are there check around in that disaster of an office of hers and see if there are any notes or letters or anything to Matt or from Matt. I won't be home this evening, but we can talk tomorrow. I have to go. Bye."

The woman was once again knocking on the door about the phone.

"Are you in a bad mood or something? I just need to use the phone for a minute, please."

"I don't know what you mean. I am just very busy."

"Is Matt coming over today?"

"I am…"

"Never mind, I have to go. Oh by the way there was a strange woman at the door the other day."

Sarah was caught totally off guard but before she could pursue the subject further the woman just disappeared. Things seemed very strange at the house today; a strange woman appearing from nowhere wanting to use the phone, and then something about someone else at Lydiel's door the other day. In the back of her mind Sarah wondered if

Allison had been stupid enough to be seen while she was at the house.

The boys were on the swings at the rest area and Matt joined Allison at the table.

"It has been a while since we were together."

"Whose idea was it to sleep on the sofa, Allison? Whose idea was it to avoid me? Who played head games?

"I miss you Matt. I feel like being close. I want…"

The boys interrupted Allison's speech.

"We're ready Dad."

"Okay. You guys get into the van and your mom and I will be there in a second."

Making certain the boys were in the van, Matt turned to Allison.

"Let's get something straight. You chose to stop making love with me. You chose to leave the bed. You chose to play stupid games. Now I no longer need you. I am no longer interested in sleeping with you; however, on those rare occasions that you do visit our bed, please don't bother waking me up asking me if I need anything. What I need is for you to leave me the hell alone like you have been doing for the last several years. Now can we please finish this day with the boys with a modicum of civility?"

Without waiting for an answer, Matt returned to the van and waited for Allison. As she watched Matt walk way she asked herself what kind of fool did he think she was? He had a sex life with that writer bitch, and his rejection of her had all the sting of a housefly. Soon my darling, soon, your life will be totally devoid of sex and Ms. Lydiel Sommers, and that you can take to the bank! Allison had to laugh at that last line of thought.

Sarah still couldn't figure out why Lydiel needed her to clean today. The bathroom really didn't require much cleaning. Lydiel was a very neat person. The kitchen floor needed light sweeping and damp mopping. Once again she was interrupted by a knock at the door.

"Yes?"

"I need to use the phone just one more time, I

promise."

All Sarah wanted was to finish and get to the mall. Instead she was entertaining a most irritating pest who always seems to in a state of emergency.

"The floor is wet right now.

"Oh that's okay, I'll just go to the front door."

Sarah met Kat at the front door and handed her the cordless phone through the door and closed it. As promised her wages were in an envelope on the dining room table, one a crisp one hundred dollar bill. This gig was getting more rewarding by the day. At last the pest seemed to have addressed her emergency and concluded her phone call. She knocked again, this time to return the phone.

"Thanks for the phone. What prompted the cleaning thing today? Expecting company, huh?"

"Not really. I am just very busy so please leave the phone in the mailbox. If you are finished I have work to do so if you will excuse me..."

The bed was neatly made; robe carefully draped across the back of the chair, and Matt's picture on the nightstand. For an older guy he was a hottie. Sarah could see why Lydiel was in love with him.

After vacuuming all three areas, she decided to do Allison's bidding and look through Lydiel's personal papers. There was another picture of Matt on the computer desk and folders with what appeared to be notes for books. Sarah opened one of the folders and began to read. She decided the easy chair in the bedroom would be more comfortable. Taking the folder back to the bedroom, Sarah settled in the chair and began to read a few chapters.

She was totally engrossed in the book when the sound of a lawnmower interrupted her concentration; just what she needed, the smell of fresh cut grass. Rushing to close the windows, she thought something fell from the folder but didn't see anything. She secured the windows, finally figured out the air conditioner and returned to the bedroom.

Like so many old houses, even with the windows closed air still managed to seep inside, and today the smell of the freshly cut grass became overpowering, and the loud rattle of the old air conditioner was distracting. She decided the air conditioner had to go. It really wasn't cooling off the bedroom at all. She had no choice but to open the windows.

It wasn't like Lydiel to forget things, but today was an exception. Jack had her so rattled she could barely remember her own name. She knew exactly where the file folder was. She would grab it and be on her way in less than five minutes. Even Jack could wait that long.

She didn't see Sarah's car so maybe she finished the chores and left to enjoy the day. Had it not been for her neighbor, Ed Lowe cutting the grass, it would have been a perfect day. Fresh mowed lawns and asthma were a bad combination.

Sarah Turner heard a key in the lock of the back door and panicked. How many people had a key to Lydiel's house. In a matter of seconds she came face to face with Lydiel.

"Oh my goodness, Sarah! I didn't see your car and thought you had gone. I didn't mean to startle you. I am so sorry."

"It's okay Ms Sommers. I thought you were gone also."

"I did also, but I forget an important folder.

Why are the windows open and why isn't the air conditioner running?"

Sarah was a quick thinker and knew that now was not the time to be truthful. She was sure Lydiel would take great exception to her reading her novel.

"The air conditioner was so loud I decided maybe to risk it and open the windows even though cut grass and I don't get along well. I am almost done anyway, and will be out of your hair."

"Take your time dear. I need to get something from downstairs and my office, and I will once again be on my way."

Sarah watched Lydiel go down the basement stairs and hurried to return the novel file to her office. She heard Lydiel wheezing as she entered the house. She didn't look like she was in any shape to drive and her voice quivered.

"Sarah, would you mind helping me to the bedroom and bringing me a class of water?"

As they walked through the living room Sarah began to wheeze a little herself. The smell of the grass was now all over the house. She helped Lydiel to the side of the bed while she went to get the water.

Lydiel knew she had to get it together and pretty quick. Jack was a demanding bastard and although she had her doubts about meeting him and not telling Matt. She knew it was her chance to get her book out there. She reached under the pillow and retrieved her inhaler. A couple of puffs would make her as good as new. When she returned, a new air conditioner was the first thing on her list. Lying on her bed she was deep in thought when Sarah's presence in the doorway startled her.

"Here's the water, Lydiel. Is there anything I can do for you before I leave?

"Yes, dear, please sit here with me for a minute while I collect myself. I have to be on my way soon for my appointment."

Chapter 14

Francesca took one last look in her compact, grabbed her purse and locked the door. The elevator was out of service so she took the stairs. She felt exhilarated as she looked forward to spending the day with Henry. The driver was waiting for her as she left her building.

Henry decided to forego brunch and opted instead to pick up a picnic basket from his favorite restaurant. There was a blanket in the trunk of his car in case he had an emergency and a cooler as well. He would surprise Francesca by wearing the jeans she picked out for him. It had been over twenty years since he had worn a pair of jeans. He paired them with his favorite Pushman golf shirt. He was anxious to tell her the news at dinner. He had carefully considered his generosity, but in the wake of recent events he felt that he was helping a noble cause. Francesca was generous in her own way and the fact that a young woman would enter into a relationship with an old married fogey said a lot. She appreciated the little things he did for her and he liked doing them. He also liked doing her. The feel of being inside her was something he would never get used to.

On the ride to meet Henry, Francesca decided to check on Connie since she knew she would be alone. There was no answer on the cell phone so once again she tried the house phone. After three rings she hung up. She had a sinking and sick feeling in the pit of her stomach. What if…? The buzzing of her cell phone did not let her complete her thought. She checked the caller ID and was relieved to see the number.

"Connie, where were you? You scared me."

"I was out on the patio and forgot to take the cordless. What kind of mischief are you up to today?"

"No mischief, just the usual Saturday errands. What about you?"

"I have a garden club luncheon later this afternoon and dinner with the planning committee for the next golf outing."

"Such a busy woman. I am concerned about you. How was your evening?"

"It was the strangest thing. I woke up this

morning and Henry was lying beside me with his arm around me. There was no sex of course but for some reason I found it comforting."

Francesca knew cancelling plans with Henry was the right thing to do for many reasons. Connie was at high risk for suicide. Now if she could only get her hands on sixty thousand dollars before Matt figured things out, Connie would be out from under Allison's threats. It was a long shot and a very big if.

"I'm glad he was there for you."

"It was very awkward waking up and finding him there. We have not shared a bed in a very, very long time, and he told me recently that he had found someone that makes him happy. Whoever she is I'm glad she is in his life."

Francesca thought about how good it felt to make love and fall asleep with Henry beside her or to reach out during the night and feel him there. For most of her life she had felt so alone. How could a woman feel awkward waking up beside her own husband? She also felt guilty hearing Connie's comment about Henry's happiness and knowing that she was the one responsible.

"Let's have lunch Monday and map out a strategy. In the meantime, enjoy your social functions."

"Lunch sounds great and thanks for caring Francesca. Good bye."

"Good bye Connie."

Henry was waiting for her as the car approached. Opening the passenger door and extending his hand he helped her out of the car and pulled her close. The first thing Francesca noticed was that he was wearing the jeans.

"I missed you last night Miss Francesca Sommers."

"I missed you as well Mr. P." How about a hug and a kiss?"

When Henry held Francesca in his arms he felt her warmth melt into him and touch his heart. He had never experienced that feeling with any other woman. He felt her warmth in many places and standing here like this made him want her more than ever.

"How are things at home?"

"It's funny how awkward things were this

morning. It has been so long since my wife and I slept together. It was like two total strangers waking up together instead of two lovers greeting the day. I realized that we had absolutely nothing to talk about other than our work. She has her interests and pursuits and I have mine. I have a wife but not a marriage."

"I understand how that happens. I was married once, unhappily so. It seems as if marriage should be a situation where best friends take that next step. How do people fall out of love with each other?"

"That my dear is a question too complex to consider on such a beautiful day with such a beautiful companion."

Lydiel always told her girls that people didn't fall out of love with each other. They either never loved each other or they simply stopped trying to be good to each other.

"My mother likes old movies and a common line back then was 'you say the nicest things' and that is true of you. You are a very nice person Henry Pushman"

Lascivious would better describe Henry's current persona. He may be nice but he was also a man, a very horny man.

Looking around, nothing about this place seemed familiar to Francesca.

"Where are we, Henry?"

"I thought perhaps instead of brunch, you and I could spend a little quiet time together so I took the liberty of having a picnic basket made up for us. It's such a beautiful day out and it seems a shame to spend it cooped up inside with a lot of noise and people shouting over each other."

Francesca couldn't remember the last time she went on a picnic. Her mother loved to make picnic fixings and drive them to a rest area off the highway. Once they were somewhere and there was a farm adjacent to the area. She and her brothers and sisters were feeding the cows apples through a fence. Lydiel was the last person she wanted to think about at this moment.

"Are you all right my dear?"

"I'm fine. Now tell me what's inside that basket?"

Chapter 15

The McNultys drove the remainder of their trip in relative silence. Allison was dying to know what juicy tidbits Sarah had uncovered in the clutter on Lydiel's desk. If her printouts were any indication of the communications between Matt and Lydiel, there had to be more concrete evidence somewhere-greeting cards, gifts, something.

Matt wanted to be anywhere but where he was. For Allison to think for even one second that he was desperate enough to fall for more of her BS was ludicrous. How long did she think it would be before he discovered the missing money, and if he confronted her directly what sort of tale would she spin in an attempt to justify her actions?

"We're here boys. First things first; we unload the van, pitch the tents, inflate the air beds and then take the bikes out."

Before Matt could get out of the van, the boys were scrambling to unload it. As scouts they knew how to pitch the tent and anchor the tarp in case it rained. Allison saw one final opportunity to persuade Matt of her good intentions at reconciliation.

"I'll help you with our tent Matt."

"The boys and I will set up the other tent Allison. You may want to check to see if you have everything you need to fix lunch and dinner."

Allison McNulty didn't appreciate her husband's dismissive attitude. In spite of what he said she knew she could still get to him if she really tried. They were miles away from Lydiel and the city. She decided to check out the camp store and check in with Connie and Sarah.

"I think I will take a walk down to the store. Lunch will be ready in about an hour."

Connie was not answering her cell phone. Maybe she and one of her girls were spending a day rolling in the hay. Sarah's cell phone immediately rolled over to the voicemail. Damn! Didn't that girl have the common sense to leave her phone on?

"Great job, guys. You can take the bikes out if you want but be back here in 30 minutes. Sean, do you have your watch on?

"Yes, sir."

"Have fun but be careful."

"We will dad, we promise."

Matt unfolded one of the camp chairs, placed it under a tree, lit one of his favorite cigars and took the folded pieces of paper from his pocket. The golf outing was in two weeks at one of the best courses just outside of town. He remembered the last time he played there - the sand traps and the lake. Just as he was turning the page, he heard a loud shriek. Replacing the pages in his pocket he ran in the direction from where the sound emanated. Sean met him half way, arms flailing, gasping for air.

"What is it? Sean, calm down and tell me what's wrong. Where is your brother? Where is Liam?

"Liam, Liam, Liam…"

"Liam what?"

"Liam got stung!"

"Calm down Sean, and show me where he is."

Matt checked his cargo pocket for the EpiPen and followed Sean down the bike path. Twenty feet ahead he saw his son lying on the ground beside his bike. Whatever stung Liam, it was not in the bee family.

"What happened, Liam?

"I was riding my bike, and...and... and a grasshopper or something hit me in the face and I fell off the bike. I just got the wind knocked out of me is all."

Matt helped his son to his feet, examined him closely and thought it best that the boys returned to the campsite.

"Get your bikes and let's see about getting some lunch. Maybe we can take a hike later."

"Can we look for frogs?"

The unison boys were back and ready to get into mischief. After lunch Matt would help them look for frogs and other icky things little boys liked. For now, he just wanted a little peace and a little time to collect his thoughts. Allison had the Coleman stove going and beans and wieners was the lunch menu. As good as it smelled, Liam was anxious to get started on the adventure.

"Dad said we could go hiking after lunch and look for frogs and things. Do you want to come too, mom?"

One look at Matt's face and Allison knew that the boys extended the invitation and that she should do the motherly thing and decline. Two things were obvious, one -that Matt did not welcome her company on the hike, and two -he wanted to spend quality time with the boys. What was the harm in staying behind? After all, soon they would have to learn to live without him.

"I think I will take a nap and let you do 'guy things' with dad. Have fun and no surprises please."

Matt and the boys ate in record time, leaving the dishes for Allison. Trailing the boys into the woods Matt wondered how Allison could live with the deceit. After all these years he thought he knew the woman he had been married to for nearly 20 years. Apparently he didn't know her at all. What he did know is that from now on any dealing with Allison would be quid pro quo. He was still trying to find the right scenario in which to confront her about the missing money.

"Wait up for your old man, guys. The ground is soft in spots so be careful. Did you bring your canvas bags?

Liam held his empty bag up for Matt to see. Sean held up a bag full of wiggly croakers. They were having fun like boys should, and Matt was glad he was spending time with them. He was also glad that Lydiel knew how important these times with his boys were. He missed her laughter and her warmth. She was adventurous like him and not afraid of icky boy things. She would have been teasing him with a frog. She would have also made a fun tent mate. Matt noticed that there was a small clearing ahead and a group of tree stumps.

"Let's sit down for a second. Then you can count your frogs before you let them go." Sean was visibly upset.

"Aww Dad, we just started and we want to show Mom how many we found."

"Boys, this is the natural habitat for the frogs. It is their home. Their food is here and their family and friends are here."

The unison boys looked at Matt as if he had lost a major portion of his mind.

"Frogs don't have friends, Dad."

"Sure they do! Why do you think they croak

the way they do?"

Sean and Liam looked at each other and then spoke.

"So their moms know when they are hungry?"

Matt tried to choke back the laughter. Their logic was above reproach. Adults could learn a lot about the carefree, sincere rationale expressed by children."You guys know that if we take them back and scare mom, we won't get dinner and we will all go to bed hungry."

As soon as Matt opened his mouth he knew the battle was lost, and the boys did not miss a prime opportunity to remind him of a few things, logical things. Liam was quicker on the draw.

"You could cook dinner like you do at home. We like it when you cook."

"I tell you what. Let's rest here for a few minutes and then we will start back. You can show mom the frogs, watch her scream and then turn them loose at the edge of the woods. How's that? If she freaks too much I will cook dinner."

Matt was very good at pacification and logic, except when it came to dealing with Allison. What the hell was she hiding? He used the rest period as an opportunity to read the pages that printed with the golf outing information. He relit his cigar and began to read the pages. When he finished the last page he silently refolded them and put them back into his pocket. Whatever doubts he may have had before had all been removed. It was difficult to deny the truth. The time for a full-scale confrontation was at hand.

Chapter 16

Francesca held the glasses and Henry poured the Pinot Noir. She was continually amazed by Henry's romantic nature. He truly believed in wining and dining her in grand fashion and she enjoyed every moment.

"Here's a toast to you, Miss Francesca Sommers. Thank you for being in my life."

"And to you, Mr. P for being such a romantic, such a gentleman and such a good partner"

Henry looked at Francesca, and his heart was full. He reassured himself that he had done the right thing setting up the line of credit for her. For some reason he trusted her and he enjoyed making her happy.

"Are you ever going to show me what is in that basket or do I have to faint from hunger first?"

"We can't have that now, can we?"

Henry began unloading the basket -plates, cutlery, pate, water crackers, cold seafood and pasta salad, and baguettes with dill butter. The last time

Francesca had pate was at a fundraiser she attended with Connie.

"I hope this is all to your liking my dear. I planned a light lunch since we are having a very special dinner this evening. By the way, thank you for agreeing to meet earlier and spending the day together."

It was more than to her liking and the fact that Henry always tried to please her did not go without notice. There was a kindness about him that she was not used to and she appreciated everything he did for her. Her most pressing issue now was the sixty thousand dollars for Connie. At this moment she felt tremendous guilt.

"Everything is wonderful as are you, Mr. P. Have you been spying on me? You seem to know all my favorite things."

At that moment Henry found it difficult to look her in the eye. When they first met he had had an extensive background check run on Francesca. He knew she was adopted, dropped out of high school, worked as a dancer in a few bars, and had been married once. He knew where she currently worked, how much money she made and that he liked her very, very much. She was worldly beyond her years and quite an accomplished lover. He just wasn't quite sure what or where her place was in his life over the long term.

Connie and the kids had been his life for so long and he never really thought what it would be like without them in his on daily basis. He missed the twins terribly. They were the reason he looked forward to going home. Now that they were gone, things were awkward between him and Connie. She seemed to be so absorbed in some project with Allison McNulty. He had all but given up on ever having a home cooked meal again.

"Hello, earth to Mr. P."

"I'm sorry dear, I was engrossed in thought. Please don't take it personally. I have a lot on my mind these days."

"Not a problem and no offense taken. Lunch was delicious. How about taking a walk to help digest that great meal?

Packing up the picnic basket Henry wondered if a walk would take his mind off the missing funds and the questions surrounding them.

"A walk sounds good. I can show you what is on the other side of the woods if you are up to it."

Henry stood and extended his hand to Francesca. As she stood, she kissed him quickly and they began their adventure through the woods. Henry pointed out every bird and identified every piece of foliage as they followed the path, which ultimately ended at a huge crystal clear lake. There was a small pier and a small cottage nearby. Walking down to the lake Francesca could see the fish jumping in the water. From where she stood they seemed to be white bass but it had been years since she had gone fishing. Henry led her to the pier where they sat and watched the sail boaters and the always irritating jet skiers. Heput his arm around her and she rested her head on his shoulder.

"I'll give you a penny for your thoughts Miss Francesca Sommers."

"I was thinking of the last time I was at a lake like this. It was over fifteen years ago when we went on a camping trip in Olympia Washington. My dad bought each of us a fishing rod and warned my brothers about breaking them. We caught a bunch of little fish and somehow my mother cleaned them and grilled them for us. My brothers did break the rods though…"

Francesca felt tears welling as she recalled the trips out west. Looking back she realized that she had experienced things other kids her age wished for but at the same time she had appeared less than grateful for the opportunities. Henry sensed that Francesca's memories might not all be happy ones.

"Do you miss your family? I know I miss my mom and my dad. They were so creative in keeping us entertained and enlightened. I tried to do the same for the twins but Connie isn't much of an outdoors person. I remember once we went camping. She had perfume on and the bees loved her!"

Francesca could just picture Connie with all sorts of netting on running from the bees. What a sight that would be! She also noticed a little sadness cross Henry's face and she understood.

"I remember once one of my brothers kept playing around a hornet's nest. My mother reminded him over and over not to play with them. About five minutes later he was running and screaming towards the house with a swarm of hornets chasing him right to the door. What a day that was."

Henry watched in fascination as Francesca suddenly came to life reminiscing about her childhood. He wanted her, right then, in that blissfully serene place. "Come with me, I want to show you something."

As Francesca looked around she didn't see anything except more woods on the other side of the lake. She held Henry's hand tightly as he led her to the small cabin. He reached over the ledge and removed a key. As soon as he opened the door the smell of roses permeated the air. Once inside she noticed a freshly made bed that had been turned down and there were rose petals everywhere, a chilled bottle of champagne with two flutes. Before they opened the door, Henry had remotely activated the small CD player and the soft sound of strings filled the room. She once again felt the sting of forming tears.

"When on earth did you do this?

"Do you like it my dear?"

"Oh, Henry, I love it. I don't know what to say. I am slightly overwhelmed I think."

"Then come here and let me totally overwhelm you."

Francesca hugged Henry as though she were holding on for dear life. She knew she didn't deserve any of this. She was not the person Henry thought she was. How could she ever tell him the truth? Worse yet, she cared deeply for him. Henry began to slowly remove her shirt and her bra, kissing and nuzzling her neck as he did so. He lifted her onto the bed and removed her jeans and the tiny thong, kissing her thighs as he spread her legs apart. Stopping briefly to remove his clothing, Francesca could not help noticing how hard he was. She wanted him to just take her and ravage her and hold her.

She didn't have to wait long. Gently holding her wrists above her head Henry lightly flicked his tongue across each nipple. He knew this was driving her wild. Slowly moving down her body, his tongue was everywhere-across her belly button, and making hot wet circles on her inner thighs before suckling her sweet spot until she was as hard as he was. Henry knew what she wanted and he knew how bad she wanted to feel him inside of her. He could smell how bad she wanted him. Kissing her as he slowly moved down her body and then parting her dark lips, Henry's tongue flicked back and forth like butterfly wings until she was as hard as he was. Rolling onto his back, Francesca took her cue, easing herself onto his cock.

Holding his hands, Francesca gave Henry the ride of his lifetime, meeting each thrust until neither had anything left to give. Lying on his back with her head resting on his chest, he considered telling her about the line of credit but decided not to further overwhelm her.

"I suppose we should be getting back to town and ready for dinner."

Getting no response, Henry turned slightly into the sleeping face of Miss Francesca Sommers. It was amazing how angelic a sleeping woman could appear -vulnerable, fragile and harmless.

Chapter 17

Allison tried in vain to reach Sarah and Connie. Where the hell was everyone? At that moment she heard the bells ring tone of her cell phone. Connie was on the line.

"Hello, Allison? Where are you today? I stopped by the house but no one was home. Where are Matt and the boys?"

"Did you forget? This is our big camping weekend."

"Ahhh, yes. Roughing it in the great outdoors. Sleeping under the stars with a man you can't stand and two kids that seem to irritate you greatly lately. How are things going?"

"How do you think they are going? Matt is very cool and distant and the boys are being little boys, out catching icky crawly things."

"Oh my! Imagine that! Matt being cool and distant. Has he taken a page from your book, sweetie?"

"Very frigging funny Miss Bitch Witch. Just remember how deep you are in this."

"Are we in a snit today? Maybe you need to get laid. Of course right off the top of my head I can't think of anyone who would oblige you. How long has it been now?"

Allison was not going to give that dyke bitch the satisfaction of a response, so she changed the subject.

"I have been trying to reach Sarah but there is no answer on her cell phone. Have you heard from her or Francesca?"

"No, but then again I have been very busy all day."

Allison saw it coming and resisted the urge to shoo the boys away but that would only have made matters worse so she braced herself for the interruption she knew was coming.

"Mom, Mom, look what we caught."

Allison knew it would not look good for Matt to find her on the cell phone and the boys weren't going to wait.

"I have to go Connie. The boys are back. Bye."

Connie would never understand why Allison was so bitter. She chose to cast aside a great guy to play the role of the celibate saint. For the last ten years all Allison talked about was church, yet she was the designer of a most vile murder plot to eliminate the one person who made her husband happy; so much for all those commandments. There appeared to be no limit to her selfishness and self-induced bitterness. What a waste.

Allison McNulty wanted desperately to go home. She needed to know what was going on and if that writing sexpert was dead yet. Why didn't Sarah just answer the phone? Why couldn't everyone just do what he or she was supposed to? For now she had to find out what was so important with the boys.

"Hi guys. Did you find anything good? No surprises, please."

Matt leaned against the tree smiling. He had a very good idea what was going to come next.

"Look what Sean and I caught!"

Just as she leaned over to look, two frogs leapt from the bag, one hitting her on the nose. As she flailed and swatted at the frogs, the boys' giggles could be heard echoing in the nearby woods. Matt wondered how anyone could be so dumb. They did the same thing last year. Maybe church had claimed the last shred of brains Allison possessed. He turned his back so she would not see him laughing. The boys were rolling on the grass, totally consumed by guffaws as they watched their mother's face turn three shades of red.

"WHAT DID I TELL YOU TWO? NO FRIGGING SURPRISES! JUST FOR THAT, NO DINNER! WHERE IS YOUR FATHER? ANSWER ME!

Matt decided that for the sake of his offspring now would be a good time to intervene. Trying desperately to wipe the smirk from his face, he approached the campsite.

"Okay, okay boys, that is enough. Your mother does not appear to be enjoying the joke."

"But Dad..."

Matt tried his best to sound stern but the whole scene was so justifiable.

"I know. I know boys. Get rid of the rest of the frogs, please. The joke is over."

Matt saw the rage in Allison's face and knew she would blame him.

"I SUPPOSE YOU KNEW ABOUT THIS? CONDONED THIS BEHAVIOR? MAYBE EVEN ENCOURAGED IT?"

"Allison, for god's sake stop shouting. They are little boys doing what little boys do. Besides how could you fall for that trick?"

"Since you think it is so damn funny, you cook dinner tonight. I am taking a walk."

"Yea!

The unison twins had struck again. Sean and Liam loved it when Matt fixed dinner.

"Maybe you should take the flashlight Allison."

"Maybe Matt, you should enlist the assistance of YOUR precious sons to help with dinner."

The boys practically hid behind Matt in an effort to escape eye contact with Allison. Matt felt Liam trembling and did his best to lighten the mood.

"Okay you two, give your old man a hand here."

As Allison looked back she thought how much they deserved each other but not for long. This was the last of the camping trips, the last of the frog jokes and hopefully the last of Lydiel Sommers.

Connie poured herself a double shot of Tequila and listened to the phone messages. She walked to the oversized double closet and tried to decide what to wear to the fundraiser. She would make the appropriate apologies for Henry's absence and try to have what may the last good time of her life. Why on earth did she ever let herself buy into this whole thing? She had never met Lydiel Sommers nor read any of her books. If it was just about Henry, Connie would have dismissed Allison's threats, but Allison had threatened to leak the information to the press and that would hurt Pushman and Associates. Wherever Henry was, Connie hoped he was enjoying himself.

Chapter 18

The afternoon had passed blissfully fast. Francesca brought back a few of the rose petals from the cottage to spread around the bedroom in the penthouse. Henry had mentioned that this was to be a very important evening and that he had ordered dinner in, if she didn't mind. The only thing she minded was that they were not in the penthouse, naked and screwing each other's brains out. The interlude in the cottage was like a small appetizer and now she was hungry for the main course.

Henry placed Francesca's left hand on his right thigh. The ache and longing were almost uncontrollable. In his mind he wanted to rip her clothes off and devour her inch by inch. He wanted to make this a night to remember. He had made special arrangements as a surprise for her.

As he pulled the car into the valet parking circle at the Renaissance, his pulse quickened as he exited the vehicle. The doorman assisted Francesca from the car and they both looked straight ahead as they entered the penthouse elevator. Once the doors closed, Henry slid his hands down the front of her jeans and began to slowly stroke her. She was wet and hot and he was hard. As the elevator doors opened the scent of roses greeted them and Francesca saw two dozen red roses on the table. There was also a black silken tether. She looked at Henry quizzically, but before she could speak, Henry spoke.

"Do you trust me Miss Francesca Sommers?"

"I do implicitly Mr. P."

"Fine. I am going to blindfold you and I want you to hold my hand and follow me."

Francesca remembered the last time she was blindfolded. It happened during a very dark event in her life. It was to prevent her from identifying her rapist. She trusted Henry but the fear was present. Henry felt her tense and begin to tremble. Perhaps this had not been such a good idea. The bathroom was to be their stage. There were small votive candles burning and as Henry flipped the wall switch, hundreds of tiny white lights twinkled against the dark backdrop of the bathroom walls and ceiling creating an almost ethereal scenario. Henry let go of Francesca's hand just long enough to disrobe and remove her clothing.

"You may remove the blindfold now my dear."

As Francesca removed the blindfold, she blinked a few times and each time she could not believe her eyes. It was as if the bathroom had been transformed into a wonderful starry night. Henry held her hand as she stepped into the warm water that filled the Jacuzzi tub. Sitting with his back against the huge tube, Henry pulled her close, facing away from him. He leaned her head against his chest and began to slowly soap her neck, kissing first one earlobe and then the other. He let his fingers walk down her body until he reached the doorknob to her pleasure zone.

The blue was doing its job and he did not want this interlude with Francesca to end yet. He stood in the tub and grabbed hold to the special bars he had had installed. Francesca held onto the lower set of bars and began to lick and suck Henry's hardness. As good as it felt, Henry stopped her. He reseated himself in the tub and with her facing him he pulled her close. As she hugged his neck, Henry gently slid deep inside her. She began to rock back and forth quickening the pace. He couldn't hold back any longer and exploded inside her. Holding her in place for several minutes he could feel Francesca's orgasmic waves continue. Tilting her face slightly Henry kissed her and lightly massaged her back until her breathing returned to normal.

"How are you feeling Miss Francesca Sommers?"

"Like I am in the middle of a wonderful fairy tale dream and I don't want to wake up."

"Not even long enough for dinner and a surprise?"

This had been a day full of surprises and Francesca couldn't imagine what Henry could possibly do to top this. She had never dreamed of making love with a man with Henry's stamina.

"I am a little hungry after that workout Mr. P. What are we having?"

"Let's get dried off and I will show you."

After putting on the thick terry cloth robes, she and Henry returned to the dining room just as the elevator doors were closing. Dinner was lobster bisque followed by Beef Wellington and an Alsatian plum tart for dessert. Once again Francesca was out of her league but chalked it up to a learning experience and the food was really quite good.

"I want to tell you something my dear."

Francesca's heart skipped a beat. Had she done or said anything wrong? Was there a major misstep that she was not aware of? Her basic insecurity was rearing its ugly head.

"Did I do something wrong?"

"Oh God, No! I'm sorry if I frightened you. You are absolutely wonderful. I have never felt so alive in my life, thanks to you. No, what I wanted to talk to you about is the situation with your sister. I know how much she means to you and how hard you have tried to keep things together for her."

Henry took Francesca's hands into his and looked deeply into her eyes. He saw fear there and that was never his intention. She had been very good to him and he wanted to do something to lighten her load a little. He knew he needed to allay her fears and just tell her what he had done.

"I have taken the liberty of opening a one hundred thousand dollar line of credit for you at First

National Bank on First and Main. All you need do is go there Monday morning, ask for the manager and sign the signature cards. There is no daily limit on withdrawals and there should be a little left over for you."

No matter how hard she tried Francesca could not hold back the tears. The last few weeks of her life had been incredible. She never expected anyone like Henry to come into her life. He was everything she could have ever wanted or hoped for in a man. The trouble was he belonged to another woman who was her lover also. Was it possible that they could all be winners?

"There, there. Everything is fine. Your sister won't lose her house and you won't have the stress of trying to find ways to help her now."

"I don't know what to say Henry. This is far too generous of you. I have no way to pay you back."

"A line of credit is money for you to use as you see fit. I have taken care of all of the financial details. You just help your sister."

The only thing running through Francesca's mind was that now Connie would be bailed out and safe from disclosure of her participation in the whole miserable mess.

"I have a question Henry. Do you think you could put your arms around me and just hold me until I fall asleep?"

"It would be my supreme pleasure to do so my love."

She wrapped herself in Henry's arms and blissfully drifted off to sleep. Henry felt satisfied that he had done a very good thing for Miss Francesca Sommers.

Chapter 19

Matt thought about the events of the last couple of months. So much had happened in his life, and most of it totally incomprehensible; a new job, unexplained thefts and a complete loss of faith and trust. No matter how bad he thought things were before, he shuddered to think of what lie ahead. He definitely wanted out of the marriage or rather the farce that substituted for it. He was beginning to think that Allison was unstable. She deliberately overloaded her schedule to avoid contact with him and for reasons unknown misappropriated forty-seven thousand dollars from their account. Connie was obviously hiding something to the tune of some sixty thousand dollars, and Francesca was having an affair with his boss. The only constant at the present seemed to be Lydiel.

Allison was more than ready to go home. This trip had been a miserable and cruel joke, frogs notwithstanding. Sharing the tent reminded her of how she was forced to sleep with Matt when they traveled, for the sake of appearance. She missed her sofa and her television. She missed church. She hated being out of touch. It made her feel as if she were not in control of the situation. She had tried for two days to reach Sarah and each time she got the answering machine. Where could she be? Most likely shacked up with some woman's husband. Was the whole world one big sexual cesspool? In her opinion sex was highly overrated.

Matt decided to get the show on the road. The sooner they got home the sooner he could once again try to unravel the mystery of the crashed Pushman website and the missing money.

"Time to strike the tents and go home boys."

"Aww Dad, so soon? Do we have to?"

"Yes we have to. There is work and school tomorrow."

"We're hungry."

The unison twins were at it again. Sometimes Matt thought they did it to deliberately irritate Allison.

"We will stop for pancakes on the way."

"Can we have the banana pancakes with the peanut butter?"

"If you get everything packed up and loaded in the next 20 minutes, you can have any kind of pancakes you want."

"Yea! Thanks dad!"

Allison cut Matt a venomous look before heading off to the camp store. Soon my darling, soon. She dialed Sarah's number once again. Damn! Still no answer. She decided to call Connie.

"Allison, do you know what time it is? What is so damn important?"

"I can't get hold of Sarah. I don't suppose you have heard from her?"

"No, but why would I? It is the weekend you know, and I'm sure she has a life. Perhaps she just turned her cell phone off. Maybe she didn't want to hear from you or Lydiel. God knows the two of you can create havoc in people's lives."

"She hasn't seen havoc. It is my understanding she left her last job without giving notice, and if that is the case it is fine with me and to hell with her. She did what we needed her to do."

"Give it a rest Allison. There are more important issues on the front burners for some of us.

The one that comes to mind is your husband resolving the computer issue and the missing sixty thousand dollars at Pushman."

"Nothing will happen, trust me."

Connie threw her hands up in disgust. If it didn't impact on Allison directly it wasn't important to her. Everything around her could crash and burn but as long as she was not caught in the flames, she could care less. What a selfish, self-centered woman she had become.

"Now that I am awake, perhaps I should give some consideration to breakfast. How did the boys enjoy camping out?

"They loved it of course. Matt indulges them. They showed up with a bag of frogs to surprise me of course. They enjoyed a good laugh at my expense."

Connie could just imagine a frog in Allison's face. She suppressed a laugh as Allison detailed the trip. It didn't take long, however, for Connie to grow weary of Allison's rambling.

"I really need to get showered and dressed. We'll talk tomorrow. Have a safe trip home. Good bye Allison."

"Bye Connie."

The McNulty boys were growing restless and looking forward to the banana and peanut butter pancakes. The fact that Allison seemed more interested in the phone call than leaving was irritating. She seemed to always be interested in anything and everything but them.

"C'mon, mom. We're ready to go!"

Allison walked slowly to the van. This was definitely not the life she envisioned - a husband she despised, and two kids who had become tiresome, needy interruptions in her life. At this moment she wished they and their father would just disappear, but one of the problems would be resolved much sooner than later.

Henry Pushman leaned up on his elbow and watched Francesca slowly come to life.

"Good morning sunshine girl. How did you sleep?"

Francesca opened one eye and with half a smile greeted Henry and the day.

"I slept like a log. What time is it?"

"It is eight-thirty a.m. Why, do you have someplace to be?"

"Not that I know of. I'll be right back. The bathroom calls."

`Francesca had to pinch herself. Had yesterday been a dream or had Henry actually given her access to one hundred thousand dollars? Brushing her teeth, she looked in the mirror and hardly recognized herself.

"Are you okay in there? It is very lonely out here."

Francesca returned to the bed and straddled Henry. Leaning over she took her tongue and licked his bottom lip before she kissed him. Henry's hands grabbed her hips and adjusted her onto his morning wood. In his estimation nothing was better than sex in the morning unless it was sex at night or sex anytime with Miss Francesca Sommers. He had taken a blue pill earlier, making sure he was ready for his hot little playmate. This was the most lovemaking he had ever done is his life and he was making up for the lost years.

Henry was so hard that each time she rose and

fell on him, Francesca experienced incredible orgasms. Rolling her over and onto her knees, He found his mark and literally drilled her until they both reached the point of no return. Collapsing in a small heap beside him, Francesca caught her breath and marveled at what an unbelievable lover Henry was. His seemingly endless stamina and sexual appetite was at times somewhat disconcerting. Before him she never thought much about old people having sex. Before him she never knew what great sex was. She was always teasing Matt about people over 50 having sex and he always told her that age had nothing to do with it. She disagreed. Age had everything to do with it. She had a feeling Matt was just as hot if not hotter than Henry.

"What would you like to do today my dear or am I being too presumptuous?"

"No, not at all, Henry. Eating sounds good. Making love with you makes me hungry. Do you like movies or bookstores?"

"I like them both but it has been quite a while since I visited either one. Tell you what, let's get dressed first and then decide on breakfast."

"That sounds mahvelous dahling. Care to join me in the bath?"

She didn't have to ask twice. There was a double shower in the penthouse and a variety of soaps, washes and lotions. As they washed and teased and massaged each other Henry wondered how long the honeymoon would last. Things always started off so well and then for some unknown reason they seemed to fall apart.

Thanks to Henry, Francesca had quite a wardrobe to choose from. Selecting a soft green sweater, black dress slacks and low cut black boots, she was ready for breakfast. Henry also chose black slacks and a black polo shirt. Waiting for the elevator he noticed Francesca was not wearing jewelry.

"I seem to have forgotten something my love. Why don't you go ahead down to the lobby and I'll join you there in a few minutes."

"Are you sure Henry? I don't mind waiting."

No, please go on and I will be along shortly."

Once inside the penthouse Henry took a small box from his briefcase, checked the contents and waited for the elevator.

Entering the lobby Henry signaled the valet to bring his car around and within minutes they were on their way.

"I always choose where we go and what we eat so today you are in charge of the entertainment, Miss Francesca Sommers."

"Don't you ever get enough?"

"I wasn't speaking of that form of entertainment and no I never get enough of you."

"Let's go to IHOP. I love pancakes."

"IHOP it is. There is one on 30th and Main I believe."

"How about some music Mr. P?"

"Choose whatever you like my dear."

Francesca found the classical music station. Her mother used to play this station and she grew to love some of the music. Romeo and Juliet was playing. Henry was more than surprised at her selection.

"Interesting choice my dear. I would expect a young woman like you to…"

"To be into loud, obnoxious music? Not me. I like classical, jazz and Elvis."

Henry shook his head and let out a hearty laugh. He listened to Elvis on Sunday mornings. Connie hated it. She always accused him of having plebian tastes. Plebian or not, he loved Elvis.

Finding a place to park was no small task at IHOP. The Sunday morning crowd was out in force. Henry maneuvered the car into a space at the rear of the lot, checked his pocket for the little box and helped Francesca from the car. He braced himself for the onslaught of stares and whispers when they entered the restaurant and he was not disappointed.

As soon as they were seated he produced the small box and placed it on the table. Since she had been with Henry, Francesca never knew the bounds of his generosity. She raised an eyebrow as if questioning the contents. He was smiling at her trepidation and felt he needed to end the suspense.

"I assure to you it is safe to open my dear. I noticed you weren't wearing jewelry when we left, and I thought this might work."

As she opened the box, Francesca saw a pair of antique emerald earrings. The waitress stood and watched as Francesca removed the earrings and put one in each earlobe, then leaned over and kissed Henry softly.

"Thank you very much. I am now completely dressed."

The waitress cleared her throat loudly and spoke just as loudly, her voiced tinged with disgust.

"Some people! I swear! If you two are finished with the mush, would you care to order?"

Chapter 20

Doreen had been trying to reach Lydiel since Saturday morning but continued to get the answering machine. It was unlike her mother to leave for days without letting her know, especially since she met Matt. She was usually glued to the house, making herself available for his unknown availability. Doreen decided to send Matt an e-mail.

Matt's mind was on Lydiel, the printouts he inadvertently discovered, and the missing sixty thousand dollars. He was anxious to get home and try to get a little work done before he reported back to Pushman in the morning.

"We're home everyone. Let's get unpacked and put everything away."

"I have some errands to run so you will have the boys. You will also probably have to make dinner."

"No, Allison. I have a lot of work to catch up on and I need quiet to work. The boys will have to go with you."

There was that word again! When would he

get it? After all the years of marriage, he knew better. No problem. A couple of days from now things would be so very different.

"Fine. In that case you put everything away. I need to leave in a few minutes."

"No, WE will put everything away and then you and the boys can go."

Allison felt it best for the moment to control her anger and put everything away.

"Have fun boys. See you later. Don't give mom any problems."

Matt went to his office turned on the computer and began to check his mail. There were three messages from Doreen, asking if he knew where Lydiel was. He had some time so he would take care of his mail first and then surprise Lydiel.

Kat Garcia stood on first one foot and then the other outside the door as she waited for Lydiel to answer. She needed to use the phone desperately and although she was a big pain in the butt interrupting Lydiel at work, she was always allowed in. She knocked again, this time harder, still no response.

Maybe she was in the front of the house and couldn't hear. Walking around to the front door Kat noticed the windows were closed, as was the door. Lydiel must be away. She always opened all the windows and front door as soon as she was up and about. Kat decided to knock anyway. When there was no answer, she knocked harder and the door gave way, and Kat entered the living room.

"Hello? Is anyone here? Lydiel?"

The house smelled strange. Not a true stench, but just unpleasant. The bedroom doors were open and Lydiel was still in bed. It seemed odd that she would fall asleep without securing the front door, and that she would be sleeping this time of day. For as long as she had lived here Kat could count on Lydiel stirring around at six a.m. She must have had a very late night.

"Lydiel? Hey Lydiel, are you okay?"

A cool shiver ran down Kat Garcia's back as she moved closer to the bed. She shook Lydiel's shoulder but there was no response and she felt cold. Rolling her over, Kat stifled a scream. She picked up the phone and dialed 911.

Chapter 21

It was one of those days where she felt like something wrong was waiting to happen. The radio had been relatively quiet until the call came through.

"Jemison, what's your 20?"

"IGA Plaza at 10th and Main. What do you have?"

"A 10-46 with a 10-44 at 8191 Spearhead Drive."

"Copy. ETA seven minutes.

By the time Detective Nikki Jemison arrived on the scene, the gawkers had all but taken over the street. Two black and whites were on the scene, and thankfully the media had not arrived. Accompanied by her very own boy wonder she entered the residence. In all of her years as a detective these were the calls she hated the most. Her first contact was with the uniformed officer on the scene.

"What do we have here?

"Dead woman found by the upstairs neighbor sitting over there."

"Do we have a name?"

"We do. The deceased is one Lydiel Sommers. The neighbor is Kat Garcia. She came down to use the phone and found the dead woman."

"Was anything touched?"

"That's a negative."

"Thanks Sergeant. We'll take it from here. We will need a car posted outside and Sergeant… NO one is to be given any information until further notice. Do I make myself clear?"

"Blatantly clear, Detective."

Nikki looked into the face of the dead woman as she did a cursory check of the body for any signs of trauma and found none. There was no sign of distress or of a struggle.

The Medical Examiner arrived shortly with his regular crew.

"Detective Jemison, always good to see you. What have we here?"

"A dead woman and I was hoping you could tell me why she's dead."

George Cates had been the Coroner before Nikki joined the force almost 25 years ago. Considered an expert in his field, he deftly examined the lifeless woman and like Nikki, could find no signs of trauma. It appeared that she died from cardiac arrest; the cause would have to be determined later in the morgue.

Nikki searched the room for any signs of forced entry, weapons, and drugs. She found two vials of prescription medications, Ibuprofen and Trazedone along with an asthma inhaler that she handed to the ME

"Could it have been an accidental overdose or deliberate overdose?" Could she have died from an asthma attack?"

"I know what you're thinking Nikki but I need to do tests of her gastric contents to determine if drugs were involved. As for the rest, a complete post mortem has to be done."

The assistant assigned to Dr. Cates unfolded the collapsible gurney, zipped up the black body bag and loaded the body onto the cart.

"I'll know more in a couple of hours. I know what these situations do to you Nikki. Maybe you should consider handing it off to another detective."

"I'm fine George and I appreciate your

concern."

Once the body was removed and the door secured, Nikki turned her attention to Kat, who was rocking in the corner of the living room, mumbling incoherently.

"Miss Garcia? Can you tell me how you came to find Ms. Sommers? Miss Garcia? Miss Garcia, are you okay?"

Katherine Garcia continued to rock back and forth totally non- communicative. Nikki called for an ambulance to check out the only known witness to the discovery of Lydiel's body.

"We need a 10-41 at the scene here at 8191 Spearhead Drive."

"10-4. ETA 5 minutes".

"Minter, can you check the upstairs residence for family members of Miss Garcia's?"

"I'm on it, boss."

Returning a few minutes later and visibly out of breath Minter informed her that there appeared to be no one home in the second floor apartment.

"That's a negative, boss.

"Please stop with the boss stuff Minter. You

may address me as either Jemison or Detective.

Nikki wanted to wait until Kat Garcia had been transported to the hospital. She didn't want to further traumatize her only source of information. The paramedics assisted Kat to their unit, examined her and decided to transport her to the hospital across the street for observation.

Gary Minter always thought suicide investigations were a waste of taxpayer money. His biggest problem was verbalizing those thoughts.

"Interesting way to knock yourself off- OD'ing on an asthma inhaler."

"Don't be so presumptive, Minter. There is no note and we aren't sure what happened here. There were other meds found in addition to the inhaler, but to answer your question, there are lots of reasons. People get depressed. They feel taken advantage of, and no one ever listens. Your friends become dismissive and the pain increases until a person feels they have no other options."

For a brief moment Nikki thought back to her own aborted attempt a few years ago. Every call like this refreshed her memory of that period of her life.

The scars in the bends of both knees were constant reminders of how dark that day had been for her. With precision, she had made two slices with an X-acto knife nearly severing the two main arteries.

It was the usual story - love affair gone wrong. For nearly eight years she had enjoyed a wonderful relationship with a married co-worker. Then one day a new guy joined their team. He took an instant liking to her and relentlessly began to pursue her. When she told him repeatedly that she was not interested, he began a campaign of retribution that resulted in her lover's wife learning of the affair. Threats were made, the relationship ended. Without him, she had no life, so she made the decision to end hers. The officer was later fired for repeated complaints of sexual harassment filed by Nikki and other female officers. George had been there for her while she recovered, offering encouragement and support.

"Maybe this will change your mind, detective."

Minter was waving a piece of paper as if it as if it were a map in the hands of a lost traveler. With unmasked disdain, Nikki removed the note from his hand and sat down to read it. Most suicide notes were apologies to love ones or a half-hearted explanation but this one was different:

"This is neither an apology nor an excuse, for in reality no one would really care. Each person who has entered and exited my life knows how his or her presence impacted on the quality of that life. No matter what the perceived crisis was I was there. No matter how dark the day, I provided light. No matter how cold or empty, I warmed and filled. A series of events took place recently and as a result the shadows seemed to forever block the light. As with most living things I too needed the light and the warmth to survive and thrive. Unfortunately love given was never reciprocated and the endless supply of kindness and generosity was mistaken for an incurable weakness that was exploited at every turn.

On so many occasions I looked for a reason-one thing that would inspire me enough to overcome the emotional adversities and to continue on, but that one thing was never revealed to me. Thus, it has become apparent that I am waiting for an invitation that will never come; to be a part of something, to be a priority in someone's life. To that end, I have decided to relinquish my place here, not to embark on another journey that causes my heart pain and my soul to suffer. Instead I shall leave this place to those more suited to its harshness and stark realities." - LS

Nikki folded the note and placed it in her jacket pocket. She felt the tears. She knew it was considered unprofessional to cry so she began to examine how Lydiel Sommers lived in an attempt ascertain how and why she died.

To accomplish this she started at the scene of the crime, the bedroom. Obviously this was a woman who loved purple. Come to think of it Lydiel was known as the reclusive Lady Lavender. There were no pictures of her anywhere. Almost everything was some shade of purple. There was a picture lying face down on the nightstand. As she righted the picture, she recognized the face. Matthew McNulty! How long had it been and what connection did he have to Lydiel Sommers? The last Nikki heard, Matt was married to some woman named Allison Woodall and had a couple of kids. Now she was puzzled.

The bedroom was functionally furnished.

There was a bed draped in purple bedcovering, two tables, and two lamps. There were books, candles and a black satin robe folded neatly over the arm of a sitting chair. Everything in its place.

Although there was a formal dining room, the living room seemed to be the most used room. Aside from the usual sofa, end table and lamp, there was a small dining table with two chairs for intimate dining. The table was set for two, complete with stemware, an unopened bottle of red wine, corkscrew and small lamp. It was as if she was expecting a guest for dinner. There was a small collection of teapots, clocks, and candleholders that adorned the lower shelf of a portable electric fireplace.

Lydiel's interest in the occult was obvious in the deck of tarot cards and crystal ball neatly placed on a small table. Small piles of unopened mail flanked the television and revealed her lack of involvement in her own life. There was also a crystal candy dish with a few pieces of wrapped candy and a cigar lighter.

The dining room did not appear to have hosted a meal in quite some time. There were no chairs at the table and exercise equipment took up most of the space. The kitchen smelled of freshly baked cookies though none were present. There was another inhaler identical to the one found in the bedroom lying on the spice shelf. A few more bottles of prescription medication and a large bottle of vitamins also lined the shelf. With gloved hands Nikki bagged and tagged the medication. It wasn't that the house was uncomfortable, it just appeared rather sterile and unlived in. There was very little food in the cabinets or the refrigerator. There was a half eaten sandwich and a half full glass of what appeared to be lemonade. The forensics team would dust for prints and have the contents analyzed.

"How long are you going to be boss? It is dinnertime and we already know she killed herself."

Minter's nasally voice screeched across the empty room. His impatience and inattention to detail were extremely irritating.

"What makes you so sure she killed herself?"

"Duh! The note?"

Minter's tone was monotonous and condescending. Nikki's aggravation was close to spilling over. Rookie detective or not he should know better than to make assumptions. The ME had made no diagnosis as to the cause of death.

"Things aren't always black and white or obvious. We have work here yet before we can secure the scene, so check the bathroom and I will take care of her office."

Gary Minter did not like Nikki Jemison at all. She was smart, self-assured and too damn good at what she did. She was tenacious. This was her lifeblood and she made him feel incompetent, and that was unacceptable. She became personally vested in every case and had an uncanny knack for thinking like a killer. She always got her man or woman, whichever the case may have been. To him, this Sommers case was open and shut -woman leaves note and kills herself, probably over the guy in the picture.

Chapter 22

George Cates and Jonathan Woodson had run the Coroner's Office for almost thirty years and as they examined the remains of Lydiel Sommers both agreed that they had never seen anything like this in their careers.

"Are we in agreement here George? This woman did not knowingly or intentionally kill herself, and that the methodology suggests foul play.

"We are in agreement and I will notify Jemison. This is incredible and let's pray that it is an isolated incident."

"I don't know which is worse George, the fact that it is perhaps an isolated incident, or that there is the technology and the evil out there to repeat it on a mass scale."

George Cates' next duty was to notify Nikki of his findings. He picked up his police radio and hailed Nikki.

"Jemison here. What do you have for me George?"

"Nikki, we have a problem. Get to a landline

and call me ASAP!"

By the urgency in his voice Nikki had a sinking feeling that something was terribly wrong. Her hands trembled as she dialed the ME's office. When he answered the phone, she knew…

"Give me the straight scoop. George."

"Nikki, I have never seen anything like this before. Your Ms. Sommers died by her own hand but not by calculated deliberate intent. She was murdered. The cause of death is cardiopulmonary failure secondary to a massive overdose of inhaled capsaicin."

The air inside the house suddenly seemed thick and fetid. Nikki felt her stomach begin to churn violently.

"Are you telling me she was sniffing red pepper?

"No Nikki. I am telling you that she inhaled the stuff somehow through her asthma inhaler. Search the house and collect all of the inhalers there. Seal them and secure them. It is important that you collect them all. Is that understood?"

"Yes, yes, of course. Thanks George."

"Nikki, I talked to your boss and he agrees with me. We do not want any leaks to the media. There will be no yellow taping of the crime scene. An officer in an unmarked car will be posted at both the front and rear entrances of the residence and the hospital police will continually patrol the area. Continue to collect the evidence, bring it in when you secure the scene tonight, and be there no later than six-thirty a.m. to meet with the forensics team to conduct a fresh search with an extremely fine tooth comb. As bad as the situation is, let's hope that it was just an isolated incidence of someone creatively disposing of someone else and not some sinister terrorist thing. Do you understand?"

"George this goes against department protocol."

"At this point kid, we are doing a public service by not inciting panic until we know more. Get some rest and we will talk in the morning."

Nikki didn't understand anything. How was it possible to inhale a massive overdose of red pepper?

"Minter! Minter!"

Where the hell was he? The house was not that

big.

"Geeze, I was in the can. What's your problem Jemison?"

"The Sommers woman was murdered. Just got the word from the ME. We need to bag all of the inhalers and other meds. "

"How was she done in?"

Nikki had no time for his adolescent Dick Tracy BS. The sooner she could get some answers, the sooner she could piece the puzzle together. Standing in the middle of the dining room, Nikki tried to understand fully what the ME told her.

"We need to carefully check and recheck every room; every drawer, cabinet, nook and cranny."

Gary checked the medicine cabinet, the over the can cabinet and the under the sink cabinet and found nothing that could be remotely construed as evidence. The bathroom waste can was empty and the room showed signs of recently being cleaned. There was the fresh smell of toilet bowl cleaner and soap. Jemison had started checking the kitchen but was interrupted by the phone call. The bagged inhaler and meds were lying on the kitchen counter.

Just to be thorough Minter checked the trashcan.

"Detective, I think you should see this."

What was his problem now? Couldn't he even do a simple search and bag? Nikki decided she might as well see what he found.

"What is it Minter?"

"Take a look at this Detective. I think we have something here."

Gary held up a brown paper bag. Inside were three small boxes, one ripped open and some crumpled paperwork. The boxes once held and albuterol inhaler and the date it was refilled was three days ago.

"Good work Minter. Let's handle the boxes as little as possible. Put them back into the brown bag and bag the entire package."

Gary Minter hastily bagged the evidence, neglecting to secure the Ziploc seal.

Although it was very early in the investigation, there were so many things about this case that bothered Nikki Jemison. The suicide theory never fit. The eloquence of the suicide note belied a woman hell bent on taking her own life. There is an impulsivity associated with the act, even when thought out well in advance. The activities of life often get in the way and may delay the action, but in the end, it is a split second decision.

The attempt was clumsy and amateurish as evidenced by the boxes and paperwork found in the trashcan. Whoever the killer or killers were their suicide scenario had been very poorly staged. Was Lydiel the innocent victim of some twisted terrorist plot to sabotage pharmaceuticals by targeting asthma sufferers, or was she the victim of something less sinister but equally as deadly? If it were the former the drug company would have to issue a recall of all albuterol inhalers currently in stock. This might invariably cause mass panic.

Had some disgruntled fan become a deadly stalker or killer? Or…? How did Matthew McNulty figure into the equation? Why was Kat Garcia the one who discovered the body? Nikki Jemison would carry these questions to bed with her

"Let's call it a night Minter. Word from Brass is that we need to report here at 6:30 a.m., renew the search of the apartment BEFORE we call the CSI unit in. Two unmarked cars will be posted at the entrances."

"But boss, er Detective, doesn't that violate protocol."

"We all answer to someone higher Minter, and the higher ups have made their wishes known. Our job is to follow orders. Go home and get some rest and be here at six-fifteen a.m. tomorrow. I am on my way to the office to log in the evidence we've collected so far."

The morgue staff was working overtime on the Sommers case. No one had ever seen such severe lung necrosis. The toxin literally ate its way through the lung tissue. There was massive cardiac damage and severe scarring of the esophageal tissues. Death had occurred quickly after inhalation. There was no sign of a drug overdose or anything that would indicate suicide. In the final analysis Lydiel Sommers died as the result of a cruel illegal manipulation of a common asthma medication. The word HOMICIDE was stamped across her file. She was stitched up and returned to the cold steel drawer in the holding cabinet.

George Cates knew two things: First, if the media was told that Lydiel Sommers died from a massive dose of commercial strength capsaicin as a result of using a common asthma medication panic would ensue, and second this situation called for containment, containment, containment. A decision would have to be made as to the official public cause of death. For the time being he knew what his recommendation would be. He had just closed the folder when Nikki Jemison knocked on his door.

"George, I know it's late but I found these boxes at the Sommers house. They have been logged in. Brass wants to know if you can analyze the contents ASAP."

George Cates signed the log and re-entered the lab. In less than an hour he had the results - each canister had been filled with capsaicin.

Matt McNulty gave up. He couldn't handle any more theories tonight on why two women needed to steal a total of one hundred seven thousand dollars from their husbands. He also couldn't understand how transcripts of conversations between him and Lydiel ended up in his printer. He decided to go for a short drive to clear his head before bedtime. He had some time before Allison and the boys returned home. In the morning he would pay a quick visit to Lydiel if for no other reason than to see for himself that things were well and that Doreen had no reason to worry.

On the drive he was still unable to free his mind. He mentally mapped out a strategy on how to dismantle the ball budget to make sure that an accounting error was not to blame for the missing money. Henry was a nice guy and Matt had seen the pain in his face when it appeared that Connie had taken the money. Turning into his drive Matt noticed that everyone was home. The lights were out in the boys' rooms indicating they were in bed already. As soon as he opened the door he saw Allison glaring. Tonight of all nights he could not handle a scene.

"How was she?"

Matt headed for the stairs without comment.

"I know you were with her."

"Get over yourself Allison. If there is a 'her', there certainly is no doubt as to why, is there?"

Matt continued up the stairs, checked on his

boys and collapsed into bed. This had been a very long day and his mind needed rest as much as his body did.

Ordinarily Allison would be upset but not tonight. Tomorrow she would track Sarah down and find out when Lydiel would be away from home again. She wanted to find the missing piece to her skirt and the gloves. Matt would be at work all week and she would have extra time at lunch to review more transcripts.

The affair of affairs would be over in a matter of a few days and then the real games would begin. She made herself a margarita and settled on the sofa with the remote. She knew Matt and there was no way he could hide anything from her. His emotional state was always transparent. In her mind she had it all worked out. The missing money would never be discovered, Matt would be the primary suspect and disgraced, and people would empathize with her as a single parent and as the long suffering wife of a philanderer.

Of course her mother would say "I told you so", and her family would rally around her. She would explain things to the boys and life would go on. Allison smiled, polished off the margarita, switched off the lamp and settled in to watch her favorite stories. Within minutes she was asleep.

Chapter 23

After staring at the ceiling for hours Matthew McNulty reluctantly decided to start his day. He showered, dressed, and looked in on the boys He covered Liam up, and went downstairs to make coffee. The television was on as usual and there was some breaking news story being announced.

Reaching for the remote to turn the set off, Matt caught a glimpse of what looked like Lydiel's street, more specifically her house. The last thing he wanted was to awaken Allison but he wanted to know exactly what was going on. He turned the television off. He couldn't call Lydiel and he noticed she was not online. That in itself was strange. While waiting for the coffee he decided to send Henry an e-mail informing him of his late arrival and requesting a conference for later in the morning. He took his coffee with him and quietly left the house.

Traffic was very light but Matt's mind was in full churn. Had there been an accident or had that crazy woman upstairs had a run-in with her drug dealers? As he parked on the pad outside Lydiel's house Matt saw a strange car with a sleeping man inside. He really needed to talk to her about moving to a better neighborhood.

He reached into the secret compartment in the glove box, retrieved the keys and walked towards the house. He noticed the lights were on and that was reassuring. As he opened the door, a gun-toting man and woman he had never seen before greeted him.

"Stop right there and raise your hands where I can see them."

"What's going on? What happened here? Where is Lydiel and who are you?"

Nikki recognized Matt right away and also recognized both fear and concern in his face.

It's okay Minter secure your weapon. I know this man."

"I'm Officer Minter and this is Detective Jemison and this is a crime scene."

"Crime scene? What crime? Where is the woman who lives here? "

"If you mean that Sommers babe…

"Minter! I'll handle this. Go back to what you were doing and don't forget to bag and label everything."

"Matt? Matt McNulty? It is you. What are you doing here?"

"Do I know you and will someone please tell me what is going on?"

"You don't remember me do you? Of course there is no reason that you should. I am Nikki Jemison, Detective Sergeant Nikki Jemison now. You and I dated a little in college."

At this point recalling old paramours was the last thing on his mind. He wanted to know what the police were doing here and where Lydiel was. The Nikki Jemison he knew was some skinny girl with frizzy hair and long legs. The woman he saw before him looked totally different.

"Yes it's me, the same Nikki, and you need to sit down. You have inadvertently entered a crime scene. How did you get past the officer posted outside?"

"You mean the sleeping guy in the strange car parked on the pad?"

"Yes, the same. Minter? Could you check on our friend outside please?"

"I'm on it, boss."

"How do you know Lydiel Sommers?"

"We are friends. Has something happened to her?"

"I'm afraid so. There is no easy way to say this, but the body of Lydiel Sommers was discovered yesterday afternoon. Apparently she was murdered."

Matt heard nothing Nikki Jemison said. He could only see her mouth moving. She said something about a body, whose body? Body found where?

"Matt? Matt? Did you hear what I said? The body of Lydiel Sommers was discovered late yesterday afternoon. She was the victim of a homicide."

Matthew found it hard to breathe. It was as if someone had turned the sound off and the heat up. Homicide meant dead. Someone was telling him that Lydiel was dead. The funny girl he made love to three days ago was dead. The woman with that giggle that made people laugh, was never going to laugh again. He felt as if his heart was drowning. He was trembling as he took a deep breath. Who would kill Lydiel and why?

"Where is she and how was she …killed? Are you sure?"

Clearing his throat, his words came out in measured clipped tones.

"Um we were… we were… we were friends, very good friends."

"Matt, were you and Lydiel lovers?"

"I am very sure. She was murdered, Matt."

"Who found her and how do you know it is her."

"The upstairs neighbor found her and called 911. She identified the body."

"Matt, how did you know Lydiel Sommers and why do you have keys to her house?"

"She loved me, yes, very much. I cared for her deeply, very deeply. We were friends."

"Matt, this is very important. Were you and Lydiel Sommers lovers?"

"I am married and I have a family, and I do not want them dragged into this. I cared for her deeply and I don't understand why she is dead."

"She lived alone is that correct? When is the

last time you saw her alive?"

Alive? Alive? Lydiel was always so alive. He kissed her three days ago. He made love to her three days ago. Matt's brain did not comprehend any of this.

"She lived alone. I saw her three days ago. She was alive then. Very much alive."

It was obvious to Nikki that Matt was in shock and she was not sure that he had fully grasped the scope of what had happened.

He remembered her body, warm and soft against his. She always said how much she liked lying naked in his arms. That is the only body he wanted to remember.

"Where is she now? I want to see her. I need to do things."

"Do what things? I don't understand. You just told me that you were married and have a family."

"I am and I do but we had an agreement. If anything happened I was to take care of things the way she wanted them done."

"Take care of things how?"

"She wanted to be cremated and for me to

spread the ashes. But I think it is too soon for that. I need to get to work. I need to talk to her daughters. I need to take care of things. I need for this to all be one big horrible mistake."

"Matt we need to talk more. Perhaps we can talk at your place of employment?"

Matt wrote his information down.

"I will cooperate with you but please do not call my house if possible, please."

"As you know the story is on the news but for now there is no reason to involve your family. Are you okay to drive?"

"I, I, I'm fine." Good-bye. Are you sure she is dead?"

"Unfortunately yes, I am quite sure."

For a minute Nikki felt numb. Matt McNulty was a man who cared for a woman who was now gone and for whom he could not openly grieve, and she knew that there was much more to the story.

Matt got into his car, turned the key, laid his head on the steering wheel and took several very deep breaths. He needed to get to work but he didn't want to leave here. Just three days ago, three short days, he and Lydiel were happy; laughing, loving, talking, and sharing. He remembered her voice but not the last thing she said. Who remembers that stuff? He should have. She was so excited about the book, her first true murder mystery. She had dreams of striking it rich and whisking him away to Belize. The joke between them was they only had one hundred twenty minutes to get there and back. Who was going to make him laugh with crazy little gifts, and seduce him with cards and stories? Who was going to hold him and tell him how wonderful he was?

The questions would not end. Who would want Lydiel dead? The first person that came to mind was Francesca, but not even she would take things this far. How did she die? Did she die alone? How would he tell Doreen? How could he grieve inwardly and not give Allison the satisfaction of seeing him sad or upset? He would need to ask Henry for a few hours off tomorrow to take care of things, and he would have to take him into his confidence and tell him what had happened. No matter how he tried he knew he would not be able to keep this from Allison for very long.

Chapter 24

Francesca was awake earlier than usual. What a glorious weekend she had and all thanks to Henry. She couldn't wait to tell Connie the news and to tell her a few other things also. She quietly eased out of bed, showered and dressed. This time it was she who ordered breakfast and left a note. Today she and Connie would be free of Allison and her threats forever. She felt that her relationship with Henry was secure, and more than likely Allison would back down from the plot to kill Lydiel. Francesca had been very careful not to do anything that would implicate herself in the scheme. She was feeling very good about things as she hailed a cab. Her first stop was the bank and then Connie's house. She needed to call her to make sure she would be home.

"Hello?"

"Connie, this is Francesca. I wanted to stop by before you went to work. We need to talk."

"Francesca have you seen the news or read the paper this morning?"

"No, why?"

"No reason dear. I will wait for you. We can have breakfast together if you haven't eaten."

"That sounds great. See you soon. Connie? Is everything okay?"

"See you soon Francesca."

The cab stopped in front of the bank and Francesca asked the driver to wait. Once inside the bank she asked for the manager and explained who she was. After signing the signature cards she was presented with a cashier's check for sixty thousand dollars. She gave the driver Connie's address and had a very good feeling about the day. She was doing a good thing. The old Francesca would have run a scam, pocketed the money and skipped town.

She saw Connie in the yard as she arrived at the house. She paid the driver and walked briskly to Connie's door. Connie had turned the television off before Francesca's arrival.

Once the boys were gone to school, Allison turned on the television to watch the news and the latest jewelry bargains. What she saw was a breaking news event. She turned up the sound to hear the reporter.

"We have learned that an unidentified woman was found dead in her apartment on Spearhead Drive. The name of the victim and the cause of death are not known at this time. Stay tuned to News 9 for further updates."

Spearhead Drive was where Lydiel Sommers lived. Was it possible that the deed had been done? Allison reached for the phone. Since Connie was the early riser perhaps she had more information.

"Good morning."

"I just saw the news Connie. Do you think…"

"I will have to get back to you on that but it is my understanding that things are as they appear to be."

"I take it you can't talk now?"

"Yes that's it exactly. I will get back to you later this morning."

"Have you heard from Sarah?"

"I'm sure I haven't. Goodbye."

Turning to Francesca, Connie wanted to know the nature of the early morning visit. Lately the two of them had not had meetings at the house.

"What brings you by so early, dear?"

"Who was on the phone Connie?"

"No one important dear."

"Connie?"

"Yes Francesca?"

"I'm here because I have something for you."

Francesca reached into her purse, pulled out the envelope and handed it to Connie.

"What is this?"

"Open it please."

When Connie opened the envelope she slowly removed the check and read and re-read it.

"You are free Connie. You are free of Allison. Now you can put the money back and Henry will never know. Matt will see that it was all a mistake."

"Francesca, I don't know what to say. How did you ever manage this?

"I have my ways and the less said the better."

"Francesca, I need to tell you something. This will affect us all and you need to be very careful now."

"I don't understand Connie. Has something happened?"

"Lydiel's body was found last evening."

"Found? Found where and by whom? Connie what are you saying?"

"I'm saying that your mother is dead. I'm saying that there is no turning away from this. I'm saying that it is done and God help us all."

Chapter 25

The sound of the elevator doors awakened Henry. He smiled as he read Francesca's note, stretched and started his day. He was anxious to get back to the office and begin to unravel the mysteries of the missing funds and the strange shutdown of the company website.

As he stood in the shower he closed his eyes and thought of the woman he had shared the last three days with. Life was so strange and right now so good, so very good. He shaved, dressed, and sat down to breakfast and the paper. After perusing the business pages he took a cursory look at the local news. There was a small blurb about an unidentified woman found dead. That was an everyday occurrence in the city and Henry turned the page without giving it a second thought. He worried about Francesca and the neighborhood she lived in but now was not the time to raise the issue.

While waiting for the valet to bring his car around Henry caught a glimpse of the morning news. There was more about the discovery of the dead woman. The story seemed to be front burner news everywhere. Whoever she was, Henry hoped the perpetrators would be caught and suitably punished. His main concern at the moment was meeting with Matt in another attempt to locate the missing Pushman funds and who misappropriated them. He simply could not deal with the possibility of Connie being a thief.

The fundraising plans had fallen behind and everyone needed to get on board and pull together to make the project a roaring success. Hopefully the site would be up and running today. Henry checked his e-mail and noticed a message from Matt. Maybe it was good news. After reading the message Henry paged the front desk.

"Please have Matt McNulty report to my office as soon as he arrives."

"He is walking in now Mr. Pushman."

"Good morning Maureen."

"Good morning, Matt. The boss wants to see you ASAP."

Apparently Henry had read his e-mail. Better to get this over with. Of all people Henry should understand the situation. Matt knocked on Henry's door.

"Matt, come in my boy. What seems to be the problem? Nothing wrong at home I hope.

In Matt's estimation everything was wrong and some of it could never be made right again. Over the course of the next hour Matt informed Henry of Lydiel's death, the nature of their relationship, and the impact this could have on his home life and his working relationship with Pushman and associates.

"How well do you know Ms. Sommers' family Matt?"

Matt knew Henry was fishing. He also knew that now was not the time to fudge on the truth as he might need Henry's support in the weeks and months to come.

"I know a few of her daughters fairly well."

Henry thought about Francesca. Was she one of the daughters Matt knew and how well did he know her.

"Matt, I…"

"I know about you and Francesca, Henry. I

saw you together one day recently. The particulars aren't really my business but believe me I do understand how these things happen."

"Connie and I have been married a very long time. We raised a set of twins together who just started college. When I met Francesca I was at an all time low and she..."

"You don't owe me any explanation Henry. I only confided in you because of the possible media backlash down the road. Allison and Connie are friends and no doubt when this hits the fan they will put their own spins on it."

"I promise you this Matt, the full resources of the Pushman legal department are at your disposal should you need them. I have very good connections all over town and I am not above calling in a few markers if need be. I can't begin to imagine how you feel, but if there is anything I can do, please do not hesitate to ask. If you need time off that is not an issue. The site is not up yet and you have things you need to take care of. I have to be there for Francesca. This is going to devastate her."

"Thanks Henry. She is going to need you."

If Francesca had anything to do with this she was definitely going to need Henry Pushman because no power on earth would keep her safe. Henry's private line was ringing and Matt felt this would be a good time to leave, but to go where and do what he didn't know.

"I need to take this Matt. I'll be in touch later this afternoon."

Matt did not envy Henry and he had no idea how he was going to break the news to Doreen. Of all the kids he knew about, she and Lydiel were the closest. He felt certain Francesca would inform Remey and the others.

Chapter 26

Matt switched the car radio to an all news station in hopes of learning something about Lydiel's death that the detectives hadn't told him.

"We interrupt our regularly scheduled programming to bring you this news update. The county coroner has ruled the death of Lydiel Sommers a homicide. No further information is available at this time. We now return you to our regular program."

Matt needed to go back to the office but first he had to see Doreen.

The few times Matt had visited Doreen he never noticed how steep the stairs to her door were. At this moment he felt old and tired, and the stairs seemed like climbing a mountain. He stood at the door several minutes collecting his thoughts before knocking.

"Who is it?"

"It's Matt, sweetie."

Matt? Why was he here at this time of day? She looked a wreck.

"I'm really not dressed or anything. Is something wrong?"

Any other time Matt would have said okay, I'll catch you another time but he didn't have the luxury of doing that today.

"Just throw something on. We need to talk. It's important."

Pulling on her robe, Doreen opened the door.

"I apologize for the way I look. I was up late with the kids. Can I get you some coffee or anything? Why aren't you at work?

"Sit down for a minute Doreen. I need to tell you something."

From the look on his face and the tone of his voice Doreen knew there was something seriously wrong.

"You're scaring me, Matt."

"Doreen, have you seen the news this morning? Something has happened."

"Something like what?"

"It's your mom."

"What about her? Was she in an accident? Did someone break into her house? Oh, no, no, no...

Please tell me she was not assaulted."

"Stop, please. Just stop. There was no accident. She was not assaulted, she was murdered."

The silence in the room made it feel like a vacuum; insufferable and sucking the life from its occupants like an emotional maelstrom. He knew he was going to asked to explain the unthinkable.

"How do you know this?"

"After I read your e-mail last night I became concerned. When I was leaving the house this morning I saw a story on the news about an incident on her street so I went there. The police were there and told me what happened."

"Why would anyone want to kill mommie, Matt? She was working on the book and things were getting better between you two. Is there something you aren't telling me?

"I'm telling you everything I know so far."

"Matt, why wasn't her family notified or you? Have you… have you seen her yet?"

This was the one question Matt dreaded. He didn't want to see Lydiel that way. He wanted to see her laughing and warm and alive, however, he knew that ultimately he would have to see her and take care of things…lots of things.

"Kat found the body and identified her. You know how your mom was. She didn't have family pictures or phone numbers in the apartment."

"Kat found mommie? What was she doing in her house?"

"Knowing Kat she probably wanted to use the phone. I have a few things I need to take care of. Can I call anyone for you?"

"There was only one person and she isn't here anymore."

Matt hugged Doreen and made a mental agenda of things he wanted to discuss with Detective Jemison. There were so many loose ends even at this stage of the investigation.

Chapter 27

The kitchen clock read eleven forty-five a.m. and Allison McNulty decided to fix lunch before the noon news came on. Details had been very sketchy about Lydiel, and Allison was hoping for a major update soon. Settling herself on the sofa she began surfing through the local channels hoping to catch an early news preview. She didn't have to wait long. Adjusting the volume she saw a reporter on the scene in front of Lydiel's house.

"Good afternoon. We are here live in front of 8191 Spearhead Drive, which was home to writer Lydiel Sommers. Sommers' body was discovered yesterday afternoon by an upstairs neighbor, Katherine Garcia. The official cause of death has been listed as a homicide. Now back to the studio."

At last, confirmation! Lydiel Sommers was officially gone bye bye forever. Allison was beginning to wonder if this day would ever come. She had her celebration dinner all planned and it was time to get started. Before she could click off the television there was another 'breaking news' crawler on the screen.

"Makers of a popular asthma drug are recalling inhalers with the batch numbers…"

Allison laughed as she put the roast in the oven. Good luck schmucks trying to find those inhalers. They were a very limited run. And now Mr. Matt, let the fun begin.

Matt was at Mirelli's watching the noon news. Lydiel's death was beginning to take on a circus atmosphere with the constant newsbreaks. He had agreed to meet Detective Jemison for lunch. He used the wait time to mentally re-create that last day he and Lydiel were together.

"Excuse me, Mr. McNulty is it? Could I bring you something to drink or a menu perhaps?"

Matt looked up to see Giorgio standing at the table. The guy had a remarkable memory as they had only met once before.

"Coffee would be great and a menu."

Matt had a gut feeling Francesca knew something about the murder, but why would she take things this far? That thought had to be put on hold as Nikki Jemison approached the table. With so much going on it was small wonder that Matt did not remember her at all.

"Thanks for agreeing to meet me, Matt."

"Detective; won't you sit down?"

Nikki knew she would have to tread lightly with Matt. He looked worn and tired and confused.

"Matt, I need to ask you some questions. How long did you know Lydiel Sommers?"

Another question Matt had trouble with. Marking time was something women did. They were the ones who remembered anniversaries. They celebrate everything from the first time a guy spoke to them to the first time they make love with him. They clung tenaciously to every misstep made, and remembered every argument. Matt couldn't recall the exact date they met. All he recalled was how full of life she was.

"Matt?"

"I'm not exactly sure- months, several months."

"Months as in less than a year; more than a

year, two years?"

"Yes."

"You told me you were married. Did your wife know about your relationship with Lydiel?"

"No. At least I'm pretty sure she didn't."

"Pretty sure?"

"Positive. She has her suspicions that I might be seeing someone but nothing concrete. It has to do with an old phone call."

"Were you familiar with any of Lydiel's friends, family?"

Matt was more familiar than he ever felt comfortable with, especially her daughters.

"She was a very private person and didn't have a lot of friends. As for her family, I know a few of her daughters."

"Were the relationships good between them?"

Giorgio saved Matt from answering that question by arriving with the coffee, water and two menus.

"Would you care to order now?"

There was a very pregnant pause as Nikki accepted the menu. Matt used the time to think of a response. Although he suspected Francesca of playing a role in things, this was a card he didn't want to reveal at this time.

"As I recall the Cobb salad here is excellent so I think I will have that. Detective?"

"A BLT and diet soda for me, please."

"Now where were we, Matt?"

"As far as I know they all got along. I really didn't spend that much time with them as I'm sure you can understand."

Nikki got the distinct impression that Matt was hiding something but decided not to press the issue at this time."

"Aren't you going to ask me where I was at the time of the murder? Isn't the lover always the prime suspect, Nikki?"

"Matt, I..."

"I was camping with my family all weekend. There were witnesses at the campground."

Nikki had to stifle a laugh. Matt had been watching too many reruns of Columbo. She felt as if she should put her hand to her eyebrow and say 'and another thing...'

Giorgio brought their food and in between bites of Cobb salad, Matt would make eye contact with Giorgio. For some reason each time he visited Mirelli's the Maitre 'D seemed to be in almost constant attendance or lurking. Matt wasn't sure if he was stationed there or just nosey. It was distracting and he felt as if he should be talking in hushed tones.

Nikki continued the conversation with Matt.

"We took Lydiel's computer in as evidence. Apparently she was quite the romantic, and very organized. She archived every communication between the two of you so we have a pretty good idea what was between you. We also discovered something else. There was stealth software installed on her computer. It hasn't been there long but it has been accessed recently. Do you know of anyone who would have access to her computer?"

"I know absolutely nothing about stealth software or anything like that, and to the best of my knowledge no one had access. She was very particular about her computer, and was always worrying that her work would somehow be compromised."

"Stealth software is used to monitor Internet activity. Once installed, Internet activity and communications can be monitored remotely and transcripts of e-mails and instant messages can be viewed as well as all of the websites visited. As you know nothing is ever 'deleted'.

Matt checked his watch. It was nearly three o'clock. He needed to think about getting home to meet the boys.

"I need to be home when the kids get there. This remote access business, is it a form of hacking?"

"Usually parents buy it to see what their kids are up to online, but occasionally we have had spouses install it on their home computers also if they suspect the other of straying."

Matt thought back to the pages that printed out with his golf outing e-mail. At the time he didn't give it a lot of thought although he was puzzled as to how they ended up in his home printer.

"I see… Can we talk more about this some other time? I really need to get home."

"Of course. You have my card and thanks for lunch.

Chapter 28

Nikki Jemison had assigned Gary Minter the task of interviewing the pharmacist who refilled Lydiel's inhaler scripts. The first thing he noticed was the plastic container filled with asthma inhalers. The clerk behind the counter was a young female who seemed more interested in the current edition of Cosmo than she was in assisting customers.

"Good morning. I am looking for the pharmacist that was on duty Friday afternoon."

Without looking up she mumbled something that sounded like the name Tom.

"Excuse me?"

With a deep sigh of resignation, she slowly put the magazine down and finally acknowledged Minter's presence at the counter.

"Tom. Tom was working that day. He is on duty now if you want to talk to him. I'll get him for you,"

A slightly overweight ruddy-faced man made his way to the front counter. His arms were loaded with boxes of asthma inhalers, which he unceremoniously dropped into the plastic box.

"I understand you wanted to speak with me?"

"Yes. I'm Sergeant Minter and I am investigating the death of Lydiel Sommers. I understand you refilled her asthma prescriptions a few days ago."

There was a marked change in Tom's demeanor. Almost tearful and with his voice cracking, he related how he and Lydiel had been on friendly terms for over fifteen years. They would often discuss her writing projects, politics and other topics of interest.

"When she came in on Friday morning I was busy in the back filling the scripts and on the phone with other customers. The pharmacy tech took care of her and informed her that there had been a change in the dosage. I will miss her greatly. I still can't imagine who would want her dead. Say, do you know anything about this recall thing? I have been getting phone calls all morning from my customers."

Minter felt as if he had wasted the morning and accomplished nothing. There had been no reports of any capsaicin related deaths but it would take a day or two to analyze all the inhalers. As terrible as Lydiel's death was, Minter was almost certain that it was an isolated incident. He wondered if super detective Jemison was having any better luck with the McNulty guy. He seemed so devastated at the news but Minter had a feeling that Matthew McNulty figured prominently in the death of Ms Lydiel Sommers.

After spending the entire afternoon with Matt, Nikki felt certain that he was hiding something aside from his affair with Lydiel. How relevant it was to the case was difficult to ascertain at this point, but she could not rule him out as a suspect. He seemed fairly certain that his wife had no knowledge of Lydiel, but years on the force told Nikki that this might be a case of wishful and hopeful thinking. If Allison were aware of the relationship, she would be joining Matt in the suspect pool.

Nikki didn't tell Matt that she knew about Lydiel's ongoing estrangement from two of her daughters, Francesca and Remey. Lydiel also archived messages between the three of them and there were feelings of ambivalence, especially between her and Francesca. Francesca seemed to be the one who was especially disapproving of the relationship between her mother and Matt. Remey, who was virtually adopted by Lydiel after being abandoned by her own mother, was jealous of the relationship. It was hard to tell whom she wanted to be with more, her husband, Matt or Lydiel. Remey was scheduled to fly in later in the week. Francesca was nearby, and on her list of people to interview tomorrow. Now it was time to check in with Minter to see if he had any luck. The phone rang once and he was on the line.

"Sergeant Minter here."

Gary was the only person Nikki knew who answered his personal cell phone as if he were on duty 24/7.

"It's Nikki. Did you have any luck with the pharmacist?"

"If you call watching a parade of people come in dropping off their asthma inhalers, then yes I had luck. If you mean could he shed any light on things, then the answer is no. Turns out he never waited on the Sommers babe; the tech took care of her. How was the interview with McNulty?"

Minter was a law enforcement nightmare. His sarcasm overshadowed the thimbleful of investigative ability he possessed. He had no objectivity and for the life of her Nikki had no idea how on earth he passed the test to become a police officer and get promoted to detective idiot with a badge.

Chapter 29

Henry was slightly out of breath as he rushed across the lobby to the penthouse elevators. He was anxious to see how Francesca was and to make sure the doctor was available as promised. He had no idea what to expect. As the elevator doors opened he heard music and smelled food. Turning the music down, Henry looked around the living room and bedroom and saw no sign of Francesca. He checked the bathroom and found her soaking in the tub sipping a glass of wine.

"How are you my dear? I got here as soon as I could."

"Hi Henry. Care to join me?"

Unsure of what to make of her demeanor, Henry seated himself on the small bench adjacent to the tub and took her hand in his.

"I'm so sorry to hear about your mother. Do they have any clues as to who did this? What can I do to help you through this?"

"You can start by taking off your clothes and

joining me in the tub."

As he began to undress, Henry thought how strange Francesca's request was. Perhaps she was in shock. At any rate he joined her in the tub. Sitting beside her he placed his arm around her shoulders and pulled her close. Without so much as batting an eyelash Francesca was like an animal in heat. He had never seen such wild abandonment in a woman and he found it overwhelming. Holding onto the bars, she rode him deep and hard, stopping just before he exploded, only to suck him tightly and deeply until he could hold back no longer. Now it was he who felt as though he were in a state of shock. He felt weak and drained and somewhat confused.

"Francesca, are you okay?"

"I'm fine Mr. P. How was it for you?"

"It was wonderful as always, dear. Tell you what, why don't we get out of the tub and have something warm. I could order coffee..."

"No need for the coffee, I have something that will warm you up just fine."

Grabbing his hand Francesca led him to the bed. This was all so totally unexpected and Henry was ill prepared to deal with her raging libido. He knew he should call the doctor but every time he reached for the phone, Francesca would wrap herself up in his arms until he finally gave up. Perhaps if he just went along with things she would calm down a bit.

"Do you want to talk about it?"

"Talk about what Henry?"

"What happened to your mother, the arrangements?"

"My mother is dead. She was murdered. Matt will take care of things. No point in wasting anymore tears over it."

Earlier in the day Francesca had seemed inconsolable and now she seemed resigned to the loss.

"Matt who? Have you talked to the police to see if they have any leads?"

"Your golden boy, Henry. Matthew McNulty! He was banging the hell out of my mother every chance he got. You didn't know about that did you? Poor, poor Matt. Mommie's dead. No more whiney syrupy sweet Lydiel to take care of him. Do you think he is sad, Henry?"

If he had any doubts before he now knew for certain that Francesca needed sedating. She was acting irrational and Henry felt an obligation not only to her but also to Matt as well. A quick phone call to the front desk and the medication was delivered. Exhausted and cradling her in his arms, Henry soon fell into a deep sleep.

Connie Pushman couldn't bear one more conversation with Allison or one more minute in the house. She had come to the conclusion that it was time to consider severing times with Allison for good. Her joy at the death of a woman whose only crime per se was having an affair with her husband was disturbing. Poor Matt. His grief had not yet begun.

Francesca had been so distraught when Connie first told her of Lydiel's death. As strange as it was, she felt that she owed her at least a shoulder to cry on. It had been a very long time since she used the Pushman penthouse at the Renaissance and with Henry being away for a few days this would be the perfect place to console her. She would order dinner and they could enjoy a girls' night out. They both needed a break from all of the madness.

Connie tried Francesca's cell phone but there was no answer. Maybe she was in the shower. No matter, they could meet at the penthouse. After turning on the outside lights, checking the answering machine and changing the battery in her cell phone, Connie Pushman was off for a night she would not soon forget.

Chapter 30

Matt was surprised to see Allison's car in the garage. The engine was cold indicating that she had been home for a while. She probably blew off work again. Why the insurance agency didn't let her go he would never know. Maybe she anticipated it and planned to use the money to make him believe she was still working. He knew he was giving her way too much credit at being that devious or was he? He didn't really know her anymore. Summoning every bit of strength he could muster, he opened the door, which in time would become the entranceway to hell.

The room was filled with the smell of meat roasting, there were candles on the table and music playing. What the hell was she up to now? Not another weak attempt at seduction he hoped. Today was definitely not the day for that.

"Hi sweetheart. How was your day?"

Matt was certain that his wife had been kidnapped and replaced by one of the bots from The Stepford Wives. Sweetheart? He needed a drink and quickly. Things were more amiss than ever.

"Allison, are we having company for dinner and you neglected to tell me?"

"No silly. It's been a long time since we sat down to a nice dinner and I thought tonight would be a good time to do that."

Matt was highly suspicious and not impressed. Something was terribly wrong with this picture and he was not buying into it.

"I had a very long day and I'm not very hungry. When did you have time to do this? Did you have a short day today?"

"I decided making my family a good dinner was more important so I called in today. You seem like you could use a drink. Would you like me to fix it for you?"

Ignoring her attempt at whatever insane game she was playing, Matt headed for his office.

"Where are the boys? Is the bus late?"

"My mother took them for the evening so that we could spend some time alone. We really need to talk."

Bingo! At last the plot was revealed; dinner

and talking. He wasn't hungry and if she wasn't going to come clean about the forty-seven thousand dollars, he had nothing to say.

"Can I have a rain check? I have work to do. I will be in my office."

There it was again, that rejection. Why was it that all of a sudden everyone felt the need to say no? Now it was her turn.

"No Matt, you may not have a rain check. You may not refuse dinner, and you damn sure may not refuse to talk to me. I worked hard preparing this dinner and I think you should join me eating it."

If he hadn't been so tired, so depressed trying to understand the loss of someone he cared for, he would have laughed hysterically. The only appetizing thing in the room was the bottle of scotch. Pouring himself a double, downing half of it in one swallow, he pulled out his chair, sat down and waited…

Sipping tequila in the kitchen Allison was lost. She had expected quite a different man to show up. Matt seemed tired but no different than every night recently. One thing was for sure; he had not been with HER. Taking the plates to the table she tried to figure out how to engage him in conversation. They were on anything but good terms these days.

"What did you want to talk about Allison?"

Matt was moving the roast around on his plate as if it would miraculously disappear. He finally put the fork down and looked her in the eye.

"I am not in the mood for games Allison, especially not tonight. If you have something to say please do so."

"I asked you earlier how your day was and you didn't answer."

"Look, you give less than a damn about my day. What's going on here?"

"Did you see the news today?"

Matt wasn't sure he liked where this was headed. That long put off confrontation seemed to be looming like overfilled storm clouds waiting to open up.

"I can't watch the news at work. That is why it is called work not entertainment."

Obviously Matt was not taking the bait. She hated waiting him out but if she pressed the issue right now it could backfire.

"Was there something on the news that would be of interest to me?"

"There was a murder over near the south side, some writer, found dead in her house. There were lots of news break-ins about it. I just thought you might have heard about it."

"Is that what you did all day, watch TV? Really Allison, I don't understand you at all. People get murdered somewhere every day. The only reason it is news is because people like you sit around watching the gore of it all. I really think they're going to fire you if you persist in calling in all the time. Now if you will excuse me..."

"Matt, wait. Can we spend a little time together?"

"We spend a little time together every day, Allison. We eat dinner together. We do things with the boys together. We live together. How much more together do you want under the circumstances?"

"Fine! One thing is for sure, you won't be spending time with her anytime soon, will you?"

"Goodnight Allison."

She was fishing for a reaction and Matt refused to play that sick game with her. Whether she knew anything or not, he was not playing along. Tomorrow came early and he had a lot of things to take care of, like having his hard drive checked for stealth software.

Chapter 31

Connie Pushman was surprised to find the lights on in the Penthouse. Maybe the cleaning staff forgot to turn them off. Standing in the foyer she decided to try Francesca again. There seemed to be some sort of echo when her phone rang. She could swear she heard the phone ringing in the bedroom. No one but the front desk clerk knew she was here. Maybe it was room service. Waiting for Francesca to answer, she walked towards the bedroom. To her surprise there was people sleeping in the bed. Maybe Corporate had arranged for guests to stay there. Feeling like a voyeur she tiptoed back to the foyer. She decided to try Francesca once more while waiting for the elevator and once again she heard the ringing echo in the penthouse. There was still no answer so it seemed she would be dining alone at home tonight.

It had started to rain when she came in so she decided to grab an umbrella from the closet. Easing the door open, she noticed a light flashing on a cell phone lying beside a woman's handbag. Bending down to pick it up she saw her number in the message window. Searching the closet, she found women's shoes, purses, lingerie and clothing. She also found a briefcase with the initials HP, and a shirt with some very familiar cuff links in the sleeve. Closing the door, Connie waited for the elevator to arrive. Hurrying across the lobby, she waved off the valet and walked the short distance to her car.

Washing the dishes was anything but cathartic for Allison. The tiny veins at her temples were throbbing as she fought to control her anger. Tired or not, Matt was going to spend time with her tonight. She had at least two hours before the boys would be home which was more than enough time to spend some quality time with her husband. She turned the volume up slightly on the television hoping to get one final update on Lydiel before going upstairs to join Matt. She turned the lights off in the kitchen and went to join Matt in bed. The lamp was out in the bedroom and for a brief moment she thought he might be asleep. Reaching over to put her arm around him, she soon realized she was alone. Where the hell could he be?

The night air was cool and refreshing. Smoking one of the cigars Lydiel had given him, Matt stood at the lake and allowed himself to grieve. Whoever did this would be caught. Whoever did this would be punished and punished severely. The more he thought about it the more he was convinced that Francesca and Remey were behind it, but thinking it and proving it were two very different things. He missed her. He missed her touch. He missed her laughter.

Allison tucked the boys in, plopped down on the sofa and began to watch the jewelry auctions. This was not over by a long shot. She could rest well knowing that wherever he was he was not with her. He would never be with her again and with a little luck, he would never know the pleasure of a woman again. Allison never heard the door open or the footsteps. Matt slept alone as usual, but this time the loneliness he felt saddened his heart. The events of the day wrapped themselves around him like a roughdried blanket. Sleep came quickly, and he willingly surrendered to it.

Connie decided to skip dinner. She looked at the glass of tequila on the table, and lying naked in her bed she once again fingered the pills in her hand. It would be so easy…so very easy. Henry had no idea about her and Francesca but Francesca knew who Henry was. Now she understood the check. Francesca had rolled Henry for sixty thousand dollars to give to her to replace the stolen funds. How laughably ironic; Francesca had to be the most expensive piece of ass around. There was no doubt in her mind that Francesca was the source of Henry's new found happiness, and Connie was a firm believer that no good deed should go unpunished. She returned the pills to the bottle, sipped the wine and finally slept.

Chapter 32

Remey Anderson carefully checked off the items on the packing list. News of Lydiel's death was followed by a request from a Detective Jemison to make herself available for interview. She had been very careful loading the canisters, disposing of the scale and tools and limiting her contact with either Connie or Francesca. As far she was concerned her tracks were well covered and there was nothing connecting her to the murder.

"Doug, can you get the hat box down for me? There is a special hat I want to wear to the service."

Like all women, Remey packed for a short trip as if she were going on a month long cruise. They would be gone four or five days at the most. Why she needed some stupid hat was beyond him.

To say that Douglas Anderson was less than thrilled about interrupting his life to attend a memorial service for someone he hardly knew would be an understatement, but Lydiel was responsible for his new job, and Remey had insisted they make a unified presence. He was also at a loss as to why the police thought his wife could contribute anything given the fact they lived over three hundred miles away. He was, however, curious about Matt. Remey seemed to think the guy walked on water. For awhile it was Matt this and Matt that. One person Doug definitely was not looking forward to seeing was that wench Francesca. She had caused so many problems between him and Remey lately.

The last time Francesca visited she had taken Doug to a place he should never have gone. She had a way of making men do things they never planned on doing, like that day in the garage. The day Francesca showed up without notice or invitation, Remey invited her to stay for the evening meal. All during dinner Francesca found some way to touch him. She had insisted on sitting next to him and her left hand seem to constantly fall into his lap, stroking him ever so lightly. He never welcomed her advances but his body involuntarily responded. He had planned a different sort of evening that included him and Remey spending quality passionate time together. They both had been so tired lately that lovemaking had been moved to the bottom of the list of things to do. Francesca was always spoiling things!

Remey was anxious to finish packing and get the show on the road. She was not looking forward to seeing Francesca again. For her part in the plot, Remey had done what was required and walked away. She did not grieve the loss of Lydiel. It was what it was. When she needed her most, she had not been there for her, so now in death perhaps the spoils left behind would assuage her feelings of neglect and oversight.

Doug had relived that day far too many times. He and Francesca were clearing the dinner dishes while Remey put the girls to bed. Standing at the sink, Doug once again felt Francesca's hands, touching, kneading, fondling…He wanted to tell her to stop but he knew it was like treading water. He dried his hands and headed for the garage, knowing she would follow him there. He needed his laptop and briefcase. As he popped the trunk latch he could see Francesca draped over the hood of the car.

Damn her! Damn her to hell! Walking around to the front of the car and behind her, his hands went underneath her skirt and it was no surprise that she was wearing no underwear. She was so warm and so willing. He let his trousers and briefs fall to the floor as he pulled her close. He was so hard and he wanted her; right then and there he wanted to drive deep inside her. Before he could give it a second thought Francesca began backing into him, gyrating against his hardness and before he knew it he was inside her and after a few quick thrusts it was over. Satisfaction was tinged with extreme guilt as he dressed silently and returned to the house. Unlike most of her previous visits, Francesca left a lasting reminder of her presence in the Anderson household. Remey's irritating whining interrupted Doug's unpleasant journey down memory lane.

"Did you find the hatbox yet? Doug? C'mon. I want to get this show on the road and the farce over with as soon as possible."

The one thing Doug never understood was the rift between Remey and Lydiel. Coming from a warm and loving family he could only imagine what it must have been like to be abandoned and virtually shunned by your kin. Lydiel had taken Remey in, given her a home and under her tutelage she had turned out to be an intelligent, warm and loving person to some. However, there was an underlying bitterness that belied her caring nature.

"Hold on Rem. This closet is packed like a sardine can. Are you sure there is a hat in here?"

This was one of those occasions where Remey appreciated the wisdom in the old adage about if you want anything done, do it yourself. Marching into the bedroom and moving Doug aside she retrieved the hatbox.

"Yes dear, I am very sure. Are you all packed and ready?"

Amazing! His wife could literally find the proverbial needle in a haystack! As to her question, packing was easy for Doug. Toothbrush toothpaste, shaving stuff, comb, shower toiletries, a couple of pairs of Dockers, a couple of shirts, suit, tie, dress shirt, shoes, underwear and he was done.

"I'm finished packing, just waiting on you."

Remey needed to go over her list once more making sure she hadn't forgotten anything. Maintaining her focus on packing was difficult because for some reason the butterflies were beginning to kick up in her stomach and she was experiencing the onset of a severe anxiety attack.

"Why don't you take the girls' things to Lenore's and I will be done when you get back."

Doug's discomfort increased significantly at the thought of dealing with his ex. He and Lenore at one time had joint custody of their daughters and then thanks to Francesca everything fell apart. It was Remey who did the damage control and at least now everyone was on speaking terms. All three girls would be staying with Lenore while he and Remey were away.

After driving the short distance to her house, Doug was relieved to learn that Lenore was not home. She had left instructions with the housekeeper to accept the girls' things and to inform Doug after she picked them up from school. He would never let it show, but Douglas Anderson had a very bad feeling about this trip.

Remey took one last look around, put the bags on the sidewalk and locked the door. The butterflies seemed to be taking up residence in her chest now and her heart was racing. She found herself breathing in short gasps. Fortunately she was distracted by Doug's arrival and her thoughts shifted to loading the luggage and getting the trip underway. It was a six-hour drive and with any luck they would be there by mid-afternoon.

Chapter 33

Henry Pushman felt stiff and sore as he stretched himself awake. Francesca was still sleeping peacefully, thank goodness. He remained confused at the events of the day before. Wild sex with Francesca was the last thing he expected. For some reason he expected her to be tearful and overcome with grief, and instead she was hotter than he had ever seen her. He was not prepared for her passionate aggressiveness and he found it difficult to keep up with her.

For the first time since they had known each other her advances had not turned him on. She had been almost savage, attacking him rather than seducing him. Apparently she handled devastating news in her own protective fashion. He became concerned when she began to talk about Matt and her mother. He needed to discuss the situation with Matt as soon as possible as this was information best left within the confines of this room. Given the circumstances he felt it best to contact Matt via e-mail.

The night had definitely been too short. Matt felt jittery and sleep deprived. Coffee was not working its usual magic, and in general at this point life sucked. Nikki had kept her promise about not calling his house and because he was listed as Lydiel's healthcare agent, the ME's office had e-mailed him letting him know the body was ready for release. He would, however, need to come in and sign the appropriate forms and designate a mortuary to pick up the body.

Sitting in his office he had to laugh, albeit briefly, at how he and Lydiel talked about when the time came she wanted to be cremated and, as he smoked one of his favorite cigars, he would put her on the big barbecue grill and baste her with his favorite barbecue sauce. Realizing that scenario was like a bad clip from Texas Chainsaw Massacre, they agreed on him spreading her ashes 'three sheets to the wind' while riding his bike. At the time it seemed like nothing more than a dark joke. He never really considered the possibility that it would happen. Come to think of it he always thought things would turn out differently for some reason; one of those walking off into the sunset hand in hand deals. Obviously that was never going to happen now.

Before Matt could call the morgue, e-mail arrived from Henry, unfortunately with a new wrinkle - Francesca's medicated ramblings about his relationship with Lydiel. Henry was convinced he could handle things for the present but admitted the obvious. This was only a stopgap measure at best. Sooner or later the whole truth was bound to come out. Henry once again pledged his support to Matt. As soon as he deleted the message, he noticed one from Remey announcing her and Doug's arrival later in the day. Could this day get any worse? The answer to that question was knocking on his office door.

"You can't avoid me forever you know. Sooner or later we will talk."

Allison had impeccable timing and any confrontation would have to be later. Matt literally had places to go and people to see and he did not plan on making his day any more miserable than it had to be by indulging Allison in some argumentative diatribe.

He opened his office door and brushing past her he grabbed his briefcase and almost made it to the front door. Apparently Allison had difficulty interpreting his message and followed him to the door. Turning on his heel, he was close enough to kiss her if he had been so inclined, but at this particular moment nothing could have been further from his mind.

"I'm leaving now. I have things to take care of. Have a good day. Going to work would be a great start, and if you get ready now you won't be late."

Matt closed the door and in so doing evoked the wrath of a woman who never ever took no for an answer. It was time to start phase two and Connie was just the person to help her.

Book Three:

The Beginning of the End

Chapter 1

Jeffrey Williams rarely had a chance to watch the news or read the newspaper, and had it not been for overhearing a conversation between fellow employees, he would have never known about Lydiel Sommers' murder. He was still nursing the broken ankle he sustained while visiting his sister in Milwaukee. He had been away for three weeks and this was his first day back. Assigned to light duty he had more down time, and that allowed him an opportunity to catch up on things. The murder of Lydiel Sommers remained front page news. He could only imagine how many gawkers had lined the street when news of it got out. He never understood how tragedy brought out people's voyeuristic nature. He didn't recall having ever seen any real signs of life in her house, but writers were by nature reclusive.

The alleys running behind the houses allowed the residents to go and come and never be seen by the security staff of the hospital. Spearhead Drive was a very quiet street with mostly elderly infirmed residents and virtually no children living there.

Occasionally an overzealous fan would park in front of her house and as a courtesy the security officers would make them move along. Some were stubborn diehards determined to get a glimpse or an autograph. One in particular came to mind.

The call had come in around lunchtime. Jeffrey had been on his way to the cafeteria when he was asked to check out a female reported to be lurking in the bushes surrounding the north parking lot. The entrance to the lot was on Spearhead Drive and was used for medical resident parking. When he got there he found a woman crouched down staring at the house across the street. She claimed to be a tabloid reporter trying to scoop a story on Lydiel. He remembered how resistant she had been to leaving and how he had escorted her to her car. He also remembered thinking that for a reporter she wasn't very smart because she parked in front of a fire hydrant and never saw the cop put a ticket on her windshield.

Jeffrey wondered if she was one of the gawkers when the body was discovered. She could have done a first on the scene piece and probably sold it to TMZ or Access Hollywood. He also wondered if the camera tapes from that day were still available. Checking the logs he found the tapes for the week before Lydiel's murder; now if he could just remember what day it was…

Chapter 2

Connie Pushman arrived at the Pushman complex before seven a.m. She needed time to process the scene in the penthouse the night before. Never in her wildest dreams did she expect to find her husband with her lover or to be more precise, their lover, the one and only Francesca Sommers. That woman gave new meaning to the term double dipping. The biggest question was did they get together accidentally or did Francesca set out to use Henry as nothing more than a sugar daddy? She intended to get to the bottom of things.

The security guard on duty waved her through the gates and buzzed her in. The place was like a tomb and since everyone was off for three days the only lights on were the security lights. The only light in her office was from her computer. There were phone messages and e-mail messages waiting for her and before she could answer the first e-mail her cell phone rang. No surprise - it was Allison.

"You must be riding high this morning Allison, so much so you are blowing off work."

Why did Connie always have to be so acerbic, and especially this early in the morning? So far things had gone better than expected. There was nothing to link them to Lydiel's murder and soon with Connie's help and a little bit of luck fingers would begin to point towards Matt.

"Good morning to you, too! Yes I am pleased with the way things are going and I will be leaving for work shortly. I may need your help with something."

"Let me guess. Matt didn't fall for your seduction attempt and now you want to feed him a poison apple, collect his insurance and pay me back the money you owe me. Does that about sum it up?"

"Are you alright this morning Connie? I've never heard you quite so bitter before. Matt seemed preoccupied and not interested in talking or eating the wonderful dinner I prepared. No I don't want to poison him but I do want to toss a few crumbs to the police. I will get the money for you as soon as possible. I promise."

"Leave it alone Allison. Just leave well enough alone and let the investigation take its course.

Tempting fate could backfire. I needed the money the day your husband started snooping into Pushman financial affairs. I have work to do. Maybe we can have lunch later or something."

"Not today. I have a lot of work to catch up on at the office. We'll talk soon. Bye."

"Have a good day Allison. Good-bye."

Connie Pushman never wanted to talk to Allison McNulty again. She knew that in all likelihood she would never see her money and at this point it didn't matter. What did matter was the pain of betrayal she felt by Francesca's actions. Seeing her in bed with Henry had triggered anger she was unaccustomed to feeling. Until she had a firm plan in place, she was going to take her own advice and leave things alone.

Matt had his morning all planned. It was just a little after seven a.m. so he had lots of time before going to the morgue. First, he needed to make a quick stop at Pushman to review the folder outlining Lydiel's last wishes -which mortuary, the service etc. That always irritated him - how she could so casually discuss these things. She said the intent was to make it easy for him in case something happened, and to reduce the potential for outing him to Allison. Since discovering the missing money he had moved all of his important papers to his office at Pushman. As he approached the gate, the security guard left the guardhouse and walked over to his car.

"Good morning Mr. McNulty. We were informed that everyone had three days off. The building is pretty much shut down. Has anything changed? Mrs. Pushman is here also."

"No George, nothing has changed. I just have a few messages I need to take care of. How long has Mrs. Pushman been here?"

"Just a few minutes. Please let me know when you both are ready to leave as I am the only one here and I may be on rounds throughout the building."

"No problem. I will be sure to let Mrs. Pushman know."

The question of the day - why was Connie here and at this hour? Maybe the system was up and he could check the fundraiser financial pages. He would stop in on his way to his office. The door to Connie's office was open and Matt tapped lightly before entering.

"Oh Matt! You startled me. I didn't think anyone was here but me. I thought you knew Henry gave everyone three days off because of the computer problems."

"I didn't mean to frighten you Connie, but I thought if you had a few minutes we could see if the system was up and try to find the missing funds. I'm sure it is an accounting error."

Connie Pushman was surprised at how calm Matt seemed. It was as if nothing had happened. She also tried to hide her discomfort at his suggestion. With no employees to interrupt, she felt boxed in and out of options.

"I thought the IT people said it would be at least 72 hours before the system was up and running again."

"It never hurts to try. Let's boot up your computer and see what happens."

Connie turned on the computer, entered her password and the Pushman site appeared on screen. Clicking on the link to the financial pages the entire ball budget spreadsheet appeared.

"I guess you were right, Matt. It seems to be working just fine. What exactly are you looking for?"

"There seems to be a sixty thousand dollar discrepancy in the ball budget. It looks as if a vendor may have been paid more than once. Give me a few minutes while I take a look at all of the related accounts, then maybe we can get a handle on things."

Connie could hear her heart pounding in her ears as Matt scrolled through the pages. Those few minutes were turning into an eternity.

"I found the problem, and it was just as I suspected; an accounting error. It seems as if someone transposed the account numbers and sixty thousand dollars was either transferred from or deposited in the wrong account. Henry will be pleased and relieved. I have a few things I need to take care of so if you will excuse me… oh, by the way, the guard at the gate asked if you would let him know when you were ready to leave since he is working alone today. Have a good day."

Matt had no idea how good Connie's day had become, no idea indeed.

At last, she was free of Allison and soon she would be free of Francesca also.

Chapter 3

After he made the call to the funeral home, Matt returned phone messages from the country club, answered a few e-mails and left for the morgue. In spite of everything, he felt better knowing that the missing money was no longer missing, and that things could now get back to normal, at least for some.

The morgue was an old brownstone with cathedral windows;, and the commercial steel doors had replaced the original oak doors. He hesitated briefly before pressing the intercom button. A voice answered asking the nature of his business. Matt found it strange that someone would have to be buzzed into a building that housed dead people. After giving his name and reason for being there he heard the latch release on the door and he went inside.

He was surprised to see Nikki Jemison at the registration counter. She was in an animated discussion with the attendant when Matt signed in.

He wasn't sure why she was here and instinct told him it was not for consolation.

"Detective? Working on another case here?"

"Actually I was waiting for you, Matt. I thought I would accompany you to the holding area if you don't mind. I have a few more questions and I would like to witness the identification."

"I was under the impression that the body had been positively identified by Kat Garcia and this was just a formality."

Nikki was more interested in Matt's reaction to seeing Lydiel's body than anything else. Kat Garcia was a credible witness given the fact that she saw Lydiel everyday, and she never doubted her identification. Nikki instructed the morgue attendant to retrieve the body.

Matt took a deep breath as the stainless steel door was opened and the drawer rolled into view. As the sheet was slowly pulled down he felt his heart skip a beat. She looked ashen and so very cold. Her arms were down at her sides, the same arms that used to hug him and hold him. It was just a week ago that they were together and yet she was so very different,

different aside from being dead. Different as in something wrong but what could be wrong? Lydiel was dead, so very dead; that's what was wrong. He reached out to touch her, to take her hand in his one final time but pulled back. He had only seen her once without her earrings. Her only pieces of jewelry were the single pair of small gold hoops.

Turning away, he saw the funeral home courier waiting in the vestibule. He quickly scribbled his name on the forms and left the room. He didn't want to watch her body removed from the drawer. Back at the registration desk he signed out and started walking towards the door. Nikki had to run to catch up to him.

"Matt wait. We need to talk. I have a few more questions. I only need a few minutes, please."

Matt found it odd that Nikki would pick now to ask him more questions. He didn't want to spend any more time here than was absolutely necessary.

"Do we have to do this now? I need to let everyone know about the service. I've told you everything I know."

"Have you told your wife yet?"

Matt knew that question coming and also he knew that he needed to take care of it but now was just not the time.

"No, not yet. I will, soon, perhaps after the service."

"How are you going to make all of the necessary arrangements and attend the service without your wife, Allison, is it, finding out?

"I will manage, detective."

"You have two days. I am under orders to interview your wife day after tomorrow."

"I need three days, please. Do you know when I can claim Lydiel's personal effects and gain access to her house again?"

"I can't promise you anything. I suggest you tell your wife and soon."

With time working against him Matt needed to take action. As soon as he got home he e-mailed Henry with the details of the service for Lydiel. He also informed him that the missing funds were no longer missing and that the website was up and running. His next task was to talk with Allison.

"Allison McNulty…"

"It's me. What time will you be home tonight?"

"About five-thirty, why?"

"I think we need to talk."

"I see…"

"Please Allison. I'm very tired and I am not in the mood for sarcasm. I'll see you when you get home. Bye."

Were it not for the fact that the district manager was coming for a conference, Allison would have left immediately. Something was going on and her imagination was working overtime. Was he finally, finally going to confess his affair with his dead writer lover?"

Now that he knew where Allison would be for the next four hours or so Matt could get to work. It was time to call his favorite forensic information expert. Once the phone was answered Matt waited for the prompts, keyed in the codes and thank goodness the next voice was a familiar human one.

"Yes, Mr. Matthew, what can I do you for?"

It was good to hear Walter's voice again. They had been friends for over thirty years and although they didn't talk often, when one was in need the other was at his disposal.

"I need a favor old buddy. I am in a jam and I could use your help. I need you to hack into my computer at home and tell me exactly what is on my hard drive. Use my secure line at Pushman and Associates and I need it no later than 1400 hours."

"Since when are you working at Pushman? I thought you were doing the thermonuclear gig. What's your fancy shmancy title - chief suit in charge?"

He and Walter used to tease each other about never wanting jobs that required suits and the equally hated designer noose around the neck. Neither was the button down shirt corporate type. What they both were very good at was keeping the trust.

"Since the thermonuclear job blew up. Connie Pushman is an old school chum of Allison's and after months of looking for a job an opening came up in her husband's company. After awhile you start to think of the greater good like the mortgage, food, clothes for the boys; you know the drill."

Ah yes, Allison. Walter knew more about

Allison than he ever wanted to know and he had bore the brunt of her wrath the first time he told her no.

"Between you, me, and the gatepost, I had a gig at Pushman myself recently. What's going on there with the mainframe? I know your Mrs. Pushman. She summoned my help for a little site crashing. Seems some hot shot was this close to discovering some awkward financial manipulation on her part. You wouldn't know anything about that would you?"

That explained the rolling shutdown thing and the site being partially up and then totally down. It also explained why the site suddenly went down the day he was in Connie's office, and it may explain how the missing money really was missing at one time…

"Sorry, buddy, I was not privy to that activity. How long will it take you to do my computer?"

"Give me an hour or so and you will have everything. Given what I've just told you, are you sure want it to go to Pushman?"

"Good point. If you're certain that it will take no longer than an hour, send it here. I'll connect the fax machine. I owe you."

"Your debt and all future debts were paid in full when you saved my ass in the Orient, Matt. May the Force be with you."

Matt had a little over three hours to accomplish everything. There had to be some trail of the forty-seven thousand dollars somewhere in the house, but where? Allison didn't use the computer for the transaction. Where would she hide something like a receipt? He chose the bedroom closet as a starting point.

Moving aside shoes, boxes and bags, his watch caught on something, a skirt or dress. Freeing his arm he removed the hanger from the rod. He recognized the skirt. There was a rip near the hemline and a small piece of fabric was missing. Behind the skirt was the same bag Matt had seen that day near the printer. Ordinarily he wouldn't dream of going through her things but extreme circumstances dictated extreme measures. He replaced the hanger on the rod, and dumped the contents of the bag onto the bed. Rifling through the papers there were more transcript printouts but nothing relevant to the missing money. There was also a computer disk and a brown paper bag.

Sitting on the side of the bed he began to read the printouts. There were several hundred pages. So she knew! Now he understood why she was blowing off work, and he had a good idea of how she came into possession of the transcripted messages between him and Lydiel. At that moment Matthew McNulty hatched a plan, but he would have to put it on hold long enough for him to answer the door. In his haste to get to the door, several items spilled onto the floor.

"I hope I'm not disturbing you Matt. I wanted to drop these things off for the boys."

If there was one thing he didn't need right now was a visit from his mother-in-law. When he and Allison were first married Hannah had a bad habit of just dropping by at strange and inopportune times. This was one of those times.

"Thanks Hannah. I would invite you in but I am in the middle of a huge project and I need to finish before the boys get home."

"Oh that's fine, Matt. I'm on my way to the mall anyway. Allison asked me to pick these things up. Kiss them for me. Bye."

"Hannah, wait. I hate to ask but would it be possible for you to get the boys this evening? I'll feed them when they get home. Allison and I have some serious talking to do and it would be better if the boys weren't here. I know this is short notice and for that I apologize."

"Not a problem, Matt. We'll do homework together and enjoy some ice cream."

"Thanks Hannah and thanks for understanding."

"I'd better get to the mall now."

Why was Allison asking her mother to do things she should be doing herself? Why? Because she was too busy snooping. Now that she knew about the affair what was her game plan? Was she planning to leave him and take the boys? Lydiel was certain that the money was not being used to leave him, but rather help Connie out of some financial difficulty that she couldn't discuss with Henry. Matt could hear the fax machine beeping, signaling the transfer of information from Walter. As promised, it had taken less than an hour. He suddenly remembered the papers spread on the bed. Quickly putting everything back the way he found it, he closed the closet door and went downstairs to see what Walter had turned up. As he removed the last page, the phone rang. What now?

"Hello."

"Hey there old buddy. Did you get a chance to look at the information yet?"

"I was just about to do so. Why? Did you find anything?"

"You, my friend have a serious bugging problem. There is stealth software on your machine. It hasn't been residing there long but it has been accessed frequently. It seems that someone is very interested in your e-mail and instant message communications."

"I see. Is there any way you can remove it remotely?"

"Of course I can and I did. I figured since you had such a tight timeframe for the download, you wanted me to debug your machine as well. I also washed your hard drive by downloading a virus. I used an external hard drive and transferred all of your files and information. I will overnight it to you.

Remember though, the only way to completely remove data on a hard drive is to either blow up the hard drive or bury it."

"I am truly in your debt, Walter. It's almost 3 p.m. and I still have a couple of things to attend to."

"Glad I could help. Take care my friend."

"You too and thanks again."

"Matt? Do you know who did this?"

"I can't talk about it now, Walter. I'll be in touch. One more thing, do you remember when Connie first contacted you?"

"Yeah, about three weeks ago or so."

"Thanks buddy. I'll be in touch."

Matthew McNulty had a lot of work to do and a very narrow window of time to get it done. The first thing he did was to print out an old thermonuclear application plan. Next, he inserted Allison's disk into the CD drive and ripped the information from it to his computer. After the process was complete he hit erase, deleting the entire program. He replaced the pages of transcripts with the thermonuclear plans and the disk into Allison's bag and put it back in the closet as he found it.

Chapter 4

Francesca half-heartedly ate the soup and grilled cheese sandwich Henry had ordered for her. The sedative was finally wearing off and she was beginning to feel more like herself. Remey phoned earlier to let her know they would be arriving shortly. Francesca was not looking forward to seeing Doug. Their last meeting, although interesting, had not ended well. She got the distinct impression that she would not be welcomed back. When she told her sister about Henry, Remey reminded her of what a hypocrite she was, not only for her attitude towards Lydiel regarding Matt but the fact that she was sleeping with Connie's husband. She needed to get dressed and check her voicemail messages.

"Henry, have you seen my cell phone? I think it was in my purse but I can't find it there."

Henry seemed engrossed in work on his laptop and without looking up responded that he thought he last saw her purse in the closet.

"Henry?

"I'm sorry dear. I wasn't ignoring you. I was

taking care of a rather important business matter. I believe I saw your handbag in the closet. Would you like me to check for you?"

"Thanks. I need to jump in the shower and get dressed. My sister and her husband will be arriving shortly."

Henry was grateful that she had not asked him to join her. He wasn't feeling well. For some reason the shortness of breath he experienced yesterday had returned and he wouldn't have been up to a repeat performance. For the last two hours he had been pouring over the financial pages of the Pushman site, which was once again up, and running. Matt was right, and through an accounting error of some sort the money ended up in the wrong account. He experienced a fair amount of guilt for even considering Connie to be a thief. He was very happy that business could once more return to normal. For now he needed to get Francesca through the service for her mother.

The first thing Henry noticed when he opened the closet door was that one of his cufflinks was on the floor. Although he usually removed them when he took his shirt off, yesterday was a very different sort of day for him. Picking up the cufflink he found Francesca's purse. The message light was flashing on her cell phone and he recognized the number as Connie's cell phone number. Why on earth would Connie be calling Francesca? He put the phone back into her purse and placed it on the dining table. The chest tightness was still present. The pills weren't working as well as they used to. Henry made a mental note to speak to his doctor.

"Henry can you do my back for me, please?"

"But of course, dear. I am on my way."

Francesca had not slept well and the warm water felt good as did Henry's hands on her back. Whatever drug Henry had given her last night had produced strange dreams. Each dream was the same- Lydiel was reaching out to her but her words were inaudible. Each time she got close to her mother's apparition, it would disappear, only to reappear more grotesque each time. She was the color of death with watery vacant eyes that seemed to see through Francesca's soul. She woke up several times clammy from the cold sweat and palpitations. Once she imagined she heard the elevator doors open but soon realized it was just a part of a dream.

Chapter 5

Remey Anderson slid the keycard through the lock and opened the door to a well-appointed room that overlooked the river. Doug unloaded the bags from the luggage cart and thought about what an opportunist Francesca was. He would have felt better staying at a Holiday Inn Express. He was less than impressed with the opulence on display and felt very sorry for Henry Pushman. Knowing Francesca, she would be the death of him. He knew he was expected to accompany Remey but he hated being here. He hated everything about here and that was why he left. Every memory was a bad one.

Remey removed an apple from the welcome basket, and began munching loudly. She couldn't help but wonder who would attend her mother's memorial service. Lydiel had become a recluse and she seemed to have alienated every friend she ever made. She wrote to the exclusion of living, that is with the exception of her relationship with Matt. Doug was visibly uncomfortable and she hoped that he and Francesca would at least be civil to each other.

Francesca's last visit had nearly destroyed their marriage. Neither Doug nor Francesca was aware that she had seen them together in the garage. Never one for confrontation, Remey said nothing to either of them but she had become emotionally distant from Doug. Being together in close quarters for the next few days was not going to be easy. On the positive side she would finally get to meet Matt. Online he was a really hot guy and she was curious what he was like in person. She should call Francesca and let her know they had arrived.

Fresh from her shower and still wrapped in the warm robe, Francesca snuggled against Henry on the sofa. For some reason he didn't seem like himself. He was preoccupied and a little distant.

"Is everything okay Mr. P? You seem a little out of it."

"Yes, my dear, everything is fine. What time are your relatives arriving?"

"I was just about to give them a call. Did you find my cell?"

"It spilled from your purse in the closet. I put them both on the bed. I think I will give you some privacy and go check on the dinner preparations. I won't be long."

"You don't have to leave. Calling my sister is no big deal."

"I don't mind dear. I could use a little air."

Francesca was becoming concerned about Henry's health. He was pale and although the room was cool he was perspiring. Whatever was going on at work was spilling over into his off time. Enough of that, she needed to talk to Remey. The front desk attendant informed her that the Andersons had indeed checked in and were in Room 512.

The telephone rang so loudly it startled Doug.

"Hello?"

"Hello to you too."

Without uttering another word, Doug silently passed the phone to Remey. The look on his face told her that the caller was Francesca.

"Hi there. We made it in a little over an hour ago. Yes I know I should have called right away but we needed to wind down a little after the drive. Have you heard from Matt about the service? You know Doug. He isn't happy at all about being back. Have you talked to the others? Six sounds fine. I am anxious to meet both Henry and Matt. See you at six."

Upon hearing that dinner was at six p.m., Doug decided he might as well shower, shave and get dressed. This was a very long day that promised to get even longer as the evening wore on.

"Francesca says dinner is at six and Matt has yet to call with the time of the service."

"I gathered that. Isn't your Matt married? How is this entire scenario going to play out tomorrow? Surely his wife must have some idea about everything by now and I am not in the mood for domestic drama."

"First, he is not MY Matt. He was Lydiel's Matt. As to whether Allison knows or not, I have no idea. I doubt seriously if Lydiel's service will provide or provoke any drama, domestic or otherwise."

"How do you know his wife's name is Allison?"

Remey realized the slip as soon as she made it. Doug could never find out that she knew Allison

McNulty, or about her relationship with Connie Pushman or the role she played in Lydiel's murder.

"Francesca told me. She talked about her the last time we were together."

"Remey, as you know Lydiel and I had very limited interaction but it was a huge mistake to ever let Francesca find out about Matt. She is the most mean spirited, vicious, evil woman I have ever…"

"Doug, do we have to do this now? We should be getting ready for dinner."

With a sigh of resignation Doug let the matter drop. Damn that bitch! He wanted all of this to be over already.

Satisfied with the dinner arrangements, Henry waited for the penthouse elevators. The tightness in his chest seemed to be abating and that was a good sign.

Francesca was dressed and watching television when he returned to the penthouse. He checked his e-mail and found one from Matt detailing the arrangements for Lydiel's service.

"I've heard from Matt. Your mother's service will be tomorrow at 2 p.m. in the gatehouse on the edge of Whistler's Woods. There will be a reception afterwards at Mirelli's. I have an idea. Why don't you and I wait for Doug and Remey in the bar? I think we could both use a change of scenery."

Chapter 6

Why wasn't this working? Allison drummed her fingertips out of frustration as she tried the password over and over and was still unable to access the home computer. Just this morning she had been able to download more transcripts but nothing this afternoon. If she left now she had time to get to the electronics store and talk to the salesman before going home. What the hell did Matt want to talk about? For weeks she had demanded to talk to him and he always blew her off. Now that his slut was dead he suddenly wanted to talk. Maybe she didn't want to talk.

There were very few customers in the store when Allison arrived. She immediately found the salesman who took care of her and explained the situation. He logged onto the system and using her password fared no better than she had.

"This happens occasionally when a drive has been washed or fatally crashes. From here it seems as if your computer hard drive has crashed and the information stored on it is irretrievable. I'm sorry.

Kids hit a site or someone sends an e-mail attachment that downloads a virus that eats up the drive, and the only recourse is to purchase a new hard drive. We sell them here and they start at around six hundred dollars."

"Are you telling me that all of the files I had stored on my computer are now lost forever?"

"I'm afraid so. Would you like to see the drives we have here?"

"One more question, if I buy a new hard drive is there someone here who can install it for me?"

"Yes, we have a technician on duty during regular business hours. There is a seventy dollar bench charge. It takes about 45 minutes or so depending on how busy we are."

Allison knew she didn't have that much left on her credit cards. Maybe Connie's computer friend could help. Without a word Allison returned to her car, lit a cigarette and swore silently. If she hurried she could get to the bank before it closed. She could buy a new hard drive, get it installed and then download the files from Lydiel's computer that were just as good if not better. Reconciling the loss of her personal files and pictures, she took solace in the fact that she had the presence of mind to download several pages of dialogue between Matt and Lydiel. Matt was going to be pissed that his files from work, resume, and pictures were all lost. Oh well, shit happens. He would get over it, just like he would get over Lydiel Sommers.

With five minutes to spare, Allison walked up the teller and handed her the withdrawal slip. Almost immediately the bank manager was calling her over to his desk. What now?

"Mrs. McNulty? I see you wish to withdraw seven hundred fifty dollars from this account?"

Allison's senses were on full alert, and she could feel her heart pounding as she searched the bank manager's face for some clue as to what the problem could be.

"Yes, seven hundred fifty dollars. I know there is enough in the account so what is the problem?"

"I'm sorry but this account has been closed and there are no funds available."

"Closed? That's impossible. How could it be closed? There was at least one hundred thousand dollars in the account. Who closed it and when?"

"I don't have that information available Mrs. McNulty."

Allison's agitation was growing as she raised her voice. The tellers were all looking her way, and the security guard was walking towards the manager's desk. She knew she should get a grip but money didn't just disappear.

"Perhaps there was a clerical error. Could you please recheck the account?"

"I'm sorry we're closing now. If you could maybe return in the morning I'm sure the matter can be resolved."

"Perhaps the resolution is to take my money and my business elsewhere."

As soon as she uttered the words Allison realized how empty that threat was since she apparently no longer had money to move. Where could it have gone? She and Matt both were very careful about overdrafts. As much as he believed in the emergency fund, there was no way he would touch it. There had to be a simple explanation for all of this. Her mood darkened considerably as she drove home.

Chapter 7

Matt cooked dinner, fed the boys early and had them ready for Hannah when she arrived. After they left he poured a drink, settled himself on the sofa and waited for Allison. He had completed the arrangements for Lydiel, notified everyone and tried to prepare himself for what lay ahead. The plan had been to disclose his relationship with Lydiel and watch Allison's reaction, but he call from the bank manager changed things.

After pulling into the garage, Allison sat in the car for several minutes. The information about the computer and the bank account situation had given her one hell of a headache. If she asked Matt about it he would want to know how she knew. Also she would run the risk of being asked about the forty-seven thousand dollar withdrawal. How could this have happened? She couldn't deal with it now, she was too anxious to see what Matt had to say.

"Hi, I'm home."

"I'm in the living room, Allison."

"Where are the boys?"

"I cooked dinner, fed them and asked Hannah to help them with their homework so that we could have a chance to talk. I would like it if you wouldn't interrupt."

There was something ominous in the tone of Matt's voice that almost frightened her. This was a side of him she had rarely seen since they were married. He moved from the sofa to sit on the edge of the chair.

"I guess there is no easy way to say this. Things between you and I seemed to have virtually come to a standstill. We share space but not a life. This hasn't been a marriage for a very long time. I tried everything in every way I know how and yet it never seemed to make a difference to you. You made all of the decisions without talking to me about it. You tell me you love me to placate me, not because you feel that way. All of this hurt me and it doesn't seem to matter to you.

A good friend of mine passed away recently and since then I have done a great deal of thinking. It was never my intention to hurt you or the boys but I don't want to live like this anymore. I'm not happy and I don't think you are either. The memorial service is tomorrow and I will be there. After that, I think we need to discuss our options."

The rage building inside Allison McNulty was like an erupting volcano and if Matt thought for one minute that they were going to end on his terms he didn't know her at all.

"It certainly took you long enough to fess up didn't it? Did you seriously think I didn't know? How stupid do you think I am? The larger question is how stupid was she? Crumbs, that's all she ever got from you. That's all any of them will ever get from you because that's all I will ever allow. Those boys mean more to you than any woman ever will and just like I allow it, I can snatch the crumbs anytime I damn well please. I'm glad she's dead. Fair punishment I would say. So you go to your memorial service and you say good-bye to your slut, but you won't be saying goodbye to me unless it's on my terms."

Normally slow to anger, Matt felt as if he wanted to just scream. Allison was truly unbelievable. He regained his composure before he spoke.

"When it comes to stupidity Allison, you are the reigning queen. Do you think I don't know about the forty-seven thousand dollars you took from the emergency account? You never discussed the need for that amount of money with me. At this point one third of our emergency fund is missing and unaccounted for. I worked hard to build that fund and as my wife I trusted you enough to add you as a co-signer. I see that not only was my faith in you misplaced, so was my trust. At one time things between us were good or at least livable, but you changed so much. There are times now when I wonder..."

"When you wonder what? I never made it a secret that I wanted to get married. It was just a matter of getting you to that point so I did what was necessary. The kids were the final knots in the laces to keep you here. If I changed it is because I stopped pretending. I never felt about sex the way you do. I don't share your love of hobbies. But mark my words; leaving me is not going to be as easy as you think. As for the so-called missing money, I have no idea what the hell you are talking about. Talk about trust- you're a fine one to talk about trust. You go say your good-byes to your dead lover. Your family will be here when you come home. Right now I'm going to get my boys."

Allison slammed the back door so hard the kitchen windows rattled. Matt had remained much calmer than he imagined he would. Initially it was not his intention to mention the missing money but he took note of the fact that Allison never admitted to taking the money but admitted to knowing about the affair. He could now add liar and thief to her character traits. His cards were on the table. He had kept his word to Detective Jemison. The next move would be Allison's and knowing her as he did, it wouldn't take very long for her house of cards to come tumbling down. Allison revealed more cards than she intended. Matt never mentioned that the dead person was a woman or that they were lovers. Now if he could just get through tomorrow…

The more he thought about it, the more Matt realized how difficult tomorrow was going to be. Not only did he have to deliver the eulogy, he would have to deal with Remey and Doug as well as Henry's relationship with Francesca. He felt certain that Allison's joy at hearing the news of Lydiel's death had more to do with her idea that she was 'getting her husband back'. In his heart of hearts he knew she was involved somehow. He had been less than honest with Detective Jemison but tomorrow he would have another discussion with her. One thing was for sure, these last few days had seemed exceptionally long and exhausting.

Chapter 8

The Happy Hour crowd was swelling and the small bar inside the lobby of the Renaissance was growing. Francesca had one more bit of housekeeping to do before dinner. At this stage she could leave nothing to chance. Henry seemed better but not quite himself. He was much quieter than usual and still seemed pale around the edges.

"Henry? "

"Yes, my dear. What is it?"

"Can we not mention Remey's and Doug's financial difficulties?"

"It never crossed my mind to do so. I am most interested in meeting your sister. If she is anything like you Doug is a very lucky man."

Henry's penchant for tact and discretion made him all the more endearing to Francesca. He was anything but the kiss and tell type. Nothing would have been more disastrous than to have the subject of money come up at dinner.

"Why don't you call up to the room and see if our guests are ready for dinner? Tomorrow will be a very long day for all of us and we should turn in early."

More than anything Douglas Anderson wanted this farce over with. He detested final sendoffs; he detested Francesca and her never-ending schemes that always ended up hurting someone, and more than anything he hated the hypocrisy. Remey and Lydiel had a love hate relationship with more hate than love on Remey's part. The fact that her mother had refused to lend her money ended whatever shred of relationship that existed. Of course Francesca further fueled the estrangement by informing Remey that Lydiel had helped one of the other girls. It turned out not to be true but the damage was done.

"Rem? Are you almost ready?"

Before she could respond the telephone rang and against his will and better judgment Doug had to answer it.

"Let me guess…?"

"You get three and the first two don't count. Hello to you too. Are you two ready to make an appearance?"

"Not really but we will see you in the restaurant in a few minutes and Francesca- no drama, please."

"Now would I cause drama, lover? We are going to have a nice enjoyable dinner, I promise."

Douglas Anderson was losing his patience and his mind. He wanted to run as fast and as far as his fifty year old legs would carry him from this awful place and these awful people.

"Rem please, can we get this over with?"

"Geeze Louise! Why are your boxers in such a bunch? It's just dinner and yes I'm ready."

Thinking back to his last dinner with Francesca, one thing Douglas Anderson was certain of was that this time it WOULD be just dinner.

"What's the word Francesca, are they on their way down?"

Henry Pushman felt awkward meeting Francesca's family in such a public place. As many times as he had spent the night here with her, it was always in the privacy of the penthouse. He doubted if he would run into anyone he or Connie knew, but there was always that possibility. For that reason he had arranged a table in the small private dining room adjacent to the main dining room.

"Doug said they would be along shortly. You know how long it takes women to get ready."

Francesca sensed Henry's discomfort and suggested they be seated and have the Maître D escort Remey and Doug to the table when they arrived. She knew she would have to take control of the situation and once the introductions were made they managed to get through the meal amicably. Doug and Henry were engrossed in a conversation about business ventures and it seemed like the perfect time for her and Remey to retreat to the powder room. Making sure they were alone, Remey started talking a mile a minute. Francesca knew she needed to rein her sister in quickly. She couldn't have her falling apart now.

"Whoa Remey, slow down will you? All I know is that she's dead and Matt's handling her affairs. It seems her neighbor found the body. The police are being very tight-lipped about the investigation. A Detective Jemison has requested an interview the day after tomorrow."

"Are you sure there is nothing to tie us to this and why is HE handling her affairs Francesca? He isn't family. What about the will?"

"My guess is that Matt was the one person she trusted and that in all probability he is the Executor of her estate, and that makes him the one to read the will. What do you think of Henry? Nice isn't he?"

Remey had better sense than to disagree with anything Francesca said. Her opinion of Henry was that he was some rich schmuck who for some reason fell under her sister's spell; more specifically he was P-whipped. Francesca always bragged about having a power puss and given what Remey had witnessed in the garage that day perhaps she was right.

"He seems very nice, sis. I'm sure Connie thinks so too. Does she know about the two of you?"

"I seriously doubt that our little Connie would ever dream that I was sleeping with both of them. I never understood why she and Allison were friends. They are as different as night and day."

"You have a lot of nerve Francesca. Of all the men in the world, why Connie's husband?"

Remey was asking too damn many questions and now was not the time.

"I think we better get back to the men. We will have lots of time to talk tomorrow after the service."

"Before we go Francesca, who else will be there tomorrow?"

"Doreen..."

Chapter 9

Gary Minter knew they were no closer to bringing in a suspect than they had been almost a week ago. After examining all of the recalled inhalers it was determined that this was an isolated incident. Both the pharmacist and the tech had been ruled out as suspects. Kat Garcia remained hospitalized and unavailable for interview. His feeling was if anyone fit the profile it was McNulty. Any guy who is cheating on his wife has things to hide, lots of things, and was probably an expert at lying. He had no idea why Jemison was dragging her feet in bringing him in for interrogation.

Nikki's gut instinct told her that the killer was a woman. Matthew McNulty had no motive to kill Lydiel Sommers. From the e-mails and other correspondence on her computer it was obvious that he cared a great deal for her. If anyone had motive to kill Lydiel it was Allison McNulty, although Matt seemed to feel that she might have her suspicions but nothing more. Nikki knew from personal experience that most women in Allison's situation knew their husbands were having an affair, and many times they knew who the other woman was. How they handled that knowledge varied greatly, but homicide was often a result. The next 48 hours would hopefully begin to unravel the mystery. Matt had assured her that he would tell his wife about the affair and she had no reason to think otherwise. Tomorrow was going to be very difficult for him.

The worst thing about this whole case was Minter. He was virtually useless. His sarcasm and willingness to draw factless conclusions were a distraction for her. Neither Matt nor his wife was going anywhere and there were a few things she needed to do before she interviewed them. In the meantime she had dragged her feet long enough and it was time to see what pieces, if any Minter could add to the puzzle.

Gary Minter believed in God, the bible, and punctuality. He also believed in marital fidelity. The fact that Nikki Jemison was almost an hour late irritated him immensely. He had gone over his notes several times, finding not one common thread. He looked up as the door swished open.

"Is the case solved and suspects in custody Detective Jemison?"

"Can the sarcasm Minter. I've had a very long day and I am not in the mood for it. Tell me what you found out."

"Just what you would expect-nothing, nix, nada, zip. We know the pharmacist and his tech are in the clear. We know that this was an elaborate underground deal with lots of money being exchanged. It ain't easy to find pre-filled hot pepper inhalers so someone had to put it all together. They had to have a way to get them inside the Sommers' babe's house and there is only one person who could do that-your cheating ex-beau."

My theory is that the Sommers' babe was pressing him to end it with the little woman. He resisted so someone dropped a dime to the wife; she gave old Matt an ultimatum: 'keep your cock behind the zipper and ditch the bitch or else I'm taking you to the cleaners'. McNulty tried to break it off once more, the Sommers' babe threatened him and he dusted her. He has connections."

"My, my, my. Are you including gift-wrap and ribbon on that package? You never cease to amaze me Minter. The less work you do, the more creative your conclusions are. First, if I hear you refer to the deceased once more as 'the Sommers babe' I will have you taken off the case and transferred to traffic where you don't have to deal with people. Second, other than your personal bias against men who have affairs, you have no basis to assume Matthew McNulty was the only one who had access to her house. After all who was it that discovered the body? Third, why would Matt eavesdrop on his conversations with Lydiel? Makes no sense. Your theory has more holes in it than a sieve. Now what say we get down to real police work.

Tomorrow while everyone is attending the memorial service let's interview the wife, Allison McNulty. The service is scheduled for two p.m. so plan on being ready to go about two-thirty p.m. or so, and Minter, warehouse that unprofessional demeanor of yours. I need you to be sharp tomorrow, and oh by the way, that so-called 'note' you found turned out to be a page from a new novel she was working on, so much for conclusions."

Nikki had been very careful about revealing too much to Minter. When they were together she could muzzle him when necessary, but left to his own devices he was a very scary man. She deliberately neglected to reveal the discovery of a swatch of fabric that matched nothing in Lydiel's closet and the pair of cotton gloves.

So the game plan had changed. Minter distinctly remembered Nikki saying the McNulty's were being interviewed together. Now she was planning to corner the wife. What did she know that he didn't?

"I understand the Sommers' house is no longer a crime scene and that her family has access?"

Minter was fishing and Nikki knew it. It was common practice to clear a crime scene after a week or so, especially a residence. She was not going to give him what he was looking for.

"True. The forensic guys are done, including the coroner. Her personal effects will be released to Matt McNulty tomorrow."

The guy had too much control over things for

Minter's taste. Lydiel Sommers had a family yet she left McNulty in charge of her affairs. Something was not right with that picture.

Chapter 10

Jeffrey Williams was working a double and on his fourth break of the day. The extra shift provided him additional opportunities to search the security tapes. Most people had no idea that in a thirty-day period there were almost five hundred tapes to review from different cameras positioned to cover the entire hospital campus. To the best of his recollection, which was not always the best, the incident occurred in the third week of the month. His biggest problem so far was being able to watch a tape long enough to find what he was looking for.

The second shift guy called off, as did the patrol officer so Jeffrey was doing double duty in more ways than one. This was the last tape from that time period. As the tape began to roll, he thought about Lydiel Sommers. There was no longer a patrol car stationed outside her home and no more gawkers. He read that a private memorial service would be held for her tomorrow. What a way to meet your maker, murdered in your own home.

He fast-forwarded the tape to the approximate

time of the call. Slowing the tape as much as possible, he saw himself confronting the reporter. The picture wasn't as clear as he would have liked but you could clearly see what she wearing. Jeffrey stopped the tape, marked it with a small piece of red tape and inserted the next cassette. With any luck this one would show her car, and the police officer that ticketed her. Advancing it to the approximate time, he saw the cop placing the ticket on her windshield. He let the tape run a little longer and saw the woman remove the ticket and enter her vehicle. He tried zooming in but could only make out her right hand fumbling with something in the car. Maybe the woman saw something while she was watching the house that might prove useful to the police. Ejecting the tape, he marked it with the red tape and placed a rubber band around the two cassettes. His next move was to call police headquarters to get the names of the investigating officers. Before he could make the call, he heard a familiar voice.

"Wellll, look who's back and with a gimp leg to boot? If it isn't the real Bat Man! How did Gotham City ever survive without you?"

Sgt. William Jemison had known Jeffrey since he was eight years old and had never missed an opportunity to tease him since helping him get the job at the hospital. Bill considered security officers wannabes.

"Very funny you old coot. I see they have you working afternoons now. Since you are here, maybe you can give me some info. Who is the investigating officer in charge of the Lydiel Sommers case?"

"This is your lucky day sonny boy. It is none other than my little sis Nikki."

Great. The last time Jeffrey saw Nikki he made a fool of himself. Why he ever thought she would go out with him...

"I see. How is the investigation coming along?"

"Not sure Jeffrey. She isn't confiding in me these days and the investigation is ongoing. My time here is up. Catch you later and take care of that leg."

Why did it have to be Nikki? He would have to swallow his pride for the greater good and give her the information. She was the best investigator on the force and if anyone could get to the bottom of this case it was her. It was nearly five p.m. but maybe he could catch her before she left for the day. He dialed the number from memory.

Nikki Jemison signed off on the last report, grabbed her bag and was almost at the door when the phone rang. Her first inclination was to just let it ring but unanswered phones were a pet peeve of hers.

"Homicide, Detective Jemison…"

"Nikki, it's Jeffrey, Jeffrey Williams."

Oh no, just what she needed, the lovesick security guard from the hospital. What could he possibly want? Her brother Bill had tried to fix them up numerous times but Nikki always found a reason to cancel the date. She hoped it was not another invitation out.

"Jeffrey. What a surprise. What can I do for you?"

"Yes, I'm sure it is. I'm working a double shift today and I was wondering if you could drop by the hospital. I think I have something you might be interested in."

"And just what might that be Jeffrey? I have had a very long day and the hospital is a twenty-minute drive out of the way for me. Can't you please tell me what it is?"

"I think it might help with your investigation of the Lydiel Sommers murder."

"I am on my way, and Jeffrey, this had better not be some scheme you and my brother cooked up. I am not in the mood for games."

Rush hour traffic was almost at a standstill on the beltway. Nikki reached for the magnet light, put it on the roof of her Ford Taurus and inched her way through traffic until she found a clear zone. She tried to imagine what it was Jeffrey knew that would help her. Maybe he knew Lydiel or spoke with her. Whatever it was she hoped it would be enough to conclusively exclude Matt as a suspect.

It took less time than she anticipated and Jeffrey was waiting for her when she arrived. He explained the events of that day and why he thought the tapes might help her locate the woman in them.

"I know it could be a wild goose chase but she was watching that house for quite a while before I was able to answer the call. I didn't think anything about it at the time because crazy reporters are always hanging around hospitals looking for a story, but she was different. She was too well dressed, and I didn't see a camera, a note pad or a tape recorder. I wish I could stay longer and review the tapes with you but I'm the only one working this evening. Let me know if you need anything else and please get the tapes back ASAP. Take care Nikki."

Why would a well-dressed woman hide in the bushes to stake out Lydiel's house? Her reclusiveness was hardly fodder for the tabloids, and she was far from being a major player in the literary world. Tossing the cassettes into her bag, Nikki realized she hadn't eaten since breakfast. Lydiel Sommers would have to take a backseat, at least until after dinner.

Chapter 11

Francesca resented the fact that there was going to be a memorial service. Why prolong things? Matt had insisted that it was Lydiel's last wish but she had a feeling that he was doing it for other reasons as well, namely to meet Remey and Doug.

Francesca deliberately seated herself between him and Henry and took every bit of license that she could to remind him of the last time they met. Fighting with his free hand underneath the table, he let her know that he was not buying into her little scheme, but no matter, she knew there would be other opportunities. Doug was weak. Right now a shower and the comfort of the king size bed in the penthouse snuggled against Henry were uppermost on her list of priorities.

Henry was thankful to see the evening end. During dinner he soon discovered that Remey and Francesca were nothing alike. Remey chatted incessantly about their other siblings and why in all probability none of them would say good-bye to their mother. Francesca was unusually quiet and restrained, and Douglas Anderson had the most vacant stare Henry had ever seen in anyone. Quiet and sullen, he contributed sparingly to the conversation. There was undeniable animosity between the three of them and their not so subtle attempts to mask it were disheartening to him. Agreeing to meet for brunch at eleven a.m. the next morning, Henry and Doug shook hands and the two couples parted for the night.

As soon as they returned to the penthouse Francesca wasted no time getting undressed and slipping into the shower. The hot water soothed the aggravation of the evening. Doug was such a piece of work. Poor Remey.

"Would you like to join me in the shower Mr. P?"

The tightness in Henry's chest seemed to be playing cat and mouse. All during dinner it was blessedly absent, only to return in the elevator. He had excused himself at dinner to make a quick call to his physician who advised doubling the dosage of his medication until he could be seen later in the day tomorrow after the service. He didn't want to disappoint Francesca; after all it was only a shower.

"Certainly my dear, just give me a few moments please."

Henry felt the pulsing in his neck as he slowly unbuttoned his shirt. He sat down on the edge of the bed to remove his trousers and felt the tightness intensify. He forced himself to choke back the fear as he took several slow deep breaths.

"Henry? Are you okay?"

"Fine, Miss Francesca Sommers, just fine."

Remey Anderson was just as animated and as talkative in the elevator as she had been at dinner, commenting on everything from Henry's tie to the es-car-got. She talked as she opened the door to their room, as she undressed, and even when she was lying down.

Douglas Anderson was not a passionate man. To him making love to his wife was done either out of necessity or the result of her intimate cajoling. Remey had never been sexually adventurous, just available. Having sex with her was a mediocre short-lived and unrewarding exercise in exchanging bodily fluids.

Tonight, however, for the first time in a very long time he was almost savage with her; sucking her nipples so hard he heard her wince. Pulling her hair back, he bit her neck as he pushed her thighs apart. He entered her deeply, ravaging her and taking her over and over until the throbbing ache ceased.

Clutching the covers and moving to the far side of the bed, Remey looked at her near rapist husband as if he were a stranger.

"Wh, wh, where did that come from?"

"Thank your sister. Good night."

Chapter 12

Allison McNulty tightened her grip on the steering wheel as she gunned the engine of the car. Pity the fool who truly believed confession was good for the soul, and pity Matt if he thought for one minute that she felt any responsibility for him having an affair. Lighting a cigarette, she replayed the day that changed everything in their marriage and her life. Although it had been ten years, the memory was as fresh as if it had occurred yesterday. He created the issues, not her. She had tried to go along but she resented him for it. He was the selfish one, not her. Fortunately the biggest issue had been dealt with. She knew she needed to calm down before picking up the boys. She noticed Connie's lights were still on.

Braking the car to a screeching halt, she decided to call her first. As soon as she heard Connie's phone ringing, she heard a beep. As soon as she clicked over she realized who it was.

"Alli, we need to talk. There has been a change in the plan."

Allison could barely hear the message over

Connie's yapping mutt. That was the most irritating canine.

"What's going on? Has there been some sort of change in the service?"

"Not that I know of, but the plan has changed and there is nothing I can do about it. I need to go."

"Wait! Did you take care of that little matter we discussed?"

"No. The time wasn't right."

'Thanks for letting me know. Take care of yourself. Bye."

"Be careful Alli."

As Allison McNulty sat in Connie Pushman's drive she seriously wondered if this evening could get any worse.

"Allison? What on earth are you doing sitting there? You are driving the dog nuts. Please, come in."

Connie could only hazard a guess as to what had set Allison off THIS time. She should be very happy knowing that Lydiel's memorial service was tomorrow and that so far the investigation had turned up no viable suspects.

"What is it Allison? What NEW thing has set you off?"

"I'm not in the mood Connie. Matt and I had a talk, or rather he talked and I listened. He confessed to his affair with his slut. He had the nerve to try to make it seem as if I was the reason he cheated. Can you imagine that? His cock gets restless and he blames me. Then, as if to add insult to injury he told me that after the service tomorrow he and I needed to sit down and discuss our options. What options? He will be locked up."

"Seriously Allison, after ten years who could blame Matt for having an, um, 'restless' cock? You are the one who doesn't like sex, not him. Frankly I'm surprised he hasn't left you before now."

"Go ahead and be smug. At least I knew who he was fucking. Can you say the same thing about Henry?" You think people are your friends and then one day you see them for who they really are?"

"Allison, you are rambling. I told you that I knew Henry was seeing someone and that he told me about it."

"Yes, but did he tell you whom he was seeing?

Did he tell you he was fucking the brains out of your dear, dear friend Francesca Sommers? I saw them together weeks ago. There is something else also."

Connie was certain that whatever emotion Allison saw registered on her face was definitely misinterpreted. If there was ever any doubt as to how vicious Allison could be, her latest tirade confirmed it. Allison caused pain with reckless disregard and if there was any justice in this world…

"Yes dear, I know all about it, all about Henry and Francesca. You said there was more?"

Connie never ceased to amaze. When Allison first learned of Lydiel and Matt she was livid and she wanted to hurt them and hurt them badly. Connie acted as if it were the most normal thing in the world for Henry to be screwing her young protégé.

"I went to the bank today to get money to buy a new hard drive. As it turns out there is no more money in our emergency fund. For some reason the account was closed and no information was available as to why.

"Did you mention it to Matt?"

"Of course not. Then he would know that I

was messing with the account."

Allison had just given Connie the key to the escape hatch. It was now obvious that she would be unable to repay the sixty thousand dollar loan.

"I see. How does this impact on your ability to repay me the money I put up for your little murder plot?"

"Money! Is that all you care about? My God, things are falling apart like straws from an old broom and all you worry about is money. I don't know where the money is coming from. Have your IT buddy screw around with the computers again for awhile."

"Forgive me Allison, was this your final destination for the evening or were you on some other mission of madness?

"Oh my God, the boys! I forgot all about the boys! They are with my mother. I have to go. Can we talk in the morning?"

"Of course dear. Do drive safely. "

Connie watched Allison back out of the drive and made a mental note to type a letter tomorrow…

Chapter 13

Holding her double-decker sandwich in one hand and the remote in the other, Nikki watched the first of the two security tapes. Just as Jeffrey described, there was a woman who appeared to be lurking in the bushes. She did appear overdressed for a spy. Zooming in didn't help much. She finished her sandwich and ejected the tape. Black and white security tapes are always grainy and often make identifications difficult. Before she had a chance to start the other tape the phone rang.

"Coming mother, well not really but coming, whoever you are."

"Hello?"

"Sorry to call you at home Nikki but your brother gave me your number. Did you get a chance to look at the tapes?"

"Hi Jeff. No problem. I just reviewed the first one. I do see the woman seemingly hiding in the bushes and you approaching her. Can you tell me anything in the way of a physical description or maybe what she was wearing?"

"I just got a call I have to take care of but if you can come around in the morning, we can sit down and I will tell you as much as I remember. I have to go."

Nikki refreshed her drink and put the other tape in. Rewinding it a few frames to better understand the scene Jeff marked, Nikki could plainly see Jeff escorting a female east on Spearhead Drive. Slowing the tape down as much as she could she was still unable to make out the woman's face but like Jeff she too saw the woman remove something from the windshield, enter the car and reach over to do something inside the car. If she had to make an educated guess, it appeared that the woman reached into the glove box. The camera angle did not provide a clear shot of the license plate so first thing tomorrow she would have the guys in traffic run every ticket issued on that date on Spearhead Drive and then try to match it up with the description of the car. Hopefully this would lead to the identification of the mystery woman.

Nikki ejected the cassette, replaced the rubber bands and dropped them into her bag. Tomorrow was shaping up to be a very busy day.

Jeffrey Williams leaned back in the chair, propped his injured leg on the edge of the desk and closed his eyes. He tried to recall the events of the day he saw the reporter watching Lydiel Sommers' house. He remembered how startled she was to see him and also how resistant she was when asked to move along. There was nothing remarkable about her looks. What was noticeable was the fact that she was wearing all the wrong clothes to be hiding in bushes; a long skirt and sweater. Jeffrey prepared a rough sketch for Nikki, answered his last call and left for home.

Chapter 14

Standing in front of the full length mirror, Matthew McNulty could swear he felt her lips brush past his ear. He could hear her laughter, and he could feel her tears, soft and warm, trickling down her face. He wanted to hold her once more, to kiss her, to make love to her, and to tell her that he missed her. There were many things left unsaid between them but she understood. The trouble was he didn't understand and he wasn't sure if he ever would.

After trying to straighten his tie for the millionth time, he decided to ditch it. He hated the tie, he hated the suit, and he hated what this day would hold. How does a man eulogize his mistress? For all these months he had been so careful not to lose himself in the relationship. He tried with everything he had to remain detached, as though he were observing his own life from a distance. This was how he protected his heart. He had been so careful not to do or say anything that would construe any type of commitment. Whatever had been between them was genuine and sincere and it never should have ended like it did.

Matt checked his pocket for the CD she wanted played at the service. He opened the jewel case and found a note. Damn her! Damn her! Even in death she was having the last word.

"Hi handsome. If you are reading this I guess it's a done deal. I hope the ending suited the story. So what barbecue sauce did you decide on? I hope you are smoking one of your favorite cigars as you read this. I did my best you know. No flowery send-off please, just be yourself and wow them all. I know how you hate it but I get to tell you for the last time- I love you. You were the best part of my life. Take care of your handsome self and my girl. Kisses lover, Lydiel."

Whoever did this, whoever killed her would pay and pay dearly, but for now he needed to get to Mirelli's to check on the luncheon arrangements.

Allison McNulty had been up for hours going over the conversation with Matt. He had chosen a dead mistress over her and his family. The irony was that his choices and his options meant nothing because soon he wouldn't be free to exercise either one. The luckiest break was the fact that the mousy and nosey neighbor Kat somebody was so traumatized from finding Lydiel's body she was unable to speak so there was no way she could recall seeing Allison at Lydiel's. She had been watching Matt prepare for the big sendoff and thought how utterly laughable the situation was. Her husband was trying to secretly mourn his dead mistress.

Matt grabbed the folder he needed for the service and headed for the garage. He had been very careful to avoid any confrontation with Allison. His first problem of the day came into view as the garage door opened - a flat tire, and whether he liked it or not he had to deal with *her*.

"Allison, I need the keys to the other car, mine has a flat. I called road service but I can't wait for them to get here. I should be back in an hour or so. If you need to go somewhere maybe Connie could drop you off or you can wait until I get back."

"What makes this my issue, Matt? What difference could an hour make one way or the other?

It isn't as if she's going anywhere."

Matt was determined not to play her game. He was trying to remain as calm as possible, take care of business at Mirelli's and pick Doreen up for the service.

"I really don't have time for this, Allison. Where are the keys?"

Allison tossed the keys to Matt and went back to her auction show. A huge smile crossed her face as she heard the door close. She wondered where Sarah had disappeared to - maybe she was double dipping and doing a play at the same time she was working for Allison, or maybe what happened frightened her and she left town as suddenly as she arrived. She made a mental not to ask the girls.

Matt backed the car out of the garage, closed the door and reached for his cigar. Damn! He left his lighter in his bomber jacket. Maybe Allison had a lighter in the glove box. As soon as he opened the small door, papers started to fall out. Moving things around he found the lighter, picked up most of the papers and closed the door.

Chapter 15

Connie Pushman sat staring at the blank screen of her computer monitor as she organized her thoughts. She spent most of the night thinking about the turns her life had taken recently - dishonesty, betrayal and the loneliness. Allison had been almost manic in her cruelty. She had known for quite some time that Matt had been seeing someone and that Lydiel was not the first, but it had never once crossed her mind to tell Allison. She felt it was not her place and in her own way she quietly championed Matt's cause.

Over the years Allison had become so punitive, taking her meanness and bitterness out on everyone including her own mother. The boys preferred the company of their dad and even their grandmother to that of their mother. Work had been replaced by her obsession to kill her husband's mistress, church and alienating her friends. Allison Woodall McNulty was on a course of self-destruction and she was unceremoniously dragging everyone with her.

With the twins grown and away at college and

Henry entrenched in his liaison with Francesca, it was time for Connie to look out for herself. She poured herself another cup of coffee and began the letter…

For Henry Pushman the sight of the morning sun signaled the survival of another night. He knew he was being foolish and reckless taking Viagra with his heart condition, but he was enjoying hot steamy sex with a passionate woman who was only too willing to fulfill his every desire. Many times recently he wished he had met someone like Francesca when he was younger. As successful as he was, he considered his life an unhappy waste. He did love Connie when they were married, but he soon realized that it was all wrong and for all the wrong reasons. He thought about ending it on more than one occasion but there were the twins to consider, and the business and a thousand other useless excuses he used to convince himself to stay. He was weak and he paid the price for it.

Francesca was like a dream, but so young; too young in fact to be saddled with someone Henry's age. He cared so very much and he enjoyed doing things for her that lovers do for each other. These last few days had been eye openers and he knew it was time to make some changes. Most of them had been taken care of but there was one important one that remained. Henry picked up the telephone and completed the one final task.

Remey Anderson was stiff and sore and she hurt in places long married women should not hurt. Her breasts were bruised as was her neck and other places she couldn't see. She had no idea what horny bug had bitten Doug but she found nothing passionate about brutal savage sex that felt like being raped. Where was the nerdy quiet guy she fell in love with? Douglas Anderson was an innocent and for the most part boring, but last night it was as if all of his pent up frustrations had been released.

So much had happened in the last few months; the planning, the preparation and finally the end of Lydiel. Truth be told Remey was more interested in being within reach of Matt than she was memorializing her mother. With Lydiel out of the way maybe she could be a source of comfort to Matt.

For her it seemed as if the morning was creeping along far too slowly.

Douglas Anderson felt ashamed. Self-loathing had always been his strong point but today even more so. Sitting at that table last night with Francesca's hand in his lap, slowly stroking him through his trousers, it was all he could do not to fuck her right then, and there with total disregard to the others. She had a way of triggering an ache like no other woman he had ever been with. When he was in the elevator with Remey he wanted to tear into her; he wanted to pin her against the wall and fuck her until she screamed. As it was he did the same thing, albeit much more savagely in their room. He needed to feel her warmth and wetness wrapped around his hardness. He needed to feel the hardening of her nipples as his tongue played in circles, and the taste and feel of her breasts as he suckled them like a baby. Remey never refused him sex but she never gave life to it. He wanted to feel her mouth engulf him, he wanted to feel her hands caress him and instead he got an almost wooden response. Damn that Francesca! Damn her to hell!

Upon awakening Francesca Sommers stretched like a sleeping cat. Her long slender limbs flexed and relaxed as her eyes adjusted to the lamplight in the room. Last night had been her first attempt at selfish love with Henry and he seemed genuinely pleased with her efforts. Her stint as a paid companion had paid off handsomely and she knew how to please a man. It was obvious during dinner and even before that Henry was not himself and definitely not up to a night of wild physical sexual activity. Her hands and mouth had worked their magic and Henry had bathed her throat with his warm, delicious orgasmic release. Before Francesca was out of the bathroom, Henry was sleeping peacefully. As for her, the little battery operated purple pill did the trick, and not too long afterwards she too fell into a deep restful sleep; the first one since hearing of Lydiel's death. Tomorrow was going to be quite a day as she would actually meet Matthew McNulty in the , and who knows, with any luck if she played her cards right she might get to press that handsome flesh.

Chapter 16

Nikki Jemison was up early and at headquarters before 7 a.m. She had lots to do before her interview with Allison McNulty and she wanted to be prepared. Last night she e-mailed a request for the ticket search and with any luck the results would be in by now. Taking one look at the 'sludge pot' as she called it, she opted to pass on coffee this morning. She turned on her computer and searched for the record of parking violations for the day in question. While she was waiting the desk sergeant appeared at her door.

"There's a woman on the phone for you. She wouldn't give me a name but she said it had to do with the Sommers case. She's on line one."

Nikki pressed the button for line 1 but there was no one on the other end. The day was off to a strange start. The violation search still wasn't completed so she decided to stop by the hospital and get the description of the mystery woman from Jeffrey.

On the drive to the hospital she tried to figure

out who the woman on the phone could possibly have been. It would be too much to hope that someone, anyone, including the mystery woman was suffering an attack of conscious and decided to come forward with vital information. In light of the way Lydiel died Nikki felt certain there were no witnesses to her death, but there had to be someone who knew how she died and who was responsible. Routine calls like that one are never traced, however, Nikki had left instructions that if anyone called for any reason the calls were to be forwarded to her cell phone immediately.

Jeffrey was waiting for her with a sketch and a detailed description of the woman. Bob was wrong about Jeffrey. He was anything but a wannabe. During her years on the force Nikki had seen cops who weren't as observant and detailed as Jeff. The first one that came to mind was Minter. As promised she returned the tapes but asked if he would keep them handy in case they were needed again for the case. Thanking him profusely for what might turn out to be the first real lead, Nikki was off to meet Minter.

Gary Minter finished his prayers, dressed and prepared to meet Nikki Jemison for breakfast at the usual cop hangout. A hopeless compulsive obsessive, he wiped the cover of the old bible clean, neatly replaced it on the bedside table and wiped the doorknob as he secured the front door. He was not looking forward to the events of the day. He thought it was a huge mistake interviewing Allison McNulty without her cheating husband present. You could tell a lot about a person by their reactions and responses, and he felt it was high time Matthew McNulty was put on the hot seat. Obviously Jemison felt otherwise. It was strange not to have one solid lead this late in the investigation. Canvassing Spearhead Drive had proven fruitless. It was as if Lydiel Sommers only existed in her house and maybe her books. Jemison was being very closed mouthed about things on her end, which made Minter more suspicious of her relationship with Matt McNulty. He saw her turning into the restaurant parking lot just ahead of him.

Chapter 17

Mirelli's was totally empty when Matt arrived. He discussed the arrangements for Lydiel's repast with the manager. Henry had paid for the luncheon with a company check that Matt promptly handed over. Satisfied with everything, Matt decided to call home to check on his tire. He needed his car. As he reached into his pocket for his cell phone Allison's keys fell to the floor. As Matt picked them up he noticed one seemed much newer than the other. It was a door key- a Schlage key. The only locks those keys fit were the ones found on older homes. As a matter of fact, it looked a lot like his keys to Lydiel's house. Before he could dwell on the keys any longer he heard Allison's voice on the line.

"Hello?"

"Hi, it's me. Any word on the tire yet?"

"The guys were here about twenty minutes ago and it's all done. I need to go out later so when are you bringing my car back."

"I'm leaving Mirelli's now so I should be there in say fifteen minutes. Bye."

Allison held the phone for a couple of minutes after Matt hung up. Good-bye to you too. Settling back on the sofa she returned to her auction shows. At one point she considered calling Connie but given the exchange between them last night she felt maybe she should give her a little space. Although she denied it, Allison was sure it was a shock to Connie to learn that Henry was screwing Francesca Sommers. For God's sake, didn't either of these men have a conscience?

There was something about that key that was bothering Matt. Why would Allison have a new door key on her key ring and whose door did it unlock? After parking Allison's car next to his, he decided to enjoy a few puffs of his cigar before going inside. Reaching over to the glove box he noticed a scrap of paper lying on the passenger side floor mat. The piece of paper turned out to be a parking ticket and it was at least three weeks old. How many times had he told her to always pay traffic tickets promptly? Being inconvenienced by having to walk a little was a lot cheaper than a ticket and this one was for parking in front of a fire hydrant.

Matt stubbed out the cigar and threw the ticket back into the glove box. As he got out of the car he noticed a new tire on his car. He slid in behind the steering wheel and opened his glove box. Feeling for the button to the secret compartment he had installed, he found the keys to Lydiel's house. He was right-her keys were Schlage as well. Why would Allison have a key to someone else's house, unless…? He was positive his Holy Roller wife was not having an affair. Holding the keys on top of each other they appeared to be the same key. How could Allison possible have a key to Lydiel's house? Why would she have a key to Lydiel's house? He didn't have time for the questions now and besides a lot of those old houses had the similar keys but they didn't fit the same locks. Right now he was running late and he needed to drop off Allison's keys.

"Allison? I'm back."

"Thanks for the warning. May I have my keys now? I wouldn't want you to be late for your mistress' sendoff. Where is she buried anyway?"

Matt sidestepped Allison's questions and went into his office to grab a tie. He heard the doorbell ring and saw a FedEx truck parked outside his house. Before he could get to the door Allison was signing for the package. Turning the box over in her hands she searched for a sender address and found none.

"It's for you..."

Matt took the small package from her hands and carried it into his office. Without opening it, he picked up his keys and left. Doreen would be waiting for him and with any luck he would just make it.

Allison watched Matt back out of the garage and as soon as he was out of sight she was ransacking his office. Where the hell was the box? Surely he didn't take it with him. What was he hiding now-her ashes? That had to be it. He was taking the ashes to the service.

Several times during the day Allison suppressed the urge to attend the service. She wanted to see the fake tears and phony sympathy that would be shown by Remey and Francesca. Those two were real pieces of work. How they could show their faces was beyond her. Maybe Connie would go with her.

They could hang back in the shadows and no one would know they were there. She really should call Connie.

Chapter 18

Doreen Bell closed the door after the babysitter and touched up her make-up. No matter what she tried the tears wouldn't stop, and she had repaired the streaks several times. She wished Matt were here. She knew how hard this had all been on him and yet he managed to take care of the cremation, and make all of the arrangements. Doreen hated the fact that her mother wanted to be cremated but she always said she didn't want to be put in a cold hole in the ground to become worm food. For Doreen this provided no place to "visit" Lydiel. She missed her mother and she was not looking forward to spending the afternoon with two people who were always wishing her mother dead. She decided to save Matt a trip up the stairs and wait for him outside.

Matthew McNulty navigated the traffic as if he were playing a video game, skillfully maneuvering lane changes. After he picked up Doreen it was a twenty minute drive to Whistler's Woods. He didn't have a speech prepared. Anyone as free spirited and unconventional as Lydiel would never want a prepared speech. Instead she would want to be remembered for her humor, her generosity and her understanding. He inserted the CD into the player. No one figured Lydiel to be a Rimsky-Korsakov kind of girl. There were, however, a few surprises on the disk. She had asked for his input also. Why he went along with her cockamamie death planning, he would never know. Maybe she knew something he didn't. If that was indeed the case he wished somehow, some way she could tell him who did such an awful thing. Matt had tried to contact Sarah Turner numerous times but after hearing about Lydiel's death she probably took off like a frightened jackrabbit. He had also made several attempts to reach Lydiel's agent, Jack Bass. How Lydiel ended up with such a jerk as her literary agent and representative was beyond Matt's comprehension. The guy always seemed so phony and self-serving. No matter where he was certainly he had heard about Lydiel's death and yet there was no response of any kind.

Doreen flagged Matt down as he pulled up in front of her house. He looked so tired and worn. He got out and opened the door for her.

"Hey there. I'm sorry I made you wait. I had a flat earlier. I borrowed Allison's car to check on the arrangements at Mirelli's and I had to get it back to her and pick up mine. How are you holding up?"

"As well as can be expected I guess."

That response evoked a new round of crying. Matt reached over and gave her a hug and tried not to let her see how he felt at the moment.

"Buckle up. We are on our way. Have you heard from Remey or Francesca or the others?"

"Matt? Who is Allison?"

"Allison? Allison is my wife, why?"

"You never mentioned her by name before. You always referred to her as "the wife" or "my wife" but never by Allison."

"I guess you're right. I usually call her Allison outside the house or when I'm at work talking to her best bud Connie or some business associate. It's probably better that way."

"Matt? Did my mommie know her name?"

"Sure she did, why?"

"No reason, just asking."

Doreen's mind was one big blur. Allison.

Connie. It was just a bizarre coincidence. Right now she needed to concentrate on how to deal with her sisters and not let them upset her. Matt must have sensed her unease.

"Things will be fine. I'll keep it short I promise and before you know it we will be at Mirelli's tossing back a few."

"Matt, do you know why mommie picked Whistler's Woods for this?"

Matt laughed out loud and debated whether or not he should reveal a lovers' secret to Doreen. Lydiel had very few fantasies but Whistler's Woods was one that he turned into a reality. He remembered that day. She was so happy and so surprised. It was a good day for them, one of the last.

"Oh, it was just a place she always wanted me to take her and you know what? I did. We should be there in another five to ten minutes. Now sit back and try to relax a little. Mr. Matt is in charge."

Chapter 19

The mood was uncharacteristically somber as Remey, Doug, Francesca and Henry rode in the limo to the gatehouse. Henry had taken a double dose of his medication per doctor's orders and was feeling almost like his old self. Francesca had her head on his shoulder and Remey and Doug sat like strangers. Francesca spoke first.

"How long do you think this will take Mr. P? I'm not very good at these things. They are so very morbid."

"I don't anticipate a long drawn out affair my dear. Matt indicated to me that he would be brief and tasteful, and I have no reason to doubt his word. Can I do anything for you?"

"No, I'm fine, thanks."

Doug glanced at Remey and the guilt stuck in his throat like a piece of lodged food. How could he have done that to her? For the second time in a matter of months he had let Francesca come between him and his wife and he vowed it would never happen again. At this moment he wanted to be anywhere but here. It seemed as if they had been riding for an eternity.

"Do you know how much farther the place is, Mr. Pushman?"

"Not much farther and please call me Henry, Doug. I think in some sense we are all family here."

Remey wanted to laugh hysterically. They were all family all right. If Connie had any idea that Francesca was boinking her husband, family would take on a new meaning. Henry seemed very nice but she knew Francesca. She could tap into a man's weakness and make him forget all about common sense. Henry Pushman was definitely pussy whipped. The scene in the limo reminded her of a scene from a very dark and scary movie where something unexpected just popped up from nowhere.

Finally the car turned to a well-traveled dirt road and came to a stop in front of a small stone gatehouse sporting a sign 'Welcome to Whistler's Woods'. Remey recognized Doreen. The man standing next to her had his back turned but from pictures she had seen she knew it was Matt. There was a single row of folding chairs in front running across the path. Scheherazade was playing from somewhere as a light breeze flittered through the trees.

Henry and Doug escorted Remey and Francesca towards the chairs when Matt suddenly turned around. Remey and Francesca were now face to face with the man their mother loved. Doreen sat alone at the end of the row and the others took their seats. Matt introduced himself and over the next forty minutes extolled the virtues of Saint Lydiel. The more Francesca looked at Matt the more she wondered what he saw in her mother. He was gorgeous. Francesca's eyes were focused on Matt's package. It was difficult to size him up from where she sat but there was no doubt in her mind that the opportunity would present itself later at Mirelli's.

Finally it was over. Doreen seemed to take it the hardest but then again she would. She never knew what it felt like to be denied.

Playing the perfect corporate host, Henry facilitated the introductions. Matt only offered his hand to Doug, which seemed strange but somehow understandable. The four returned to the limo and

Doreen helped Matt with the chairs and the music.

"Some nice relatives you've got there Doreen."

"You have no idea, Matt. You just have no idea. My sisters are looking at you as though you were something good to eat."

"So I noticed. Doug seems strange, very quiet."

"This was the first time I have ever seen or met him. He and Remey used to live here before they moved to Chicago. Can we get out of here? This place is giving me the creeps."

"Sure honey, sorry for taking so long to get things together."

Once they were in the car Doreen turned to face Matt. The fact that his wife's name was Allison and she had a friend named Connie seemed to be too much of a coincidence.

"Matt, this is going to sound crazy but do you remember when we used to talk to mommie and she sounded garbled and scary sometimes

"Yeah. I used to tease her about and she was going to write a story or book about it. Why do you bring it up?"

"Do you remember me telling you that I could hear another conversation when she and I would talk, almost as if we were on a party line? I told you I had tapes and you agreed to listen to them when you had time."

"I guess. Yes, vaguely. Sorry. I have been a bit preoccupied lately."

"Could we stop at my house before we go to Mirelli's? I'm sure the others won't mind if we are a little late."

"I suppose. What's going on?"

"I want you to listen to something. It won't take very long."

Matt looked at his watch. It was already after 4 p.m. He had no place to be. Allison knew where he was so why not.

"To your house it is, mademoiselle."

Chapter 20

Connie finally finished the letter that was tantamount to a full confession. It had taken the better part of the day to write and was a detailed accounting of the death of Lydiel Sommers. As she sent it to the printer she called the courier service. She looked at her watch and realized that the service was probably over by now. She was certain that Matt had done a fine job. Now she was at loose ends as she waited for the messenger. Within ten minutes he was there. She handed him the envelope, gave him the instructions and decided to go for a walk.

Nikki Jemison ordered a sandwich and took a good look at Minter. His sarcasm far overshadowed his association with religion. He was always quoting the scriptures, and after ordering his food he arranged and rearranged, wiped and re-wiped the flatware until she broke the silence.

"The security officer at the hospital gave me a pretty good description of the woman who was watching Lydiel's house a few days before the murder. I reviewed the tapes and got a description of the car. Apparently the car was ticketed for a parking violation, and last night I e-mailed a request for them to run a history of all violations issued that day on Spearhead Drive. Right now I'm waiting for the printout to make a match and run it through the BMV. What do you have for me?"

"Is there anything left? I think we need to bring McNulty in for questioning. As far as I'm concerned he is the primary suspect."

"Based on what proof, Minter? Having an affair does not automatically make a person a murderer."

"No, but it sure makes them a liar with things to hide. It is a violation of the commandments. Do you really believe he came out to his wife? My money says no. This guy is so smooth, and it's as if you have blinders on. In my opinion you have lost all objectivity."

Nikki was surprised at the rage displayed by Minter. Sarcasm was one thing but this was something totally different.

"Tell you what Minter. Let's talk to Mrs.

McNulty first and then Mr. McNulty and see who had motive. Hold that thought."

Nikki took the call parked on her cell phone. It was headquarters.

"Jemison here. I see. Did you do a match with the BMV? Can you let me know when that's done? Minter and I are heading over to the McNulty residence. Please put the document in my in-basket. Thanks."

Listening to one side of the conversation made Minter feel like a kid eavesdropping. From the look on Jemison's face there was news on the case.

"What's going on?"

"It's getting late. Let's go interview Allison McNulty before her husband gets back from the memorial service. I want to talk to her alone."

"Can I finish my sandwich at least?"

"Get a doggy bag and let's go."

Minter's discomfort with Nikki's silence was blatantly obvious. He felt out of the loop and more like a third wheel.

The McNulty house was one of those stately colonials in a high rent development. Minter hated the pretentiousness of it all.

Nikki pulled her badge out and rang the doorbell. It wasn't long before a woman appeared with a cigarette in her hand. Nikki took a long look at Allison McNulty before she spoke.

"Good afternoon. I'm Detective Jemison and this is Sergeant Minter. We are looking for Matthew McNulty"

"He isn't here. Is there something I can help you with?"

"Would you excuse me for a moment Mrs. McNulty? I have a call I need to take."

The fact that Minter avoided eye contact with Allison McNulty did not go unnoticed by Nikki nor did his nervousness. He could have used the time to question her but he didn't.

"I apologize Mrs. McNulty. Here is my card. Would you please have your husband call me at his earliest convenience? Thank you for your time. Minter…?"

Gary Minter had no idea what had just transpired. He never heard Nikki's phone ring and he didn't understand why, after all the talk, Nikki didn't question Allison McNulty. He wondered if this had anything to do with the earlier call at the restaurant.

"Was that call about the case?"

"Minter, I need you to go back to the station and follow up on the traffic violation. By now the information should be in the computer. Give me a call on the cell when you get it. I need to take care of something and I'm not sure how long it will take."

Nikki dropped Minter off at his car and drove back to her apartment. The first thing she did was to download the picture she took of Allison McNulty while pretending to take the phone call. She decided not to interview Allison until she showed the picture to Jeffrey. Allison McNulty bore a striking resemblance to the woman on the security tape and dressed in the same fashion. By the time she arrived at the hospital, Minter should have the report for her.

Chapter 21

Doreen handed Matt a cup of coffee and turned the cassette player on. She had the tapes dated just in case no one ever believed her about hearing strange things on the phone. She put the first tape in:

"I'm telling you Allison, we need to discuss this. Let's do lunch. I will call the others. How about noon at Mirelli's?"

"The time for discussion has long passed. "That bitch needs to disappear and I mean forever!"

Doreen removed the cassette and put the next one in.

"Hello? Connie?"

"I thought you were coming to play cards."

"The bastard wouldn't watch the kids and just drove off."

"Oh dear, I'm sorry. I wonder where he went. Henry gave him the afternoon off and the day off tomorrow."

Matt felt as if a volcano was threatening to erupt in his chest. A light suddenly went on and for the first time he saw the big picture and it was ugly-terribly,terribly ugly.

"Stop the tape Doreen."

"There are more Matt, lots more."

"I'm sure but I've heard enough. I know who the two women are."

Matt instantly recognized both voices and they belonged to his wife and Connie Pushman. He didn't want to believe anything he heard. Who did Allison want to disappear and who were "the others?" So many questions but at least now he knew how Allison knew he was off those days.

"Matt, is the Allison on the tape your Allison?

His Allison? He had no Allison. The Allison he knew disappeared almost ten years ago, and the woman who took her place was almost a total stranger. She looked the same, sounded the same, but was so very different. The warmth was gone. The passion was gone, and lately he had begun to question whether it ever really existed. Right now there were people waiting for him at Mirelli's.

The look on his face told Doreen that the Allison on the tape was Matt's wife. In her heart

Doreen felt that Allison McNulty had something to do with her mother's death. The other tapes were much more detailed.

"What do you think I should do with the tapes, Matt?"

Matt had been thinking about that same thing. An idea was forming and perhaps he could force Allison's hand.

"Can I borrow the tapes for a few days? I want to listen to them in detail when I have more time. After that I'll let you know what to do with them. For now we need to make an appearance at Mirelli's before the rumor mill goes crazy."

Chapter 22

Things were in full swing by the time Matt and Doreen arrived at Mirelli's. Doug and Henry were engaged in a lively conversation about investment opportunities and Remey and Francesca were huddled, talking in muffled tones. On the surface no one would ever guess that these people had just attended a memorial service for a murdered family member. Matt watched as Doreen showed signs of breaking under the strain. Maybe it hadn't been such a good idea to suggest she come after all. Her sisters barely acknowledged her presence. It was Henry who noticed them first.

"Matt, Doreen! We were just about to give up on you two. Grab a chair. Giorgio! Giorgio! Libations for my friends. Henry seemed to be in an exceptionally jovial mood, and from the shadows a rather surly Maitre 'D appeared carrying a bottle of Pinot Noir and two glasses.

"It's nice to see you again Mr. McNulty. I'm sorry it is under such solemn circumstances."

"It's Matt and thanks. Could you bring out

more appetizers please, and when you have a moment I wonder if we could have a word in private?"

"I will put the order in with the cook and be back in just a few minutes."

This was a switch, Matt wanting to speak with him. Whenever his wife came in she was always less than complimentary, in fact more times than not she was curt and verbally abusive. It had been awhile since he had seen all four ladies in for lunch together but never one to make assumptions, Giorgio had his suspicions.

Matt was outside his comfort zone on many fronts and he was growing increasingly concerned about Doreen. His identification of the voices, especially Allison's had shed new light on who may have possibly wanted Lydiel dead. For now, however, he needed to make Doreen feel a part of things.

"Henry, I don't believe you have met Lydiel's eldest daughter Doreen. Doreen, this is Henry Pushman, my boss."

Henry staggered slightly as he stood and

extended his hand to Doreen. As Doreen took his hand she noticed how pale he was. He seemed more ill than intoxicated.

"The plethsuure is all mmmine. Franthesca hasth mentioned yyyouu"

It was readily apparent that something was seriously wrong with Henry. Matt got up and helped him to his seat, loosened his tie and unbuttoned his shirt collar. Taking charge he ordered a glass of water and asked someone to call 9-1-1. Giorgio brought the water and remained at the table until the paramedics arrived.

"Giorgio, can you take care of things here please? Please see to it that everyone has dinner and transportation back to the hotel. I'll go to the hospital with Mr. Pushman."

"Certainly, Mr. McNulty. You may depend on me."

As Matt passed the ambulance he noticed Francesca climbing inside. There was definitely something wrong with this scenario and he intended to correct it before any further damage was done.

"Excuse me, but what hospital are you taking

Mr. Pushman to?

"Southeastern General. We should be arriving in ten to fifteen minutes. It appears that your friend has suffered a stroke. I'm sorry sir, but we really need to leave now."

"Thank you. Francesca? I believe you may be more comfortable riding with me."

The paramedics helped Francesca from the truck, closed the doors and sped off with Henry clinging to life inside. Matt knew he had to deal with Francesca firmly and leaving no room for misinterpreting his words, he began:

"What exactly is your problem or rather how stupid are you? How do you think it would look with Henry's mistress riding in the ambulance with him? Don't you have any sense of propriety? I don't want to see you anywhere near Henry or that hospital, do you understand? Now do everyone a favor and take your opportunistic self back inside with your family. I will keep you informed but it seems to me as if your free ride is over."

Matt left Francesca standing outside the restaurant as he drove off to meet the paramedics at the hospital. His priorities had shifted and he genuinely hoped Henry made it. He needed to call Connie to let her know what had taken place. Francesca had more balls than a brass monkey.

Chapter 23

Nikki Jemison lightly tapped on the door to the security control office. Jeffrey was on the phone but waved her in and signaled that he would be free in a minute or two. She looked around the small room and noticed how many different camera angles were captured on video. A thought occurred to her. If the mystery woman was indeed Allison McNulty, was it possible that she made more than one visit to Lydiel's house? It was a very long shot but at this point she had to explore every possibility. Jeffrey ended his phone call and faced her with his trademark grin.

"This is a pleasant surprise. What's up?"

"I want you to look at this picture and tell me if this is the woman you saw that day in the bushes?"

Jeffrey only had to glance at the picture to know positively that that was the same woman.

"Where did you get this picture? Not only is it the same woman, she is wearing the same clothing."

Nikki bowed her head slightly and issued a silent thank you. At last, a break, a break big enough to make Allison McNulty a person of interest. Now, if only Jeffrey could go through the tapes for the week following the first time he saw Allison, maybe, just maybe her suspicions would be confirmed.

"Jeff, I need a huge favor. I need you to review the tapes from the camera focused on Spearhead Drive and the visitor parking lot for the week after your first encounter with our mystery woman. If you find anything, please let me know."

"Anything to help. Nikki, I have something else for you. I know how busy you are so I asked one of the cruiser cops to run a parking violations search for that day. Here's the printout."

Nikki wanted to hug Jeffrey. He just gave her the best twofer a girl could hope for. Her bet was that either Allison or Matthew McNulty's name would be on that list.

Sitting at the spare desk she went down the list. She had no idea so many tickets were issued on Spearhead drive in one day. The traffic guys must just camp out on the corner and wait for violators. Making things easy for herself she zeroed in on the time frame in Jeffrey's report. Finally, there it was. Nikki circled it in red, folded the pages and put them into her bag. Why hadn't Minter called her? A 'wannabe' found a way to get information that a detective sergeant couldn't seem to find. Maybe he got tied up at the station. She decided to give him a call before heading back in. Just as she was leaving she saw Matt pull into the emergency room parking lot. He seemed in a hurry.

Nikki caught up with Matt at the registration desk. He was giving information on a patient. Her first thought was that one of the guests from the memorial service had become ill. She had no idea it was Henry Pushman.

"Matt? I heard you give the nurse information about Henry Pushman. What happened?"

"Nikki. What are you doing here? Apparently Henry suffered a stroke at the reception following the service. I don't know what condition he's in but he didn't look good. Can you excuse me while I call his wife?"

"Sure. Would you like to use my phone?"

Matt went out to the parking lot and phoned Connie. She wanted details but Matt thought it best that she get to the hospital as soon as possible. Matt also thought he should probably call Allison. The day was going to be longer than he thought and he wasn't going to be there for dinner.

"Allison, something has happened and I don't know when I'll be home. Henry suffered a stroke and I'm at the hospital. I called Connie and she's on her way. No, I don't think it would be a good idea for you to come here. Just take care of the boys and I'll be there when I can. The police were there? I see. I'll call them and we will talk when I get home."

Matt handed Nikki her phone. She knew he had questions and she wasn't sure he was ready for the answers right now. No time was ever a good time to tell a man that his wife was possibly a suspect in the death of his mistress.

Matt knew that Nikki overheard his end of the conversation with Allison. This whole day had been filled with 'not a good time' moments and he had the feeling he was about to add to them.

"We can talk but I need to stay at least until Connie gets here. Why were you at the house today? I thought you were going to talk to both of us together and you knew I had the service today."

Before Nikki could explain, a very distraught woman ran through the double sliding doors. Matt walked over to her and gave her a hug. Apparently this was Henry Pushman's wife. He escorted her to Henry's room and returned to the lobby. Nikki was touched by Matt's compassion.

"That was kind of you Matt. Connie is lucky to have you for a friend."

Connie Pushman was lucky all right, due in large part to Matt's thoughtfulness. He could only imagine the scene that would have taken place had she walked in and found Francesca comforting Henry. He never considered Connie a friend and in fact he didn't trust her. His conversation with Walter convinced him that Connie had somehow found a way to replace the missing sixty thousand dollars. After listening to the tapes he also knew that Allison was involved in some way but he just couldn't quite connect the dots.

"I hope Henry pulls through. He's a nice guy. I need to get back to Mirelli's. Can we talk there? I think you will find the Maitre'D to be quite interesting,"

"That would work out great actually. I haven't eaten and it is quiet there. Do you mind if my partner joins us? We have been out of touch most of the day and he has information I need."

"I have nothing to hide, Nikki. Do whatever you need to do and I'll meet you at the restaurant."

Chapter 24

Gary Minter spent the afternoon doing what he considered good police work. He deleted every copy of Allison McNulty's parking violation and shredded the traffic report along with Connie Pushman's letter; a long detailed account of the who, why, when and how concerning the death of Lydiel Sommers. From the one and only time he met her he knew she was too weak for this sort of thing, but he also knew that without her financial input the plan would have fallen apart. He just wished she had been more of a silent partner. In his estimation Connie Pushman was nothing more than an irreverent clit kisser who preferred women to men. The Bible had a name for women like her.

Nikki decided to give Minter a call on her way to Mirelli's. She was annoyed that he never called her with the information, just another indication of his lack of commitment to his job.

"Homicide, Sergeant Minter."

"Minter, where are the reports I asked for? They should have been in my inbox a long time ago."

"I've been here all afternoon and they still haven't arrived. Where are you now?"

"Minter, I'm en route to Mirelli's restaurant and I need you to meet me there. Matt McNulty will be there and it will be a good opportunity to informally interview him. It will also give us an opportunity to catch up and compare notes. I should be there in about ten minutes."

Minter shook his head in dismay. There she went again, trying to soft peddle things with McNulty. The guy was a cheating bastard who deserved no compassion just like the asshole who was responsible for his sister's death. He threw the bag of shredded paper in the trunk of his car and made his call.

"Hello…"

"It's me. I took care of everything. I'm sorry about this afternoon but I didn't have time to call. Did you get rid of everything like I told you?"

"Not yet but I'll put it in the trash tomorrow before the pick-up. Anything else I should know about?"

"Yeah there is. I am on my way to meet Nikki

at Mirelli's to interview Matt. I will keep you posted but for now I have to go. We will talk more Sunday at church"

Things seemed very quiet when Matt pulled into the parking lot at Mirelli's. He was hoping to have a few minutes alone with Giorgio before Nikki arrived. As luck would have it the majority of patrons were clustered around the bar watching a barely audible news program. Matt seated himself and before long the hovering Maitre'D appeared.

"Welcome back Mr. McNulty. How is Mr. Pushman?"

"Holding his own. Giorgio, I need to ask you something. You were working most days when my wife and Mrs. Pushman met here for lunch. Can you tell me who else was with them? Trust me I am not just another jealous husband. This is very important."

Giorgio knew more than any waiter should know but over the years he had made a very good living eavesdropping, sometimes as a request and other times for future reference, like now. He hated Allison McNulty and recently had lost a great deal of respect for Connie Pushman. He knew what Matt wanted. The only thing to be determined was how much it was worth to him.

"Tips haven't been very good lately and it's difficult living paycheck to paycheck. Good stories usually come with a price tag."

"In that case, perhaps we should just wait for Detective Jemison. Now that I think about it that would probably be best. I'll just wait over there."

As Matt attempted to stand Giorgio grabbed his arm and urged him to remain seated. He proceeded to inform Matt of the nature of Allison's and Connie's frequent meetings at Mirelli's, including their guests, two of whom were members of the funeral party and sounded a lot like Remey and Francesca. On one occasion two men joined them. What surprised Matt the most was that Connie knew Francesca. He assumed that Remey had been in town visiting and tagged along as her guest. It also meant that Allison knew that Francesca and Remey were Lydiel's daughters. Before he could process anything Nikki came in. Matt knew there was more but he needed to talk to Nikki.

"Giorgio, what time are you off duty?"

"I'll be around for awhile and if you order I will be your waiter."

Nikki ordered a club soda at the bar and walked over to Matt's table. She noticed the exchange between Matt and Giorgio.

"You must come here often. I saw you talking to the Maitre 'D. I'd be willing to bet you two are on a first name basis. Have you had any updates on Mr. Pushman?"

"Nikki we need to talk and now I'm not so sure here is the best place. In fact here might be the worst place. How soon will your partner be along?"

There was an urgency and concern in Matt's voice that almost frightened her. What did he mean by this being the worst place to talk? This investigation was taking very unusual turns. As much as she wanted to talk to Matt, she wanted to talk to Minter more. He lied to her about the report. Jeffrey had the report hours before she asked Minter to pick it up from the station, yet he told her the report never came in. He also failed to check in all afternoon.

"I don't understand Matt. Why is this not a

good place to talk? I thought you wanted to meet here and I really need to eat. Has something happened since we left the hospital?"

Before he could answer any of her questions, Gary Minter was at their table waving Giorgio over. Matt didn't like him and it had nothing to do with the fact he was a cop. Minter's demeanor around Matt was always hostile as if he held a grudge of some sort.

Giorgio was taken aback as he walked to the table. He recognized Minter as one of the men seated with Allison, Connie and the two other women. He was the one Connie handed the envelope to. Why was he here with Matt and the woman?"

"Can I get anyone anything? By the way Mr. McNulty, my boss would like a word with you about the reception."

Minter and Nikki placed their orders and a very confused Matt followed Giorgio to the galley area. He was certain the check from Henry had taken care of everything and at this hour he was certain Mr. Mirelli was long gone for the day.

Nikki was grateful for the interruption. She needed to get at the root of the report issue. There was something about Minter lately that was sending up lots of red flags that perhaps police work, especially on the detective level was not his strongpoint. His constant inattention to detail, his reckless assumptions and presumptions made it difficult to compare notes and move the investigation forward. She made allowances for his quirky OC disorder and the endless biblical quotes, but outright lying was suspicious and unacceptable.

George Cates had expressed his concerns to Nikki about working the case with Minter who seemed to have never gotten over his sister's relationship with a married guy, and the fact that she killed herself as a result. Although the department shrinks had cleared him to return to duty, George was never convinced of Minter's stability. For now Nikki needed to warehouse Cates' concerns as she needed to ask Minter a few questions.

"What happened with the report, did it ever come through?"

"No, the report never came through. I waited all afternoon and then Brass had me doing housekeeping on my case backlog. If you ask me, this seems like a long shot. That woman was probably just some snoop sister who wanted to get a look at a celebrity. I hardly think the wife would waste time spying from across the street. We should be focusing more on the real suspect - McNulty.

"Assuming again are we? Just because there was no match for Allison doesn't mean whoever our mystery woman is can't tell us whether or not she observed anyone going into the Sommers' house. This is one reason why I wanted to see the report and to run the cross check with the BMV."

"I suppose I can try to order the report again and run it tomorrow. I just assumed..."

This was just what Nikki didn't need, more of Minter's insistence that Matt was the culprit. Tomorrow she was going to ask Brass to reassign Minter. He was becoming a liability she couldn't afford at this stage of the investigation.

Matt stood idly by as order after order was taken to the tables, including the ones for Nikki and Minter. He had no idea what was going on and he was beginning to develop a rather serious headache from the aggravation of the day. He also needed to get back to the table. Just as he was about to give up on the Maitre 'D, Giorgio appeared and took a very deep breath.

"I apologize Mr. McNulty. All of a sudden we got very busy. The man sitting with your friend is one of the men who met with your wife and Mrs. Pushman. One evening not too long ago Mrs. Pushman and the two young women from the funeral reception were here for dinner. Two men joined them and the gentleman sitting there was one of them. At one point Mrs. Pushman slid an envelope to one of the men. He and one of the young women left soon after, but not together. Then your wife came in and joined Mrs. Pushman, the other young woman and the man over there. Mrs. McNulty handed the man an envelope. They spoke briefly and then he left."

The headache Matt was experiencing earlier now felt as if an axe had become embedded in his skull. Was Giorgio saying that Allison, Connie, Francesca and Remey were paying off a cop and for what? The matter at Pushman was being handled internally and who was the other man? He was too tired and not thinking straight.

"Giorgio, did you hear any part of the conversation?"

"I heard about some bitch needing to die. I heard about canisters and I heard things about you I would rather not repeat. I'm sorry but I need to attend to a few things. I must say that I don't like your wife very much. I realize I am out of line and I apologize. Good night."

Matt's legs felt like rubber and his head felt as if it were in a spinning vice. He gripped the edge of the stainless steel table to steady himself. A waiter just told him that his wife paid off a cop to do what, kill someone, kill .... He couldn't bring himself to finish the thought. He needed to go somewhere, anywhere but here. He would tell Nikki he needed to get to the hospital to check on Henry. After making his excuses to Nikki and Minter he sat in his car and slowly went over the events of the day. First the tapes at Doreen's and now this new information from Giorgio and to top it off a dirty cop. He needed a drink and a bed and Lydiel.

Chapter 25

Connie Pushman sat beside the hospital bed holding the hand of her dead husband. The doctors told her Henry was brain dead on arrival to the hospital, and she made the decision to have him removed from life support. Henry tempted fate by taking Viagra knowing he had a heart condition, but he always wanted to please, and at his age it was difficult to keep up with a woman half his age. He tried so hard and was so patient with Connie, and although she knew how much the continuous rejection hurt him, she could never bring herself to tell him the truth.

She wanted to blame Francesca but she didn't believe the affair happened to hurt her. If that was the case Francesca would never have given her the money. Now she was all alone and soon the police would read the letter and she would be even more alone because she was weak. Her weaknesses surrounded her like an old worn coat, her need for friendship, her need for marriage, her need to be somebody, her need to be… loved. She really should call the twins but it was late. She wanted to call Allison but she couldn't. She needed to tell Matt how sorry she was for her role in Lydiel's murder. She needed to lie down and sleep forever. She needed to be with Henry.

Sitting on the side of the bed, the computer issue was nagging at Allison McNulty. Maybe the clerk was wrong. Maybe she should try using the disk to access the program on the home computer. The memorial service was probably running longer than anticipated considering Henry had been rushed off to the hospital. She was certain she would have enough time. She knew she should also dispose of the skirt and the inhalers.

After opening the closet door Allison pulled the skirt from the hanger and placed it into a garbage bag. She began to move things around in the closet to find her work bag when she heard the garage door close. She stashed the bag in the closet, hastily closed the door and quickly ran downstairs to wait for Matt to come into the house.

"It must have been a very long service to keep you away so long. I trust it is now a done deal?"

"It is quite done Allison. Henry Pushman died tonight."

Matt brushed past Allison and slowly walked up the stairs to his bedroom. As he removed his jacket he noticed something hanging out underneath the closet door. He was too tired to unravel one more mystery or take off the rest of his clothes. He slipped off his shoes, fell into bed and stared at the ceiling. He recalled his conversation with Giorgio - another why with no answer.

Allison McNulty was certain that if Henry was dead Francesca had something to do with it, and that Connie would have called. She checked the answering machine for messages but there were none. She took the cordless phone out onto the deck, lit a cigarette, and called her.

Connie Pushman sat in the old rocker, sipping a glass of wine and listening to the echoes of ringing telephones throughout her house. She didn't notice the cold or the dark. All she felt was a terrible aching loneliness. She let the machine pick up the call.

"Connie, if you are there please pick up. Matt

told me something about Henry. Please, I need to know if you are all right."

Connie lifted the receiver and sighed deeply as she answered Allison's questions.

"Yes Allison, Henry is dead. He suffered a stroke while attending the funeral reception. Now you have your confirmation. You should know that I sent a letter to the police detailing the entire plot surrounding Lydiel's death, including the money I took from Pushman and the money you took from Matt. They know everything and now if you will please excuse me there are things I need to take care of. Goodbye Allison. Please don't ever call me again."

"Connie, wait. I think we should talk."

"No Allison. No we don't ever need to talk again."

Allison McNulty crushed out her cigarette, went back inside and poured herself two fingers of scotch. She shook her head and smiled silently. Minter had taken care of Connie's "confession" letter and the ticket which were the only links that could possibly tie her to the murder. She switched off the kitchen light, finished the scotch and turned off the television.

Allison McNulty felt a total sense of exhilaration as she bounded up the stairs to the bedroom. She thought out loud how bad things happen to bad people. Henry cheated and now he was dead. Matt cheated, his mistress was dead, and he was going to be blamed for it. A wicked smile teased the corners of her lips as she reached the top of the stairs.

Sleep would not come to Matthew McNulty. The more he tried to relax, the more he thought about Giorgio's remarks and the tapes from Doreen's. He had just closed his eyes when Allison opened the door. Surely she couldn't be thinking…

"What are you doing here Allison?"

"I'm tired and I'm going to bed."

"Fine, then I suggest you sleep where you usually sleep, downstairs on the sofa."

"Matt, I…"

"You what? Whatever it is forget it. You are not sleeping here tonight or any other night. Get whatever it is you came for and go. I am very tired and I need to get to sleep."

Allison opened the closet door and stepped on her sweater. She must have pulled it off the hanger when she was searching for the disk. She grabbed the garbage bag and her work bag, covered them with her robe and slammed the door on her way out. That makes two people in less than an hour who had told her no.

Seated on the sofa, she dropped the garbage bag on the floor beside her, and went over the events of the last two days. Everything was wrapping up nicely, just as she planned. All that remained was the disposal of the skirt and the inhalers. She was still puzzled about the disk malfunction. Tomorrow she would take the disk with her to the electronics store to see if it was defective or damaged.

She searched inside the leather work bag and removed the disk, and noticed that the brown paper bag was missing. It must have fallen out inside the closet earlier and there was no way she would risk waking Matt. She would search the closet tomorrow after he left for work. Allison eased the kitchen door open and tossed the garbage bag with the skirt inside into the closest trashcan. So much for evidence!

Dreams haunted Matt. They were always the same. Lydiel was kissing his neck and whispering into his ear in tones so hushed he could never understand what she was trying to tell him. She was so close he could smell her, feel her, and touch her. As soon as he tried to pull her close, his eyes opened and he realized he was alone. Leaving the bed, he stood at the window engrossed in thought and staring at the stars. The why's seemed to be adding up and the answers nowhere in sight. Just as he turned away he saw Allison toss something in the trash. What could be important enough to throw away at this hour?

It was just after two a.m. and Nikki Jemison was trying to put the edges of the puzzle in place. Matt had something he wanted to discuss with her but when Minter showed up he suddenly didn't feel comfortable talking. Then there was the fact that Minter lied about the report and the BMV match-up. She had solid proof that Allison McNulty had been watching Lydiel's house a few days before her murder, and someone had been using stealth software to spy on computer communications between Matt and Lydiel. It was definitely time to talk to Allison McNulty.

Remey Anderson held her sister's hand as Douglas called the hospital to check on Henry's condition. After several nods and I understands, Doug put the receiver down. Francesca knew the answer before he spoke.

"He's dead isn't he?"

"Yes. Apparently he was brain dead when he arrived at the hospital and his wife had him taken off life support shortly thereafter. He seemed like a nice guy with very poor taste in women."

"Doug! This is not the time or the place! Can't you see what this is doing to Francesca?"

"What it's doing to Francesca? Henry Pushman is dead. What about what that does to his family? Francesca is nothing more than a selfish opportunistic bitch that only fucks a man if there is something more than an orgasm in it for her. Now I suppose we will have to hang around for another funeral. I'm going up to the room and go to bed. You stay as long as you like Remey."

Remey watched in silence as Francesca wept uncontrollably, and knew in her heart that everything Doug said was true. If Francesca were telling the truth about not knowing at first that Henry was married to Connie, why did she continue the relationship after she discovered the truth? What did she possibly think was in it for her when she had sex with Doug in the garage? Was she holding it over his head to insure future encounters? Whatever Francesca was feeling at the moment, Remey found it difficult to empathize with her. If anyone discovered the role they played in Lydiel's death Francesca would have more cause to weep. She couldn't watch any longer.

"You should get some rest Sis. I'm going to leave now. Doug and I have had a very long day. We'll talk more in the morning. I'm really sorry about Henry."

Francesca never looked up as the door closed after Remey. How this could have happened, and did she really cause Henry's stroke? She had no idea he had a heart condition. He always seemed so lively and so horny. Better it happened in a public place than in bed with her. She knew she should call Connie but she couldn't. Tomorrow she would clean her things out of the penthouse before Connie got there. She would never be able to explain things to her. She turned off the lights, hugged Henry's pillow and fell into a tortured sleep.

Chapter 26

The early morning air was cool and crisp. Matt noticed the smell of burning wood as he drove down Spearhead Drive. The only sound was that of helicopter blades as the chopper landed on the pad at the hospital. He found a parking space on the street and sat looking at the little house. He had been putting off packing her things because he didn't know what to do with most of them, and now was as good a time as any to take care of that. It was also a good time to see if his suspicions were right. He had taken Allison's keys on the way out, and now he tried the new key on her ring in the lock and the door opened. He was hoping against hope that it wouldn't work. It was freezing inside and as he turned the heat on he saw his lighter in the candy dish. He hadn't thought much about it that first day, but now he realized how it got there.

As he walked through the house he realized how much he missed the good smells that always came from the kitchen, the music and most of all the life she brought to the place. It felt strange not to see her typing away at the computer, totally frustrated when writer's block halted the creative process. He sat on the edge of the bed, their bed, and felt as if he was sitting on a grave marker. Although everything was as she left it, it was so cold and empty. Strangers had touched what they shared together and one had dared to take it away. He knew for certain that Allison had been here, touching things, insinuating her presence in the space he and Lydiel made love in. He knew she killed her. His headache had returned and as much as he hated to admit it, sitting here like this he realized that the answers to most of his whys were staring him in the face. It was time to call Nikki Jemison.

Nikki Jemison was on her third cup of coffee and nursing one hell of a headache when the day officer came to her office. He apologized to her profusely for any misunderstanding from the day before. He had given both reports to Minter as well as a letter addressed to her and delivered by courier.

"Who signed for the letter, Johnson?"

"I did, Detective. I brought it into your office and Sergeant Minter was sitting at your desk so I handed it to him along with the reports."

"Do you by chance recall the name of the courier company?"

"Yes, ma'am, I do. It was Winged Heel Courier Service and the logo was a picture of Mercury, you know the Greek god."

"Approximately what time was the letter delivered, officer?"

"At about 12:30 p.m., ma'am. I remember because I was just about to go to lunch when it arrived."

"Thanks Sergeant. Sorry to pull you away from your desk. I know how much you love it there."

"Yeah right. If I can be of further assistance…"

Why didn't Minter tell her about the letter and where was it? The first thing she needed to do was to call Winged Heel and find out where the letter was picked up. She decided not to have Minter reassigned. She needed him where she could keep an eye on him and she needed to talk with Matt ASAP.

Her cell phone rang as she was dialing the courier service; it was Matt.

"Nikki, I need to see you. I'm at Lydiel's and

at the risk of sounding like a line from an old movie, I would appreciate it if you came alone."

"I understand. I need to take care of a couple of things here and I should be there in about forty-five minutes."

The dispatcher at the courier company told her the letter was picked up from 6790 Ridgecrest Lane from a Mrs. Henry Pushman. Why would Connie Pushman courier a letter to Nikki, and why would Minter not tell her about it? Before the end of the day she expected to have the answers to these and other questions. For now she needed to find an assignment for Minter.

Why was it that the phone seemed to ring at the most inopportune times like when someone was using the can, in the shower or making love? Gary Minter seemed to have been a victim of all three, albeit the last time he had been with a woman had been over three years ago. He was in the middle of a hot shower when Nikki called. His assignment for the day was to show the Sommers woman's picture in some of the stores in the IGA mall in an attempt to piece together the final day of her life. This was bullshit duty and he knew it, but it would give him time to tie up a few more loose ends like making absolutely certain Allison had followed his instructions. He knew from years of police work that it was the little things that resulted in an undoing such as careless disposal of murder weapons and confessional letters to the police.

On numerous occasions he had had to keep her focused. She hated Lydiel Sommers with a passion he was unaccustomed to. He remembered when he met her in church that Sunday. She talked about her marriage and about her husband's dalliances. She told him about Lydiel's relationship with Matt. He shared the details of his sister's fall from grace and her suicide. As far as he was concerned the devil got his due, and his sister had paid the wages of sin. Over time he and Allison had gotten to know each other well and one day she confided in him about Lydiel and her plan.

He had been the one to show Allison the way to dispose of Lydiel in a manner almost impossible to trace. He also told her over and over to stay away from Lydiel's house, but she went anyway and left a paper trail. Fortunately he was able to delete all traces of the ticket. Now he needed to deal with Connie Pushman.

Chapter 27

"Damn it! Couldn't Matt at least take the trash out?" Allison swore silently under her breath as she dragged the can to the curb. She supposed she should get used to doing it since he wasn't going to be around much longer. Minter promised he would take care of everything. When she returned to the yard to get the other can Liam was standing there in tears.

"Mom my throat hurts, and my head hurts and I don't feel so good. Where's Dad?"

"Dad isn't here right now and you need to go back inside. I'll be there in a few minutes. I need to get the trash out."

"Mom, I don't feel so…"

Allison stood in the doorway and watched Liam vomit all over the kitchen floor. Just what she needed! The trash was going to have to wait. Sidestepping the mess, she led him to the bathroom, helped him clean up and put him back to bed with a cup of tea. She saw the garbage truck drive past her house before she could get the other can out. She put the can back in the shed and went inside. This day was off to a great start. She poured herself a cup of coffee and switched on the television. The lead story on the local news was the sudden and untimely death of entrepreneur and philanthropist Henry Pushman. The cause of death was listed as a massive stroke. Allison couldn't help but wonder how much of a role Francesca played in Henry's death.

Connie Pushman walked aimlessly around her house. She stared at the yellow envelope that contained Henry's personal effects. How do you reduce a life to a single envelope? Henry was so much more than that. He died never knowing what kind of monster he was married to. She had just settled at her desk when the doorbell rang. She opened the door and was confused to see the man from the restaurant standing there. How did he know where she lived and more importantly what did he want?

"Good morning Mrs. Pushman. I'm Sergeant Minter from the Homicide Division and I would like to ask you a few questions about the murder of Lydiel

Sommers."

A cop! The man from the restaurant was a cop! Something was definitely wrong and as Connie tried to close the door, Minter threw his weight against it sending her sprawling into the foyer. Locking the door after himself, he pulled Connie up by her hair forcing her down onto the sofa. Training his gun on her he began a rambling conversation.

"You and I need to talk Mrs. Pushman. Your friend Allison and I are worried about you and your letter writing activities. You let us down. You defended that philanderer McNulty. Fortunately Detective Jemison never saw the letter. I made sure of that. Now you are going to type another letter incriminating Matthew McNulty. Get up and move slowly to your computer."

Nikki Jemison turned onto the parking pad and knocked sharply on the back door of Lydiel's house. Matt let her in and offered her coffee. Over the course of an hour he told her how he discovered the missing money from his bank account, how he found Lydiel's door key on Allison's ring, computer printouts of conversations between him and Lydiel, all the tapes Lydiel's daughter, Doreen, made of conversations between Allison and Connie and his conversation with Giorgio. He also related how he saw Allison toss a garbage bag in the trash late last night.

Nikki realized that Matthew McNulty had just given her nearly all the pieces to the puzzle of Lydiel's murder. What was lacking was substantiation; witnesses and concrete evidence.

"Matt, how was it possible that Allison obtained a key to Lydiel's house. Could she have found your key? Was there anyone else who had a key?"

"Aside from me just the part-time housekeeper she hired, Sarah Turner, but she was only here a few days. There's no way Allison could have found my keys. I had a secret compartment installed in the glove box of my car."

"I need Allison's keys Matt. Do you know where the garbage bag is now and do you know where Sarah Turner is?"

"I have the bag in the trunk of my car along

with an external hard drive containing everything that was on my home computer up until yesterday. I thought anything worth tossing at two a.m. must be suspect so I grabbed the bag as I left home this morning. As for Sarah Turner, she only worked a few hours a week but there was something very unique about her…"

Before Matt could finish his sentence Nikki got a call.

"Excuse me, Matt. I need to take this."

While Nikki took her call Matt washed the cups and cleaned the coffee maker, and thought how Lydiel would never have allowed him to do any domestic chores. In some ways she was very traditional and in others so progressive. He used to think about goosing her as she stood at the sink. Unlike Allison she would have welcomed the advance, and wanted him to make love to her right then and there.

Nikki had to move and move quickly. She needed search warrants for the McNulty house, the Pushman house, and Francesca Sommers' house. This would take at least two hours or so. In the meantime she needed to know exactly where Allison McNulty was as well as Gary Minter. Then she needed to get to Giorgio before he disappeared.

"Matt, we need to get to Mirelli's quickly. But before we do I want you to call home and find out what Allison is doing. Tell her you will be home in a couple of hours so the two of you can pay your respects to Connie Pushman. Ask her to take your boys to their grandmother's. Do whatever you have to do, get them out of the house."

Without so much as a 'why', Matt called Allison. He repeated Nikki's story. Allison argued about taking a sick child to her mother. Trying to remain calm he reinforced the importance of why they needed to talk and hung up. Nikki tried without success to raise Minter on the radio.

Connie Pushman's fingers trembled as she tried to type the letter Minter dictated. There was a small part of her that wanted him to pull the trigger and another part that knew she had to take care of the details of burying her husband. She owed him that much. Apparently Allison neglected to tell her about the relationship between the "pharmacist" and herself. She knew she had to think fast.

"Please, Detective Minter, is it? I need to use the restroom. You can follow me if you like."

Minter waved the gun motioning for Connie to get up. Grabbing her by the hair he followed her to the bathroom. Once inside she attempted to close the door but Minter's foot allowed only for partial closure.

"Look you clit-kissing bitch, do whatever you need to do and get back out here. You have five minutes."

Connie turned on the faucet to muffle the sound of the telephone on the wall beside the toilet. She pushed speed dial and heard the 911 operator ask the nature of her emergency. She whispered, "kidnapped", flushed the toilet, washed her hands and met Minter at the door. The 911 line remained open. Once again grabbing her hair he led back to the living room.

"You recall what God did to abominations like you? Abominations and purveyors of sin were all destroyed with the twin cities. When's the last time a man dumped his load in you? Did your husband know you liked sucking puss?"

Connie tried desperately to show no fear as Minter continued to wave the gun and caress his crotch. She watched the bulge in his pants rise, as did his level of irritation. She continued to type and hope that the 911 operators heard her.

Minter continued to dictate the letter, pausing briefly to quote bible scripture. Connie's fear of Minter had been replaced by her fear that the call didn't go through to the 911 dispatcher. Minter paced as he talked. Then suddenly he stopped and leaned in the direction of the kitchen. Brandishing the weapon he ordered Connie away from the desk.

"I need a glass of water, NOW!"

Rising slowly from the chair , Connie walked towards Minter. She heard the voices coming from the bathroom at the same time as Minter. Turning back towards the desk, she felt the sting and then the warmth as she hit the floor. Minter watched as the pool of blood permeated the pristine white carpet. He holstered his weapon and let himself out the back door. The woods behind the Pushman house led directly to the McNulty house.

The police radio crackled to life as Nikki Jemison drove towards Mirelli's. The emergency dispatcher reported an incident at 6790 Ridgecrest Lane. Officers were to approach silently and with caution. Nikki and Matt both recognized the address as Connie Pushman's. Nikki was close and took the call, requesting a black and white for back up. She dropped Matt off back at Lydiel's and headed to Ridgecrest Lane.

Once she arrived at the residence Nikki pulled the light from the roof of her car and motioned to the black and white to remain out of sight. She checked her weapon and rang Connie Pushman's doorbell. When there was no response, she waved the officers in the black and white towards the back of the house. She tried the doorknob first before she broke the small windowpane over the lock. Connie Pushman was lying face down on the floor, bleeding and barely conscious. Gently nudging the injured woman, Nikki spoke gently and reassuringly.

"Hang on Mrs. Pushman, help is on the way. Can you tell me who did this to you?"

Connie Pushman felt cold and numb. Her mouth and throat were dry and her words were barely audible as Nikki Jemison leaned close to hear her.

"It was the man …from Mirelli's…the cop…"

Nikki called for an ambulance and requested the two officers remain on the scene. Minter was on the move and his most likely destination was Allison McNulty's house. She called for backup as she headed for the McNulty house and called Matt at Lydiel's house.

"Matt, call your mother-in-law on your cell phone and make sure the boys are there. I'll hold on."

"Allison dropped them off about twenty minutes ago so she should be almost home by now. What's going on Nikki?"

"Minter shot Connie Pushman and I have every reason to believe he is headed towards your house. Stay where you are until you hear from me again. Matt, please, stay where you are."

The line went dead as Matthew McNulty sped away from Spearhead Drive. Something bad was happening at his house. Nikki called Brass and requested a search of Gary Minter's apartment.

She also requested a supervisor to meet her at the McNulty house. She prayed that Matt had taken her advice.

Chapter 28

Allison saw Minter's car as she pulled into her garage. Before she could get out he was standing at the driver's side door.

"Gary? What's wrong? Why are you here?"

"Hi Alli. I had a little time this afternoon and I thought we could have lunch and talk."

"Matt will be here in a little over an hour so now is really not a good time."

"Consider it a formal police request. Move over."

The look in his eyes told Allison that refusal on her part would be a bad move. She slid over to the passenger side as Minter pulled out of the garage.

"Gary what is it? Why are you doing this? Everything was going so well, just as we planned it."

"Yes I know. I just don't think it is safe for you here anymore. McNulty knows we're onto him. Connie Pushman wrote a letter explaining everything. Your house will be crawling with cops soon looking for him. "

"You mean...you mean they are going to arrest

Matt and charge him with the murder?"

"Yes, and you and I will be having lunch at Mirelli's when it goes down."

Allison had known Gary Minter for over four years and had never known him to lie about anything. When the whole murder plot started he said that the earth should be cleansed of adulterers; the whores should perish, and the men should suffer in solitude for the remainder of their days. Somehow at this moment Allison McNulty took no solace in those words.

Matthew McNulty arrived at his house at the exact same minute Nikki Jemison did. Police cars swarmed around his car as he tried to get out. Guns from every angle were trained on him until Nikki ordered a stand down.

"Matt, didn't I tell you to stay at Lydiel's? We have no idea what we are dealing with here. Give me your keys and get back in your car."

Matt handed his keys to Nikki and watched as she first knocked and then let herself and several other police officers into his house. After what seemed like an eternity, they emerged as they had entered – empty-handed.

"Matt, call Allison's cell phone. Find out where she is."

Matt watched as one by one the police cars left and his neighbors closed their curtains. He was prepared for a dressing down from Nikki and she didn't disappoint him. She decided since he couldn't be trusted to follow instructions, the safest place for him was with her. A radio check let her know that Minter remained on the loose and that Connie Pushman was in surgery. Now was as good a time as any to have that talk with Giorgio.

Gary Minter parked the car in Mirelli's parking lot and opened the door for Allison. Giorgio seated them in the nearly empty restaurant and took their orders. Holding Allison's hand he repeated one verse of scripture after another, rambling on endlessly about faith and redemption. Subtle attempts to free herself were fruitless. Screaming would only make matters worse and it was clear that for the first time in a very long time, Allison Woodall McNulty was anything but in control.

Matt spotted Allison's car before Nikki turned into the parking lot.

"That's Allison's car! Something's wrong. She was supposed to meet me at home right about now. Call the restaurant and ask for Giorgio."

After a short conversation with Giorgio, Nikki called a silent alarm to the restaurant. Cuffing Matt to the steering wheel she entered the back door of the restaurant. She quickly grabbed one of the restaurant flyers from a rack on the wall and folded it to look like an official document. She rushed to the table where Allison McNulty and Gary Minter were seated. Waving the folded paper in front of him, Nikki made her move.

"Good job Minter! We have a warrant for Mrs. McNulty's arrest so you get to do the honors. Read her her rights and cuff her. This is going to look very good on your record."

Allison searched Minter's face for some sign that this was a joke or at the very least a horrible mistake. There was nothing, no evidence connecting her to Lydiel's murder. He promised her had taken care of everything.

Caught totally off guard, Minter seized the opportunity to buy himself a little time. Nikki handed him her cuffs and watched as he arrested Allison Woodall McNulty for the murder of Lydiel Sommers.

Matthew McNulty's wrist ached from his handcuffed connection to the steering wheel. Nikki had been inside for quite awhile, and a couple of black and whites were babysitting him now. A variety of scenarios played out in his mind as he waited. Suddenly he noticed movement as Nikki, Minter and a handcuffed Allison appeared in the parking lot. He watched as Gary Minter put Allison in the back of a cruiser. She never saw him. Nikki waved for one of the remaining officers on the scene. Matt saw the officer handcuff Minter and usher him to the remaining cruiser. Nikki flashed thumbs up to Matt and he knew this was the beginning of the end of the nightmare.

Chapter 29

Giorgio Pieri was sequestered in an undisclosed location with a police sketch artist in an attempt to identify the "paper man". He confirmed everything he told Matt that night in the restaurant. Now Nikki's attention was focused on Matt's progress with his IT friend.

"How did things go with your techie friend, Matt? Was he able to find anything that would help us?"

"Walter was able to retrieve and fax a copy of Connie's confession along with Henry and Connie's banking transactions for the last 60 days. I also asked him to run Allison's and Francesca's as well as mine. I'm not a cop but it seems like the dates correspond with the payoffs to Minter and his friend. Henry opened a line of credit for Francesca, part of which she gave to Connie to replace the previously stolen sixty thousand dollars with a little left over for herself of course."

Nikki thought about how much planning and scheming went into killing Lydiel and she began mentally forming a psychological profile of the people involved.

"She must have really done a number on poor Henry Pushman."

"I don't like Francesca and I never have. Her hatred for her mother was so big that it consumed her. But I know what it's like to be lonely, unappreciated, ignored and generally unloved. I was like that so I can understand how Henry appreciated the warmth and the pleasure of pleasing someone and being pleased. He simply had no idea how devious Francesca was."

"The way things look now, your wife may be looking at some serious prison time. How do you feel about that?"

"Allison sucked the life out of me. She took what I felt for her and twisted and mishandled it to satisfy her own selfish agenda. She caused me years of pain and angst, and then she took something very important from me because of her own jealousy and insecurity. Do you have any idea how many times she told me she loved me and then ignored me? All those times lately when I was babysitting she was scheming and planning a murder, Lydiel's murder. My boys mean the world to me and I shudder to think that for all these weeks they have been in the care of a woman who would resort to murder rather than let me go. At this point I have pretty much reconciled myself to the way things are. Allison created this situation and now she has to deal with the consequences. My concern is the boys. What happens now with Francesca?"

"Hopefully the search of Minter's apartment will give us what we need to bring her in as well as strengthen our case against Constance Pushman. Beyond that, I don't know at this point. I will stay in touch and let you know what the investigation reveals. Of course the DA will be contacting you also. Take care of yourself Matt and take care of the boys. I'm sure your Lydiel Sommers knows that you are thinking of her."

Chapter 30

For Nikki Jemison the Lydiel Sommers case was far from over. Allison McNulty and Gary Minter were only two players in the murder. According to the Maitre 'D at Mirelli's, Francesca Sommers, Remey Anderson, Constance Pushman and another unknown man all figured prominently in the murder as well.

The search of Gary Minter's apartment turned up several old case files, all dealing with individuals killed as a result of extramarital affairs. Each was labeled and contained various pieces of evidence that would have made a difference in the outcomes of several trials. Each case would now have to be reopened and re-investigated. The most significant findings were the cache of syringes, inhaler canisters, scales and several vials and containers of commercial strength toxins, including capsaicin.

Gary Minter was a meticulous record keeper. Several journals were discovered including one detailing the planning of and his participation in the murder of Lydiel Sommers. Of particular note to

Nikki were the entries regarding his meetings with Allison McNulty and two meetings with someone identified only as J.B. The information was enough to secure warrants for Francesca, Remey Anderson and Constance Pushman.

The shooting of Constance Pushman, the arrests of Allison McNulty and Gary Minter in connection with the death of Lydiel Sommers was the news of the day. Lounging on the sofa in the penthouse, Francesca felt confident that no one would be able to tie her to her mother's murder. Since Henry's death she had remained in the penthouse sucking up the last of the freebies before she would be asked to leave. The little money she had left from the line of credit was her nest egg in case she had to leave town. She missed Henry. She never really thought about life without him, and her sister and brother-in-law had been less than sympathetic about her loss. Maybe she needed a change of scenery. She got dressed grabbed her purse and waited for the elevator.The two cars pulled into the valet circle in front of The Renaissance. A few words were exchanged between the valet, the woman and the two men accompanying her. The valet escorted the trio to the penthouse elevators and used his passkey to call for the car. Once inside the officers said very little to each other until the doors opened. The female was the first to speak.

"Are you Francesca Sommers?"

"I am and who are you? If you are looking for Henry Pushman, I'm afraid he isn't here."

Nikki Jemison had waited weeks to say the words and now without hesitation she reached for her cuffs and addressed Francesca.

"Francesca Sommers, you are under arrest for the murder of Lydiel Sommers. You have the right…

Douglas Anderson loaded the last piece of luggage on the cart and looked around the room one last time.

"Rem are you ready? I have had enough of this place and I want to get an early start. I want to be home when the girls get out of school."

"In a minute Doug…"

"I'll meet you in the lobby. I'm taking the cart down and I will have the valet bring the car. Please don't be long."

As he stood in the elevator lobby Douglas Anderson experienced a brief moment of foreboding. He paid no attention to the woman and man getting off the same elevator he was getting on. He never saw them knock on the hotel room door, nor did he hear the conversation that ensued.

Remey Anderson heard the knock at the door and was already upset with her husband. He must have forgotten the keycard. As she opened the door and saw the couple standing there she felt a sinking feeling in the pit of her stomach. The woman spoke first.

"Are you Remey Anderson?"

"I am. Has something happened?"

"Remey Anderson, you are under arrest for the murder of Lydiel Sommers. You have the right..."

Chapter 31

The fallout of the arrests and trials of Francesca Sommers, Remey Anderson, Allison McNulty, Connie Pushman and Gary Minter had significant impact on the lives of their family members.

To the bitter end Allison McNulty defended her actions, repeating numerous times that Matt was to blame. She detailed the history of their marriage in that very public forum, and on numerous occasions her mother, Hannah, had to be escorted from the courtroom. Allison insisted she could prove Matt's infidelity with the transcripts obtained from the stealth software, but she could never explain what a thermonuclear application or a blank disk had to do with discovering an affair between her husband and Lydiel Sommers. She alleged that Matt placed the key to Lydiel's house on her key ring to make her look guilty.

Matt tried with everything inside him to remain stoic throughout the process. Sadness and pain consumed his heart, and he barely listened as his wife finally related how she planned the murder of a woman she didn't know; a woman who had done her no harm, and a woman who only brought pleasure to him and the world.

Doreen Bell tried to hold back the tears of anger as the taped conversations were played, and as Francesca told the court how she tried on numerous occasions to kill her mother, and how she provided Allison with vital information to carry out the murder plot. Her attitude was often times flippant and sarcastic with no sign whatsoever of remorse.

Douglas Anderson seemed to be in a perpetual state of shock as the trials wore on. The prosecution told the court how his wife, Remey Anderson took painstaking care to prepare the murder weapon. This was a woman he left his wife for and entrusted the care of his children to. He rocked in his seat, tears streaming down his face, asking why.

Gary Minter's defense of emotional instability was disregarded as Nikki Jemison read entry after entry from his journal. His ex-wife testified against him and recalled a marriage of jealousy, verbal abuse and obsessive religious ideation.

For her part Constance Pushman had been

extremely forthcoming, and readily admitted her role in the murder as well as her sincere remorse for "being weak and needy". The injuries sustained during the shooting by Gary Minter had left her partially paralyzed. She was sentenced to five years of court ordered supervision.

As the mastermind of the plot, Allison Woodall McNulty received life imprisonment without the possibility of parole and no contact with her sons. All parental rights were terminated. Gary Minter received a similar sentence. Remey Anderson was sentenced to twenty years in prison without the possibility of parole. Francesca Sommers was given the same sentence. Each of the defendants would spend Lydiel Sommers' birthday and death day in solitary confinement for the duration of their incarceration.

Chapter 32

In the three months since the trials, Matthew McNulty and his boys had begun to make the adjustment to life without Allison. The boys didn't understand any of what happened, and Matt tried to explain to them how sometimes people do things that hurt other people, sometimes people they love.

The publicity surrounding the trial made it difficult for them in school and some of Matt's old friends stopped talking to him. The "paper man" remained at large and Sarah Turner seemed to have vanished into thin air. The consensus was that perhaps the women had disposed of her as well.

Matt still not come to terms with Lydiel's death. There was a little place within him that could not accept the fact that he would never see her again, or hold her again, and he desperately wanted to make love to her again. That day in the morgue he was convinced that the woman on that cold steel tray was not his Lydiel, but then he realized that death changes people and had signed the mortuary release. When he received her belongings the little gold hoops she always wore were not among them. He wondered if some morgue attendant had stolen them.

Henry Pushman changed his will a few weeks before he died and Matt was now the Chief Operating Officer at Pushman. Obviously the discovery of an alleged misdirected deposit did not dispel his suspicions that his wife was a thief, and this act of betrayal was something he could not tolerate.

Plans for a new expansion were underway and this time someone else was in charge of the day-to-day planning. Doreen had become his administrative assistant and buzzed him just as he leaving for a meeting.

"Yes, Doreen, what is it? I'm late for a meeting."

"There is a government official from the embassy in Belize demanding to speak with you."

"Put him through but please go to the conference room and make my apologies. This shouldn't take long."

"This is Matthew McNulty. Hello? Hello?"

Book Four:

With Love

From Me To You

Chapter 1

The plane from Corozal touched down just past noon. The slush and cold were such a striking difference to the warmth and humidity of the Belizean rainforest. How very different things looked here.

The cab driver put the luggage in the trunk and asked the woman her destination.

"The Renaissance, please."

Matt tried several times to reconnect with the embassy but was forced to assign the task to Doreen, who fared no better. The city planners were restless and wanted to finish the meeting before lunch. Doreen put the slideshow up and as usual everyone was impressed with Matt's plans and timetables. Business at Pushman was better than ever but he was always just slightly preoccupied with thoughts of Lydiel. He began to wonder if it would ever end.

The meeting ended and Matt thought today might be a good day for him and Doreen to have lunch together. Her life had changed greatly since

Lydiel's death and things were looking up for her, finally.

"Doreen, how about lunch with me today? I'm sort of at loose ends and could use the company."

"As much as I would like to Matt, I have a date. Can you believe it – a real date."

"I didn't know you were seeing someone. Would I like this guy? I'm supposed to look out for you, remember?"

Doreen had to laugh. She and Matt were such good friends but there were times he acted like a dad.

"I'm sure you would. I need to go. Make sure you eat something, okay?"

Matt stood in the doorway and thought about the last lunch he shared with Lydiel. How long would it take? How long indeed. He returned to his office before heading off for Mirelli's. He thought he might as well check his e-mail first. It was then that he saw the blinking light of an incoming instant message but before he could click on the message the phone rang.

The person on the other end had a rather thick accent making it difficult for Matt to understand what he was saying. He was calling a number given to him by Lydiel Sommers. There had been some sort of incident and more information would be available soon. The caller terminated the call and no matter how many times he tried, Matt was unable to re-establish the connection. He even tried calling Nikki Jemison, but she was away on a case for a day or so. The old headache was back. Rubbing his temples as he popped a couple of aspirins and he saw the instant message light flashing and read the screen.

> Ly_Som: Hi handsome. You probably had given me up for dead. Long story but I discovered that even a quick trip to Belize takes a lot longer than 120 minutes. A lot has happened Matt. The embassy tried to call, but Allison always answered the phone.

> Ly_Som: I guess you are too mad to talk to me. I have a very good excuse, really. Matt? Matt?

Matthew McNulty felt ill. Who hated him enough to do this? He wanted to hit delete, but something was stopping him. Why now, why today?

He closed out the screen, put his jacket on and left for the restaurant.

The valet signaled for a cab and opened the door for the woman. She seemed familiar but he couldn't quite place her. He gave the driver directions to Mirelli's and prepared to serve the next waiting guest. During the ride she couldn't help thinking the more things changed, the more they stayed the same, except for her - she was much different. She prepared herself for the meeting. She hadn't wanted it to be this way but knowing him his reaction would be the same regardless of where they were. The receptionist at Pushman had informed her that he was having lunch here today. Mirelli's - the place they never had a chance to go to. She collected her thoughts and paid the driver.

She opened the door to the restaurant. She had never been here before and she was surprised at the promptness of the Maitre 'D who offered to seat her. She pulled a note from her purse and asked him to deliver it to the gentleman seated at the rear table.

Matt toyed with the blue cheese in his Cobb salad. The instant message was weighing heavily on his mind. He was so engrossed in thought he didn't look up as Giorgio approached the table.

"Mr. McNulty, er, Matt. I was asked to deliver this note to you."

Matt took the note from Giorgio, read it and re-read it. He recognized the handwriting. He recognized the scent. He didn't understand why.

"Giorgio who gave this to you?"

She took a deep breath and found her voice- the voice he knew.

"I did, Matt…"

Chapter 2

"Good morning Mr. McNulty."

"Good morning Ms. Sommers."

"I tell you, the things a girl has to do to spend a night with her hero."

Lydiel was once again in her comfort zone; naked and in the arms of Matthew McNulty. She almost pinched herself to see if it was all real. The hospital in Belize had cleared her to fly and she and Matt were together again. It was hard to believe that people she never met, along with her own relatives wanted her dead so badly. Matt tightened his hold and she snuggled into him as if she never wanted him to let her go. They had lost so much time together and it took some getting used to, to learn that the world thought her dead.

She told Matt how she got the call from Jack Bass and how he assured here they would be gone no longer than forty-eight hours. She thought that she would be home by the time he returned from the camping trip, and she could give him the good news about the book deal. She related how on that day she had to return home because she forgot the book file, and encountered Sarah Turner. The smell of fresh cut grass was all over the apartment, and when Sarah went to get her a glass of water, she used the inhaler she kept under the pillow and then dropped it into her bag.

She finally met Jack and they boarded the plane. However, once they arrived in Belize everything went wrong.

Jack virtually disappeared during lunch, along with her laptop, her passport and her book. While attempting to look for him she took a wrong turn somewhere, was mugged and robbed. Her purse and her other identification were stolen as well as her earrings. She had been hospitalized for a few weeks and Jack was never found. The Belizean embassy had tried to contact him several times but for some reason he was never available.

As much as he regretted it, Matt told her about the murder plot and the trial. Looking at her face he couldn't begin to fathom what it would feel like to have your family as well as everyone else think you were dead.

Matt kissed her neck gently and nibbled at her neck. It felt so good to hold her again. He made a mental note to buy her a new pair of earrings. He rolled her over and stared into her eyes. He teased her mouth softly before kissing her deeply. He felt her melt into him and their lovemaking was warm and tender and lustful and passionate. The silence between them spoke volumes. Matt was the first to break the silence.

"All those weeks and months there was something deep inside me that refused to accept the fact that you were gone forever. I signed off on everything, conducted a memorial service you would have been proud of."

"Stop. All that matters now is that I'm here and you're here and the bad people are where they can't hurt anyone anymore."

Before Matt could respond the phone rang. It was Nikki. How did she know he was here?

"Doreen Bell told me where I could find you. I take it things are going well with you and Lydiel? I can only imagine the shock and joy of seeing her alive. I'm really happy for you Matt. I just thought you'd like to know that we now know the identity of the dead woman found in Lydiel's house. George Cates still had tissue samples from the body. Apparently she parked her car in the hospital lot and security became suspicious since it had been there so long. Samples taken from the car matched the DNA of the tissue samples at the morgue. It turns out the body was that of an actress who had been reported missing several months ago. She and Lydiel could have passed for twins. Well, one case closed and another one opened. Take care my friend and be happy."

Lines of worry crossed Lydiel's face as she listened to Matt's side of the conversation.

"Matt? Is everything okay?"

"Yes. Everything is fine babe. That was Nikki Jemison. The DNA from the dead woman was traced to a missing actress who was a dead ringer for you."

"Well sweetie, what was it Shakespeare said about all the world being a stage and the men and women merely players? Apparently our Sarah Turner or whoever she was, played one role too many. Now how about a kiss handsome?"

The End

For Now…

The story continues in the sequel to The Crumb Snatcher, The Unpunished Deed by Deana Walters, available December, 2015

Chapter 1

Jack Bass looked out the window and loaded the expensive English cigarette into the holder, flicked the flint wheel of the Zippo lighter and inhaled deeply. This was an eccentricity he could not bear to give up, and he would be the first to agree that the British knew how to take a drag on a fag. He remembered the first time he visited London. He was fascinated at the way the people there held their cigarettes, and the fact that they called them fags made it all the more endearing. Indeed there was nothing better than seeing a fag smoke a fag. That was the inside joke between him and his friends both in England and in the States. The tolerance for alternative lifestyles made things so much easier there, unlike the relentless persecution of those uncloseted souls in his adopted country. After an extended coughing spell he booted up his computer and began to mentally compose the letter.

Every day for five years he had written a letter, all the while scouring the newspapers for any information on the fate of his friend. Were it not for the fact that he was still in hiding, he would have made the trip to see her in that dreaded penal institution. He had followed the trial religiously and was not the least bit surprised at the verdict. What irony it was that a woman so vile had been convicted of a murder she didn't commit. There was no doubt in anyone's mind that a murder had been committed. The trouble was that the presumed victim was not only very much alive and well, but was the current paramour of the incarcerated woman's husband.

Easing the chair back and away from the keyboard, Jack reread the article about the impending release of Allison McNulty and her co-conspirators. Apparently the legal system's endless efforts to keep her locked up had failed, and a magnanimous anonymous donor had deposited sufficient funds into the bank account of Hannah Woodall to allow her to post the necessary funds to bond her daughter out of prison. According to the newspaper article Allison would be released within a week and that new charges would be filed in the death of actress Aisling Lavery. Jack smiled as he thought of the impact that release was going to have on the lives of Lydiel Sommers and Matthew McNulty.

Lydiel had been such an easy mark. She was so honest and trusting, and more than anything she wanted to be recognized as a published author. Even as a novice writer Jack knew she had a best seller on her hands. He made his living off hijacked manuscripts, and since the dead don't talk it was easy to pass the works off as his own. The routine was always the same. He set up a dummy corporation to lure new writers under the guise of teaching them how to write a best seller. His services were free and he courted them every step of the way, demanding copies of each chapter as it was written. Oblivious to the warning of 'caveat emptor', the writers all sent chapter after chapter for his perusal and approval. Under normal circumstances things went smoothly and the books would be published by a second dummy corporation using one of his many "nom de plumes". Such was not the case with Lydiel

Sommers.

Matthew McNulty was not only Lydiel's lover, he was her muse and confidante. He was also a busybody who convinced Lydiel not to send anything to anyone without copywriting it first, thus Jack could only get his hands on the first three chapters as they were written. Finally he had had to employ the services of a hacker to extract the information from Lydiel's computer.

Things were progressing well and he had the release date for the book all set until once again McNulty interfered with his plans. For some reason that was never made clear, McNulty had someone install an impenetrable firewall on Lydiel's computer. The only files accessible were her e-mail and instant message transcripts. Jack's hacker informed him that most likely it was some type of software utilized by the military and far too expensive to attempt penetration. He was then forced to hatch a new plan that involved whisking Lydiel off to Belize under the pretense of meeting people interested in her book. Even as the plane departed the runway all Lydiel was worried about was the white lie she told her beloved

Matt. She went on and on ad nauseum about her feeling of disloyalty.

Once they landed in Belize everything had gone according to plan. They ordered lunch in the little out-of-the-way restaurant, and he excused himself just long enough to give the well paid assailants opportunity to kidnap Lydiel and finish her off. He then returned to the restaurant to collect her belongings which included her laptop and her purse containing all of her identification. Shortly thereafter Jack learned that Allison McNulty and three others were on trial for Lydiel's murder. How that all came to be remained a mystery, but Jack decided not to look a gift horse in the mouth. Confident Lydiel Sommers had been dispensed with and that he was in the clear, Jack set up shop for an extended stay in the former British Honduras.

Several months passed and life was good. The book was published, distributed and doing quite well on the bestseller list until the bottom fell out. The New York Times reported author Lydiel Sommers was alive and well after surviving a kidnapping ordeal in Belize and that her agent Jack Bass was now the prime suspect in the crime. Reuters picked up the story and Interpol got involved. Jack was forced to use the income from the advance and the book sales to go deep underground where he remained. Folding the newspaper and tossing it aside he began his letter to Allison:

My Dear Allison,

Imagine my delight at the news of your impending release from that dreadful place you have called home these last five years. From the beginning your innocence was never a question and alas the authorities have come to their senses and are allowing you to leave.

As promised the funds were deposited by a third party and include enough to mount a suitable defense in your next trial. I do so look forward to talking to you by telephone as a face to face is not possible at this time.

As we discussed previously we must attend to the matter of Lydiel and Matthew post haste after your release. I will be in touch and enjoy and savor those first few breaths of freedom my dear.

Your loyal and trusted friend,
Jack

With one final keystroke Jack Bass sent the letter to the printer and decided an espresso would just hit the spot.

Chapter 2

"McNulty! Step forward, hands behind your back."

After five years of wearing prison khakis, there were two things Allison Woodall McNulty had learned: to take "no" for an answer, and that she was no longer in control of anything. The years had not been kind to her. The gray hair now framing her face was a stark contrast to the dark locks she sported when she entered Marysville Correctional Facility. Her eyes had taken on the watery look of age, and the stamp of crow's feet marked the corners of her lids. Gone were the well-manicured hands - now replaced by fingers that showed nails chewed to the quick, and blood coursing through ropey blue veins barely covered by wrinkled dry skin.

The guard placed the cuffs around Allison's wrists and led her to the waiting room. There would be no family to greet her there, only one of the many lawyers her mother had hired to plead her appeal. She had lost count of how many "suits" had listened to her story. It wasn't so much that her case didn't have merit, as it was her attitude that had driven most of them away.

Looking around the visitor area she noticed the families visiting their inmate relatives. One boy looked to be the same age as her Liam and for a brief moment there was a tinge of sadness in her heart. Liam was now fifteen and as tall as his…

Thanks to her mother, Allison received letters from Liam and pictures of both boys. At her sentencing the judge had issued a no contact order as he severed her parental rights. Sean had chosen not to contact her, and Allison was certain that her husband was behind it. She knew all about Matt and his writer slut. How could she have known each time she met with Sarah Turner she was staring into the face of Lydiel Sommers? Adding insult to injury was the fact that Remey and Francesca knew all along and said nothing. How could Matt humiliate her so? Lydiel wasn't even "one of them", making her the laughing stock of her circle; but with any luck all of that was about to change.

She seated herself in the dirty molded plastic stack chair, and came face to face with a woman she assumed to be her new solicitor, one Caitlin MacGregor. One look at her and Allison McNulty felt renewed anger seize her throat as if a hand were placed there. Apparently everyone at home had decided to give the knife in her back a few good twists.

"Good afternoon Mrs. McNulty. My name is Caitlin MacGregor and your husband, Matthew McNulty has retained me in a divorce action filed against you. I decided to serve you personally so I could entertain any questions you might have."

Caitlin MacGregor's appearance belied her heritage. Her complexion reminded Allison of smooth polished mahogany wood. There was not a single blemish visible. Her dark brown eyes looked through Allison as if they could read her every thought. Her eyelashes were long and soft, like two feathery little brooms. Caitlin's hands were small, too small in fact for the diamond adorning the third finger of her left hand. Looking down at her own hands, Allison thought about her wedding ring. It was locked in the property room along with the rest of the reminders of the life she once had.

So Mr. Matt had decided to divorce her had he? Allison wanted desperately to laugh but even that urge stuck in her throat. He seemed determined to be with *her.* He deserved *her.* They deserved each other, but no one deserved her boys. Reading through the copy, Allison knew she had nothing to fight Matt with. He was exercising his "options" as it were, for now at least. With any luck Allison Woodall McNulty would be exercising her options when she walked through the prison gates and back into the lives of her husband Matthew McNulty and Lydiel Sommers. Caitlin's questions interrupted Allison's reverie.

"Mrs. McNulty? Mrs. McNulty do you have any questions? Do you plan to counter sue?"

"No Ms. MacGregor. If you summon the guard, I will sign the papers now and my husband can have his precious divorce."

Placing the signed papers into her briefcase, Caitlin had a strange feeling that the divorce was only a formality. She was aware of Allison's request for a new trial, and she was also aware of something sinister in the person of the woman seated before her.

The relationship between Allison and her estranged husband was far from over and possibly portended more drama to come.

Walking back to the cellblock, Allison now had one more task to complete when she left Marysville - destroy Matthew McNulty and his writer slut once and for all.

Chapter Three

Lydiel Sommers had a busy day ahead. Matt had given her his list of people to contact, and it was going to take the better part of the morning to get through it. So far she lucked out with the caterer. Several calls had resulted in either busy signals or voicemails. Why he insisted on using a caterer was beyond her. She offered to prepare everything, but he was adamant that she focus on enjoying their special day. Next on the list was the printer. The invitations were two days overdue. Just as she reached for the phone it rang. It was Doreen.

"Hello Ma?"

"Hi there. How's my girl this morning? Is Matt playing the taskmaster today?"

"Very funny Ma. Matt is a dream to work with. Come to think of it, he is a dream, period. We have lots of meetings today so he probably won't call until later this afternoon. How are things going with the catering and all? It's going to be a big day for you two. Have you decided what to wear yet?"

"I am on top of everything here. The

invitations are late, but not to worry. I have a backup plan. As for what I am wearing, the jury is still out on that. I am thinking some shade of lavender or purple..."

"C'mon Ma. This is going to be a very special day. Why purple? Why not something lighter?"

"We'll see Doreen, but for now, I need to get back to work here. I need to have results to report to you-know-who. Talk soon chickie, okay?"

"Okay Ma. Ma? Be careful okay? Make sure the cell is fully charged when you go out, and don't forget to call and let us know when you leave and when you get back. I love you Ma."

"I love you too. Bye Doreen."

The more things changed the more they stayed the same. Since her return from Belize Matt and Doreen seemed to call twice as much as before. They both knew how difficult her readjustment had been.

Every night when Matt slept at home, Lydiel's eyes would open suddenly at four-fifteen a.m. like a vampire coming to life. For some reason this is when she was most afraid. The only time she slept well lately was when he was with her, and on more than one occasion he had awakened her from a nightmare.

Each time it was the same – she would find herself staring into her own face, but she was dead. She would reach out for Matt and there would only be space - cold, empty space.

A tear rolled down her cheek and dripped onto the list, smudging the ink, and Lydiel knew that the ordeal in Belize was not over. She lost so much during her stay there. Her manuscript was gone, some of her memory and most importantly, her time with Matt.

Enough of this! The florist, printer and caterer were all waiting and she needed to get a move on. She checked her bag to make sure she wasn't forgetting anything; eyeglasses, pens, pad, calendar, calculator, cell phone, wallet, address book and an unopened inhaler. Since the murder attempt she had become almost phobic about her inhalers; so much so that Matt had installed a safe to store the refills. Additional locks had been installed and a security system for the windows.

Lydiel sat on the side of the bed staring at Matt's picture. This was going to be a big step for her and she was beginning to have second thoughts. After all that had happened, she knew it was the right thing to do, but still… Why did she do this? Why did she always over think everything? Why couldn't she just be happy? Grabbing her bag, she was determined to leave the house. It was right at that moment when the phone rang.

"Good morning. This is Lydiel Som…"

"Hi Sweetie. How are ya?"

"I'm okay Matt. How are you? I thought you had meetings all morning."

Matthew McNulty could count the times Lydiel Sommers had called him by his name, and he didn't need all his fingers to do it. He was becoming increasingly more worried about her, and he deliberately gave her the list as a distraction. Allison, Francesca and Remey no longer posed a threat to her, but the fact that Jack Bass had never been found had put them both on edge. It was for this reason that a Pushman car and driver had been assigned to her.

"What's the matter sweetie? Having a hard time getting started today, huh?"

"I'm okay baby. I have things under control,

and I am on my way to the printer to check on the invitations, then to the florist. How is your day going?"

"Oh you know – the life of a busy corporate executive is filled with the usual; tons of meetings and people to meet. I would be lost here without Doreen. Connie was here earlier to pick up a dividend check. Be careful today but don't worry, okay babe?"

The mere mention of Connie Pushman's name triggered a near panic attack. Lydiel realized that the woman posed no direct threat to her per se, but the fact that she helped orchestrate her murder disturbed her greatly. Connie Pushman's paralysis did not evoke sympathy from Lydiel.

"I'll be fine, I promise. Not to worry."

"I know you will, babe. I need to get a move on here or else your daughter will hunt me down. Let me know when you get back, okay…

www.ingramcontent.com/pod-product-compliance
Lightning Source LLC
LaVergne TN
LVHW010222110826
845148LV00022B/1228

* 9 7 8 0 9 7 9 3 1 7 1 2 5 *